False Flag · Brown

MW00935670

False Flag

Henry Brown

Cover design by Logotecture.

ISBN-13: 978-1511932608

ISBN-10: 1511932600

False Flag - Brown

False Flag - Brown

TECHNICAL NOTE

TIME DESIGNATIONS:

Historically, military planners have designated the day of a major operation as "D-DAY," and the hour of the kickoff as "H-HOUR." The schedule is then adjusted so that surrounding times and dates reflect their distance from D-DAY and H-HOUR.

Going back to the allied invasion of Normandy (0600 on June Six 1944), for instance: the fifth of June, 1944, was designated "D MINUS ONE." The ninth of June, 1944, was "D PLUS THREE." A quarter after midnight on D-DAY (when Allied Airborne operations in force commenced behind Hitler's Atlantic Wall) was considered "H MINUS SIX." At 1000 hours (or "10 a.m." when Omaha Beach was finally secure) the Operation Overlord planners thought of it as "H PLUS FOUR."

In this novel, all listed dates and times are similarly designated by their temporal relation to one specific operation. In fact, as some chapters occur years prior to said operation, their place in the timeline have been measured according to their distance from the "Y-YEAR," going back as far as "Y-MINUS 20."

ACROMYMS:

Some acronyms have periods in between the letters; some don't. This is not inconsistency or oversight. This is to distinguish between terms which are spoken like a normal word, and terms which are verbally spelled out in normal conversation.

For instance: "PDQ" is not separated by periods because it can't be pronounced like a normal word without adding vowels. However, "S.O.P" is always spelled out verbally, even though it has the vowel needed to be pronounced as a normal word: "sop."

False Flag - Brown

"ASAP" is usually spoken as if a normal word in conversation: "ay-sapp." The letters are not separated by periods unless meant to be spelled out verbally.

More examples:

GPS

S.U.V.

SNAFU

C.I.A.

DHS

A character reference is at the back of this book.

False Flag - Brown

It was determined some years ago that 0300 was the ideal time to raid a home.

That was when normal people enjoyed their deepest sleep. They would be slower to wake. When they did wake, they'd be disoriented for a few crucial moments.

The assault transports, which looked like unmarked SWAT vans, rolled up on the gate at 0245. The gate was simply a cable hanging across the driveway, suspended from trees on either side. Hanging from the cable was a metal sign which read: "NO TRESSPASSING." An officer hopped down from the van, unhitched the cable and let it fall across the road, taking no small satisfaction that the sign would be run over by multiple vehicles momentarily. He jumped back into his seat and the small convoy rolled onto the rough snow-covered dirt drive.

The DomTer's house was a ways up the mountain from the road, and isolated enough that it made surprise more difficult than normal. The sound of engines straining to pull heavy vehicles up the steep drive could potentially give warning to the perps. Helicopters would be faster to put boots on the ground, but were even louder than their assault transports. Helicopters were also of limited availability, and in high demand these days. In any event, somebody high up had decreed this operation go in on wheels.

The assault transports and the supporting armored vehicle and communications van arrived at the end of the drive at 0303. Doors flew open and a full platoon of federal agents burst out of the transport to deploy.

It was supposed to be an especially cold winter this year, and up here it already was. Thick white clouds hung overhead, threatening more snow any time now. Their black uniforms stood out in stark contrast to the white landscape.

All was quiet. No lights were on. Good--likely the perp was still asleep or only just stirring--if he heard the truck engines at all. Either way, there was nothing he could do now that wasn't suicidal.

Satellite imagery of this property hadn't been a terrific help, as the buildings were well-camouflaged. It took a few confused moments for the agents to locate the house--a dome-shaped structure back in the trees.

Funny though—no sign of the dogs. They'd been worried that shooting them would also tip off the perp prematurely, but that seemed to be a non-issue. Everything was working out in their favor today.

False Flag - Brown

The breech team went forward, bristling with weapons, explosives, armor and night vision devices. The blocking team circled around to close off any escape routes in back. The other teams dispersed to search the barn, sheds, and the rest of the property. The breach team leader got confirmation via his radio headset that the blocking force was in place. His team stacked on the front door, primed and chomping at the bit. The ram was passed forward.

"Go!"

The two agents closest to the door swung the ram back, then forward with all their strength, at the door.

The door didn't give way, but they never had a chance to wonder why, or batter at it a second time.

From a distance the explosions didn't seem that impressive. There was no fireball, and though the blasts all occurred simultaneously, the report was loud but not ear-splitting.

Up where the breach team stood, however, it was hell on Earth for a split second that would forever alter their lives permanently...and end some of them.

Big bore armor-piercing rounds tore through them from the front, sheering the bone of one agent's arm, passing between armored sections of another and punching through his torso. But the worst of it was underneath them.

The very ground they stood on erupted. White-hot shrapnel streaked upward all over the kill zone. It ripped through boot soles and feet, through legs, buttocks, and at angles through their bodies, blowing tunnels through vital organs allegedly protected by their state-of-the-art body armor.

Other blasts sounded around the property as agents evidently stepped on mines or tripped booby-traps.

The commander, sitting in the passenger seat of the communication van, surveyed the scene in wide-eyed horror. "Ambush!" he cried. "It's an ambush!"

False Flag - Brown

1
Y MINUS ONE
TEXAS PANHANDLE

Jimmy and Bill stopped by the game warden's office, went through the usual routine, then headed for their favorite diner with the eight-point white tail gutted and wrapped in a tarp in the back of Jimmy's pickup.

At the diner, the two ravenous hunters ordered coffee and lunch.

Jimmy and Bill knew each other from high school, but hadn't been especially close friends. After 9/11 Bill joined the Marines and Jimmy became a medic in the Army. After returning home they ran into each other at the V.A. Since agonizingly long waits were standard at veteran's hospitals, they had plenty of time and nothing better to do than talk.

It turned out they had a lot in common. Both liked to hunt. Both were firearms enthusiasts. Both were disillusioned about the "war on terror." Neither of them liked the way V.A. doctors were trying to classify them as PTSD. Nor did they like nurses and doctors asking them if they owned firearms. And both were pissed off about what was happening to their country.

A strong friendship developed after that, and many of their conversations centered around speculations on what kind of country America was going to be in a few more years, how the transformation might take place and what, if anything, they could do about it.

They hunted together; went to the range together; introduced girlfriends; invited each other over for Superbowl parties. Now and then one of them met others who shared a lot of their concerns over the state of the Union. Sometimes those others made it a habit to join them at the range and at bull sessions in the diner. Sometimes they brought wives and/or sons. A few times they asked Bill to talk about what he'd done and seen in the Sandbox. He obliged by explaining small unit tactics at length. A few quizzed Jimmy on combat medicine, and techniques he'd used in Ass-Crackistan. A lot of those folks bought weapons and gear, showing it off to the two veterans, or sometimes seeking advice and approval before buying. All of them bought ammunition with every available dollar, including Jimmy and Bill.

When the two friends entered the diner, they left their cellphones in the truck--even though both phones were rooted, and they had removed the hidden backup batteries which allowed third parties to remotely turn the microphones on.

As they discussed the hunt, the buck, and what Jimmy would do with the hide, the meat, and the antlers, a Toyota Tundra swung into the parking lot and pulled up right next to the GMC. They sat facing each

7

other in the booth, but both noticed the new arrival through the window.

Arden Thatcher exited the Toyota's cab and wandered up to lean over and look into the bed of the GMC, flipping up the tarp to snoop under it. He was a little below average height, thin and bowlegged, but compensated with cocky swagger for what he lacked in stature. With clod-kickers, a cowboy hat and a Rebel flag on his Levi jacket, he was the poster boy for Texas rednecks.

Arden had come upon Bill engaged in a conversation with some other folks at a survival expo, and jumped right in. He talked like a gun enthusiast, who hated the present administration. After that first meeting he bumped into one or the other of them by coincidence--like the way he just happened to show up at the diner just now.

Jimmy and Bill watched him turn from the GMC and saunter toward the diner's front entrance.

Arden Thatcher didn't leave his smartphone in the truck. Nor had he taken it apart and removed the hidden backup battery. He stepped inside the diner and swept his gaze over the patrons until he found Jimmy and Bill. Jimmy was dark-haired, with a big crooked nose. Bill was a redhead with Scotch-Irish features. Both still wore woodland cammies with matching baseball caps.

Arden smiled and nodded before heading their way.

Jimmy nodded back. That was a good sign. Maybe they were warming up to him. They still hadn't invited him to go shooting with them or otherwise hang out with their local gang.

He felt sure he could earn their confidence in time.

"Hey Jimmy," he said. "Howdy Bill. Mind if I pull up a chair?"

"Howdy Arden," they mumbled, neither of them scooting over to make room on their booth seat.

Arden found an unoccupied chair at a nearby table and slid it over to sit perpendicular to the two veterans. "About due for a bad winter, I hear."

Jimmy and Bill nodded, chewing their food.

"Who bagged the eight-pointer?" Arden asked.

Bill chinned toward Jimmy, who grinned. "We knew it would be winner-take-all," Bill said. "That first shot would scatter all the game for 20 grid squares."

"I hear the mating cry of the sore loser," Jimmy remarked, smirking.

"Grid squares," Arden repeated. "Does that mean you had a military topographic map of the area?" He seemed to be a little proud that he knew about military grid, and had shown them he knew his stuff.

"Naw, <u>USGS</u>," Bill said, blowing on a spoonful of soup. "Gotta use latitude, longitude and minutes. It's just habit to think in military grid."

"Oh," Arden said.

Silence fell over the table for a moment. The waitress came over and asked Arden what he'd like. He ordered a cup of coffee and a slice of cherry pie.

"Y'all hear this latest thing about the illegal aliens?" Arden asked.

Both men grumbled in the affirmative.

"More and more people are rejecting the mass media brainwashing," Jimmy said, finishing off his enchilada. "The globalists have to bring in more illegals to cancel out their votes."

"Ain't enough that the sheeple get to vote five or six times every election," Bill added.

"Elections are a total sham anymore," Jimmy said. "And what choice do we get every time? Communist or Communist Lite."

"Tastes great!" Bill blustered, drunkenly.

"Less filling!" Jimmy blustered back, pounding his fist on the table and adding a hiccup for effect.

Arden's coffee arrived and he took a big gulp, oblivious to the once-famous beer commercial referenced. "It ain't just about elections," he said. "It's genocide against white Europeans."

Jimmy and Bill both raised their eyebrows, shared a glance and looked back to Arden.

"Genocide?" Jimmy asked.

"Sure," Arden replied. "It don't always take gas chambers—if that even happened. They'll breed the white outa' the world if they have to. The whole country'll be one shade a brown or 'nother, it keeps goin' the way it is now."

"What 'they' are you talking about?" Jimmy asked.

"You know," Arden said. "The NWO. ZOG, or whatever you wanna call 'em."

"NWO are lily-white Europeans themselves," Bill said. "Why would they want to 'breed out' their own race?"

Arden shook his head. "Most of 'em are Jews. Don't you know that? Besides, even the ones that are truly white protect their own blood lines. They just want the rest of us to lose our racial purity."

Jimmy fidgeted, visibly uncomfortable. "What is 'ZOG,' anyway?"

"Zionist Occupational Government," Arden explained. "Our government is controlled by the Israelis. Ain't it obvious?"

Bill set his coffee cup down, leaned back in his seat, and wiped his face with a napkin, exchanging another glance with Jimmy. "Arden," he said, "We got nothin' against you. But it's fairly plain there's some matters we don't see eye-to-eye on. If you're lookin' for like-minded

False Flag - Brown

people to hang out with, you should go on and look somewhere else."

Arden looked crestfallen, his jaw slack. "What? What's the matter?"

"Nothing's the matter," Jimmy said. We believe what we believe. You've got different opinions, and you're welcome to them. We'd prefer not to argue with you or anybody who believes like you do. We just want to do our own thing."

"What are you?" Arden demanded, blushing. "Jew lovers?"

Maybe Jimmy was a Jew. He sure did have a big nose. The dark hair might mean he had a Mex somewhere in his family tree. Arden had determined to let that slide. But if they were going to cop an attitude just because he was fed up with the Z.O.G...

"No offense, Arden," Bill said, staring hard into Arden's eyes. "But it'd be best for everybody all around if you just left us alone."

The waitress arrived with the slice of pie. Jimmy smiled at her and said, "If you would, please, serve that to him at a different table."

AMARILLO, TEXAS

Many miles away in a secure commo room, Jason Macmillan, along with the comm tech on monitoring duty, sat listening to the conversation via the microphone in Arden Thatcher's cellphone.

McMillan's power and fortunes had increased significantly over the last 20 years. Too bad his health hadn't prospered proportionally. He had most of the ailments common to men in their middle age now, including a degree of obesity, high blood pressure, and erectile dysfunction. What hair hadn't fallen out all turned gray. But people respected him more than ever. He had the power to step on just about anybody from 95% of the population, should he need to. And even if he retired today, he'd be set to live comfortably for the rest of his life. Not that he wanted to retire. Ever.

Macmillan tore off his headset and swore. "More candy-asses," he declared, shot to his feet, and marched to the door. He turned back to tell the comm tech, "They wouldn't even let him eat a slice of pie at their table. When he gets far enough away, tell that stupid redneck the assignment is terminated."

"Should he report to his handler for a new assignment?" the comm tech asked.

"No. Let him cool his heels for a while. Tell him we'll be in touch if another assignment comes along."

"Yes sir," the comm tech said, and Macmillan shut the door.

Macmillan cussed under his breath as he made his way to his own office-away-from-home. They had wasted months working their informant into the confidence of that DomTer cell, and Thatcher blew it

10

False Flag - Brown

over the course of a few minutes.

Every potential target city had its challenges. Around Amarillo it was infiltrating the organized groups. Not the racially motivated gangs--those were easy, and conventional departments already had informants planted. But the groups that posed a real threat were proving tough nuts to crack.

The problem this time was, Thatcher had a long enough leash to improvise. But he wasn't smart enough to improvise. He didn't know the marks as well as he should have. Plus he actually believed in all that Jewish conspiracy business; so he assumed others would, too.

Macmillan didn't care whether there was a Jewish conspiracy or not. It didn't change the parameters of his job. But it occurred to him how he might be able to turn Thatcher's belief in it from a liability into an asset. He would work on it with the handler before they attempted to give Thatcher another assignment.

False Flag - Brown

2

Y MINUS TWO
BAGHDAD, IRAQ

Jake McCallum hadn't had many visitors since he'd been in the hospital. A few guys from Security Solutions, International, including the president of the private military company, dropped by. Ingrid--a field surgeon and his on-again, off-again girlfriend, checked in regularly. But his closest friend in SSI, Leon Campbell, was stateside. And after the first few days there was little break from the bedridden monotony in the cool, white room.

At six-foot-eight and with a massive, carefully-sculpted musculature, it was agonizing for Mac to lay here and feel himself atrophy. His arm was broken and his knee recovering from surgery. In a civilian context he would have been released to recover at home; but here he was treated like a wounded soldier because it wouldn't be safe for him in-country in his vulnerable condition.

A black man, who was not Leon, appeared in the doorway and rapped his knuckles on the jamb. He was a little shorter than Leon, and huskier. "What's up, my brotha?" the man greeted.

Mac noted his business formal attire, despite the environment. His shoes were in the latest style. The creases in his pants were razor-sharp, and his jacket was tailored to his V-shaped torso. With perfectly trimmed mustache and goatee, he looked like a model for the cover of *Jet* or something. Mac had rubbed elbows with plenty of Agency guys over here. Agency guys usually dressed business/casual Nobody except politicians dressed sharper than that.

From his bed, Mac chinned an acknowledgment of the visitor, who then entered with a very subtle three-legged swagger.

"DeAngelo Jeffries," the man said, extending his hand. Mac wrapped his own huge paw (the one he could still use) around the offered hand and pumped it once.

"I'm in town for a while, checking things out," Jeffries said. "Guy I'm with was assigned to debrief your girlfriend—tall Swedish blonde—so I thought I'd come by and holla at ya."

"Debriefing" meant Jeffries was working for the Agency in some capacity. McCallum had wondered if his trip to Indonesia would get their attention.

"Nurse said they had to do some work on your knee," Jeffries said, sliding the chair over to seat himself at bedside.

"Yeah," Mac said. "I can get around on crutches for now. Hopefully I'll be able to put weight on it before much longer."

False Flag - Brown

"Knee injuries are no joke, man," Jeffries said. "I had to have mine scoped a few years back. It's like the most critical joint in your body. Has to withstand the most abuse."

"Hurt it playin' ball?" Mac asked, slipping into a 'hood accent without conscious thought.

"Yeah, you know it," Jeffries said. "But nothin' like yours. Speakin' of ball, I know you had to play somewhere, with your height."

Mac shrugged massive shoulders. "High school. A little college, before I went in the Army. So if somebody's debriefing Ingrid, that means you're here to debrief me."

Jeffries shrugged this time. "Naw, man--nothin' official. Wouldn't do that here, anyway. But rumors go 'round, and I'm supposed to ask you some questions. That's all."

"What you wanna know?"

"You know: routine stuff. Like were you injured here or somewhere else?"

"On vacation," Mac said, technically telling the truth.

"Where'd you go?" Jeffries asked, in a friendly, conversational, none-too-concerned tone of voice.

"Indonesia," Mac replied, wondering how much Ingrid was telling this guy's partner. She didn't know everything, but she knew enough to raise some eyebrows in certain circles where a smart person never wanted to cause eyebrows to be raised. "My first time over there."

"SOCOM never sent you over there, huh?" Jeffries asked, surprised.

So Jeffries had read Mac's dossier.

"Not me," Mac said. "They always had me focused on the Middle East. Taught me Arabic; oriented me on Islam; all that."

Jeffries nodded. "I guess it makes sense you got a Private Military Company over here. Ain't too many brothas got that kinda' juice at War, Incorporated."

"I'm only vice president," Mac said.

Jeffries chuckled. "Looks to me like you do all the work at SSI, while the president just handles the administrative end."

Mac shrugged again. "Nigga behind the trigga. You know."

Jeffries shook his head, sadly. "We come all this way. Even got a brotha into the White House. But the white man still has the white collar."

"Even in a war zone," Mac agreed, chuckling himself, relieved that Jeffries didn't seem to be hungry for details about his "vacation."

"I don't know what you've heard," Jeffries said, suddenly serious. "But there's a new development here. *Al Qaeda* is reorganizing; working on changing their name."

False Flag - Brown

Mac knew "former" *Al Qaeda* cells were instrumental in a lot of regional mischief. And white people were making entirely too big a deal that American tax dollars were buying weapons which found their way into the hands of the late Osama Bin Laden's jihadists. The issue was much more complex than who was behind the 9/11 attacks and whether the new regime in Syria would be more hostile to the US than the old one was. Now, evidently, the jihadists were getting ready to topple the precarious post-Saddam regime here in Iraq, too.

"The withdrawal is a done deal," Jeffries said. "The day is coming when you won't have the Army or Marines here to back you up."

"I go to the briefings," Mac said.

"You ever consider working domestically?"

"In the States?" Mac nodded. "I tried to get on a SWAT team after I left the Army. Wound up a contractor instead."

Jeffries shook his head, frowning. "I ain't sayin' you wouldn't be good at it, but SWAT—that's local stuff. The Man wants to keep us local and small scale, but we need to get in where the power is, on the federal level."

"You mean like what you're doing?" Mac asked.

Jeffries nodded. "I'm at the federal level. I got my finger on the pulse; feel me? And if bad stuff goes down, I'm in a position to do somethin'. Look at the whole Eric Garner thing...did you follow that?"

Mac shook his head slowly. "Yeah. Man, that jury..."

"That jury was just the start, man. You know I can't talk about everything, but trust me, my brotha: it's gonna get real ugly before too long. The man sees us movin' up, now, and he don't like it. I mean, we even got one of ours into the White House. White House. White. It's their house, the way they see it. And they're frothin' at the mouth to make make sure us uppity Negroes don't ever get up there again. There's gonna be a backlash sooner or later, and you can kinda' see it happening already."

Mac considered his white friends. Some of them were just consumed with hate for Obama. They could rattle off facts and statistics to justify it, but what was the real reason? Then there were loose cannons like Josh Rennenkampf, who Mac was sure must be a closet Neo-Nazi.

"You got too much talent to waste on a SWAT team," Jeffries went on, laughing derisively. "Or to waste bein' a contractor." He swept his hand in an arc--not to indicate the room they occupied or even the whole hospital, but the volatile country surrounding it, along with the chaos and military/political quagmire it represented.

"I dunno," Mac said. "Contracting has been a good fit for me."

"Well you might wanna think it over, my brotha. I might be able to hook you up, you ever decide to give it a try."

"I appreciate it, man," Mac said.

Jeffries stood from his chair. "Tell you what: I'm not gonna pry into your personal business about the vacation right now. You're in the hospital, on pain meds. I'm just gonna say you fell asleep before you told me much. You get with Ingrid, find out what she said, then you can get your stories straight. Then we can finish debriefing. Sound good to you?"

Mac nodded, dumbly. When they shook hands again, it was in the familiar street method passed down and constantly revised by young men ever since the Vietnam era.

After Jeffries left the room, Ingrid came to visit him. She was a tall, well-proportioned, attractive Scandinavian woman, with a lab coat on over a nice casual blouse and pants. She asked how he was doing, and if he'd been questioned.

"Yeah. And he's not done, either. What did you tell them?"

Ingrid shrugged. "What I know, which wasn't much. I was on the boat when all of you went ashore. But I did see the one firefight."

Mac groaned. Why did she have to mention that?

Well, he guessed the Agency probably knew about it already, anyway. "What did they seem **most** interested in?"

"Who all was there," she said. "They knew about Tommy Scarred Wolf and his brother. And about you. They wanted other names, but I couldn't remember them. I just gave physical descriptions."

"Alright. If they come back to ask if you remember anything else, say no."

They chatted for a bit, then she kissed him and left.

Mac pondered the whole strange encounter with Jeffries. The agent had saved Mac a whole lot of hassle, not asking questions there probably weren't any safe answers for. In fact, if somebody really wanted to be a jerk, they could classify Mac as a suspected accomplice in the murder Tommy and Vince were framed for back in Medan, Indonesia.

Something bothered Mac about how easy Jeffries had made it for him. On the other hand, he was grateful to finally find an ally who saw things how they really were in this white man's world. The negative possibilities surrounding Jeffries' behavior paled in comparison.

False Flag - Brown

Trooper Jason Macmillan, 29 and fit with a full head of brown hair under his Smokey-the-Bear hat, turned his halogens on bright, then adjusted his side spot onto the little Chevy S-10 pulled over in front of him. After the make was run on the vehicle's owner and radioed back to Macmillan, he got out of his cruiser and approached the S-10's passenger window.

He turned on his big Maglite and shined it through the rear window into the cab. He didn't see anything incriminating inside.

But that was kind of the point: he couldn't see everything inside.

The driver rolled his window down. Already squinting from the bright light of the cruiser's headlights and side spot in his mirrors, Joe Tasper was now completely blinded when Trooper Macmillan fixed the Maglite's beam directly in his eyes.

"Driver's license, registration and proof of insurance," Macmillan said. "And please turn your engine off, sir."

"I've got battery problems," Tasper said. "If I shut it down, I'll need a jump to get going again."

"Do me a favor and shut it down," Macmillan ordered. "Then please comply with my request, sir."

Tasper turned off the ignition, dug out his wallet and leaned over to open his glove box. Macmillan rested one hand on his holstered sidearm. He'd never had to pull his gun in the line of duty, but could never tell when the opportunity would arise. Tasper handed over his papers and Macmillan took them, relaxing just a bit.

"The reason I pulled you over is that your windows are illegally tinted," Macmillan said.

"I just bought the truck today," Tasper replied. "I was on my way to get a new battery for it. I can take the tinting off Monday after work. You'll give me a jump when you're done, right?"

"You sit tight here," Macmillan said, waving the license, insurance card and registration form. "I'll be back in a few minutes."

"The store is gonna be closed in a half hour," Tasper said. "I have to get there quick to get the new battery."

Macmillan ignored him and returned to the comfort of his patrol car. He called in the additional info, but Tasper's record was clean, except for normal traffic citations, and his story checked out about buying the pickup that day.

Macmillan took his time filling out the ticket. When he went back to

False Flag - Brown

the suspect's vehicle, he asked to see the bill of sale, then looked it over. He questioned the suspect about why someone in northwest Texas had driven so far to buy a truck in Louisiana, but failed to trip him up or get him to admit anything. Macmillan added a seatbelt violation to the citation and got the suspect to sign. The suspect asked again about getting a jump start, but Macmillan ignored him and returned to his patrol car.

Normally he waited for the suspect to drive away first, but knowing Joe Tasper wouldn't be able to start his vehicle now, MacMillan drove away without waiting. He decided to come back this way at the end of his shift and see if the S-10 was still sitting here. Who knew? Maybe it would be abandoned and he could schedule it for impound.

It turned out to be Trooper McMillan's lucky night. A county mounty called for backup on a resisting arrest code. MacMillan floored the accelerator, flipping on his light beacon, and got the Crown Victoria rolling down the fast lane at 120. The incident site was only a few miles away. He would get some stick time tonight.

MaQuon Lutrell was pulled over for a "no turn on red" violation. The sheriff's deputy asked to search his car. MaQuon had a bag of weed under the passenger seat and didn't want to go back to jail. He heard people say that cops couldn't search a vehicle without either a search warrant or the driver's consent, so he didn't give his consent. The deputy asked what he was hiding and the conversation soon turned into an argument.

When the deputy ordered him to get out of the car, MaQuon feared it might get ugly. And it did.

The scenario ended with the deputy and an increasing number of arriving cops beating on him with police batons. One of the arriving cops was a young State Trooper.

The beating took place in a well-lit area on a street connecting residential and industrial areas. Across the street, hiding behind a cluster of bushes, was a group of preadolescent boys. They were friends from school who got together to hang out one last time since Mrs. Thatcher was moving tomorrow and would be taking her son, Arden, with her to Texas.

The boys laughed and joked among themselves, watching the black grown-up getting the crap beat out of him. Arden bragged that he would be a cop one day himself, and get paid to beat up niggers.

False Flag - Brown

Brigadier General Clayton P. Vine, USMC, looked up from the training schedule when the intercom buzzed. One of his staffers told him the civilian V.I.P. had arrived. Vine had played power games when he was younger, forcing people to wait unnecessarily on him when they were on time for appointments; but he had grown out of that. The military--and the government in general--wasted entirely too much time with stupid little games designed to prove who had more power.

"Let him in."

The door opened and one of Vine's marines announced the visitor before shutting the door behind the State Department errand boy.

The errand boy was a mid-30s nerd with one of those fancy new Blue Tooths and a haircut that appeared downright unsanitary. He glanced around the office--which was tastefully built of stained wood—not that cheap paneling that simulated the real thing. The walls, of course, were bedecked with a few framed photos and several framed awards. There was also a US flag and the Colors of Vine's present command.

The errand boy strode forward and shook the general's hand. Vine encouraged him to have a seat, and he did.

Vine asked him all the polite garbage like how his flight had been, if he had any trouble finding Vine's headquarters,and so forth. He had entertained errand boys before, and knew these pleasantries were expected. One never wanted to piss off anyone from the State Department.

The errand boy made a few polite comments about formations of marines he'd seen marching as he passed on his way here.

Finally the errand boy got around to business...in a bureaucratic way. "Well, as I'm sure you've noticed, the domestic situation is a bit worrisome."

Vine said nothing, unsure what the errand boy was referring to. He wondered what exactly Washington was worried about. There were issues with police and demonstrators in various cities, but that was hardly a concern of the Marines. He could be referring to the influx of radical Muslims, hiding among the hordes of Latin refugees invading the country. But that was unlikely, since the administration he worked for obviously wanted to make the situation on the border worse, not better. None of it made sense to Vine, but then politics rarely did. Most of what the Marine Corps did made sense; which was one reason Vine loved

False Flag - Brown

being a marine.

"The President and Secretary thought it important that we touch base with our senior commanders in all the Armed Forces," the errand boy said. "And I thought it best to meet with you face-to-face."

"That's good," Vine said, resisting the urge to demand he get to the point. "I appreciate it."

"Even with all this technology nowadays, I still think it's the best way to communicate." The errand boy checked something on his beeping smartphone, then slid it back in his pocket. "First of all, I want to personally thank you for your service to the President over the years."

Vine nodded. His career had spanned the terms of a few presidents, and he considered his service as to the Corps anyway, but he went along with the assumption, hoping the errand boy would spit out what was on his mind.

"I understand you're up for promotion."

Vine nodded and smiled, which was not what he wanted to do. This civilian dweeb mentioning specifics of his career made his stomach queasy.

"Obviously my superiors and I understand how important it is to retain quality leadership," Errand Boy said. "My uncle served in the Marine Corps, so I know the deal."

You don't know your sphincter from a gopher hole, kid. You should have sent your uncle to talk to me.

"So with the situation like it is, it's imperative that the President knows he can count on you."

"You lost me, son," Vine said. "I've been in the Corps so long I can't remember life before it. I've served with honor and been faithful to my duty. Is there some reason the President—or anyone else—suddenly questions my ethics?"

"Of course not," the errand boy replied. "I took a look at your records, and your ethics are peerless...except, of course, for that brief dalliance with the young woman in Japan about 30 years ago."

The queasy feeling got worse, and Vine's blood ran cold. How did the State Department know about the affair? His wife never found out, and neither had his commanding officer. He would certainly have heard about it if they had. He'd felt guilty about the moral lapse for years afterwards, but finally chalked it up to youthful recklessness—no harm/no foul—and forgot about it.

"So it's not really about ethics," the errand boy said. "It's about loyalty."

The cold, sinking sensation intensified. Vine couldn't very well swear to his own loyalty when they knew he'd once cheated on his wife.

False Flag - Brown

The errand boy chuckled and held his hands up, palms-forward. "Hey, don't worry. I'm not here because anybody's upset that you got a little side action when you were young."

"Why are you here, then?" Vine asked, losing his ability to maintain the polite tone.

"As I said, the domestic situation is getting ugly, General. Not everybody out there welcomes change. And change isn't always easy-- sometimes it makes things uncomfortable, even though it ultimately works for the greater good. And sometimes bringing change requires some people to adjust their methods, and perspective."

Now it was dawning on Vine what this was about. He'd heard scuttlebutt about a purge taking place across all the branches of the armed forces. He knew about a few of the senior commanders who were sacked a while back—vocal critics of how *Benghazi* was handled. He assumed that was the extent of the purge. Obviously not.

"What specific change are we talking about?" Vine asked.

"Well," Errand Boy said, "there are some old traditions and rigid ideas about what the military can and should be used for. We need to take our concept of the armed forces to a whole new level. Times like these call for flexibility. For thinking outside the box."

"All right," Vine said, in a tone meant to coax out more information.

Errand Boy crossed his legs the way a lady does, removed his glasses, and polished the lenses with a handkerchief "The ways of war are changing, as I'm sure you know, General. There's no more one nation against another, sending bomber formations at each other's factories; soldiers stabbing each other with bayonets; that sort of thing. At least not in the developed world. We've got modern technology; a different definition of victory; and different threats. Our men and women in uniform won't necessarily be tasked with fighting enemy soldiers...or shipping off to some faraway land to do it."

"Let me spell out what I think you're driving at," Vine said, his face heating up. "And you tell me if I'm right: the President wants to know if I'm willing to command my marines to fire on American civilians, based on his say-so."

The errand boy's head rocked back on his neck as if he'd just received an invisible slow-motion blow to the face. "Well, I wouldn't..."

"And you all believe that what I did in Japan is an insurance policy just in case I don't want to dance to the President's tune," Vine interrupted. "Is that it?"

"I assure you, nobody in Washington thinks any less of you because of some harmless booty call in the previous century," the errand boy said, nonchalantly.

False Flag - Brown

"And furthermore," Vine continued, "my promotion, and therefore my career, depends on me agreeing to this. Does that sum it up?"

The errand boy shrugged. "Perhaps that's not the most delicate way to phrase it. But yes."

Vine wanted to tell him where to stick delicate phrases. Vine had never concerned himself with politics. There were only a few times he even bothered to vote, and he'd never even watched a presidential debate. The only campaign promises that motivated him had to do with the military budget.

Vine's father, however, had been different. A marine, for sure, but he also considered history and politics to be important. In one of their last conversations before he passed away, Vine's father reminded him that Clayton had taken an oath to uphold and defend the Constitution. Vine had never read the Constitution, and only knew what other people claimed that it said. His father said that it was the law of the land--the fundamental core of American government. His father said America was unique because, here, individual rights were sacred whether laws were written acknowledging them or not. In America, government's purpose was to protect those rights.

His father would go on at length about this, and Vine couldn't remember all the details, but that was the gist of it.

Vine hadn't studied what his father had; and didn't agree with him about everything...but something just struck him as wrong about using the Marines as a weapon against Americans.

"I'm curious," Vine said. "Why are you so sure we're going to need to fight a war against our own civilians? The country's what—240 years old or so? There's never been a need for this before."

The errand boy frowned and checked his watch. His whole demeanor changed as the pleasant, respectful facade was dropped. He paused before speaking. "It's obvious from your hesitation that you're not the man for the job. I thought you were smarter than this. But not everybody can handle the adjustments necessary to make change work."

"Why won't you answer the question?" Vine asked. "Why are you so sure you'll need my marines to kill civilians? I mean, even in the Civil War, armies fought other armies. What do you anticipate?"

The errand boy stood from his seat and gave a curt nod. "Of course I don't need to tell you that the subject and details of this conversation are classified; not to be disclosed to anyone without the expressed permission of the President."

Vine rose to his own feet. "We didn't discuss anything of strategic significance, young fellah—there's no national security concerns here. I'm not legally obligated to keep any of this secret. But then I suppose that's where the implied blackmail threat comes in."

False Flag - Brown

The errand boy already had his back to Vine by then, but flashed him a wry grin over the shoulder on his way out the door.

The errand boy walked back to his rental car using one thumb to compose a text message. Once behind the wheel, he finished it.

"Nix Vine. Won't play ball."

He sent the message, started the engine, and scrolled through his notes to find the next senior officer on the list.

And just like that, Clayton P. Vine's career in the United States Marine Corps was over.

Within the next few days Vine would be notified that his second star had been pinned on somebody else's uniform.

Someone who passed the litmus test.

Vine would be thanked for his service and forcibly retired. If he leaked the reason behind his sacking, his affair with the young lady in Japan would be leaked, adding disgrace to injury.

For the rest of his life, Vine would wonder if he'd done the right thing. Was his instinctive moral resistance important enough to throw away what he loved most of all?

For the first time in 40 years, he felt the urge to cry. The Marine Corps was his entire identity. Wasn't it worth keeping, at any price?

Despite the anguish of his shockingly crushed spirit, he suspected it wasn't.

False Flag - Brown

5
D MINUS 88
POTAWATTOMIE COUNTY SHERIFF'S OFFICE, OKLAHOMA

Tommy Scarred Wolf finished reading the email from his niece and was organizing a reply in his mind when a knock on his office door roused him from his thoughts. He glanced up to see Deputy Janet Bailey leaning around through the doorway.

His door was usually open, but his people were polite enough to knock anyway.

"Have you got a minute, sir? Janet asked.

He had never got used to being called "sir," preferring to be called by his first name. Janet knew that, so this was her way of telling him something serious was going on.

"Yeah," Tommy said, nodding toward the vinyl sofa opposite his desk. His office was tidy and Spartan, with little in the way of decoration save for an American flag, a framed photo of all his deputies between two prowl cars, and some other cop stuff. He didn't clutter his work area with family memorabilia.

Janet entered, followed by a girl who looked to be about 15. The girl glanced at Janet tentatively as if making sure it was okay to sit down. Janet shut the door behind them.

Tommy straightened in his chair. This was serious, alright.

The sheriff had a lean, sinewy build, a little below six feet in height, but tall for a full-blooded Shawnee. Shaving had never really been necessary for him, and it was a good thing since his red-bronze face was now full of more pits and other terrain features than ever. He still kept his black hair short, but not high-and-tight for a long time, now.

The young girl was mixed, like Janet. Maybe a quarter-breed or less. Her hair was brown with streaks of different colors. She wore a cumbersome volume of jewelry as so many in her generation did; stylishly torn jeans; a tank top showing off her pierced beer belly, and some of those retro-hi-top sneakers kids wore because they thought they made them look street savvy or something. Her fingers had nicotine stains and it was obvious she chewed on her fingernails.

"This is Diana," Janet said, sitting beside her.

"Hello Diana," Tommy said, trying to smile warmly to put her at ease.

"Diana," Janet said, "I'm going to tell the sheriff what you told me, okay? Feel free to add anything new you remember."

Janet, a mother of three, wasn't great at police work, but she was a dynamite rape crisis counselor. Actually, in anything requiring the human touch, Janet was his go-to superstar. She faced Tommy as she spoke, with

23

frequent glances at the young girl to coax nods of agreement and include her in the conversation.

"Diana found me at the gas station," Janet explained. "She had just left the house of one of her teachers and ran about six blocks before she found me."

"Is it normal for you to see your teachers on the weekend?" Tommy asked.

Diana nodded.

"She's been visiting Ms. Greeley at her house for a few weeks," Janet said. "Right?"

Diana nodded.

"What's your relationship with Ms. Greeley?" Tommy asked.

"We're friends," Diana said, staring at the floor.

"She ran from the house because she was scared," Janet went on. "There were things going on in the house that made her uncomfortable."

"What kind of things, Diana?" Tommy asked. "I'd like to hear it from you, if you don't mind."

"Well, there was me, Rose—Ms. Greeley I mean—Zack and Dave," Diana said in a squeaky voice.

"Who are Zack and Dave?" Tommy asked.

"They go to my school. Zack is a junior; Dave's a senior."

"How about you?" Tommy asked.

"I'm a freshman," the girl replied.

"So what do these boys do over at Ms. Greeley's house?" Tommy asked.

"They...they're lovers," Diana said. "The three of them."

Tommy had a poker face that came in handy at times like these.

"For the last few days," Janet said, "they've been pressuring Diana into doing some things she doesn't want to do."

Tommy nodded. "Sexual things?"

Diana nodded.

"The boys are pressuring you?"

Janet cleared her throat. "The boys, yes. But mostly Ms. Greeley Right?"

Diana nodded.

"How old are you?" Tommy asked.

"I'm 14," Diana said.

"Did they try to force you to have sex, Diana?" Tommy asked.

"Well, not exactly," Diana said. "I mean, nobody got rough, I guess. But, Rose has been, like, pregnant...and, she's all into some kind of, like, alternate religion..."

The girl seemed on the verge of breaking down. Janet picked up the narrative. "It sounds like the school teacher gave birth in her house. They took this newborn baby and performed some sort of ritual. At the end of the ritual, they took a knife..."

The girl lost it, wailing and blubbering, face wet with tears. "...Blood everywhere...it kept screaming..."

Janet put her arm around the teen and patted the back of her neck, turning to Tommy with tears in her own eyes.

Tommy ground his teeth and asked, "Can her parents come get her?"

"She lives with her mother, who's at work today," Janet said.

"She's gonna have to leave work and come get her daughter," Tommy said. "And we need the address of Ms. Greeley's house."

"Yes sir," Janet said, wiping her eyes.

Tommy rose, opened a desk drawer and pulled out his shoulder rig, checking the magazine in his M1911 out of habit and clicking it back into place.

He threw his office door open and stalked down the hallway, pulling on his shoulder rig. He paused at the dispatcher's desk. "Who do we have not busy right now?"

Laura brought up a window on her monitor and scanned the list. "Jeff and Kevin don't have anything."

"Get 'em," Tommy said. "And if anyone else gets free in the next hour, send 'em to me, too. And get Judge Aragon on the phone. We need a warrant PDQ."

"Yes sir," Laura replied.

NORMAN, OKLAHOMA

Tommy and two deputies arrived at the Greeley house and checked all the exits before knocking. For most cops the girl's tip by itself would suffice for probable cause, and judges would accept it in cases like this, when time was of the essence.

But Tommy had an arrangement with the judge to get warrants quickly, and so far he'd always had one when he intended to search somebody's property.

A skinny teenage boy answered the door, with an oversize T-shirt and sagging pants, a toboggan on his head despite being indoors. "What is it? he asked, taking in the sight of his visitors, with hollow eyes.

Jeff gave him the spiel. The kid tried to stall, then his eyes came alive with hate when the uniformed men entered anyway.

As they drew closer to the door to the basement, the kid's protests grew louder. Kevin stayed with the boy during the search, to make sure he didn't try to run.

False Flag - Brown

Kevin wasn't expecting the kid to produce a knife and stab him just under his vest.

The kid screamed and came at Jeff with the knife. Jeff had his pistol out by now, and fired. The kid went down.

Jeff's eyes went wide. He'd never had to shoot before, and this was a kid.

Tommy grabbed him by the shoulder, pointing at Kevin, who was also down, crying out and bleeding everywhere. "Put your weapon away and stay with Kevin. Use one hand to put direct pressure on the wound. With your other hand, call an ambulance, and for backup. Got it?"

Jeff nodded dazedly.

The basement door burst open. Another teenage boy emerged, taller and sturdier, slamming the door behind him. He wielded some kind of curved sword and by the way he moved it, it was obvious to Tommy he was comfortable using it.

"Hold your fire!" Tommy shouted, in case Jeff decided to counteract this new threat, or if Sanford came in the back way after hearing the shot.

The boy glared at Tommy and bellowed something that was neither English, Spanish, or *Shawandasse*. Then in a guttural voice in English he said, "I'm going to carve you up and drink your blood!"

The kid definitely had the edge in speed and energy--Tommy could tell by the way he moved. His T-shirt said something about ROTC and leadership. He reminded Tommy a little of himself as a boy—maybe what some of Tommy's buddies might have looked and dressed like when young men.

"You need to put down the weapon, young man," Tommy said.

Light glinted off the blade as the boy twirled it in a figure-eight pattern while advancing.

Tommy didn't want to shoot him; but he also didn't want to be sliced open by that blade. Without warning he dropped into a deep crouch and used his leg to sweep the kid's feet out from under him. The kid fell and Tommy, springing up from his crouch, landed on his wrist, kicking the sword away.

Tommy squatted, pinning the boys arms against the floor. From here he paused to decide how he would wrestle the kid around onto his stomach, to get the cuffs on.

With strength no teenage boy of his size should have, the boy bent up from flat on his back, rising like Dracula from a coffin, lifting Tommy up with him. Tommy shoved his unbelief to the back of his mind and drove an open hand strike into the boy's jaw.

Tommy knew how to knock a person out. He could do much more than that with his bare hands, in fact. But the boy was barely even

False Flag - Brown

stunned.

Tommy hit him again, and again. He rained down blows that would send a mature man twice the kid's size to the hospital, but his lights wouldn't go out. Ideas occurred to Tommy in those few seconds: Maybe the kid was on cocaine, or PCP. But where was his disproportionate strength coming from? It wasn't like Tommy hadn't known people who were stronger than they looked. In fact, Tommy himself was one of those people.

This was something different.

In desperation, Tommy reached for a weapon on his belt he'd never used before. He drew the stun gun, poked it against the kid and pushed the button. It jolted the kid's body, but didn't stop him. Tommy sent charge after charge into the boy, who was still full of fight. But it slowed his body down enough for Tommy to roll him over and slap the cuffs on.

In amazement, he straightened and watched the kid flail around, straining with spastic desperation as if trying to break the cuffs. For some reason Tommy feared he might be able to. "Keep your eye on him," he told Jeff. "I don't know what he's on, but if you have to, taze him."

Jeff nodded, hand clamped on Kevin's wound.

Tommy opened the basement door again and stepped through. His nostrils were assaulted immediately. The air was heavy with strong incense--and something foul underneath that smell.

He descended the stairs, preferring to let his eyes adjust to the dark rather than use a flashlight. Strangely shaped objects hung from the rafters. As his eyes focused in the dim light, it became obvious why there'd been such an epidemic of pets reported missing in town. And what had happened to the pigs reported stolen by a local farmer was also explained.

The floor and walls were decorated with strange symbols and pictures. Tommy remembered Diana had mentioned some kind of alternate religion. Then he noticed something that looked like a stool, or perhaps a small end table, made of brass. Upon this platform was what appeared to be the corpse of a human baby.

Something about a collection of pillows on the floor didn't look right, Tommy studied it. A mattress lay on the floor--no bed frame, no box spring. One of the large pillows stirred, then took on the form of a naked woman. Early-to-mid forties, attractive...probably quite a hottie once upon a time. From her lower lip, trailing down her chin and neck were dark streaks. Tommy was afraid to guess what those streaks were composed of.

"You should leave," the woman said. "Forget you ever came here. You don't know what you're messing with."

False Flag - Brown

6
D MINUS 83
COCCOCINO COUNTY, ARIZONA

Dwight Cavarra measured the chemicals and prepared to mix them. In the back room shop of CBC Southwest Tactical were 21 different molds, including the one in front of him. This one was for his patented polymer pistol grip stock for the Springfield M1A.

Once the initial casting cooled, the cutting, drilling, grinding and sanding would begin. Then the bipod would be fitted, the hinged, rubber-padded butt plate affixed over the cleaning kit compartment, then the whole assembly boxed for shipping.

The cheap walkie-talkie squawked in Cavarra's breast pocket. "I need to talk to you when you get a minute, Rocco."

He held the radio to his mouth and thumbed the push-to-talk button. "I'll be right out."

Cavarra—"Rocco" to his friends—was built stocky, and his once black hair was now mostly white. His swarthy Sicilian features and cauliflower ears had earned him the ethnically insensitive nickname, which stuck no matter where he went. But whereas he once resembled a mob enforcer, he now looked more like a mafia don.

He left the shop to enter the front counter area. Waiting for him was Leon Campbell. Leon was tall, lanky, with a dark brown complexion, and coarse black hair buzzed close to his scalp.

Out in the lobby the television was on, turned to Fox News. Rocco had sworn off TV in general, and the lapdog media in particular. But customers liked to watch it while waiting around, and Fox at least allowed some diversity of opinion...up to a point. A customer sat on one of the padded chairs in the lobby, staring at the screen.

"What's up?" Rocco asked Leon.

"Probably in your office would be better," Leon replied in his lazy marble-mouthed Georgia drawl.

Just then Carlos Bojado entered through the front door, with a tricked-out SKS rifle in one hand. Carlos was about Cavarra's height, but still in really good shape, like Leon. He had a few white hairs now himself, though.

Even the young guys are getting long-in-the-tooth, Cavarra thought.

"I need to talk, too," Carlos said, slipping his radio into his cargo pocket.

Cavarra gestured toward his office. "Let's all go back, then."

The three of them entered Rocco's office. He didn't take the chair behind his desk, but sat with them on the furniture in front of it.

28

False Flag - Brown

The walls were covered with plaques, framed photographs and certificates from the Navy and Naval Special Warfare. One of the pictures, taken in a temporary encampment in the Sudan which officially never existed, captured three men in the "see no evil, hear no evil, speak no evil" pose. The man covering his mouth: Cole; and the one covering his ears: Fava-Vargas, were long dead. The man covering his eyes was Tommy Scarred Wolf. Another photo captured Tommy, Rocco, Leon, Carlos and Jake McCallum posing together on the deck of a cargo ship. They had been the only survivors (save for a couple pilots) of that mission in Sudan all those years ago.

"You first, Leon," Cavarra said.

"This cat out there," Leon said, chinning toward the door, "the one in the lobby?"

Cavarra nodded. "He's the one wants to order all the night vision and ballistic armor, right?"

An order like this one would go far toward making this a profitable fiscal quarter.

"Somethin' about the dude bothers me," Leon said. "I don't wanna sell him nothin'. I wanna tell him to hit the trail and don't come back."

"This must be the day for it," Carlos said. "This guy I got..."

Cavarra's eyebrows furrowed and he raised his hand to interrupt Carlos. "One at a time. What's wrong with him, Cannonball?"

Leon fidgeted in his seat. "I don't know, exactly. I'm gettin' a bad vibe from him. Gives me the heebie-jeebies."

"Think he might be from the Alphabets?" Cavarra asked. All three of them were careful to keep everything about the business above-board and adherent to current legislation. But of course legality didn't guarantee tolerance from the federal government.

Leon shrugged. "I mean, he could be ATF or FBI or somethin'. But I think it's deeper than that. I can't prove it, man, but I'd bet money there's somethin' dirty about this cat."

Rocco puffed his cheeks. Leon was a friend and he knew him pretty well. "It's a decent pile of money, Leon. And who-knows-how-much word of mouth."

"I know," Leon said.

"Okay," Cavarra said. "Your turn, Carlos."

"I think I know what kind of vibe my guy's putting out," Carlos said. "He smells like one of those white separatists or something."

"Anything in particular?" Cavarra asked.

"Mostly the way he looks at me," Carlos said. "And he keeps asking if we have a fourth partner he hasn't seen yet. That seems to be his biggest concern."

False Flag - Brown

"Like, 'do you have somebody white I can deal with'?" Leon guessed.

"Yeah," Carlos said. "That's the vibe I'm getting. Like just now, he didn't want to come inside with me. He's standing around outside, like if he comes in a building with a Spic and a Spade, he'll pick up a disease."

"Don't forget the Dago," Cavarra said, trying to lighten the atmosphere.

"Who knows," Leon quipped, "he might at least consider you **part** human."

"The good news is," Cavarra said, gesturing toward Leon, "we can test this theory. Hand him off to our buddy, here. See if he agrees to let Cannonball take him through the Target Course."

Leon patted his sidearm. "I got hollow points, Rocco. Make a nasty mess out there. Just sayin'."

Carlos elbowed him. "Hey, are Neo-Nazis in season?"

"Open season," Leon replied. "Got my huntin' license in the truck."

"Hey, seriously," Cavarra said. "If you decide Carlos is right, send him packing. Don't even get started."

"Want me to send this one away, too?" Leon asked, gesturing toward the lobby.

"Nah. I'll take care of it," Cavarra said, standing.

Leon and Carlos stood with him. They exited the office in a group. Cavarra marched toward the man in the lobby, but stopped when something caught his attention on the TV.

"...The Pottawatomie Sheriff's Department says they found evidence of occultic rituals in the basement of this house," the reporter was saying, as the screen filled with the image of an average-looking house on a residential street in Norman, Oklahoma, "including animal and human sacrifice. The chief suspect is a local high school teacher, also suspected of numerous sexual relationships with students..."

"Ho-lee..." Carlos intoned.

"That's Tommy's stomping ground," Cavarra said.

"I think you're right," Leon agreed.

"That's where Tommy lives?" Carlos asked, incredulous.

"Not in that house," Leon replied, with a condescending tone. "But he's Sheriff of that county."

Carlos flipped him the bird.

They continued watching, and it was reported that one deputy was injured in the arrest, but there was no mention of the sheriff himself.

CBC Southwest Tactical was located a short drive from Flagstaff. The dry, rocky surrounding terrain looked like something out of a Clint Eastwood movie. *The Outlaw Jose Wales*, to be specific. The office was a converted "manufactured home" on a concrete slab.

Back outside, Leon found the customer Carlos described smoking a cigarette over by the target shed. Leon marched toward him and checked his clipboard on the way. "Arden Thatcher?"

Thatcher glanced up, took a look at the tall, athletic black man, and his disapproval was obvious. "Yeah."

"You want to qualify on the Western Shootout Course today. Is that right?"

"Yeah," Thatcher said, taking a drag of his cigarette.

"Carlos already showed you the route, and briefed you on range safety?"

"Yeah," Thatcher said. "Doesn't anyone else work here?"

"What do you mean?" Leon asked, calm washing over him as if he was taking up trigger slack.

Arden Thatcher was a short, skinny guy with bland features and long blond hair in a pony tail. He wore jeans, cowboy boots, and a black T-shirt with some country-western musician's name on it in stylized letters. His lips now twisted into a smile that struck Leon as hopelessly phony. "It's just the two of you runnin' the show here? You and the Mexican? ...I mean, the Spanish guy?"

"Our partner," Leon said, "he's the Sicilian guy—he's busy with sumpthin' else right now. Can I get you to sign the paperwork now, Mr. Thatcher?"

Thatcher's gaze dropped to the clipboard and pen Leon held. Or was it the dark hand that held them? His stare was one a person would level at an object infected with the Ebola Virus. "What's on those papers?"

"Carlos should have explained it to you," Leon replied, patiently. "It confirms that we explained the safety rules; says you agree to not hold us liable for what happens if you violate those rules...all the usual stuff."

"That sounds almost like a threat," Thatcher said.

"Not at all," Leon said. "We're careful to advise everybody who comes here how to stay safe. If you ignore us and do sumpthin' unsafe anyway, and get hurt, that's not our fault, is it?"

Thatcher pursed his lips and continued to stare at the paperwork.

"And we're gonna need payment up front," Leon added.

Thatcher shook his head. "I ain't signin' that and I ain't payin' for shit up front."

Leon forced a smile. "In that case, thanks for visitin' and enjoy your drive."

"I drove all day to get here and payed for a motel already," Thatcher said, angrily.

"Afraid I'm not catchin' your point, Mr. Thatcher."

False Flag - Brown

"This is false advertisin'," Thatcher declared. "Your website don't say nothin' about how you really run this rinky-dink shithole."

"What is it that has you confused?" Leon asked.

"Oh, I ain't confused. And neither will the Better Business Bureau be, when I report your ass. You wanna play? Let's play."

"Just curious," Leon said, "what is it you think we wasn't honest about?"

Thatcher was red-faced and Leon could tell he normally would have tried something stupid. But his gaze kept returning to the holstered Ruger P90 on Leon's hip.

"Well ain't you just a great salesman?" Thatcher finally said, with a sarcastic tone. "I'll have to write this company and tell 'em what a good salesman you are. You really make me want to give you my business." By the time he finished saying this he had his back turned and was halfway back to where he'd parked his Toyota Tundra.

"Since I'm one of the owners, you can hand the letter directly to me," Leon said to his back. He took position by a tree that was thick enough for temporary cover in a pinch, in case this loose cannon had something hidden in his vehicle and decided to try something really stupid.

The Titan started and Thatcher was heavy on the gas tearing out of there,

"Don't let the door hit you in the fourth point on the way out," Leon muttered, half aloud.

Inside, Cavarra called the other customer to the front counter. Before doing so he had checked the background of both questionable customers on internet databases while in his office. Both of them had clean records.

Almost too clean.

But now, as Terrance Handel approached the counter and Rocco studied his face, he understood what Leon had meant.

Handel was a strapping dude--over six feet tall and muscular, with a handsome enough face. But he gave off a vibe that suggested something ugly and cold.

Cavarra gave himself this assignment automatically despite the fact that he dreaded it. He'd never had to do this to a customer and didn't want to. Not only did it mean turning down money; but also casting judgment on somebody for no defined reason.

Although CBC Southwest Tactical was a partnership between the three of them, he still usually had the final say in business decisions. One of the costs of leadership was playing the bad guy in situations like this.

"I'm sorry, Mr. Handel, but we won't be doing business with you."

Surprise registered in Handel's narrowing eyes, but not to the degree that would seem normal. "Excuse me?"

Cavarra repeated himself.

"I don't understand," Handel said. "Why? I'm willing to pay your asking price."

"I appreciate that, sir," Cavarra said. "I'm afraid we'd just rather not do business with you."

Handel reminded Cavarra of a robot trying to process data that "does not compute" in an old Science Fiction movie. Finally, he said, "That's not an answer. You at least have to tell me why."

Cavarra began to sweat. Inside he was squirming, but he kept his voice calm and neutral. "No sir. We're not required to disclose our business decisions."

Handel turned to study Carlos, then back to Cavarra with an appraising gaze. "That's ridiculous. You can't just refuse service to a customer."

"We're not a hospital," Cavarra said, "so we reserve the right to refuse service to whoever we please. Unless you're a homosexual, we're allowed to run our business as if this was still a free country."

"Is that it?" Handel asked, squinting in unbelief. "You think I'm gay?"

Rocco shook his head. "I have no idea; and I don't want to know. Even if you are, we don't bake cakes or hire out space for wedding receptions, anyway. Bottom line is, we're not gonna sell you anything."

Handel gave both Rocco and Carlos another measuring stare, and finally turned to exit.

Cavarra felt even more uneasy, now. For some reason it would have sat better with him had the guy been outraged, cussed and threatened for a while before storming off to slam the door behind him. This guy just took it in stride a little too well, for a civilian.

"We'll make up the money somewhere else, Rocco," Carlos said, once Handel was gone. "We've been doing real good, considering the economy. We could become millionaires just by selling ammo, these days."

Leon came in through the side door. "I'm pretty sure you was right, Carlos," he said.

"Let's mark this date on the calendar," Cavarra said, grimacing. "From now on this will be Turn Customers Away Day."

"Hey," Carlos said, pointing to the TV again, "they're still holding fast on the Garber Ranch."

Leon stopped to look and Rocco came around the counter to direct his attention to the flat screen. News cameras panned over a parked convoy of APCs and armored vans, with Alphabets in black uniforms, armor, masks and helmets, brandishing automatic weapons. Then there was a

False Flag - Brown

short montage of different armed civilians in old-school woodland camouflage. Then a shot of an ambulance making its way between the opposed forces to the ranch house.

"Somebody get shot?" Rocco asked.

"Shh!" Carlos held his hand up.

"...The elderly rancher is thought to have suffered a heart attack," the news announcer said. "Right now the rumors are that it was due to the stress over the standoff; but as yet there is no confirmation."

"Whaddya think, Rocco?" Leon asked. "They gonna throw down on each other there?"

Cavarra exhaled heavily. "You know what I believe. This is 1913 Austria-Hungary. I don't know if the whole thing touches off at Garber Ranch or somewhere else. And so far as we're concerned, it probably won't matter a whole lot where the fuse gets lit."

"Come on, man," Carlos said, waving dismissively. "This is America. That crazy stuff doesn't happen here. We always work it out, in the end."

Cavarra glanced at his friend, shook his head sadly and returned to the workshop.

False Flag - Brown

Joe Tasper pulled his boots on while his girlfriend continued to rant. His headache was getting worse.

He had to raise his voice to be heard over her tirade. "You don't need any more jewelry, Crystal. And I sure don't need to run my credit card up any higher."

"If it was something for your car or your stupid computer, you'd put it on your credit card!" she said, spittle flying from her mouth.

She was about five-foot-seven, had multicolored hair and piercings in various places. When he first got with her she seemed normal and was attractive. Since she'd been with him, her persona had grown more and more bizarre; she grew overweight; and she started fights all the time about nothing.

"Why does it have to go on the credit card anyway?" Crystal demanded. "What have you been doing with the money that you hide from me?"

"Paying bills," he said, tying his work boots. "Like the electric bill that's more than doubled since you moved in. And the phone bill, since you insist on exceeding your minutes every month."

"Oh, don't you dare blame me for your money troubles, Joe! It's not my fault that your job is for losers. Maybe if you'd have gotten an education, you could have found something that pays decent."

He finished tying his laces and stood. "Oh, like your fancy college degree is doing **you** so much good? Go buy your own trinkets if your education is so great at generating money."

Her face beet red, she stepped forward, poking her index finger toward his face, and called him a few unflattering names. "You **would** belittle my education, you pathetic moron! You're so threatened that I've accomplished more than you have; that I have a degree..."

He stepped around her, pushing her finger out of his personal space, and strode for the door. "You wanna give me something to feel threatened about? Get off your ass and find a job. Bring home some money to help with the bills for a change, instead of just spending it faster than I can make it."

"Oh, you think you're a 'real man' because you go screw around with your buddies all day and get a paycheck for it?" Crystal asked, shrilly. "I bet Jordan doesn't mind buying **his** girlfriend something nice once in a while. I'll bet..."

The rest of her words didn't register. He was blown away by the idea that she believed his grueling, dead-end blue-collar job was "screwing around with his buddies all day." She made it sound like he was at some fun party six days a week, instead of working himself half to death. Was she really that delusional?

The distraction of this thought must have slowed his stride, because she raced past him despite the weight of her flab, and barricaded herself in front of the door.

"You're not going to walk away from me this time!" she declared.

He rolled his eyes. "You're complaining about how I don't have enough money to buy stupid shit, so you're gonna keep me from going to work? How much sense does that make?"

"It's not stupid! You want to know what stupid shit is? It's spending hundreds of dollars on a stupid pickup truck you don't need!"

"Oh, I don't need it?" he retorted. "Like how we used it to move all your crap over from your mom's apartment?"

She was ready with a remark, as always, but changed gears when he picked her up and set her down over to the side so he could open the door. She screamed out as if she'd been injured, and screeched obscene insults while flailing wildly at him. One of her clawing hands caught his shirt and tore it right down the front.

Joe felt himself losing his temper, and had to get out of there. He stepped through the door and slammed it behind him, which at least muffled the volume of her tirade. Now he had to show up for work wearing only a partial shirt. He wasn't sure how serious a reprimand he'd get for that, but he knew better than to go back inside and try to get an undamaged one with Crystal on the rampage.

He got in his car and started it, itching to take off right away but not wanting to strain the engine before it warmed up. Glancing in the rear-view mirror, he saw he was bleeding from scratches under his eye inflicted by her fingernails when she clawed at him.

He heard a door slam and craned his neck around toward the source of the noise. Crystal was charging toward him. She had taken his baseball bat from inside his closet and wielded it like a weapon. He rolled down his window and shouted, "That's mine, Crystal! Put it back where you found it and calm down!"

"Calm down?" she repeated. "You want me to calm down?" While hurling more insults, she swung the bat with all her strength into his windshield.

The glass was shatterproof, but the blow cracked it into a spiderweb pattern.

Now he was pissed. He got out of the car and stalked toward Crystal. She held the bat cocked, threatening to smash his head with it. He grabbed it and yanked it out of her hands.

"Listen, bitch," Joe said, straining to control violent impulses, "get the hell away from me; get your ass back in the house and keep your big damn mouth shut! We'll deal with this when I get back." He tossed the bat in the back seat and began to open the car door again.

He wouldn't have guessed she could act any crazier, but she went completely berserk now. All she heard was the word "bitch," and she became a windmill, trying to punch and kick him repeatedly.

He caught one wrist as she was trying to hit his face. She swung with her other arm and he caught that wrist. She kicked him in the groin and spit in his face. Reeling from the pain, he let go of one wrist and wiped the spit off. She took advantage of the opportunity to slap him.

She'd slapped him several times in these stupid altercations since they'd been together, and he'd never retaliated. All his life he'd heard it was wrong to hit females, so he put up with a lot because he had no choice. But at that moment he stopped caring what he'd been taught.

He slapped her and she went down, wailing, gasping, staring up at him in horror.

He spit on her, got in the car and drove away.

Joe had almost made it to work when the cop car pulled up behind him with flashing lights.

Great. Now he was going to be ticketed for the windshield, which was going to make it even harder to scrape up the money to replace it. And it would make him late for work. He had already missed several days at his job due to Crystal's unlimited supply of personal crises, and was probably close to getting fired.

He had to get her out of his life. He was a fool for ever letting her in.

Two cops got out of their car and walked up to stand at both Joe's doors. He rolled his window back down.

"Is your name Joe Tasper?" the cop nearest him asked.

That was weird. Usually they asked for the driver's license and registration first before they let on that they knew his identity. Joe confirmed who he was and the cop rattled off his address, asking if Joe lived there. Joe confirmed again.

"I need you to get out of the car, Mr. Tasper."

Joe complied, asking, "What's going on, officer?" as he stepped out.

"Face your vehicle and place your hands on the roof, please," the cop said, with a hard ugly look.

"Whoa, wait," Joe protested. "What's going on?"

"Just do what I said, Mr. Tasper."

The cop nearest him had handcuffs in his left hand, his right hand resting on his gun butt, thumb under the holster snap. The other cop was circling around to sandwich Joe from the other side, something black in his hand.

"Are you arresting me?"

"We are placing you under arrest, yes."

"For a busted windshield? It's my own car; and I'm not even the one who did it."

"You're under arrest for aggravated assault," the cop said.

Joe groaned. Crystal again. The gift that just kept on giving.

"Listen, officer, if there was any assault that happened today, it was against me. I was kicked in the groin; slapped in the face; my clothes torn up; windshield smashed... You can see my face is bleeding, right?"

The cop coming up behind him said something, but Joe only caught part of it: "...You get for abusing..."

"No, **you** listen," the other cop growled. "I said turn around and put your hands on the car!"

Again Joe swallowed his anger. There was nothing he could do right then to avoid getting arrested, so he spun in place and began leaning forward. But before his hands made contact with the car, two sharp objects pierced the skin in his side. He had time to look down at the source of the pain and form the word "tazer" in his mind, then he was on the ground, flopping like a fish.

False Flag - Brown

8
D MINUS 83
COCCOCINO COUNTY, ARIZONA

Terrance Handel drove his Honda Pilot off the CBC property to the highway, tuning through the radio stations.

He might have spent more time pondering his treatment at CBC Southwest Tactical had he not seen the news segment on the TV in the lobby.

Finally he found a station broadcasting a news segment. He waited for the report from Norman, Oklahoma, and finally it came. "The primary suspect is local school teacher Cynthia Greeley, 45."

Terrance drove aimlessly while he listened. His day and this trip were a bust, anyway. He had nowhere to be, and would have to figure out what the wisest course of action would be, now.

While driving through the town of Sedona he noticed a quaint old tavern-like establishment with an owl logo on the sign. He pulled into the parking lot, listened to the rest of the news report, then went inside for a beer.

When Terrance first saw Ms. Greeley, she was teaching biology at his middle school in Oklahoma City. She was maybe in her 20s then, and the sexiest woman he'd ever seen. He hoped to get her for biology in spring semester, but was assigned to Mr. Spicer instead. Ms. Greeley's class filled to capacity early--and no wonder: every horny boy in the school wanted to ogle her for a full period.

She had a fantastic body that she routinely showed off with short skirts and tight, low-cut blouses. She had a sensuous voice and walk, and boys who took her class claimed that one time seeing her uncross and recross her legs made the whole school year worthwhile. But what really pushed her hot factor over the edge was how she looked and spoke to boys. She never said anything overtly sexual in school but boys were just certain she was sending out seductive signals. When she batted her eyelashes it seemed she knew their naughtiest fantasies and was more than capable of fulfilling them.

Terrance witnessed this once when she discussed one student's homework with him. Then, toward the end of Seventh Grade, he approached her to ask about getting in her class the next year.

She smirked at him like she understood perfectly well why he wanted her class. He didn't remember much about what was actually said. Mostly he remembered her scent; her lips as they formed words; her perfectly tanned cleavage; and her bewitching eyes.

False Flag - Brown

He spent all summer fantasizing that she would turn out to be one of those teachers who had an affair with a student.

But he didn't get her for biology. The year passed and he was off to high school.

He didn't see her again for the next four years, but he thought about her constantly. He thought about her all through boot camp, too. He also convinced himself to look her up when he got back.

He returned home on leave after Parris Island and visited the school in uniform. Teachers and students alike gushed over him, but the high point was when Ms. Greeley looked at him with an appreciation he hadn't seen when he was a student trying to get in her class.

"You remember me?" he asked.

"Of course I remember you, Terrance. I was hoping to teach you some biology."

"I tried to get in your class," he said. "But they assigned me to Mr. Spicer."

"Oh, he couldn't possibly teach you about biology the way I can," she told him in a conspiratorial, sultry tone. Then she actually winked at him, shooting his imagination into overdrive.

He wanted to say, "It's not too late; I'm still willing to learn." But he chickened out.

Then, the next day, he ran into her at the bank. He decided he had nothing to lose, since he would be shipped to Afghanistan after AIT. So he flirted, and asked for her number.

She not only gave him her number, but her address.

He showed up in uniform again, which was a corny thing to do, but she apparently didn't mind. There was little preamble. When she met him at the door she immediately took his cover off his head and pulled him inside. She asked if he'd had any personal biology lessons before. He admitted he hadn't, and she proceeded to give him the biology lesson of his life.

Technically she was married; but it was an open arrangement and her husband was rarely home. By some coincidence, his job took him to the Pentagon frequently. She lived mostly alone in their house, and kept herself busy when not in school with some weird religious stuff that required Terrance to remove his shoes inside the front door.

She made all his fantasies come true, and then introduced him to some he'd never even thought of. Every time he got leave, he arranged to spend it with her. Strangely, he remembered less and less details about their love-ins as time went on. He just knew he left satisfied.

It was funny, how his memory worked. It seemed like so much was blurred into obscurity during his childhood and after becoming intimate

40

False Flag - Brown

with Ms. Greeley (she still insisted he call her that, even when they were in the most informal positions). He didn't even remember much about his deployments, or all his years in the Corps.

Come to think of it, he didn't remember how he came to the decision to visit CBC Southwest Tactical, or why he wanted to place bulk orders for gear.

So Ms. Greeley had moved to Norman. He wondered if all the stuff about sacrificed animals was true. And a human baby, too?

No. He knew her. She was only interested in bringing pleasure to others, and she excelled at that.

He thought briefly about visiting her in jail. Maybe even testifying as a character witness for her. But he'd lost touch with her in the last few years. Plus, these days he had an instinctive compunction to keep a low profile.

Ms. Greeley was no longer low profile.

False Flag - Brown

The paramedics avoided eye contact with Roy Jr. as they hauled Roy by stretcher into the ambulance. The last thing Roy Jr. heard his father say before the ambulance doors closed was "Don't knuckle under, son!"

The ambulance got turned around, then negotiated the bumpy dirt road off the ranch. Three men who had been watching everything at a respectful distance now moved in closer as Roy Jr. watched his father being taken away.

The rawboned one, dressed like a cowboy, was his neighbor, Mike, who owned the closest ranch. Mike's sons were not in sight, but likely patrolling the spread on horseback. The big, burly man in bib overalls was Roy Jr.'s uncle, Rusty. He had brought sons and grandsons, all armed, and dubbed "anti-government extremists" by the press. The stocky man in camouflage fatigues and a boonie hat was named Gary. Roy Jr. had never met him before three days ago. Gary had driven about 300 miles with a party of 11 other men who came armed and equipped to help Roy's family and friends defend the ranch, if necessary. Right then they were in hasty defensive positions facing the feds.

The Bar G Ranch spread over thousands of acres, but there were only three roads cut through the rough land. The feds had their military armored vehicles massed at the three entrances. Of course they could go off-road just fine, but for now evidently intended to stay on clearly defined avenues once they moved in. No doubt reconnaissance aircraft had caught heat signatures of armed parties waiting for them in the hills and brush, too. What they might not suspect was that some of Roy's allies were hiding among the cattle, as a sort of infrared camouflage. There wasn't nearly enough manpower to secure the entire perimeter of the property

When Rusty drew close enough, he squeezed his nephew's shoulder. "How you holdin' up, Junior?"

"I think I'm still a long way from a heart attack, if that's what you mean," Roy Jr. replied.

"Did he say anything before they took off?" Mike asked.

"He said 'don't knuckle under'," Roy Jr. replied.

Rusty and Mike chuckled.

"Hey, fellas," Gary said, looking down the road the Ambulance had taken. "Here comes The Man."

A black SUV drove toward them, a white flag tied to the antenna.

False Flag - Brown

"What the hell do they want, now?" Mike wondered aloud.

Gary looked Roy Jr. in the eye. "They want you to knuckle under."

"He's right," Rusty said, spitting into the dirt. "With Roy out of the way, they're gonna test the waters with you. Scare you or sweet talk you into givin' up."

"Don't do it, amigo," Mike said. "Don't fall for their bullshit. They got no right to even be here. They only pull this kind of stunt because folks been lettin' 'em get away with it for so long. We need to stop lettin' 'em get away with it."

"We're with you, Roy," Gary said. "Don't let them scare you. You're not alone."

Roy Jr. thrust his hands in his pockets. "They're gettin' paid to be here," he told Gary. "You guys'll have to go back home at some point to your jobs and families. They can afford to wait until you do."

"We can stay for the rest of the week," Gary said. "If it hasn't blown over by then, some of our buddies will come to take over. We'll rotate men through here, if that's what it takes. There's a guy gonna interview me for a podcast here on site. I'm goin' on a HAM radio broadcast when I get back. The word will get out."

The SUV pulled to a stop and three doors swung open. A man in a suit and two figures in black combat gear emerged from the vehicle.

Gary locked-and-loaded his AR15. "You two Nazi ninjas, back in the vehicle!" he commanded.

Mike and Rusty also got their weapons ready.

The man in the suit raised both hands, fingers spread. "Gentlemen, we came under a flag of truce. There's no need..."

"We've all seen how 'honorable' you clowns are," Gary interrupted. "Tell your goons to get back in the truck, **now**."

The negotiator nodded to the two dark figures and they climbed back inside.

"That really wasn't necessary," the negotiator said, then extended his hand toward Roy Jr. "My name is Ray Hollis. Can we speak in private?"

Roy Jr. reluctantly shook his hand and gestured over toward the tack shed. The two men walked over and faced each other in the shade of the small structure.

"First of all," Hollis said, "I'm sorry about your father. We've got him on his way to the best care available and we'll do everything we can for him."

"Who's this 'we' you're talkin' about?" Roy Jr. asked. "Do you speak for the hospital and ambulance service, too? Do they work for you?"

The negotiator's public relations facade faltered, and he licked his lips. "Hey, there's no reason to make this hostile. We're all sorry about

False Flag - Brown

your father. None of us wants this situation we've got, here. We all just want to resolve this reasonably so nobody else has to get so stressed out."

"Reasonably," Roy Jr. echoed, mockingly. "You show up here with an army of killers because my dad built a duck pond on his own property, and **you** want to talk about bein' reasonable."

With a flash of irritation, Hollis said, "Look, it won't do anybody any good to have another argument about the law concerning wetlands..."

But Roy Jr. wasn't done. "You're lyin' through your teeth about not wantin' to be hostile. Look at these goose-steppin' bastards you brought here. You don't **want** this situation? You **made** this situation! This situation is **exactly** what you people want."

"Calm down, sir," Hollis said. "We don't want any more..."

"Kiss my ass, Mr. Hollis," Roy Jr. said. "You want me to calm down? Get the hell away from our land, and we'll calm down. Put this army of yours on the border, and protect the people who pay your salary, instead of stealin' from us. I'll calm right down, then."

"I understand you're upset..." Hollis began, only to get interrupted again.

"Mr. Hollis, I'm not in the mood for any more of your snake oil. This is my family's property and you're trespassin'. I don't care what the EPA says, what the FBI says, the ATF, the IRS, the DHA. You're breakin' the law. You thought I'd be weaker than my father and you could strong-arm me. Now you got the media callin' us a bunch of Klan members. Kiss my ass, Mr. Hollis. You boys came dressed for a fight. Well, you drive one of those tanks through our fence or onto our driveway, you're gonna get one."

Hollis shook his head and gave a slight shrug of the shoulders. "All right. We tried to reason with you."

Ray Hollis walked back to the SUV. Gary snickered and called after him. "Hey, revenue man! Most of us know all about Waco. Guess what? All of us will shoot back this time. And you don't get a cease-fire when you run out of ammo."

Roy Jr. watched the SUV bump along and disappear down the road. Had he just guaranteed bloodshed? Should he have knuckled under, regardless of right and wrong?

He knew most of those standing with him were just as scared as he was. Maybe some of the boys who came with Gary were itching for a fight--he didn't know for sure. But Roy Jr.'s father, and grandfather, and great-grandfather had worked their lives away making the Chapanee Valley a profitable ranch to feed and clothe their families. Once upon a time Roy Jr. had assumed he could pass it down to his own son.

That wasn't a sure thing anymore. But he wasn't going to let some

False Flag - Brown

jackbooted Fed bulldoze his family off this land. Not on his watch.

False Flag - Brown

There was already a keg at Captain Taggart's party when Trooper Macmillan arrived, dressed in a golf shirt and Levi Dockers.

Macmillan made the rounds. There were a lot of guys he didn't get to see often because they were off when he was on, and vice-versa. There was also a fairly hot blonde and some other chicks present, mingling. He would have to check them out before long.

He got absorbed in a story Trooper Beale was telling about catching two queers going at it at a rest stop. Everybody laughed themselves silly. Then when the story was over, they got in a competition over who could tell the funniest faggot jokes. Macmillan had a few that got everybody howling.

He felt a tap on his shoulder and turned to find Captain Taggart, in a loud Hawaiian shirt and shorts, holding a beer.

"Let me have a word with you, Macmillan," the Captain said.

Macmillan followed him around the swimming pool, past the tool shed to the corner of the wooden privacy fence surrounding the back yard. His mind churned through possible reasons for this special attention. He decided it must be about the Texan he'd left on the side of the highway with a dead battery. The civilian must have complained. Somebody looked the citation up, found he'd been pulled over for tinted windows, and decided Macmillan had gone too far this time. Macmillan kept his cool and began formulating a probable cause story in his mind to justify the traffic stop.

The captain faced him and asked him a few questions about if he was enjoying the cookout and so forth. Then he said, "I've been looking over your productivity, and you've been exceptional, Jason. Just exceptional. You've been consistently proactive since you've been on patrol."

This didn't sound so bad. Maybe Taggart was praising him as a preamble to warning him to dial it down a notch, after the battery guy from Texas.

"When I pull a trooper aside for a one-on-one," Taggart said, smiling faintly, "it's usually one of two reasons. One is if he's not being proactive enough. I give him the usual talk about how each trooper should generate enough revenue to pay his own salary, and all that." He paused to chuckle, slapping Macmillan on the shoulder. "That's not the problem here, Jason, so don't worry. The other reason is to feel somebody out for possible promotion. That doesn't happen nearly as often. Both of those take place on duty, when we're in uniform."

False Flag - Brown

"Is this job-related?" Macmillan asked, confused.

Taggart took a conspiratorial look around. "Yeah. In a way. There's this program..." He paused to purse his lips for a moment. "Every so often, federal law enforcement takes a look at the Highway Patrol in different states. What they like about state and local police is that you're proven on the job. You've got a track record already; you've been screened for medical and all the other stuff. So they come down and look over entrance exams, psych profiles, interview transcripts and notes, performance reviews and the whole nine yards. Well, this time you were one of the troopers they took an interest in. A short list of badge numbers got handed to me and they're waiting on me to pick who I think the best candidate is. I don't know if I'm the tiebreaker vote or exactly how much weight they'll give my recommendation. I've never been in this position before."

Macmillan mulled this over. He wasn't in trouble at all.

I'd hate to lose you," Taggart went on, "but I wouldn't want to deny you the opportunity, either. Think you might be interested?"

"Yeah. I would," Macmillan said. His strict enforcement was getting him rewarded, not punished!

"It's a bigger pond," Taggart said. "Probably harder to get noticed. But then there's probably a lot more avenues to advancement than here, too."

"Sounds great," Macmillan said.

"Word to the wise, though," Taggart said, expression and tone now turning a bit stern. "The Feds are really touchy about all this diversity stuff. The big thing right now is sexual orientation. You have to kind of jump on the band wagon. They don't tolerate homophobia and they don't play around when it comes to that."

It only took Macmillan a moment to make the adjustment. "Consider me an advocate, then."

Macmillan would march in the next Gay Pride parade, if necessary. For this opportunity, giving somebody a blowjob wasn't even completely out of the question.

"And of course it's the same for women and coloreds," Taggart said.

"I love niggers, sir. And I was just thinking we need more women on the State Police."

They both shared a good laugh.

False Flag - Brown

11
D MINUS 87
POTTOWATOMIE COUNTY, OKLAHOMA

After the county coroner and other forensics experts had been on site for a while, Tommy made sure they had what they needed from him, and returned to the office. He watched some of the questioning of Ms. Greeley and the boy not in the hospital, took care of some paperwork, then called it a day.

He pulled into his front yard on the rez after midnight, and was greeted first by his dogs. His wife, Linda, met him at the front door and they spent a few moments showing affection before she led him to the kitchen, where his supper was keeping warm in the oven. The kitchen was old, like the rest of the house, but Linda kept it clean and cozy, in the way only feminine women could.

Tommy and Linda still usually spoke to each other in Shawandasse, to keep in practice."Where's Carl?" Tommy asked, sitting, as she set the plate in front of him.

"Out in the garage, tinkering with that dirt bike again," Linda replied, and sat across from him at the table.

Carl was their youngest, and still lived with them. Gunther and Takoda had been on their own for a while, already.

"How was your day?" Linda asked.

Tommy frowned, not really knowing how to answer that question. What could you say after seeing what he'd seen over in Cynthia Greeley's basement? He felt bad, because his job put him in an unpleasant mood more often than not, and Linda was the one who had to deal with it. It wasn't her fault that he had to see that kind of stuff...

Well, in a way, it was.

Y MINUS TWO
ABSENTEE SHAWNEE TRUST LAND, OKLAHOMA

When Tommy returned from Sumatra, he at first considered going into hiding. Maybe assuming a new identity. That's how scared he was.

He and his brother Vince had been framed for the murder of an Indonesian cop, and had to run from the local police just to escape with their lives. But after all was said and done, Vince hadn't escaped with his life.

The attempts on their lives over there made it clear they had some powerful enemies who could pull strings just about anywhere. The only reason Tommy could think of was an investigation both he and his brother had been working, which grew to include a domestic terrorist incident, and involved complicity in the highest levels of the Justice Department, implicating involvement even higher up.

So when he returned to the States, Tommy figured his enemies would come at him from some other angle. Certainly his job as a special agent of the Bureau of Indian Affairs would be sabotaged somehow, just for starters. Then what? That murder rap overseas would be the most obvious line of attack.

But against his understandably paranoid judgment, he showed himself publicly, answered (or avoided, depending on who asked) a million questions, and attended Vince's funeral service.

It was at this very kitchen table, when Tommy was deliberating with himself about what to do, that Linda made her suggestion.

"You know Sheriff Flores is up for reelection, Tommy. He's not very popular."

Flores was crooked and most everyone in the county knew it. "So what?" Tommy replied.

"So, you know it doesn't matter who the Republicans run—they won't have a chance in this county. Flores is practically running unopposed."

"I still don't see your point," Tommy said.

"You should run for sheriff, Dad," Carl said, catching on quickly and loving the idea. "As an independent."

"County sheriffs answer to the people," Linda reasoned. "You won't be under the thumb of some federal agency, or the suckups in the Tribal Police, if you go back there. As a sheriff, you'd be able to defend yourself a lot better than as a subordinate of some career slave."

"I'm not a politician," Tommy said. "Sheriffs are all political these days. I couldn't win a popularity contest against Jack the Ripper, and wouldn't want to try."

"But you could," Linda said. "You're **very** popular right now. Word's been getting around about how you rescued Jenny and Susan Pyrch, and the other girls."

Tommy's niece Jenny, Susan Pyrch from here on the rez, and some of their college friends had been kidnapped while overseas on vacation. Tommy had led an effort to get them back--and succeeded with the exception of one girl.

"What kind of word is getting around?" Tommy asked, worried. Other men had gone with him, and he owed them more than he could ever pay. If their names got out, they could suffer for their association with him.

"You're a hero, Dad," Carl said. "You're all people are talking about at school."

False Flag - Brown

"It's the same with my friends," Linda said. "I'm married to a living legend." She gave him a playful nose-honk with one hand. "Just don't let it go to your head, okay?"

"I don't know," Tommy said. "I'm not good at giving speeches or debating."

"Just be yourself," Linda said, now rubbing his cheek. "Your capable of charm, or you never would have got a second date with me."

He had to grin at that one.

"And I think you're popular enough right now, you wouldn't even have to say much," she added. "At least think about it. Unless you have a better idea."

Tommy didn't have a better idea, so he thought about it.

He ran for sheriff.

There were no debates. He gave only one speech, a week before the election, and it looked like half of the county, plus everyone on Shawnee Trust Land, came out to hear it.

"If you want a bigger jail, that's fine," he said. "I'm not gonna say you need one. And I'm not gonna seek federal or private money. If I'm sheriff, we'll handle things ourselves with the resources we have. I don't want Washington pulling strings here, so I won't invite that by begging for federal cheese. The way I see it, the office of sheriff exists to protect your rights."

This got a cheer, requiring him to pause before continuing.

"Politicians and bureaucrats get your tax dollars to serve **you**; not so **you** have to serve **them**."

Another cheer. Given the voting record of the electorate on the rez, he had expected heckling when he got to this part—or blank stares at best.

"Because most politicians see it the other way around, and usually get away with it, doesn't make it right. I'm glad you all are so enthusiastic about your rights. But your rights end where somebody else's begins. When rights get violated, that's when the police should get involved."

He spotted his family in the crowd, all toward the front. Takoda and Carl's hair was just beginning to grow back from their Mohawks. They and Gunther were typically blank-faced, but now with chests pushed out perhaps more than normal. Jenny was smiling broadly and Linda looked so excited she might faint.

"If I was sheriff, criminals would be put in jail," he continued, inspiring applause. "My deputies wouldn't be spending their time harassing people who aren't criminals. They wouldn't be engaging in random roadside checkpoints, or issuing tickets for tinted windows or seatbelt violations. If you respect the rights of your neighbor, then the law should be on your side. And it would be, if I was sheriff."

Tommy wasn't ready for the ovation he got for that short, unpolished speech. Linda threw herself at him and said, "Take me home, now, and ravage me!"

He laughed and shook his head.

"I'm serious," she said. "Have Carl spend the night with Gunther. I want you."

"I just pissed off every 'law and order' type in the county," he said. "People don't want what's right. They want..."

He was interrupted by some well-wishers who complimented him on his speech.

When he was done with this bout of glad-handing, Linda wrapped herself around his arm and said, "There aren't many 'law and order' types after Flores, Tommy. He converted them."

Tommy tried to smile, not so sure.

"Tommy, you could run for **president** after a speech like that, and even your sister-in-law would vote for you!"

Reporters crowded in to ask him questions, but Tommy ignored them. He ran the gauntlet of hand-shakers and eventually made it to his Blazer.

The election came and Tommy won, surprising him more than anyone.

His first order of business was to scrutinize his deputies. He fired all but seven of them, then sat the survivors down in the briefing room and gave them a longer speech than the one he delivered on the campaign stump.

"You men have heard the expression 'there's a new sheriff in town'?" Tommy asked, then just watched the deputies reactions as the thought sunk in.

"The reason you are the only ones here is because I let everyone else go. The first thing I want you to understand is that for every one of you still here, there's ten unemployed wannabes waiting in line, who paid to put themselves through the police academy. It will be much easier for me to teach them good habits than to correct any bad ones you might have. If you've been learning the wrong way to conduct this job before I came along, then you'd better un-learn it before I find out."

He opened the cardboard box on the desk, pulled out a handful of small booklets, and tossed one to each deputy.

"Each one of you took an oath to uphold the U.S. Constitution, and the laws of Oklahoma," Tommy said. "The Academy does an okay job teaching you the most common Oklahoma statutes you can use to trick, bully, and charge citizens. It does a disgraceful job teaching you about

False Flag - Brown

the Bill of Rights. These little books are copies of the Constitution, with the Bill of Rights and the later amendments, plus the Declaration of Independence and some other stuff. When you report to work tomorrow morning I expect you to have read the Bill of Rights. If you have any questions about it, ask me. I'm giving you one week to read the entire Constitution. You swore to uphold it, so as long as I'm sheriff, you're gonna know what's in it."

None of the deputies had worked with him before. Nobody grumbled —possibly only because they weren't sure how crazy a boss he would turn out to be.

"Until then," Tommy said, "here's some items for you to remember: if you ask for or accept any kind of bribe, you'll be fired. If you steal something, I'll put you in this jail myself. There will be no more checkpoints. No more speed traps. No more arresting people, then figuring out what to charge them with after they're brought in. No unwarranted searches; no warrants without probable cause—and probable cause does not include skin color, camouflage clothing or gun racks."

Tommy studied faces again. Some of the deputies blushed. He took note of them.

"You will not take one of the unmarked cars from the motor pool without authorization directly from me. We are not going to use unmarked cars for speeding tickets. If our objective is truly to make drivers slow down, then we want them to see that we are out there on the road with them.

"I don't want citations for seatbelt violations coming across my desk. Citizens are not our property. If they aren't endangering someone else, leave them alone. There's more than enough yahoos on the road out there driving drunk, tailgating, changing lanes without signaling, cutting people off, running stop signs, and all kinds of other idiotic stunts, for you to concentrate on. Citizens don't pay our bills to be harassed, or for you to make up excuses to cite them. You aren't revenue men anymore, so make that mental adjustment right now. From now on you are public servants, and your job is to protect and serve."

Kevin raised his hand tentatively.

"Save your questions until I'm done," Tommy said, and Kevin lowered his hand.

"If you find yourself in a situation that requires backup, then call for it. And if you need to use force--up to and including deadly force--then don't hesitate. If you're doing your job right, I'll have your back. But understand this: that badge doesn't give you the right to violate anyone's rights. If you hurt or kill somebody without good reason, then I will be your enemy. And if a suspect is truly resisting arrest, and the situation justifies a call for backup, your job is not to converge on the scene to get your sick jollies beating and tazing the suspect. You get them restrained and back here for booking as quickly, efficiently, and painlessly as possible. Is that understood?"

A chorus of sober "yes sirs" sounded in reply. This was not a happy crew.

"I'll take questions, now," Tommy said.

"Is it just us, now?" Kevin asked. "Are you going to replace the deputies you fired?"

"We're gonna work it like this for now," Tommy said. "I'll see how it goes. I might bring in a couple rookies if it turns out we truly are short-handed. But the workload will be going down now that we're out of the harassment business. This will probably be enough manpower, right here, to do the job we're getting paid to do."

Sheriff Flores had bloated the office with a small army of deputies, and ballooned the budget every fiscal year. Paying for all that excess made it necessary to generate revenue by "proactive" policing that made the locals despise and distrust law enforcement.

"Question," Jeff said. "If we're only concerned with people who violate the rights of others, how do we deal with drunk drivers?"

"Drunk drivers put other people's lives at risk," Tommy replied. "That's a violation of somebody's most basic civil liberties: the right to life—weaving all over the road and other drunk behavior will kill somebody; the right to liberty—a wheelchair is a definite infringement on their freedom; and property--the other vehicle or whatever else the drunk is going to crash into.

"Men, I spent some time in the Middle East. That region has the absolute worst drivers in the world. I wouldn't trust them at 20 miles an hour on an empty four-lane road. But they drive at 110 on two-lane, half-paved roads, with crossing livestock and blind corners. And yet they have only a fraction of the accidents as we have in the States, driver-for-driver. Why? Because they don't drive drunk. Period. They just don't do it."

Another deputy—Walker was his name—raised a hand. "You just told us to use deadly force without hesitation if we need to. Then you said you'll be our enemy if we hurt or kill somebody. That seems like a contradiction."

"Two problems, Walker," Tommy said. "First off, you didn't listen carefully to my instructions. Poor attention to detail. Secondly, it seems to me that you question your own ability to judge when force is necessary and when it's not. That's a fatal flaw in any peace officer."

"I think his concern," Harris said, "is the same as mine and everyone else's: I mean, it's our first day with you in charge and it's like you're taking the side of the civilians over us already."

False Flag - Brown

Tommy shook his head and ground his teeth for a moment. "Let me make something real clear to all of you right now: **you** are civilians. You are not soldiers; you are not in an army; and we are not at war with the taxpayers." He pointed at the booklet Harris absently played with in one hand. "I don't just expect you to read that, men. I expect you to know it; accept it; and conduct yourselves as if you believe it, for as long as you work for me."

Within the first four months, three more deputies were gone. Harris tampered with his car camera; Walker coerced sexual favors from a prostitute in Norman. The third quit.

Tommy deputized some academy graduates to replace them. One of them was Janet Bailey, who covered for the dispatcher during her shift, and also updated the website. The image of the county sheriff's office turned around, between her efforts at communication and the reformed conduct of the deputies.

Looking back on that first year, Tommy was surprised more deputies hadn't quit. What surprised him even more was that, after a few months, the Feds seemed to lose interest in the bogus murder rap. He was questioned a few times; Gunther and Jenny were questioned; then the Feds backed off. Maybe, by some miracle, an honest person was calling the shots despite the Attorney General. And the fact that Tommy had been too busy with his new duties to keep sniffing around at the Justice Department probably helped.

D MINUS 87

Tommy set his coffee down, took Linda's hand and kissed it. "It's good to be home, baby."

Linda's dark brown eyes turned sympathetic. "You want to talk about it?"

"You remember that thing you told me about the other day—some link Jenny posted on Facebook about cults?"

Linda made a face. "Oh, yeah. Sick stuff."

"Can you forward the link to me?"

Linda nodded, then her jaw dropped. "Did you find something like that?"

Neither of them ever turned on the television, unless it was to watch a movie together; so it was no surprise she hadn't seen the news.

"Yeah," he said. "I still don't know how to process what I saw, yet."

"I'll send you that link," Linda said, then moved around behind him to massage his shoulders.

False Flag - Brown

"You still think me running for sheriff was a good idea?" he asked, grunting with pleasure as she kneaded the stress knots out of him.

"I do," she said, stooping to kiss his neck.

"You're the greatest," he moaned, as she continued kneading. "Sorry if I'm more grumpy than normal. I don't mean to take it out on you."

"You owe me about 40,000 date nights, Sheriff Scarred Wolf," she said.

"I know," he said. "Let's have one Tuesday night. I found this place I think you'll like."

Later, Tommy read the article his niece had posted a link to. It reported occultic rituals all over the country with very similar characteristics to what he found in Cynthia Greeley's basement. He spent a few hours digging out what information he could on M.O.s, and the belief system which led people to commit these bizarre, disturbing crimes. He jotted down some specific questions to ask the woman and the two teenage boys during interrogation. So far nobody had stepped forward to post bail, and his deputies had little luck getting the boys' parents to come in.

False Flag - Brown

12
Y MINUS FOUR
AMARILLO, TEXAS

Ken Fowler cursed when he got to the house. It was on a cul-de-sac and the front edge of everyone's property was squeezed together. What that meant for him was that he couldn't park his work van on the street in front of the customer's house without blocking the driveway. He also couldn't park **on** the driveway, lest the company van leak oil or some other fluid on the drive.

Two houses down there was an unoccupied space where the van could fit without blocking any driveways, so he parked there. It was going to make the job take longer, walking this far every time he had to go to the van, but there was no helping it. He checked the paperwork, gathered the tools he knew he would need, and walked to the customer's house.

After knocking and ringing the doorbell he waited three minutes without an answer. As he retreated back to where the van was parked, the door finally opened and someone called to him. Sighing, because he would just as soon not have to do this job or even remain in this neighborhood, Ken turned around and headed back.

The woman standing at the door was black, middle-aged and overweight. Though it was mid afternoon, she was dressed in a nightgown and looked like she'd just got out of bed. He put on the fake professional/polite voice he used for customers and asked, "Willie-Mae Harris?"

"Yeah, that's me," she said.

"Hi, my name's Ken. Looks like you're switching over from the phone company. I'm here to give you cable, Internet and a whole-house DVR on three TVs."

"Five TVs," Willie-Mae said.

"Well, there's only three authorized on the work order," Ken said. "But if you call customer service while I'm here, they can add the outlets and adjust your billing by the time I'm done."

"Adjust the billin'? Oh no. They said I get five boxes for that price right there." She tapped the price on his work order.

This was going to be one of those jobs, Ken realized. Either the salesperson had lied to the customer, or the customer was lying to him. He'd seen both happen plenty. But he knew what the cost of the services and extra outlets should be, and the company would not give it all to her for the price on the work order.

The first half hour was spent on the phone, trying to get it straightened out between the company and the customer. When they finally came to an agreement, he went to work.

The house was reasonably clean, and he was thankful for that. He'd been in many places that were so filthy, he almost refused to work there. But he needed to keep this job for a couple more years. Then he should have enough saved to start his own business and deal with customers on his own terms, and hire somebody else to do the dirty work, if there was any.

There were several kids in the house, playing video games at different locations. Surely they had to be the customer's grandkids. They were a bunch of rude, disrespectful children. Judging by how they stared at him, they obviously didn't see many white men, or like them very much. It briefly reminded him of that time back in Kindergarten.

Eventually the other adults in the house stirred, got out of bed and began going about their business while yelling at their kids. Willie Mae Harris casually cussed at and berated the adults and children alike from time to time. Ken had seen this scenario in hundreds of houses around town.

He passed through the living room several times while assessing, gathering tools, and performing the work to be done in various parts of the house. Every time he passed by, Willie Mae was seated at her desktop computer (where it was going to be very difficult to get her an Internet connection) playing Solitaire. The desk had been turned into kind of a booth with a frame made of black posterboard arching over the monitor and keyboard. The posterboard frame was nearly covered with cut out pictures of Barack Hussein Obama; printed text of his famous quotes; pictures of Michelle; and the "O" symbol.

Ken had seen a lot of these shrines to "the first black President" in his line of work. Some of them juxtaposed pictures and quotes of Martin Luther King with those of Hussein. When he did work in houses with these shrines, in the past, he would ask questions (as neutrally as possible) to see what, if anything, the supporters knew about their messiah. None of them had even heard of the guy before 2008.

Ken didn't ask Willie Mae Harris anything regarding Hussein because she was still surly about not getting the extra outlets for free.

The job became really miserable once Ken got up in the attic. Attics were much, much hotter than even working in the direct sunlight in the summertime. At just over six feet it was hard for him to maneuver in the tight spaces and his body didn't take the extreme heat well. Progress was slow up there, and his mind often wandered as he scooted belly-down through the insulation an inch at a time. Today his mind wandered back to his first experience with race relations.

False Flag - Brown

His family moved into a housing project in Houston when he was four years old, and stayed there for almost two years. It seemed like a nice enough place to Ken for the first year—but then he didn't have much to compare it to at that age. Then, after he'd started kindergarten, one day his mother answered a knock on the apartment door and found two black girls waiting there who he recognized from school. They asked if he could come out and play, and his mother let him.

He played outside with his new friends, and had a great time.

Some days later, out in the courtyard playing by himself, he spotted the same two girls playing amidst a larger group of children. Ken didn't pay attention to the racial makeup of the group, but that would be the last time he made such an oversight. He ran over and greeted his playmates, only to be shunned. Confused, he nonetheless remained there, assuming he'd be welcome to play with them. The other kids told him to go away. Too stubborn for his own good, he decided he had just as much right to be there as they did. Then two boys ran up and bashed him in the head with a large rock and a large chunk of asphalt.

The other kids laughed and pointed fingers, which angered Ken. He found a small rock and, when he recovered, threw it at one of his attackers. He missed his revenge target, hitting instead a girl who was even younger than he—one who had probably only learned to walk recently. The toddler cried, of course, and Ken ran away.

The two girls from his kindergarten class tattled on him at school, conveniently omitting everything that happened before Ken threw the rock. When he tried to tell the whole story in the principal's office, the principal continuously interrupted Ken until he was too frustrated to even speak coherently.

Ken's family moved again, so he went to First Grade at another school, but he never forgot how important it was to pay attention to skin color after that.

Somebody yelled for him, "Yo, cable man!"

As loud as the voice was, it meant somebody must have climbed his ladder and stuck their head into the attic hatch, though he couldn't see them from where he was. "Yeah?"

"You need to move your truck, man."

This made no sense. He had parked in the only nearby spot where he wouldn't block anyone's access to anything. "What's going on?"

"Yo man, I'm tellin' you you gotta move your truck! Our neighbor's pissed off."

Ken groaned and cussed. This was the worst time for this kind of interruption. He really didn't want to have to crawl through this attic any more than necessary. He decided to finish what he was doing before crawling all the way back to the trapdoor. Twice more someone stuck their head up the hatch to tell him about their angry neighbor.

He believed people had a right to forbid someone to park in front of their property, but jerks pissed him off, even when they were within their rights.

When he finally got out, filthy and drenched in sweat, he strode out of the garage straight for his van, intending to move it without any discussion so the neighbor could get the knot out of their panties. He would have to block somebody's driveway or mailbox, pissing off the US Mail or somebody else, but he had no choice. The neighbor had plenty of room in their driveway so it wasn't like they needed room for somebody else to park. It was best to not even speak to an unreasonable jerk, lest he lose his temper and get a complaint.

There were two black men in talking on the porch of the house he parked in front of. As he went to the van one called to him. "Yo, man, you gonna move your truck?"

"Yup," he said, and kept walking.

"Who told you to park up on my lawn?" the guy demanded.

Ken stopped at his passenger door, opened it, and put his tool belt inside. He wanted to avoid this conversation altogether, but it was obvious by tone of voice and body language that the guy was going to force it.

So be it.

"I'm not on anybody's lawn. I'm on a public street, where there are no signs posted, and I'm not even touching the sidewalk, much less the lawn."

"What!"

Ken shut the door and started around the nose of the van toward the driver's side. He heard some unpleasant comments pass between the two men. Then the aggressive one raised his voice again. "I don't give a shit if it's a public street! Why you park in front of my house?"

Ken stopped and pointed back at the Harris house. "I'm doing work over there."

"So why didn't you park over there then?"

"Didn't want to block anyone's driveway or mailbox."

"That's your damn problem!"

Ken got in the van, started it, backed up to the front of the Harris house and shut it down again. He was blocking the mailbox now, but there was no helping it. He got out again and went around to retrieve his tool belt thinking the discussion was over.

"I know you don't think you're bad, right?" The pissed off neighbor

False Flag - Brown

was now off his porch, approaching Ken as he went back toward the Harris's garage. The other man...the stocky one...hung back a ways, holding his tongue.

Ken gritted his teeth and kept walking. The aggressive one was about his size and build. Maybe he could fight; maybe not. If Ken wasn't on the clock, they would have found out.

"You gonna walk right out to your truck like you bad," the guy continued. "You went straight to your truck 'cause you knew you was wrong. I don't know who you're used to dealin' with, but we don't play that at my house."

Ken stopped and faced him. "Play what? What exactly am I so wrong about? Parking on the street? Where exactly would **you** park if **you** had to do work at that house right there?"

The guy got more and more wound up, like Ken had insulted him or something. Ken could think of plenty actual insults and wisecracks, but he had to swallow them because he represented the cable company.

"You shoulda' parked in their driveway, then," the loud mouth said.

"Against company policy," Ken said. "You wanted me to move the van. I moved it. Now if you'll excuse me, I have stuff to do." And he went back to work.

Next time he had to go back to his truck, the two men were standing on the sidewalk, talking again. The aggressive one was still doing most of the talking, but didn't seem angry now--just loud and boisterous. "...Know his white ass doesn't think I'm impressed. He may have to claim workman's comp up in here."

They shared a laugh, but it wasn't a genuine laugh inspired by humor. It struck Ken as bravado.

The loud mouth looked at Ken as he said, "Parked right in front of my daughter's bedroom window. Scared my daughter half to death. Man, I ain't tryin' to have no..."

Ken stopped again, and interrupted him. "Scared half to death? Wow."

"What? You say somethin' to me?" Loud Mouth asked, taking a few menacing steps toward Ken.

"What is it about a work van that's so terrifying?" Ken asked. "Does she have this phobia about **all** vehicles? Or has she never seen an automobile before? Maybe you should put her in the hospital; cause all it takes is for her to see one more work van and she'll be scared **completely** to death."

The guy got right up in Ken's face at that point. He obviously didn't like having his statements taken literally, or being challenged about the meaning of his words. He hurled insults and feinted striking a blow several times.

False Flag - Brown

Ken knew he should have kept his mouth shut, but his buttons had been pushed. He now waited to see if the guy was going to make good on his threats.

It was hard to be heard over Loud Mouth's monologue, but Ken said, "I'm not supposed to get involved in fights, but I am allowed to defend myself if attacked. You're threatening me with physical assault right now. I suggest you back off."

"Or what, cracker?" Loud Mouth then spewed out all the euphemisms for "coward" he could think of, still feinting.

Ken wanted to pop him in the face really bad, but he at least had to avoid throwing the first punch. If the other guy swung first, he might get to keep his job.

The guy didn't swing. But Ken had to get out of there before he blew a fuse.

He felt like a yellow-bellied worm for doing it, but he got into his van and drove away, calling his supervisor to explain why he couldn't complete the job. While grumbling and cussing to himself later, he used the word "nigger," and meant it, for the first time in his life.

***

Cleveland Parker only partly enjoyed the white boy getting served. His younger neighbor, Meldrick, was a little too low-class for Cleveland's taste. Sure, it was good seeing the pink toe put in his place, but Meldrick behaved like a common thug to do it. The ghetto wasn't far away, but this neighborhood wasn't technically in it. There were classy people who lived here, like Cleveland and his wife, but you'd never know it by Meldrick's behavior, or by their welfare queen neighbor Willie-Mae Harris and her clan, to the other side of Cleveland's house.

Meldrick fancied himself a poor man's Denzel Washington, but he was missing a whole lot of class for that. The only reason Cleveland was making nice with Meldrick was because the brotha knew somebody with a late model Benz they might be willing to sell. Cleveland's Benz was pushing ten years old now and was way overdue for an upgrade.

After the white boy drove away, Meldrick finally gave him the address where the Benz was parked, so Cleveland could go take a look.

Cleveland entered his own house to put on some presentable shoes and get his car keys.

At the landing of the staircase between the first and second floors, he slowed. There was a spot on the mural about a quarter inch in diameter that looked like either a stain or a chip in the paint. He hadn't noticed it before so it must be new. Anger rose quickly as he tried to imagine who might be responsible. He didn't let just anybody in his house, so he should be able to narrow it down.

The mural wrapped around the landing. It was the scene of a tropical paradise, full of the green vegetation of Mother Africa. A lion sat on one side, a black panther on the other. Both regal cats looked toward the center of the scene, which was a life-sized portrait of Cleveland and his wife in loincloths. In the painting, their bodies were ebony perfection. He stood behind her, but their hands were joined in front in an ancient symbol for dignity. Their images stared out from the painting with stern pride.

His wife was getting her hair done downtown at the moment, so he'd have to inquire about the damaged spot later. He ascended to the master bedroom, changed shoes, came back down the stairs and fetched his keys.

He pulled a Lionel Ritchie CD from the shelf on his way out the door. In moments he was underway in his Mercedes, and put the CD in the player. The player ejected the CD right away. He pushed it back in. It ejected again. Yes, it was certainly time to get an upgrade--little things on the car were starting to give him trouble. He took the CD out for examination, just to make sure it wasn't scratched.

***

Joe Tasper couldn't afford bail, so he remained in jail until his hearing. Crystal was apologetic about the incident and didn't press charges, but he knew soon she'd start up over something else, real or imagined, and make his life a little more miserable. He had to dump the psycho bitch, but wasn't sure how to do it, yet. There was no doubt she would go batshit when he told her they were breaking up. She had previously threatened to kill him if he ever left her. At the time he assumed she'd been joking. Now he wasn't so sure.

In the mean time, he had lost his job.

He'd begun reporting for day labor gigs while searching for something permanent, but sure enough got a ticket for the cracked windshield. He was putting off paying it for as long as he could, thinking he couldn't be cited for it again at least until the payment deadline on the existing citation. But yesterday he'd been pulled over again for the windshield.

Pigs didn't have anything better to do. All the drug deals going down in this neighborhood; and prostitution; and theft; but the cops chose to make life harder for a guy trying to make an honest living.

Joe lived in a house in a black neighborhood because the rent was cheaper. But the vandalism and burglaries he suffered there made it not-so-cheap to live, after all.

Unable to risk getting pulled over for the windshield again, Joe would have to take the pickup truck. Shortly before Crystal moved in with him, he had traded his old S-10 for a full size Chevy truck. It burned more gas than the car, but he had no choice now. It was also parked behind his car in the driveway, so he would have to switch them around.

He started both vehicles and pulled the car out on the street. He left the engine running, walked back to the truck and pulled it onto the street, parking next to the curb. He got out and walked toward the car.

He saw a Mercedes speeding up the residential street toward him, but didn't think much about it because the driver had all the room in the world to stop and his own car was plainly visible. As Joe reached his car and was climbing in, he looked up and saw the Mercedes bearing down on him at the same speed, only much closer.

"Oh, no. No! No!"

He threw his car in reverse and hit the gas and horn. The cold engine hesitated. At the last second there was a squeal of tires as the Mercedes rammed him head-on.

Joe slammed the shifter back in park, turned it off and got out, walking forward to inspect the damage. His car and the Mercedes were crumpled pretty bad. The other driver got out--a stocky older black man with fancy shoes, clothes, and glitzy jewelry.

"You alright?" Joe asked.

"Man, what the hell you think you're doing, all over the street like that?" the guy demanded.

Taken aback by the guy's self-righteous attitude, Joe angered quickly. "What am I doin'? How 'bout you look where you're goin', jackass? You just ran into my car!"

The other driver said something, but Joe didn't catch it. Suddenly,Crystal was at his side , yelling at the other driver.

Crystal specialized in making bad situations worse, and she did so now, insulting the other guy with phrases like "fat coon." The guy got pissed and came after her, and Joe had to physically get between them. Finally Crystal retreated indoors to call the police.

It took nearly two hours for the police to get there. Meanwhile, several people from the neighborhood gathered on the sidewalk adjacent to the Mercedes, staring at the accident scene. The other driver spoke with them while they waited. One remark Joe caught from that crowd was, "You had the right-of-way!" like it was an open-and-shut case.

Well, it should all get cleared up when the police filled out the report. Joe wasn't impressed much with cops, based on his experience. But at least they were useful for stuff like this. If they ever showed up.

False Flag - Brown

They finally arrived. There was an older cop and a younger one. The older one went right over to the Mercedes driver when they arrived. It seemed like a familiar greeting shared by the two. The Mercedes driver spoke in hushed tones, gesturing at Joe and the vehicles. They spoke for a long time.

The young officer, after looking the vehicles over, approached Joe. Joe explained what happened, and the officer took notes.

Finally the older cop, smoking a thin cigar, came over and told Joe to sign a ticket.

"You're citing me?" Joe cried. "You're sayin' I'm at fault?"

"That's right," the cop said. "You **are** at fault."

"How you figure? My car wasn't even moving! I had just got in it and this guy rammed me!"

"He had the right of way," the cop said, nonchalantly.

"Right of way for what?" Joe demanded. "My car was on the street first!"

"It shouldn't have been on the street," the cop said.

"I told your partner I was switching vehicles in my driveway," Joe said. "You can see there's no place to park it on this street. This clown was doing over twice the speed limit through here, and wasn't looking where he was going!"

"He had the right of way. You need to sign this ticket."

"The right of way," Joe said. "You're tellin' me I can run over anything on the street, as long as I have right of way? There are kids out here all the time. He would have killed them today, if there'd been one on the street."

"Kids aren't supposed to be on the street," the cop said.

"So you're sayin' I can haul ass down these residential streets as fast as I want to go, and you're fine with it? And if I run over somebody or crash into something, that's on them?"

"You can do that," the cop said, "but if I catch you, you're getting a ticket for it."

"Do you two know each other?" Joe asked. "Is that what this is about?"

The cop breathed cigar smoke in Joe's face and said. "Listen: you sign that ticket or we can do this another way."

Joe wound up signing the citation, but was determined to fight this one in court.

He later obtained the police report and saw that the younger officer had drawn the diagram to portray Joe's car as pulling out of the driveway and slamming into the Mercedes. The report named the Mercedes driver

False Flag - Brown

as Cleveland Parker. His occupation was listed, too.
He worked for the police.

False Flag - Brown

13
D MINUS 74
LAS ANIMAS COUNTY, COLORADO

Joshua Rennenkampf let the Palomino set its own pace up the mountain slope. The sun, where it shone between the trees, was hot; but the air had a cold bite to it in the shade. A nasty winter was due, and even this far out Josh could tell it was on the way.

Josh was tall and lanky, with classic Nordic features. His blond hair was grown out almost down to his collar, and he used the beard trimmer just often enough to keep perpetual five o'clock shadow. When he entered civilian life his divorce from the Army manifested in his appearance and his sleep schedule, if not his tactical mindset.

A rifle scabbard hung hunter-style from his saddle rig, and a pistol was holstered on his hip. From the opposite hip hung a scabbard full of oversize survival knife--the ESEE Junglas. In his breast pocket was a lensatic compass.

He didn't anticipate using any of this today. Most people didn't expect to get in automobile accidents, either, but they still paid for car insurance.

Beside the horse trotted two pit bulls--a 90 pound male and a 60 pound female. The female,Valkyrie, was buckskin, with amber eyes. The male, Ragnarok, was brindle all over except for black socks and tail, and a white patch on his belly. He looked like a burglar's worst nightmare, and probably was, though he had been just a growing puppy only a month ago. Neither had ears or tails cropped, as was the fashion for the breed.

So far only one of his traps had paid off for Josh. The raccoon dangled below his saddlebags.

He rode up to a spot overlooking his third and final trap, and saw that it, too, was empty.

Josh patted his mount, Denver, on the neck. "Looks like I still got some learning to do, huh?" He turned Denver around and let the mustang pick it's own way down the slope. Both he and the horse were startled when his phone rang. The dogs both cocked their heads to the side and stared curiously. He pulled the phone out of his breast pocket and checked the caller I.D.

It was Jennifer.

"Hey," he said. "How's it going?"

"I'm here," Jennifer's youthful, feminine voice answered. "I think this is the south entrance I'm at."

"That'll work," he said. "Just hang the cable back across when your car is inside. "Keep it in low gear. First fork, make a right. After that,

False Flag - Brown

always go left. I'll meet you at the house."

"I remember," she said. "Okay."

He continued down the slope, thinking about Jennifer's tone of voice during their brief exchange. Was she still upset with him? It didn't sound like it, but then who could tell?

They'd had their first fight on her last visit when he insisted she leave her cellphone outside in her car. She'd thrown a few words at him, including "unreasonable" and "paranoid," the latter most likely applicable, but he told her that her choices were to keep it out in the car, or with her, turned off, after he had removed the secondary battery. She told him tampering would void the warranty.

He had wanted to give in, but didn't. More and more judges were ruling that, by voluntarily carrying around a device with a microphone in it, a citizen waived his Fourth Amendment protections.

When she left after that argument, he assumed it would be the last time he ever saw her. It was too bad, because she meant a lot to him.

Then, after a few weeks, she called. They began talking again, and she soon asked if he would still take her riding up in the mountain. Who could figure women? But when Jennifer sprang surprises on him, they were usually of the pleasant variety.

He heard the engine of her Jeep straining to make it up the steep driveway. His emotions were haywire. On the one hand, he missed her; but on the other, he dreaded this visit if they were just going to pick up where they left off last time.

Denver felt his own way down the trail and made it to the flat shelf a couple minutes after the Jeep. Josh dismounted and tied Denver to the hitching post in front of his dome house.

Ragnarok and Valkyrie had gone ahead and beat him to the shelf. They now stood facing the Jeep's driver door, tails wagging in sync like windshield wipers.

The Jeep door opened and Jennifer got out. "Hello, babies!" she said, stooping to pet the dogs. Valkyrie especially loved the attention and jumped up, her paws landing on Jennifer's jacket.

"Get down, Val!" Josh snapped. "You know better than that."

Val dropped to all fours, ears swinging back and head smoothing into an abashed expression. But her tail kept wagging.

Jennifer was short but shaped nicely. Her red-bronze face was pretty, but had a kind of toughness to it that Josh assumed was normal for the Shawnee nation. What he liked best were her radiant brown eyes.

They walked toward each other and she smiled, then hugged him, pulling back quickly.

Platonic. *Well, so be it.*

False Flag - Brown

"They've both gotten so big," she said, reaching down to pet the dogs as they escorted her on either side. She then held up both hands as if ready to be searched. "Don't worry—no cellphone. I left it in the car."

"Nice trip?" Josh asked.

"It was," she said. "I've really got to pee, though."

He waved toward the front door of his dome home and she headed toward it. He fell into step behind her and couldn't help admiring the scenery, glad she was wearing tight jeans, but half-wishing she wasn't at the same time.

"When you're done," he said, "we can eat if you're hungry."

"I'm fine," she said over her shoulder. "I'd like to start out right away. That gives us more riding time."

His house's exterior was painted subdued earth tones that blended in so well with the surrounding environment that it wasn't easy to see unless you knew what you were looking for.

They entered, both dogs taking a seat outside the door.

Inside were several shelves sagging with books; Josh's commo nook full of shortwave and HAM radio gear; and his server and four desktops.

Josh had removed the portrait of his ex-wife from the wall prior to Jennifer's very first visit here. If nothing else, Jennifer's friendship had helped him exorcise that particular ghost.

While Jennifer was in the bathroom, Josh fetched the pair of chaps he had bought for her. She came out and he handed them over.

"What are these?"

"There's cactus and thorny bushes out here," he said. "You may get brushed up against something with sharp edges now and then. These will protect your legs."

"Oh, these are chaps," she said. "Like the cowboys wear."

They went out to the stable and saddled Indy, the mare, and went off on their ride.

He took a trail that led farther away from his traps, with a gentler grade. Both he and Jennifer were novice riders, so he figured excessive caution was the best way to avoid doing something stupid. He hadn't owned the horses long and was learning their strengths and weaknesses even as he learned about horsemanship in general.

Only a couple miles up the trail some snow had stuck, but it was shallow enough the horses had no trouble with it. The dogs couldn't have been happier, either, licking up the snow on the run and snooping around in general.

Joshua and Jennifer didn't speak much, but every time he glanced her way, she seemed to be enjoying herself.

"It's so picturesque up here, " she said. "It's crazy to see snow this time of year."

"High elevation," he said. "If it's high enough, you get snow year-round."

"But it's worse in the winter, right?"

Josh nodded. "And there's supposed to be a bad one coming up."

Before long, the dogs' ears swung forward and tails extended down. Ragnarok growled.

"Stay on me," Josh said, but the dogs' instincts were too powerful and they bolted forward to investigate. Josh sighed and Jennifer giggled.

"Needless to say, we've still got some training to do," Josh said.

"I'm impressed that they're not barking, though," Jennifer said, always seeing the glass as half-full.

Josh noticed movement between the trees far ahead, perpendicular to the path of his dogs.

"Did you see that?" Jennifer asked.

He nodded.

"Is it a bear?"

He waited to reply until he got a better look. When he did, he saw it was another party of horses and riders moving across their path. No more growling or other noise from the dogs, nor sign of a struggle, either. "Looks like my neighbors."

The two parties drew close and Josh recognized Paul Tareen, a tough-looking hombre with a black mustache, his sons Dan and Reuben, both dark-haired and whipcord thin like their father, and his daughter Terry. They greeted each other and Josh introduced Jennifer, noticing the looks of appraisal she got from the two young men. Ragnarok and Valkyrie came back to sit at either side of Denver, panting, tongues hanging out from the run.

"This is the family that sold me the horses," Josh said, smiling at his neighbors.

"They're beautiful," Jennifer said.

"How do you know each other?" Terry asked, gaze bouncing between Josh and Jennifer.

As little as Josh understood women, he was fairly sure Terry had a crush on him. At 19, Josh considered her far too young for him, but she didn't seem to agree. Josh had always looked younger than his years, inspiring unflattering nicknames like "Baby Face" in some circles. In the past he'd tried growing his beard out to look more his age, but he didn't like how it felt when it got long. It itched and felt greasy.

"I'm friends with her uncle," Josh said, assuming he had been downgraded from boyfriend since the cellphone incident.

Terry, a pretty blonde with dimples in both cheeks, appeared to like this answer. But not Jennifer. In fact, maybe he was reading too much into it, but he had the impression Jennifer took a dislike to Terry from that moment.

"You been keepin' an eye on the Chapanee situation?" Paul asked.

"The Bar G Ranch?"Josh asked. "Yeah. Just read the latest before I went up to check the traps this morning."

"You think it's gonna get ugly?" Paul asked.

"I think it's already ugly," Josh said.

"Yeah. Man can't dig a retention pond on his own property..." Paul said, shaking his head. "The Feds will use any excuse to steal from us."

"The land owner got sent to the hospital for a heart attack," Josh said. "You know they're gonna work on his son—see if they can get him to cave in."

"What do you think about this Jade Helm business?" Reuben asked. "Is it just a cover for beginning martial law?"

"They're supposedly just carryin' blanks," Dan said. "I think they just might have live ammo."

Josh shrugged. "Hey, I'm a civilian like you. I'm out of the loop. Best I could do is speculate."

"Please do," Paul said, with a worried frown.

"I really do think it's an exercise," Josh said. "Will they springboard from it into martial law? I don't think so. For one thing, they're using SOCOM personnel—not who you'd want to earmark for occupation troops. Two things SpecOps have always done is special operations, hence the name, and military advising. So first off it's probably another psychological prep for the population—get civilians used to seeing soldiers patrolling Elm Street and Oak Street like it's no big deal. The Pentagon has been pushing more and more of these exercises over the last several years. Another thing it does is familiarize the participants with the terrain that a real operation might play out on in the future—a special operation, to take out the most dangerous leaders of a potential resistance movement, for instance."

"Night of the Long Knives," Paul mused aloud.

"Or it could be so they can advise foreign troops how to effectively pacify this region," Josh added.

"You think American soldiers would really go along with all this?" Reuben asked.

Josh nodded, feeling a pang of the old heartbreak again. "I do. Soldiers are mostly folks who were taught what to think by government schools and the idiot box, just like everyone else. They haven't read the Constitution and, these days, probably lack the reading comprehension even if they tried. So all they know about it is what they've heard."

False Flag - Brown

"From government schools and the idiot box," Paul said, frowning.

Josh sighed and nodded. "Almost nobody joins for patriotic motives. I was an oddball because I did. It's all college money, signing bonuses, and job training. The different branches recruit by appealing to mercenary instincts, so they get mercenaries. G.I. Joe is gonna do whatever he's told to do. Likely they'll have him overseas in some U.N. Or State Department manufactured hellhole violating somebody else's rights, anyway, while foreign troops are dealing with us. Bottom line is, don't put your trust in our military. It's not ours, anymore."

"The weapons and equipment ain't even made here now," Dan remarked. "We could never go to war with China—all they'd have to do is stop sellin' us what we need to fight."

"They have to do away with *posse comitatus*, too," Rueben opined. "They know police will be a joke if they come up against organized resistance. They need combat troops if they get serious about coming for our guns."

"They pretty much have done away with it," Josh said. "But *posse comitatus* was never as restrictive as we wish it was. Not that politicians will abide by even the most simple laws, anyway. And nobody appreciates the danger of standing armies anymore."

Paul turned solemn. "Josh, you reckon you could start teachin' me and the boys...um, Morse Code one of these weekends?"

Paul wasn't talking about Morse code. He obviously didn't know if he could speak freely in the presence of Jennifer. As the neighbors had gotten to know each other over the years, they found out Josh was a Special Forces vet. One primary mission for Special Forces was to train indigenous armies for war. "Advising." Paul was asking Josh to train him, his sons and some like-minded friends for a war they believed was coming right to their back yard.

"I'll drop by your place one of these days," Josh said, "and we'll talk about it."

Terry flashed a charming smile at Josh. "Maybe you could show me some orienteering, Joshua?"

"What's the matter?" Josh asked. "Your brothers don't savvy land navigation?"

"I bought compasses for all of them," Paul said. "But we haven't tried to use them much."

"You can do it without a compass, right Joshua?" Terry asked. "At night, by using the stars?"

Before Josh could answer, Jennifer said. "He can. He taught me how. I can teach you." The offer was made in a sweet tone of voice, and Jennifer's expression was innocent enough, but this struck Josh as the

False Flag - Brown

proverbial hissing and scratching of a cat announcing her ownership of the turf in question. Terry seemed to take it that way, judging by the fading smile and furrowing eyebrows.

"Matter of fact," Paul said, oblivious to all the covert saber rattling between the females, "if you're not doing anything for Independence Day, we'd be obliged if you'd come over and spend the day with us."

"You can try some of my potato pie," Terry suggested, undaunted.

"I appreciate it," Josh said. "Sounds good."

They exchanged a few more pleasantries and bid goodbyes.

Josh continued along the trail with Jennifer following. He expected either an angry outburst, or the silent treatment. Not that he had been anything more than polite with his neighbor's daughter. But since when did facts ever matter to a woman?

Jennifer surprised him again, though. She asked a few reasonable questions about his neighbors, but never escalated the exchange to an argument.

He turned back just after the waterfall so they would make it home before dark. The ride was a pleasant one, with horses and riders getting familiar with each other along the way. When they reached the house, Jennifer asked to take a shower. While she did that, he stabled the horses, rubbed them down and fed them.

Jennifer was still in the bathroom when he came indoors, but the water was no longer running. He called through the bathroom door, "You wanna eat something before you go?"

Her answer didn't come right away. "I'm staying here tonight, aren't I?"

That was the agreement originally, but judging by her lukewarm greeting and attitude, he assumed she had changed her plans. "You're welcome to stay if you want," he replied.

"I thought that was the whole idea," she said, rustling something around on the other side of the door.

"Well, yeah. But I figured you only wanted to go riding, after..." He shrugged, deciding to drop it and just play this visit by ear.

"After what?" she asked.

"Nevermind," he said, and went to the kitchen.

As he dug through the freezer, she entered the kitchen wearing a bathrobe she must have brought along, and a towel wrapped around her head. "What are you doing?" she asked.

"Trying to figure out what we're going to eat," he said.

She grabbed the freezer door out of his hand and waved toward the doorway. "Why don't you clear out. I'll take care of this."

"Cool. I'll go make sure the guest room is ready, then."

False Flag - Brown

"And call Uncle Tommy," she said. "He wants to talk to you about something."

Josh rounded up sheets, blankets and pillows, and made the guest bed for her. Jennifer was the only guest he'd ever had sleep over at this house; and he'd been convinced they were finished as a couple, so he hadn't anticipated using the guest room again.

Josh wondered what Tommy Scarred Wolf wanted to talk about. For the several months after returning from Indonesia Tommy had continued the investigation which probably got he and his brother Vince marked for ruin in the first place. But then Tommy got too busy with the whole county sheriff thing and slacked off.

Josh opened up his video conferencing program and dialed his old friend. It worked much like Skype, only it was strongly encrypted—a custom program he'd installed on his and Tommy's desktops.

Tommy was an old buddy from Josh's A-Team in 5th Group. Tommy was a living legend getting short when Josh was an FNG fresh from the Q-Course. Still, they were like-minded in those days and got tight. They remained friends even after Tommy got out, but after Josh's time in Iraq years later...things changed. Joshua's attitude soured regarding the people running the U.S. government. Over time, the more he learned, the sour attitude became seething animosity, which trickled down to nearly every bureaucrat and person with any kind of authority. Tommy had become a cop like his brother, and that strained their friendship. Then he left the Tribal Police and went over to the Feds for a while, which was when Josh completely turned his back on him.

Then Tommy showed up one day right here on the mountain, in desperate need of Josh's help. Joshua still didn't completely understand why, but he couldn't turn Tommy down.

Josh got wounded helping Tommy on Sumatra. Then everything was further complicated when Jennifer came into the picture (her father was murdered, so Tommy was even more protective of her than normal). But somehow when all was said and done, Josh and Tommy were good friends again, as if they'd never had a falling out.

"Hey Tommy," Josh greeted. "Jenny says you wanted to talk."

"Yeah, thanks," Tommy replied. "I have something new for you to keep track of. Maybe dig at a little, when you have time."

"Is it related to the secret teams?" Josh asked.

Between what Tommy and Vince dug up, plus some information their friend Rocco Cavarra had once been privy to, they had pieced together evidence pointing to an ongoing black ops division hidden inside the intelligence community. The division employed an unknown number of clandestine "tier zero" teams, a couple of which Rocco and the crew ran into overseas. They strongly suspected at least one of the secret teams

False Flag - Brown

specialized in false flag ops.

After a hesitant pause, Tommy said, "I have no evidence of that. But it's something that looks pretty big. I can't really do much more digging from here without getting The Man back on my tail."

Josh fancied himself a pro at hacking into secure resources without being detected. "Whatcha got?"

Tommy told him about an epidemic of occult rituals involving both animal and infant sacrifice. Tommy himself had traced connections from some of the practitioners to classified government programs. He wanted Josh to glean more information, on the down-low.

"I'll see what I can do," Josh said. They exchanged a little more information and hung up.

After the meal of buffalo burgers and diced potatoes Jennifer cooked, Josh thanked her and bid her good night. His plans for the evening involved some reading on the living room couch before turning in.

He wasn't ready for her to sit in his lap, wrap her arms around him and stick her tongue down his throat. It stunned him, but was certainly another pleasant surprise.

The towel-turban was gone now and she looked earthy and glorious with her long black hair hanging down.

They had been affectionate with each other before, but something was different about this time. Jennifer was really revved up, and soon had his motor running at redline. He let his hands roam over her, and she didn't protest. Her breathing became heavy, but she didn't push his hands away until he began to slip one inside her bathrobe.

She pulled away, but he tugged her back into his lap. "Don't sleep in the guest room tonight," he whispered. "Stay with me."

Her only answer was a quavering moan and he was sure she'd finally surrendered. Careful not to make any sudden moves, he climbed to his feet, cradling her in his arms, and carried her to his bedroom.

All went well until he got her out of the bathrobe, then she shook her head and began crying. "I want to, Joshua. I really want to, but I can't."

He sighed and pulled away from her. He didn't want to argue. Besides, her crying killed the mood for him, anyway. He patted her on the arm, draped the robe back over her, and stood to leave. But she grabbed at his arm and pulled him back.

"Don't go," she pleaded, wiping her eyes. "I'm sorry."

"Is this about religion, still?" he asked.

She didn't answer. Which meant yes.

She sniffled and tried to smile, sitting up to wrap her arms around him.

"Since when," she asked, "am I just the niece of a friend of yours?"

False Flag - Brown

"Since your last visit," he replied. "Our knock-down drag-out about the stupid phone. And reinforced just now. Did I miss something?"

She licked her lips. There was concern, if not fear, in her deep brown eyes. "We may not agree on everything; but I don't want to lose you, Joshua."

"That's good and all," he said. "But there are some things about me that will never change."

She tossed her hair. "The one thing about me that will never change is my faith. And I believe I should only give up my virginity when I'm married."

"Then why are you wasting time with me?" he asked, with an irritated tone. "There must be millions of church boys out there who would do everything you want."

"I'm not in love with them," she said. "I want you."

"But only on your terms."

She chewed on her lower lip. He sighed.

"I don't want to fight," he said, half-turning. "I'll see you in the morning." He pulled away again, but she tugged him back, locking her fingers between his.

He was doing just fine by himself. Why did she have to bring all this drama into his life?

She placed her palm against his face. She looked like she was ready to cry again. "I'm not willing to give up on you."

He hugged her, patting her back. Sexually frustrated as he was, he tried to give her what comfort he could.

After a while, she composed herself and asked if she could borrow a computer to check her email. He set her up, then checked his news updates on a different computer.

The item of most interest to him at the moment was the standoff in the Chapanee Valley. According to the video feed from one of his most used alternative news sites, the Feds had backed off. His fellow wingnuts were celebrating all over the country, like they'd just destroyed the Death Star and saved the galaxy from the Empire.

False Flag - Brown

Justin yawned, checked the time, and turned back to his monitor. He'd been at it for 12 hours so far today. He'd put in a couple more before calling it quits for the night.

The room he sat in was crowded with computers, separated by small cubicles. There were ten tired, uncomfortable people in there, all trying to maintain enthusiasm for this project despite the long hours.

Justin closed the file he had just completed and went back to Surveillance Photo 18F-5 from the Garber Ranch. Several more zones of the photo had been grayed out since he last looked at it. He moved his cursor over an active zone and clicked on it. The zone grew to fill his screen, and he zoomed in on the little Ford Ranger parked on the side of the road. He kept zooming closer until he could make out the license plate, then split his screen to open the Motor Vehicle database.

"We got any more coffee?" asked Barnes, from the adjacent cubicle.

"Had about half a pot left an hour ago," Justin replied, checking the blackened bottom of his styrofoam cup to ensure his last dose hadn't magically reappeared.

"Which means it's empty again, and I'll be the one who has to fill it," Barnes complained. "You'd think they could get us one of those fancy machines where you just slide a packet in, push a button and it gives you espresso, coffee, cappuccino or whatever."

"They spent all the money on these work stations," Justin said.

Frawley, the green-eyed blonde in the cubicle to his right, rolled back in her chair and asked, "Did you hear the latest about that defensive back at Miami?"

Justin shook his head. "I don't follow football that much anymore."

Frawley looked almost hurt. "But..."

Tench, the short brassy-haired black woman in the cubicle to his left, rolled back and said, "I thought you were a wide receiver for UCLA."

"Tight end," he corrected. "But I'm done with football."

Justin's love for the game had been cooling for a while even before his back injury during senior year. It had cooled even more in recent years.

"You shoulda' stuck with that," Tench said. "You coulda' been makin' big money."

"You're still in terrific shape, too," Frawley said. "Most guys put on a lot of weight after they stop playing."

False Flag - Brown

"That's Ex-Jock Syndrome," Justin said. "Guys who try to bulk up or trim down for their position ruin their metabolism. I never did that."

"So I guess you wouldn't be interested in joining a fantasy league," Frawley said.

"No. But thanks anyway," Justin said. His co-workers rolled their chairs back into their cubicles.

He ran the license plates through the database, pulling up the name and address of the person who registered the Ford Ranger. The owner had driven across two states to join the DomTers at Chapanee. Justin initiated a new file and began filling in the details.

First he checked for a criminal record. There was none. Some speeding tickets when the DomTer was a teenager, and an accident report filed 15 years ago made up the only entries on the rap sheet.

He looked up the DomTer's cellphone number and flagged it for monitoring and tracking.

Next he checked for prior military service. The <u>DomTer</u>, Gary Fram, served in the Army, in the combat arms. That moved him up the danger scale quite a few notches.

Justin looked over his medical records and filled in the requests for peripheral checks of his wife and children. He shifted to Fram's financial history and status, and confirmed his political affiliation by voter registration. The man's voting history started out typically sporadic, then he became a hell-or-high-water voter for several years. But he quit voting altogether after 2012. This would flag his profile as an extreme risk.

For variety's sake, Justin investigated his public library habits next. (Normally he put this off for later in the process, but switching around the routine helped relieve some of the monotony.) Several books checked out on the American Revolution, the Constitution, the Federal Reserve, and various survival topics all fit the profile and confirmed the risk level.

He ran the man's identifiers through the firearm sales database. Though this database was far from complete, it still showed a rifle and shotgun purchase, along with several ammunition purchases. The caliber of the ammo purchased indicated at least two additional weapons owned.

Only then did Justin begin poring through Fram's email, search engine and social networking history. This was the most tedious, time consuming portion of any profile. It generated anywhere from dozens to hundreds of peripheral requests for profiles of potential accomplices, but the intelligence rewards were too juicy to pass up.

Fram hadn't said anything that could yet be construed to suggest criminal intent, but his wife posted pictures on Facebook of him posing with a couple different weapons which did not show up on the firearm sales search.

False Flag - Brown

Justin still had a long way to go on the social networking history when time came to go home. He would have to continue that tomorrow. He estimated that it would take another day and a half before he could wrap up with an analysis of the DomTer's home, based on satellite and street-level images from Google. Only after all that was complete could the DomTer's residence be more thoroughly investigated via thermal imaging, ground-penetrating radar and other methods available by satellite or U.A.V...assuming he or his wife hadn't bought into DropCam or some other service that installed cameras inside their home, which would make everything easier.

Justin began shutting down and gathering his stuff.

"You calling it a day?" Barnes asked.

"Yeah," Justin said, logging out of succeeding security layers. "My eyes are burning. Guess I'll be back in about 10, 12 hours."

"You know what we're doing here, right?" Barnes asked, rising to his feet and hurrying around the cubicle row to where Justin stood.

Justin shrugged, not sure what his co-worker was driving at. But no doubt Barnes would do his best to enlighten him, whether the enlightenment was welcome or not.

"It's like 'reconnaissance by fire'," Barnes said, grinning at the opportunity to share his theory. He was retired Air Force, and looked for the military angle in everything. "You know those old fashioned wars...infantry attacking defensive positions and all that. Well, what you do is send a heavy patrol out at night and make contact, but just to harass —not to try overrunning the position or anything. The defenders open fire, and you take note of how their defenses are laid out--where their machineguns are; mortars, artillery; whatever. And which parts of the perimeter are only defended by riflemen. Then when you're ready to attack, you knock out their heavy weapons first, then hit them where they're weakest. Of course today you don't have to do that because we got satellite intelligence and so forth, but you get the idea: we're probing the DomTers to find their strong and weak links."

"You think we intended to back down from the standoff all along?" Justin asked, incredulous.

"Well, the whole operation may have been part test balloon," Barnes said. "If that old cowboy prick had been reasonable, we'd have just moved on and taken care of business. But these DomTers are feeling their oats. They think they won't get a spanking--or that it won't hurt that much. So we'll let them go on thinking that, while we just pin down where all their assets are."

"I wonder why we don't spend this level of effort on the folks swarming across the southern border," Justin wondered aloud. "I mean, **Domestic** Terrorists aren't the only threat we have to worry about."

78

False Flag - Brown

Barnes frowned, shrugged, and headed back to the coffee maker.

Justin left the "data mine" and exited through a series of security checkpoints until he finally made it outside the building. On the way to his car, he considered his short conversation with Barnes. He hoped he hadn't come off as critical, or the Department might decide he had tendencies that were sympathetic to the enemy.

The enemy.

It should be bizarre thinking of American citizens that way, but Justin was getting used to it. It kind of bothered him at first when reading department memorandums gave him the impression that a civil war was expected by his bosses, and their bosses. Mainstream culture was clueless that anyone even considered it possible. Yet in the minds of many intelligence professionals, it was a done deal.

Justin remembered enough world history to know that evolution of a state and its culture was inevitable. The great empires all lasted approximately 200 years before corruption ate them away from the inside, or weakened them enough to be toppled by external forces. That meant the United States of America was on borrowed time anyway.

At least his job was secure. In the emerging global order his kind of work would always be in demand.

False Flag - Brown

Jason Macmillan found the park bench in question. A moderately attractive 40-something woman sat on it, wrapped in a fur-lined parka, smoking a cigarette.

"Ms. Simmons?" he asked, when he was still a polite distance away.

She glanced up and flashed him a business-casual smile. "You must be Jason."

He shook the thin hand she offered and was surprised at the electricity that passed between them. His eyes and mind told him she was nothing fantastic on the desirability scale (especially around the Washington-New York axis, which was crawling with hot, horny women) but his body didn't agree.

He sat on the bench, with less than a yard of space between them.

"It's not that cold yet, is it?" he asked, with a meaningful look at her expensive coat.

"It's partly psychological," she said, taking another puff of her cigarette. "I keep hearing what a bad winter we're in for one of these years, so I'm bundling up in preparation. Plus I just spent a month in Hawaii, so my blood has thinned out."

He nodded toward the huge building where the Council met. "They should be out by now, shouldn't they?"

"Oh, their meeting's been adjourned," she said, with assurance. "But there's the usual hob-nobbing to do afterward. And then Lawrence goes through his dog walking ritual. Are you familiar with that, yet?"

Macmillan shook his head.

"Well, you **are** new, after all," she said. "His show champion dog has its own dedicated driver and vehicle. Can't be getting shedded fur all over the limousine, now can we? Then his dog handler escorts the dog to Lawrence and hands it off. Lawrence walks with it for exactly half an hour, then hands it off back to the dog handler, who hands it off to the doggie driver, who takes it out of sight, out of mind for the rest of the day."

She didn't seem scornful or bitter. Rather, amused. But not quite mocking.

"Has he given you the speech about Border Collies?" she asked.

"Not yet," he replied.

"Oh, then you're due for **at least** one. He's got dates and places, names of breeders and dogs. He'll tell you all about how Collies were bred to help herd livestock. They're born with the herding instinct and even his spoiled, urbanized pet unconsciously tries to herd him away from traffic and other perceived threats. Lawrence is fascinated with the whole concept of herding, in fact."

"He hasn't opened up to that extent with me, Ms. Simmons. He probably doesn't know yet if I'll work out."

"Call me Jade," she said, patting the bench surface right next to her. "Come here. I don't bite."

Macmillan scooted over until they were right next to each other.

"I hear you started out in the Louisiana Highway Patrol."

He acknowledged the question with a slight hunching of the shoulders. "Yeah. But that was a long time ago."

"Impressive that you've climbed so far."

Her voice was sensuous--almost hypnotic. He was turned-on despite himself. Forget Viagra—this broad was an effective cure for erectile dysfunction all by herself.

"I think I like you, Jason. So I'm going to share a little privileged information up front—otherwise it might take you some time to figure out: Lawrence wants to meet with both of us at once in order to foster competition between us. So don't be surprised if he seems to be pitting us against each other sooner or later. He believes we'll both work faster and harder for him that way. Ironic, isn't it? So Free Market of him."

"So you're my competition, then," Macmillan said, trying to reciprocate her subdued, playful manner.

"But I don't think it should be totally competitive," Jade Simmons told him, with direct eye contact. "I prefer cooperative arrangements." She glanced pointedly at his left hand. "So you're married."

"Is that a problem?" he asked, smoothly.

"That's up to you," she replied, patting his thigh this time.

He wasn't sure how to respond. He was used to being the sexually aggressive one.

"I'll save you some more time," she continued, chuckling. "The only reason you're in this is because your assets are expendable, whereas mine are valuable enough, Lawrence wants to save them for future operations if possible."

This sounded like an insult, which rankled Macmillan. His agents were sharp and well-trained. So elite even the CIA wasn't privy to their ops. How could her guys be less expendable than his? Maybe she meant only his civilian informants.

"I agree with him," she said, "which means I want you to succeed. So the game is rigged in your favor: if you can get your dominoes lined up, you get the operation."

Lawrence Bertrand appeared around the corner on the sidewalk,

False Flag - Brown

flanked by two imposing bodyguards, with his Collie leashed at his side. He was a tall, thickly built aristocrat with a nose like a vulture's beak, probably in his mid-to-late 60s.

As Bertrand's small entourage drew closer, someone else arrived at the park bench and stood beside it, waiting—obviously the dog handler.

Bertrand made it to the bench, handed the leash to the handler, exchanged a few words about the Collie's diet, then dismissed him. The two bodyguards wandered far enough away from their boss to provide some privacy, but close enough that they could go into action in case Alex Jones popped up out of a trash can with a video camera or something.

Jade Simmons made as if to stand. Moving quicker, Macmillan shot to his feet and made room for Bertrand to sit on the bench. Bertrand took the offered space. Macmillan stood facing the seated Bertrand and only then noticed that Jade was still seated. She smirked. She had only feinted at rising. This was some sort of power play, to establish that Macmillan was lower on the totem pole than her.

Macmillan would like to get her alone, where he'd show her exactly where to stick the totem pole.

"I trust you've introduced yourselves," Bertrand said.

"Yes sir," Macmillan said.

Jade nodded. "How was the meeting?"

Bertrand frowned. "All this oil fracking on private and state land is a nuisance. But still, we're at the point where, with or without more quantitative easing..." his words trailed off and he looked annoyed. "That's hardly any of your concern, Jade."

The reprimand didn't seem to bother her that much, but it kept her mouth closed for a moment.

"How is the initiative coming along?" Bertrand asked her.

"I've got penetration across the board," she replied. "Per your instructions I've concentrated on the DomTer cells, and we've got assets in or close to leadership in 38 states. We're pushing for full permeation, of course, but in the mean time we've got fully trained, invested assets who are ready to go right now."

Travis turned from her to address Macmillan "I've got Jade going at this from a different angle, but her priority is identical to yours. We need assets tuned and fueled up PDQ, waiting on the 'go'."

Pretty Damn Quick was a lofty goal when you had to accomplish all that was cut out for Macmillan and the people under him.

"Your predecessor not only failed," Bertrand told Macmillan, scowling, "but he managed to lose valuable assets in the process. I think part of the problem was, he promoted operators to leadership who were too hands-on. Brice Mallin was a hell of an operator; but the wrong man to run the show. Chiefs plan; Indians execute. Show your fangs a little, but I need you and your command structure where you can observe and administer. That means delegate and supervise. Unfortunately, it also means recruiting, to replace the operators we lost."

Brice Mallin had a big reputation as a bad dude. But not only did he lose three teams of shooters overseas, he wound up greased himself.

"Yes sir," Macmillan said.

"The teams we spoke of," Bertrand went on, "with the civilian assets prepped for high-profile...that is your priority until further notice."

Civilian assets. So that was it, after all. That was why McMillan's teams were considered more expendable than whoever Jade Simmons had working for her.

"I want to see significant progress very soon." Bertrand now glanced at Jade to include her in what he was about to say. "With any kind of operation like this, discretion is of the utmost concern. We can't expect the press to be able to continue damage control for us with the same success they've had in the past." His scowl deepened. "There are too many rogue elements out there now." He gestured toward the headquarters building. "We're working on that problem, but frankly, we might not be able to accomplish much until after you've done your job. Anyway, we've got to police the situation tightly, and there are these rogue elements trying to start trouble...most are crackpots, but there's this one B.I.A. agent that doesn't know his place."

"Are you saying we've been compromised?" Jade Simmons asked.

"They're all poking their noses into our business," Bertrand replied. "This one was snooping around one of our prior operations. He's not a blogger or reporter or anything like that, but he's kicked up some dust in his little backwater. The risk is, having some training in investigation, he could stumble onto current operations. Perhaps even our priority initiative."

"So you need him out of your hair?" Macmillan asked.

Bertrand coughed and made a face. "It's trickier, now. He's running for sheriff in his home county."

"Too high profile," Jade said, nodding.

"Not if he starts making waves again," Bertrand said. "For now he's backed off. So let's get what we can on him. He's got family. And if he does become sheriff, he's got that to lose. In any case, I'm putting him at the top of our database."

"Yes sir," Macmillan said.

"Understood," Jade said.

Bertrand directed his focus back on Macmillan "You should have the mission parameters already."

"Yes sir," Macmillan said.

"I want you to be prepared to operate anywhere on that list of venues. And I want every item from the criteria addressed."

That was a tall order, but not impossible. Macmillan welcomed the challenge.

"Above all," Bertrand said, "we can't have loose ends. The press can't smooth over sloppy work as well as it could in the past. They can't until we sort out this whole Internet boondoggle. Eric Varney will help us with background checks on recruits, as always. But beyond that, you need to do some careful screening of your own. And keep on top of it, even when candidates pass. Attitudes can change. Someone might decide to stop being a team player."

Bertrand was paranoid, Macmillan decided. Nothing on Earth could turn a made man once he'd graduated up through all the layers of concentric circles to get here. C.I.A. and NSA employees didn't even have the clearance needed to be a part of this organization, now operating within a subcompartment of the DHS. Most of Congress didn't even know the organization existed.

"If there's any security breach whatsoever," Bertrand said, "well, let's just say you don't want to be the person responsible."

False Flag - Brown

16
D MINUS 56
AMARILLO, TEXAS

"Oh man, I don't believe this shit," Delton Williams muttered as he swung his car around the curve and saw the po-po lined up across the road, lights flashing on their cruisers. Another random roadside spot check. Another part of the "zero tolerance policy" garbage the politicians on the local news were talking about lately.

Delton had lost his job months ago when the company he worked for downsized and outsourced their remaining labor overseas. His Unemployment Compensation was about to run out and he'd had no luck finding a job. He'd just sacrificed some gas to go to an interview which turned out to be a scam. He should have known the "no experience necessary" was too good to be true in this economy. Their job posting said he'd get paid training to be a financial consultant, when in actuality it was a door-to-door sales job and they expected him to pony up some cash to pay for the training. He'd spent the last of his cash on gas and now he wouldn't be able to buy baby formula. He and his girl already switched to cloth diapers, hang-drying them on the apartment balcony because disposables were too expensive. The easy way out would be to either start selling weed in his neighborhood, or go on welfare. He didn't want to do either, but was running out of options.

He needed to get back to the apartment soon so his girlfriend could take the car to her late shift job at the convenience store. Delton's sister had borrowed the car Sunday and he hadn't had a chance to clean it out since then. Who knew what she might have left in there somewhere? He was only a mile or so from his apartment. This checkpoint was the last thing he needed right now.

Six cruisers were parked here, in all. Most of the cops stood over by a cluster of trees shading them the late afternoon sun. They were all either white or Hispanic.

He rolled down his window as he came to a stop abreast of the two cops standing in the road. Maybe they would wave him on and harass the next guy.

"Good afternoon, sir," greeted a short, beady-eyed cop, leaning down to face Delton through the open window. "We're conducting roadside spot checks today." He pointed beyond the paved shoulder to an area in front of the trees. "Would you mind pulling off up there so we can check you out real quick?"

"Yes sir, I would mind," Delton said. "My girl got to get to work and she got no ride without this car."

85

False Flag - Brown

The cop blinked in puzzlement. Evidently he wasn't used to people treating a question like a question. "That's alright sir," he finally said. "It'll only take a second."

Just in case the cop was being honest, Delton asked, "What exactly you gonna check?"

"We just need to look at your driver's license, registration and proof of insurance, and to look the car over to make sure everything's all right."

Delton was behind on all his bills, because Unemployment was not covering his expenses. He had foregone paying the electric bill so he could send a token payment to the insurance company. He was pretty sure it appeased them for at least another month. But the premiums kept going higher and higher every year...

"You wanna search my car without a warrant?" Delton asked.

The beady-eyed cop's demeanor changed. Hard lines formed around his mouth. "Excuse me?"

"I said you need a search warrant to do that."

Beady Eyes looked over the car's interior. "Is there something you don't want us to find in here?"

Now the other cop, taller and uglier, stooped over to join Beady Eyes outside Delton's window. "Is there a problem here?"

Beady Eyes gave the big ugly cop a meaningful glance. "He's refusing to comply. Says he wants to see a search warrant."

"Have you got something to hide?" asked the second po-po.

"I ain't hidin' nothin'," Delton said. "Why I gotta be hidin' somethin'? I told this officer here I need to get home so my girl can take the car to her job."

"You could be in and out of here if you didn't give us a hard time," the second cop said. "This is just a random stop, as part of the zero-tolerance policy..."

"I ain't givin' you a hard time," Delton said. "I'm mindin' my own business, just tryin' to get home so my girl can get to work. You're givin' me a hard time."

The second cop stood to his full height and hitched up his gun belt. "Tell you what: do me a favor and pull up over there."

"No thanks," Delton said. "How 'bout you do me a favor and let me get home?"

"You need to think hard about this, sir," the second cop said. "If you insist on making this difficult, you won't like what happens."

"You guys can't search me unless you got a reason," Delton said.

"Where'd you hear that?" Beady Eyes asked, voice dripping with disgust.

"Man, it's my rights!" Delton replied, unable to keep the irritation out

False Flag - Brown

of his tone.

The two cops exchanged a look. The other cops, over in the shade, were now taking notice that something was amiss. Beady Eyes turned to them and called out, "We've got a belligerent one, here."

The other cops hurried over, stationing themselves on both sides of the car.

Why can't they just leave me be, Delton wondered, wracked with the sinking feeling of hopelessness. But he countered all their demands by insisting they produce a search warrant.

Finally one of the other cops approached to lean down in his window. "Unless you show us your license and registration, we're gonna arrest you."

"I'll show you that stuff," Delton said. "No problem. He reached across the front seat to open the glove box, where his registration was.

"He's going for a weapon!" Beady Eyes cried.

Cops flung open both doors and grabbed Delton.

"Chill the hell out! I was just gettin' the papers, like you axed!"

His words were drowned out in the shouting of the cops. More and more hands grabbed hold of him and they hauled him out. He tried repeating his protest but they didn't hear him, or paid no attention. All of them were shouting at once and he couldn't sort it out. They shoved him against the side of his car and somebody wrenched his arm behind his back.

They were going to cuff him.

Delton tore his arm away and twisted around to face them. "Back off, man! I was just gettin' the..."

Something hard hit him in the ribs. Through blinding flashes of pain he saw the one holding the night stick. His body reacted before his brain thought it over, and he planted his fist in the guy's face.

Now sticks crashed all over his shoulders and the top of his head. The only female cop in the group aimed a tazer at him. He batted it out of her hands and pushed her. She went tumbling backwards.

Blows rained down so fast and heavy it was like fireworks went off inside his head. Through the blinding pain of the beating he felt the ground come up to strike him yet another blow on the back of the head.

The perp's resistance was an unexpected highlight to the checkpoint duty. Not only did they get to see Officer Katy Hobbes go tumbling ass-over teakettle after losing her tazer, but they were getting quality stick time like most of them had never enjoyed before. Then Archuletta began yelling, holding his arms out to stop the beating.

Panting but pumped on the adrenalin, they gradually stopped

swinging. Their human *pinata* was unconscious.

They all glanced at each other and smirks were exchanged. Hobbes picked herself up and came over to take in the scene, and a couple jokes were cracked at her expense. Then Archuletta squatted to examine the perp.

"Hey guys, this doesn't look good."

"Cuff him and get him in my car," Fender said, chuckling. "Somebody can bring aspirin to his cell."

"No," Archuletta said. "I mean this looks bad. Maybe we should get an ambulance over here."

Archuletta stood again, then noticed all the civilians from the backed-up traffic standing outside their vehicles with smartphones out, taking pictures and video.

"Oh, shit."

False Flag - Brown

This was BS duty. Jake McCallum trained his team for direct action. That's what their purpose was. And yet here they were in a rented storefront doing flunky work that the local cops were more than capable of.

Local cops **were** there. And state troopers. So were the U.S. Marshalls and reps from competing federal agencies. Mac's boss had played up this assignment as a "joint task force" operation that faced a significant threat. The threat level was exposed for what it really was when they were told they wouldn't need helmets, armor or rifles.

In this little store front meeting room, local police and federal agents were busy collecting information from outraged members of a group that had been circulating a petition for secession. The perps were forced to surrender their wallets and let the agents go through their I.D., insurance cards, credit cards, cash and other personal items. Cellphones were confiscated and checked. They were grilled regarding places of employment, aliases, alternate addresses, friends and relatives. While local and federal agents recorded information on them, the group members protested, but were obviously not going to offer any violent resistance.

When Mac remarked about this bogus operation, his boss told him it was a sort of *quid-pro-quo* job. They relied on the NSA's intelligence database for some of their raids. It was a good idea to pay the NSA back once in a while with this kind of hands-on data mining that couldn't be accomplished online when the DomTers didn't advertise their personal and group information on social media.

On first glance none of these group members looked like domestic terrorists. They were all middle class; most were middle aged; they were dressed conservatively and practiced good personal hygiene. And they weren't all white. Mac couldn't imagine them carrying bombs or rifles. But they sure were carrying dangerous ideas around.

Still, Mac's men would be better employed against somebody who did look, smell, and act more like a terrorist.

While his men helped interrogate the people in the store front, Mac's mind wandered back over the few operations he'd led since taking over this team. He cringed upon remembering he'd have to write the report for the last operation.

Mac had been putting this off, because he didn't want to deal with it and wasn't sure how to spin it: The raid on the Tasper house in Texas had

False Flag - Brown

been carried out with clockwork precision--his experience as an operator had finely honed his ability to organize and lead such missions. Trouble was, the intelligence was faulty. After busting in the door at 0300, rounding up the family for questioning, and cracking the gun safe, they found nothing illegal. At least nothing **currently** illegal.

Mac's boss had offered to "season" the site. Plant evidence, in other words, so Mac would be credited with a good bust for his efforts, at least. This was something else that bothered him, but he'd give it more thought later when he'd dealt with other matters.

Other matters like one of his shooters: Samuels.

It was bad enough the operation was all for nothing, but Samuels had to stomp a baby kitten to death in the little girl's bedroom. The Tasper family was complaining about that to their representative more than about the damage to their house. How was he going to explain that incident in the report?

Mac's tablet beeped to warn him of an incoming file. He stepped outside through the back door to look it over.

Another Contingency Profile from Domestic Intel. He opened it and began reading about Gary Fram, whose profile raised just about every red flag there was to raise. Mac studied the satellite and street-level images of Fram's house. Within a few moments he had decided which SOP, with what modifications, would work best for a home raid. He'd drafted enough of these contingencies that he could get the basic plan spelled out succinctly, to be adjusted further in the future, according to situation, policy, or team assigned, if a raid was greenlighted. But before he finished drafting a contingency for the profile, his phone rang.

He recognized the incoming number as one of Jeffries'. "Yo, what's up DeAngelo?"

"What's goin' on, my brotha. Hey, I'm in the neighborhood, man. You wanna get some chicken wings?"

Mac checked the time. He hadn't eaten for quite a while and realized he was famished. "That sounds like a plan," he said. His team really didn't need his supervision to finish this data mining flunky work.

The local Hooters was packed every night, but at that time of day they had it mostly to themselves. Their redhead waitress was about a seven, but would probably only rank a five without the makeup, push-up bra and short shorts. They ordered beer and the hottest wings available.

"So how you settling in?" DeAngelo asked, dipping his first wing in dressing.

Mac nodded, tearing a hunk of meat off a wing with his teeth. After swallowing, he said, "I'm getting the hang of it."

False Flag - Brown

"From what I hear, you've got the planning thing down," DeAngelo said.

It was good to know somebody appreciated Mac's ability. He wondered who DeAngelo knew in his chain of command to get this information, though.

"That's good," DeAngelo went on. "You gotta represent, Mac. You're the only brotha up in there. Make us look good and they may hire some more of us."

"How is it where you work?" Mac asked.

"A lot like major league baseball--it's mostly a white show, with a few of us token niggas so they can say they're not prejudiced."

"The few, the proud, the nappy," Mac remarked, and they both grinned around their spicy chicken meat.

The waitress came by to check on them and replenish their beer. Both men watched her little white booty as she walked away. Mac couldn't help wondering what she'd be like. He'd heard a lot of comments about how crazy redheads could be. Crazier than white chicks in general.

Mac sobered up quickly, though, when he remembered Samuels. "You ever had to deal with a shooter who pushed things just a bit too far?"

"What's up, man?" DeAngelo asked.

Mac told him about the kitten-stomping incident. DeAngelo listened, then shrugged.

"He's just being a white boy," DeAngelo said. "Half of them are psychopaths, man. If they weren't working for the government, they'd be serial killers or something. Did you hear what happened in Texas?"

Mac shook his head. He'd been too busy to check the news.

DeAngelo frowned, his eyes flashing something dangerous for an instant. "More white cops, man. Pulled this brotha over for nothin'. Drag this brotha out his car and beat him to death right there, man."

"What set them off?" Mac asked.

"Drivin' While Black," DeAngelo said, shrugging. "They're tryin' to say he didn't have insurance, and that he attacked them first. Six different cops, man. There's video going viral, though. He didn't try to defend himself until they started beatin' on him."

Mac immediately thought of Eric Garner and grew infuriated. "This is too much, man. How far are they gonna try to push us?"

DeAngelo shook his head slowly, with a hard scowl. "I'm tellin' you: local police are nearly as bad as the Constitutionalists. And state police ain't much better. All those good ol' boy networks, man. You'd think they'd be extinct by now, but they're gettin' even stronger. It's all gonna come to a bum rush one of these days."

False Flag - Brown

Every time they talked, DeAngelo sounded a little more militant in his worldview, but that matched Mac's own evolving mindset. White people's media and entertainment might be getting ostensibly more sensitive and diversified all the time; but at the same time there were more and more bloggers, blog followers and social media participants sounding less sensitive and more separatist. Their boldness grew daily as they railed about the decline of western civilization. They called African-Americans "feral," referred to mixed relationships as "mudsharking," talked about Caucasian heritage like it was something to be proud of, and even used the phrase "white supremacy."

"You think it's any better at the federal level?" Mac asked.

DeAngelo swigged some beer down and made a face. "It's a white man's world over here. America is racist--no way around that."

Mac nodded. "I'm the Jackie Robinson where I am, seems like."

"Not even that, my brotha," DeAngelo said. "You're a Buck. I'm a Tom. At least that's how The Man sees us. They talk a lot of shit about equality and all that, but when it comes down to drawing lines, they'll side with their own. You and me are useful to them for now, but we'll just be another couple niggas to them eventually."

Mac licked buffalo sauce off his huge fingers, then stared at the texture of the skin on a drumstick while forming his words. "You hint around a lot that something big is coming down, racially. You know something I don't?"

DeAngelo sighed. "Off the record?"

Mac held his hands out and raised his eyebrows. "Just you and me talking, man."

"These cats like Sharpton and Jackson are a joke," DeAngelo said. "Nearly everybody knows it. They ain't done a damn thing for black folks, except make Whitey hate us even more. It's like two gangs getting ready to rumble out there, man. Actually more than that—the Spics already outnumber us, and it's gettin' worse every day. But imagine something like Baltimore or Ferguson, only nationwide, and our people actually throw down this time. Meanwhile, Whitey is thinkin' if he can't have us for slaves anymore, he should either kill us off or send us back to Africa."

"Race war," Mac said. "You think it's gonna come to that?"

"Oh, I know it is," DeAngelo replied, solemnly. "And like I said, we may not just be fightin' the whites. Might be a three-way fight with them and the Spics...or they may gang up on us. And that ain't even puttin' the Asians in the equation. You know there's never been any love lost between us and the Slopes, man. They'll most likely side with Whitey, too."

Mac let this sink in. It was a lot to process. He knew there would

92

always be rednecks, and some degree of white privilege, but had always assumed life would continue on pretty much as it was. Or, if anything, get better. They had finally gotten one of their own people in the White House, after all. For two terms. But DeAngelo talked about a coming attempted genocide like it was a done deal.

"That's one thing makes working with the feds an advantage," DeAngelo said. "We'll be able to see it coming a lot farther off than those poor brothas in the hood."

"And then what?" Mac asked, the pitch of his voice raising.

"Again, off the record," DeAngelo said, locking eyes with Mac.

Mac nodded.

"Me and some other brothas been gettin' together. Nothin' official, and still we're careful about what we say and how we say it. But we all know there's a day comin' when we'll have to look out for each other, y'know? Mutual protection."

Yes, Mac decided, that was smart thinking. It wasn't just a good idea —if what DeAngelo said was true, it would prove to be a necessity.

"Hey, you know the circumstances we met under," DeAngelo said, shrugging. "Like it or not, I know all about your background. And because I know it, I know we could use a brotha like you, when it all goes down."

DeAngelo was inviting Mac into some kind of clandestine brotherhood within clandestine agencies. One that might make all the difference in the survival of their race in North America.

Mac had made friends in SF, in Delta and as a contractor. Some of those friends were black; some were other minorities; some were white. But he lost touch with most of them and gave up on the rest as politics became a more and more powerful influence in everyone's life. You just couldn't agree to disagree anymore.

In Iraq the man he trusted most was Leon Campbell. But Leon got out of the contracting biz, went back to the States and started a business with friends. Mac had other guys in SSI he got along with--some who he'd even dodged bullets and eaten dirt with. But none of them knew what it was like to be black. They never would--and probably didn't want to.

DeAngelo knew. And he was in touch with others who knew. There was power in that.

"Give me a holla next time y'all get together," Mac said.

False Flag - Brown

Ken Fowler used his lunch break to drive to the polls. He took his voter's guide inside with him, signed his name on the register, and stood in line.

He recognized a young woman as she left a booth and handed off her ballot and instructions. It was Mandy Albright, a pretty girl with an outgoing personality he dated for a while when she had first moved to town. Mandy had naturally curly blonde hair—just like the girl in the Charlie Brown comic strip. Ken nodded at her.

Her eyes flashed recognition and a big smile formed on her face. She stopped to chat, sharing that she was married now and it was so nice to see him and wasn't it just wonderful the country was finally moving forward and she was so proud of him for voting.

She bid him ta-ta and breezed away.

What an airhead, he thought. And naturally she assumed that he'd be voting the same ticket she obviously was.

A louder-than-normal buzz of conversation drew his attention. A group had entered behind him. There were about 15 of them, who were all short, dark, with straight black hair, and dressed much heavier than the weather justified. A poll worker gave them the instructions she gave everyone about how to use the ballot, and a well-dressed Latino translated the instructions into Spanish for his group.

Ken shook his head, suspecting exactly what was going on. This was one of those places that didn't check ID, so the usual suspects were taking advantage by shuttling illegal aliens in to cancel out opposition votes.

Then he noticed Willie-Mae Harris standing in line in front of him, with some other blacks. He would never forget her face, thanks to that confrontation outside her house. She didn't live in this district. She had no right to vote here. Since she didn't work, she was probably spending the entire day visiting the polls in different districts to cast multiple votes.

Ken's fists clenched of their own accord.

He knew it would do no good to point this out to anyone. He would just be called a racist and thrown out for causing a disturbance. Maybe arrested. Also, the Black Panthers and other black supremacy groups were out in force today (they had some of their members posted at certain poll stations armed with clubs to scare away anybody they believed would not vote correctly), and might even have somebody outside this station, ready to beat him if he made a fuss.

Ken took no comfort in the fact that Texas wasn't really a swing state.

False Flag - Brown

There was enough of this going on in swing states to steal the election once again anyway. Everyone knew about the massive voter fraud going on, but nobody with authority would admit to it. In fact, they obviously wanted it. That's why they fought so hard to make it possible.

Requiring people to show identification was racist, they said. Requiring I.D. wasn't racist for anything else; just for voting.

When it was his turn, Ken filled out and cast his ballot. He knew his vote had been illegally canceled out, and knew he could do nothing about it.

Outside, he sat in his work van and watched. After a while the illegal aliens emerged from the building, all piled into a passenger van, and their translator drove them away.

He drove to his next job angry and depressed.

Ken's experience in kindergarten wasn't his last unpleasant encounter with the "black community." In elementary school some loudmouth picked a fight with him, but Ken was the only one to get in trouble. In junior high, three colored boys found out Ken had cash in his wallet. They waited for him after school and jumped him. In high school one of them stole his new pair of sneakers from the locker room. Another one, his junior year, cold-cocked him simply because they disagreed about something in Algebra Class.

Since then he generally avoided the black neighborhoods when his job didn't send him there. Violence didn't happen as often since his school years, but there was an attitude among most blacks that since he was white, he **owed** them. And violence was sometimes threatened when he didn't "lend" strangers money for beer or whatever. He got bum-rushed by five black dudes once because his refusal to "lend" money escalated into a pissing contest. He might have been badly beaten had a pickup truck full of rowdy white football players not swung around the corner onto the scene just as it was unfolding.

In the movies, on TV, and in their own minds, blacks were always the victims of whites. In his experience, it was the opposite.

You couldn't even point out election fraud for fear of being classified as a racist and ostracized.

Their entitlement just never ended. They were entitled to his money via theft, coercion or wealth redistribution. They were entitled to jobs he was more qualified for via Affirmative Action. They were entitled to scholarships and grants simply because of their race. They were entitled to the world's sympathy regardless of who was right or wrong in a given dispute. They were entitled to pronounce guilt on the people they hated. They were entitled to commit election fraud if they thought the end justified the means. Their politicians were entitled a free pass for

False Flag - Brown

incompetence, corruption and straight-up crime. They were entitled to media attack dogs, to smear any who dared criticize them. They were entitled to select what parts of history should be remembered, and how it should be skewed. They were entitled to select what statistics, incidents and anecdotes were valid to report, as well. And they were entitled to blame their own behavior and performance on the "racism" and "privilege" of everyone's favorite whipping-boy—the white heterosexual male.

Ken Fowler was done with it. He wasn't participating in the entitlement racket anymore, if he could help it. They would never get sympathy from him again. He would be on his guard around them at all times, and do whatever he could to protect himself and other white folks.

The black mindset was to always take the side of whoever looked most like themselves, regardless of the facts. It was time for white people to start looking out for their own, too.

False Flag - Brown

19
D MINUS 50
COCCOCINO COUNTY, ARIZONA

Rocco Cavarra hadn't done much swimming or diving since moving to Arizona. Each morning he did a few miles on the bike, though, because his knees and shins didn't very much like the jarring abuse of running, anymore. After the bike ride he would prepare and eat a big breakfast, which he'd gotten used to decades ago in the Navy.

Roberta came this way to visit him once in a while, but the visits were getting fewer and farther between. He hadn't heard from his ex-wife in many years, which was fine, but he didn't hear from his kids very often, either. His daughter Jasmine had visited when he first moved, but only once since then. He also no longer saw his old buddies. Were he a younger man, Cavarra would probably regret leaving California. But the economy and taxes there were making life less and less tenable. He could see that even his nice little suburb of San Diego was no longer very safe, and was only going to get worse.

Besides, life wasn't all lonely and quiet here. He had the business. Their age gap probably kept them from being super-tight, but Leon and Carlos were friends as well as business partners. They'd been through some stuff together and he trusted them. It didn't get much better than that these days.

Cavarra liked his eggs fried hard, along with hash browns, toast and a small cut of steak. He ate it right out of the frying pan to cut down on dirty dishes. As he ate, he checked his news feeds.

Topping everyone's list that morning was yet another police brutality story, this one from Amarillo, Texas. The news reports only gave the bare bones info: a black driver stopped by police and beaten for "resisting arrest." He later died of a brain hemorrhage or something everyone assumed was ultimately caused by a blow or blows to the head. Cavarra had quit paying attention to mainstream media long ago, and didn't even fully trust his alternative sources. So minimal details were okay, especially this soon after the incident.

But whereas the reports were bare bones so far, the people who commented shared all kind of details. Most of it was probably opinion, embellishment or rumors passed along via social networks but presented as suppressed facts. Cavarra read down through one of the comment threads just in case there was a kernel of truth to be gleaned. Of course plenty of commenters assumed that Delton Williams had been targeted because he was black; that officers used excessive force because he was black; and there would be no repercussions for the police because their

97

victim was black.

Cavarra remembered back to Eric Garner and figured they were probably right about the cops getting away with it. It was just another symptom of the contempt the ruling class had for the citizenry. But rather than recognize the problem and direct their outrage at those responsible, citizens preferred to see each other as the enemy, based on racial and ethnic differences.

"Get over yourself and quit playing the victim," one person commented. "Not everything is an anti-black conspiracy."

Several people responded by calling the commenter "racist," "redneck," "inbred cracker" and similar euphemisms. Then others responded to those comments just as ignorantly, throwing around the N-word as well as "jungle bunny" and "coon." Cavarra chimed in to attempt reasonable discussion, but was ignored and drowned out in the racist flame war that ensued.

That's what happened pretty much every time he appealed to reason in these matters. People weren't interested in reason. At least most didn't seem to be.

Cavarra realized, with great irritation and a deep sadness, that if all the people in the comment thread were physically gathered at a single location somewhere, they would be throwing punches instead of insults, and the violence would probably escalate to fatal.

He could excuse the irrational anger for somebody who personally knew Delton Williams and cared about him. But for these other dirtbags he was just a symbol--an excuse to unleash the ignorance and hatred they'd been carrying around locked and loaded for just such an occasion.

And another aspect of this bothered him.

For decades now blacks had gotten away with (in fact, were pretty much encouraged to harbor) a blatantly ethnocentric worldview. They looked at everything through a racial lens, and got a pass for their racist attitudes toward whites and others. They enjoyed Sacrosanct Victim Status by virtue of simply being born. And because they were Sacrosanct Victims, their own racism and bigotry was never recognized as racism and bigotry.

It wasn't just blacks, of course. Women and other minorities also got awarded Sacrosanct Victim Status at birth. There were scholarships, institutionalized hiring practices, de facto public relations programs in Hollywood and the press, and armies of activists waiting to rush to the defense of anybody who suffered an inconvenience. Anybody except a white male heterosexual, who was forever barred entry into the Sacrosanct Victim Club.

For the offense of being born.

For decades, white men (those without the correct political affiliation,

False Flag - Brown

anyway) walked on eggshells for fear of offending somebody, and dared not make too big an issue when they were victimized because it ran counter to the overall Sacrosanct Victim Narrative.

But now that was changing. White men were growing openly contemptuous of everyone who habitually played the victim card...and those who maybe were innocent but still shared the genetic traits of the "social justice warriors" who **did** play the victim. Cavarra wouldn't be surprised if some men started wearing shirts with "You wouldn't understand--it's a white thang" logos, or maps of Europe on their sweaters. More and more white men were speaking and behaving like the bigots they'd been accused of being all along.

That's what bothered him most. That meant it was officially hopeless.

And in another self-fulfilling prophecy, the G.O.P. was becoming the white people's party. It sure wasn't the "right-wing" party, at least by any accurate, objective definition. Republicans differed from the Democrats only by degrees; certainly not in principle.

Cavarra had never seen the country so racially polarized. Up until recently he'd assumed racial differences would decline in importance as time went on, until they were no longer a concern to most people. But there was a motivated subculture in government and media determined not to let that happen, and they were winning the struggle. When former egalitarians descended into tribalism, the prospects were grim.

Then, of course, there were card-carrying white supremacists coming out of the closet now, like the dirtbag who showed up at the office the other day.

And where would Cavarra be, if worse came to worst? Blacks considered him white; Hispanics considered him Gringo; and tribal whites would probably decide he was too swarthy to be racially "pure." He'd suffered his share of prejudice as a young man. He had worked hard to neutralize the heavy Sicilian accent passed down from his grandparents because he tired of having people assume him stupid due to his speech.

Cavarra tuned to one of his pre-programmed satellite stations on the drive to work. He cranked the volume when the virtual DJ played the Rolling Stones' "Gimme Shelter."

War, children...
It's just a shot away
It's just a shot away...

After singing along with the chorus for the third time, he couldn't help wondering if the song was an omen.

False Flag - Brown

Cavarra and Leon arrived at the office at the same time. Carlos was already there.

They got started the usual way: jokes and insults over coffee. But everyone had heard about the killing in Amarillo by now, and it didn't take long for the conversation to go there.

"You think there'll be riots?" Carlos asked.

Rocco nodded. "I'm kinda' worried it might be worse than that this time."

Both younger men gave Cavarra their attention.

"Just seems to me it's all at the boiling point," Rocco said, shrugging. "On the one side you've got agitators screaming 'America is racist' and that the Man is out to get black folks. Not only are people in the hood listening, but they've seen cops kill one too many of their own. Not just in Amarillo, but all over. And of course they've been programmed to classify the incidents like Michael Brown and Freddie Gray as more crimes against Africa. Some of them have actually assassinated police as an attempt at social justice. Then on the other side you've got these Hitler Youth cops...and judges who agree with them...who think their badge puts them above the law and that they are basically occupation troops inside an enemy nation. They're just itching to taze or beat or shoot somebody. Now they've got armored vehicles and combat gear..."

"C'mon, Rocco," Leon interrupted. "You make it sound like racism is just a figment of our imagination. And 'crimes against Africa'--what's that supposed to mean?"

"That's how **they** think; not how **I** do," Cavarra said. "I have no doubt there are plenty of racist cops. And racist judges and district attorneys and police commissioners. But not everybody with this police state mentality are white, are they? So you've got consistent behavior but inconsistent racial composition. That right there busts the myth that the core motive for their fascist behavior is racial."

"People of color don't see it that way," Leon said.

"Right," Cavarra said. "That's why I'm worried we're at the tipping point."

"Wait 'til Sharpton and Jackson and those guys get out there and start drumming," Carlos said. "Like stirring nitroglycerin"

Leon had to roll his eyes and groan upon hearing those names.

"Even when they've been provoked," Rocco said, "a peaceable population won't normally strike back without people mixed in who aren't afraid to use violence. But we've got plenty individuals who are comfortable using violence in the inner cities, don't we? And I'm worried they're not going to be content smashing a few windows and stealing a few TV sets this time."

"I'm glad I don't live in the big city," Carlos said.

"I'll tell you something else," Cavarra added. "When you look at those videos from, say, Baltimore...blacks attacking whites, but the whites won't fight back..."

"One dude did," Carlos pointed out. "They hit his girlfriend with a trash can, so he went out to throw down with the guy who did it...and like a dozen black dudes all jumped on him, man."

"But none of the white guys went to help him out, did they?" Cavarra asked. "They just wouldn't fight back."

"It's a solidarity thing, I guess," Carlos said. "White boys don't have it."

"Right," Cavarra said. "But what happens when that changes? What happens when a mob attacks some white person, and a whole bunch of white people decide that an attack on one is an attack on all? What happens when they start fighting back?"

"A race war," Carlos said, "no?"

"Look at it this way," Rocco advised. "When was it...2009? Anyway, the Fraud-in-Chief warned us he was gonna build a 'civilian' army more powerful than our military. So now we've got all these militarized police with armor, helmets, assault rifles, grenade launchers, armored vehicles, and the DHS by itself has what—maybe 100 rounds of jacketed hollow point for every human being in North America?"

"That's just the .40 caliber," Leon said.

"Right," Cavarra agreed. "So here's this huge solution looking for a problem. Along comes Ferguson; then Baltimore; now Amarillo. Ta-da! And in this corner, may I introduce...the problem!"

Leon looked as though he wanted to say something, but car doors slamming outside alerted them that their first customers of the day had arrived.

In mid-afternoon a green Corvette pulled into the parking lot. The exhaust noise was very loud--though all three partners were at different parts of the property, they all noticed the strange, lumpy sound of the engine. When the driver tapped the gas pedal at one point, it snarled like some kind of doomsday machine.

Carlos, who owned an old Camaro and knew something about cars, left his customer and walked over to investigate. Noticing this through the window, Cavarra left the counter and went outside.

As he drew close to the 'Vette, he recognized the young man now out of the car talking to Carlos. It was Takoda Scarred Wolf. He'd met him at Tommy's victory party.

False Flag - Brown

Cavarra knew Tommy's oldest son Gunther, and liked him. Takoda, however, struck him as a troublemaker.

Carlos nodded toward Cavarra and bumped fists with Takoda. "Rocco can hook you up. I gotta get back to my customer."

Takoda nodded and turned to regard Cavarra.

The young man was built like his father and brothers—all lean, ropy muscle with veins bulging through his red-brown skin. His face seemed locked into a permanent fierce scowl. He looked the caricature of an Indian warrior, only missing the feathered war bonnet and tomahawk.

Cavarra offered his hand and Takoda shook it with crushing strength.

"What brings you to Arizona?" Cavarra asked.

"This place," the young man answered. "Carlos gave me a business card back at the victory party."

"And you kept it all this time, huh?"

Takoda shrugged. "I wanted to come try it out. I have a couple days off. Figured now would be good."

"Okay," Cavarra said. "Let me show you around."

Cavarra gave him the tour. Takoda showed a keen interest in the urban target course they called "the Wild West Shootout." Rocco advised him it would be better to start out on the Jungle Walk and work his way up to the Shootout, but Takoda knew what he wanted. Rocco got on the radio and advised that whoever got freed up first should go over the targets real quick. That turned out to be Leon.

Takoda filled out the paperwork while Leon inspected the course. Cavarra advised him to run through it with a pistol, but Takoda insisted on using his AK.

The frontier-style facade buildings in the Shootout course not only made it popular for cowboy action shooters, but more serious-minded customers loved it as well, because the pop-up and moving targets presented a tremendous challenge, even painted to resemble Old West bad men.

Nobody at CBC Southwest Tactical freaked out when customers came geared up with military style weapons, as a lot of them did. And no records were kept of who brought what.

By the time Leon was done with his inspection, Carlos was freed up to give Takoda the safety briefing. When he was ready, Carlos hit the start switch.

Takoda was like a machine, running, crouching, dropping, crawling, rolling, taking a knee, running again, and using what cover/concealment was available as he moved. He missed a lot of targets, as everyone did (especially their first couple times through), but he fired at least once at every target. Including targets that most people never saw their first time through. And he kept his weapon pointed either downrange or straight up, without being reminded. He finished with a really good time, but cussed at himself when Carlos calculated the hit ratio afterwards.

"Relax," Carlos said. "You did really good for your first time through. And with a rifle, no less. Most people don't get a shot off on some of those targets, even with a pistol."

"How much to go through again?" Takoda asked.

Not everybody was willing to pony up the dough for the Wild West Shootout, but those who did almost always got hooked. Rocco gave discounts for multiple runs through the course, which encouraged repeat sales. So it was a big money maker—not even counting the ammunition sales it generated.

Carlos was surprised how much Takoda improved his second time through, even though some of the moving targets tracked the opposite direction on subsequent runs, to keep shooters on their toes. When the sequence finished, and they removed their shooting muffs, Carlos said, "You handle that rifle pretty well. You got experience from somewhere?"

"I plink around a lot," was all Takoda said.

He went through a third time, and his hit ratio was now impressive. Some recently-arrived customers had gathered to watch behind the Safe Line, and appeared intrigued.

Carlos congratulated him afterwards, but Takoda wasn't happy with his performance.

"No, trust me," Carlos said, "you tore it up. That was truth."

"I still missed targets," Takoda grumbled.

"Everybody does. Even the best shooters to run this course."

"Who is best?" Takoda asked.

Carlos sighed. "Leon's got the best score. It's like 74% hits." It was irritating to admit this, since Leon was a sniper, and wouldn't normally be expected to be so accurate with snap shots. But Carlos' best score so far was 69% and Rocco's was 66%.

"I can't afford another run today," Takoda said, grudgingly. "But I'll be back."

"Long way from home, aren't you?" Carlos asked.

Takoda shrugged and chinned toward his Corvette. "Not in that. It's nice to take her out on a long stretch of open road once in a while."

"My Camaro's set up more for quarter mile," Carlos said.

They talked cars for a while—a little about gear ratios, horsepower and top end—before Takoda spotted Leon over at the 1,000 meter range. "Excuse me," he said.

Carlos waved the paperwork in the air. "Just stop by the front counter and settle up when you're done."

"How'd he do?" Rocco asked, once Carlos joined him behind the counter.

"He's legit. It's almost scary."

"Guess the apple doesn't fall that far from the tree," Rocco said. "At least in physical abilities, huh?"

"That whole family is the truth. But I got the impression that this one spends most of his time trying to give Tommy an ulcer," Carlos said.

"Yeah, me too." Cavarra shook his head, grinning. "Well, if you want to watch the counter for a while, I can go patch up the targets."

"Sounds good, Rocco. Stretch your legs."

Cavarra pushed out the door and nearly ran into a trio of men headed the opposite way. After perfunctory apologies all around, the stocky man in front stuck out his hand.

"Howdy. Gary Fram. These two are with me."

Cavarra shook the offered hand and nodded at the others.

"We came here to try out the Jungle Walk and to dope in one of our big caliber rifles," Fram said. "We heard about this place on the Web. But we just watched your Western Shootout deal, and might want to try that while we're here."

The "Jungle Walk" was down by the *arroyo*. An *arroyo* was like a dried riverbed (in the Middle East these were called "*wadis*") which moved a lot of water during flash floods, but was usually dry. But there was enough moisture lingering under the surface at this one that quite a few juniper trees grew nearby. Cavarra and his partners had planted extra trees in between the junipers to make it seem more like a forest. It didn't look like a jungle by any stretch of the imagination, even using old black & white Tarzan movie standards, but there was enough foliage to hide targets in.

Cavarra gave Fram his friendly businessman smile and thumbed over his shoulder toward the office building he just left. "If you go in there and talk to Carlos at the counter, he can hook you up."

Cavarra made to resume his trek, but Fram followed up quickly with a question.

"Is he the one to talk to about possible discount bulk rates, if we bring a group here?"

Stopping in his tracks, Cavarra asked, "A group? Like how many?"

Fram exchanged glances with his friends and said, "About 20, right? Yeah, probably about 20 of us."

Before Cavarra could answer, everyone noticed Leon and Takoda approaching with an old ammo box full of spent brass.

False Flag - Brown

"It's a lot like the difference between the UFC and the NFL," Leon was saying. "Combat is a team sport. You may miss everything you shoot at. The man left and right of you may miss, too. But as long as you helped your unit take the objective, then you won. Maybe all you did was hold the line; cover for your buddies. But the enemy retreated 'cause they was afraid if you get close enough, you'll stop missin'. See, you can talk all day about air strikes and force multipliers and laser-guided ordnance or whatever, but even with all these science fiction gizmos we got, winnin' a war still means you gotta take and hold key terrain and resources. Only infantry can do that. So as long as there's war, there'll always be infantry."

Leon and Takoda arrived at the spot where everyone was standing outside the door, and noticed they were the focus of everyone's attention.

"What?" Leon asked, then handed the ammo box to Takoda and raised his own hands as if submitting to a search. "No brass, no ammo, sir."

Cavarra grinned, blinked his eyes, shook his head and turned back to his customer. "Come on inside, Gary, and we'll see what we can work out."

False Flag - Brown

It wound up being a good day at work, even though Leon felt like a dark cloud was lurking on the horizon, waiting to move in. On his drive home, he thought about what happened in Amarillo, and what Rocco said that morning.

Leon had checked his news feeds and social networks over lunch. Relatives in the hood, and acquaintances of theirs, were making remarks about killing cops; killing whites in general; and burning Amarillo to the ground. And pictures were being uploaded which made Amarillo look like Damascus--platoons of police in body armor and Kevlar helmets packing carbines, tear gas and flash-bangs, backed up by MRAP armored vehicles. It all looked to be going down just how Rocco predicted.

FLAGSTAFF, ARIZONA

Leon came to where the road was blocked for construction. Of course one of the few streets that was in good shape and needed no repair was the street being torn up. He shook his head and followed the arrow on the "DETOUR" sign. Anticipaing a right turn at the end of the detour, he drove in the right lane. He approached an intersection with a small side street, following a tractor-trailer. When the tractor-trailer pulled far enough ahead, he saw faded paint on the asphalt indicating he was on a right-turn-only lane.

Unlike 90% of drivers on the road, Leon actually checked his mirrors before changing lanes. When he did so, he saw other cars behind him swerving into the middle lane and accelerating. After each one got past him, he intended to change lanes, but before he could, another car would dart out and pull abreast. He was worried he'd be forced to turn onto the side street, but finally got an opening and whipped out into the middle lane just before he had to stop for the light.

A car pulled up beside him in the far left lane.

"Hey!"

Leon turned toward whoever was yelling to him. A white couple sat in the front seats of a little Nissan. The young man behind the wheel was glaring at him. "Yeah you, monkey-man! Learn to drive, boy!"

"Up yours, redneck," Leon replied.

"What?!?" The redneck's face contorted in rage. "Up yers? Up yers? Boy, I'll kick yer black a-yass!"

"You're welcome to try," Leon said.

False Flag - Brown

"What!?!"

"You got a hearin' problem?" Leon asked, "or you just don't savvy English?"

The redneck was bent down and leaned over the young woman's lap to get a good look through his passenger window at Leon and his truck. "Stupid coon, yer lucky Ah got mah baby here in the car, or Ah'd put yer black a-yass in the hospital!"

"I guess one of us is lucky, anyway," Leon said.

The light turned green. The far left lane moved faster, and the redneck sped ahead, calling Leon everything except a human being.

The more Leon thought about the loudmouth jerk, the angrier he got.

Less than a block later, the redneck got stuck behind somebody stopped to make a left turn. Leon stared at the ignorant slab of meat in the Nissan as he passed, muttering under his breath.

When the detour required him to finally make the right turn, Leon slowed and waited for the vehicles in front of him. Cars buzzed by on the left.

Something flew in his window and hit the inside of the passenger door with a violent thud. The first thought that occurred to Leon was, "Grenade!" He swerved, looking for the projectile, ready to throw his door open and dive out before it exploded.

Then he saw it was a ¾ full bottle of Mountain Dew.

Leon's gaze swung back to the left lane and he saw the Nissan speeding away, the driver flipping him the bird as he went.

In his younger days, Leon probably would have chased the redneck down and found out if he was as bad as he thought he was. But he let it go, cranking his music to calm him down.

His old compilation CD came to his only Kanye West track: "Jesus Walks."

Need ta recruit all the soldiers.
All a' God's soldiers...
We at war.
We at war with racism, terrorism,
But most of all, we at war with ourselves.

Leon appreciated the commentary.

Police were getting ready to rumble. Hood rats were getting ready to rumble. Rednecks were out for blood. And then those dudes showed up at the office, planning to bring a group numbering 20 or more to run through the combat courses? It didn't take Sherlock Holmes to guess what was on their mind, either.

False Flag - Brown

Even the Indians were convinced a fight was coming, if the Scarred Wolf kid's appearance that day was any indication. But who were they planning to fight? If they took their marching orders from television and professional victims, as most minorities generally did, they'd side with the government. But Native Americans, more than anyone else, had powerful reasons to distrust the government. And the cops were the enforcement arm of government—the same cops who were out to get minorities. But Tommy himself was a cop. It was all hopelessly muddled.

Besides, Tommy Scarred Wolf was cut from a different cloth. He didn't have a victim mentality and preferred to think for himself. His son Takoda was already skilled before he stepped on the shooting range that day. It had to be because Tommy had trained his sons. If he also believed a fight was coming, which side would **he** be on?

Or was Leon reading too much into the day's events? He'd grown to be fairly paranoid over the last quarter century.

But then paranoia had kept him alive and healthy for that quarter century.

Leon parked in his driveway and hid his sidearm in his fag bag before unassing the truck. Scarcely had the engine even shut off when the doggie door pushed open and Shotgun came running out to greet him, her tail wagging to beat the band.

He squatted to pet her. "How's my four-legged home security system today, huh?" She licked him but he kept their affectionate greeting short and regained his feet. She'd been a working dog in Iraq when he was a contractor and he still felt a compulsion to keep her sharp, not letting her get too comfortable in this lax civilian life. In fact, he should bring her with him to work so she'd stay familiar with the racket of small arms fire, but he felt his home was more secure with her here while he was gone.

His one-story house on ten acres was paid for with cash from what he'd managed to save working as a contractor in the Sandbox. And looking back, he'd got out of that business at pretty much the right time. The situation over there went from bad to worse; and just when it seemed impossible for it to get even worse still, it did. A whole lot of blood and money wasted, was how Leon looked at the Iraq occupation.

But Washington was always looking for ways to waste even more blood and money.

Leon shook the thoughts loose and unlocked the front door. Shotgun entered before he did—an ingrained habit from Iraq, to ensure there were no booby traps awaiting him.

Once inside, he heard the TV from his bedroom. Funny--he hadn't watched it for a few days, he thought, and went to investigate, pulling the pistol back out of his fag bag even though Shotgun was calm.

False Flag - Brown

"Oh, hell no," he exclaimed, after opening the bedroom door.

Lachelle was still where he left her that morning, only wide awake, with dirty dishes beside her on the bed and an open bag of tortilla chips. Some talk show emanated stupidity from the TV.

"What happened to you leavin' after your shower?" Leon demanded, feeling stupid. She could have robbed him blind because he'd been trusting enough to leave before she did.

She stretched and said, "Damn, don't shoot, Negro. Hello to you too."

Lachelle was a bootylicious ghetto princess who got over like rover in every respect. Even all the junk food she consumed went to just the right places, and her skin was as healthy as could be.

"Where is your car, woman?"

"It's my cousin's car," she explained. "He came and picked it up"

"But he didn't pick you up with it? And why you invitin' strangers over to my house?"

"He only saw the driveway. Why you gotta sweat a sista?"

"What happened to the job applications you was gonna put in today?" he asked, holstering his pistol.

"I didn't feel like it," she said, with an irritated tone, eyes going back to the TV. "I'll go tomorrow."

She had never worked a day in her life, and probably never would, he guessed, even if the economy weren't such a wreck.

"You should at least be helpin' your mama 'round the house, then."

"Damn, you sound just like her," she complained. "Who are you—Judge Judy?"

"Get outa' my bed," Leon said, turning the TV off. "Clean up them dishes and get out. No, I take it back: I'll clean up your mess; you just get out."

Shotgun sat watching the scene unfold, gaze shifting back and forth as if watching a tennis match.

Lachelle must have sensed Leon was serious, because her demeanor sweetened for a moment. "What's the matter, baby? You don't like havin' me around? You sure liked havin' me here last night."

Despite her perfect body, she wasn't all that great in bed. Like everything else in life, she was accustomed to others bothering to put in all the effort and learning to perform well.

In the back of his mind Leon knew what she was about when Lachelle made a comment about how his truck was almost 10 years old.

She had no concept of earning anything and automatically expected to receive the best anyone had to offer just because that's what she was used to.

"Guess I was temporarily insane." He gathered up the dishes and bag of chips, set them aside and yanked the covers off her. Maybe he shouldn't have done that, because she wore nothing but her underwear, and the sight of her body made it difficult to keep a clear head about all this.

But no worries--she quickly broke her own spell by copping a blackitude. She angrily jerked off the bed, shot to her feet, stuck her finger in his face and went into that Egyptian side-to-side head-shifting movement women practiced so much in the 'hood. "Nigga, I don't know who you think you're dealin' with; but don't you **evah**..."

He clamped one hand on her shoulder, turned her around until she was pointed at where her clothes lay, and swatted her on the (magnificent, he had to admit) booty. "Get dressed. You got five minutes."

She spun back around, livid. "Now I know you didn't just lay hands on me, nigga!"

Shotgun, now standing next to them, wagged her tail tentatively but growled low and quiet at Lachelle.

"Four minutes and 45 seconds," Leon said. "Your clothes are right there. Make sure you take your drama with you, too."

"Drama? You wanna see drama? I got about 40 niggas who'd come put a cap in yo' ass if I axe 'em to."

Whatever insanity she may have been capable of, she was obviously leery of the growling German Shepherd. She kept a wary eye on Shotgun even as she talked trash.

"Four minutes," Leon said.

She began dressing, but paused to rest hand on hip and challenge: "Whatcha gonna do, huh? Whatcha gonna do afta fo' minutes?"

Shotgun growled a little louder. "Three minutes 50 seconds," Leon said.

Lachelle made a clucking sound and turned back to dressing with a look of toxic hatred.

Leon escorted her out the front door. She stomped toward his truck, but when she realized he had turned back, she stopped and whirled. "Where the hell you goin'? How'm I opposed to get back home?"

"Call your cousin," Leon replied, "or take the bus."

Her nostrils flared with rage and she stalked toward him shrieking obscenities, but Shotgun's growl got loud quickly. The Shepherd bared her fangs and advanced toward the charging woman, barking and snarling. The fear was obvious in Lachelle's body language as she stopped in her tracks.

"You a punk, Leon! You **bettah** hide behind a dog, 'cause I'll jack yo' ass up!"

False Flag - Brown

If Shotgun wasn't here and Lachelle did take a swing at him, he knew which side the cops would take on a domestic violence call. Getting a dog had been one of the best decisions he'd ever made.

"I don't need another bitch to lay around my house all day," Leon said, gesturing toward Shotgun. "At least this one is willin' to work for a livin'. And she don't make a mess inside."

Lachelle screamed a few really nasty accusations, but stomped away down the drive, stabbing buttons on her cell phone.

"Bus stop is that way," Leon called after her, pointing.

She seemed to be resigned to leaving with no further drama, so Leon and Shotgun returned to the house.

"Next," Leon muttered.

He cleaned up his bedroom and washed dishes before he forgot, and gave Shotgun a few treats before settling in for the night.

Leon grew restless on Saturday.

Something was off. Something was missing.

He enjoyed peace and quiet. He thought once he became a civilian again and got a healthy dose of solitude on a regular basis, the emptiness would go away. Instead, the solitude just helped him notice the empty spot more.

It wasn't loneliness—he enjoyed good friendships during his military and paramilitary careers, and he still had a couple now. Girls didn't fill the empty spot, either. He even thought he was in love once...but the ache was always there underneath.

Alcohol didn't fill the hole—and he certainly had tried that back in his younger days, as a paratrooper. He didn't believe drugs would be any more effective.

So as Sunday got closer, he thought more and more about giving church another try. When some smiling strangers rang his doorbell and invited him to attend their worship service, he took that as a sign.

Maybe God forgave him for all the work Leon had done with a sniper rifle over the years, and this was a message

He dressed up Sunday morning and drove to the 'hood. Leon didn't want to go to the church he'd been invited to, even though it was right around the corner. The redneck in the Nissan had reminded him about skin color again, and he didn't want to be the only black face there.

Leon had gone to a few different black churches in town, previously. Although he enjoyed the music, everything else was playing to emotions; repeating catchphrases and street slang to make the amen corners laugh and affirm; and faking "spiritual gifts." Black church was mostly tribal entertainment, and a fashion show.

False Flag - Brown

On that morning Leon steered toward the one church that stood out as exceptional. The preacher and congregation struck him as more intelligent, and even humble. The music was still good, but there were no theatrics or pretentious oratory.

A few people recognized him and welcomed him back. There were some fine sitstas in attendance, too, but Leon tried to concentrate on the message.

The preacher taught from Genesis, on Cain and Abel—the first murder in human history. Of course this brought up Leon's old conundrum about killing vs. murder, and if a sniper was anything more than an assassin in uniform.

Then the preacher went off on a tagent about the "Black Lives Matter" meme.

"Sure, maybe slavery was commonplace in the 1800s," the preacher said. "But I don't think God is up there saying, 'well, it wasn't as big an affront to my people's dignity, since everybody was doing it back then. **Now** I'd have a problem with it, but **back then**, it wasn't as big a deal'."

The amen corner all voiced their approval for this line of reasoning.

When service was over, the preacher made a point of engaging Leon on the way out. He was friendly and seemed sincere, asking where he lived and where he was from and the usual polite questions. Then, after the preacher shifted to gladhanding the next person in line, one of the deacons went through almost the same routine with Leon, and asked what he thought of the sermon.

"I was curious why he fit that little part about slavery in there," Leon replied.

The preacher overheard and responded to the question. "Some of the white pastors I know tend to lean conservative, and more than one of them has tried to say we have to put slavery in context."

Leon turned from the deacon back to the preacher. "How does that come up in conversation?"

The preacher shrugged, smiling. "What do you mean?"

"Well," Leon explained, gesturing toward the members of the congregation nearby. "When I hear it come up in conversation, it's usually because some black church person says America is racist, or America couldn't ever have been a Christian country...because slavery."

Other people lollygagged to listen in. The preacher laughed nervously and shrugged again. "Well, if the shoe fits..."

Others chuckled. Some said, "That's right," and, "I know that's right."

Leon nodded. "So then the other person would probably say, 'compared to what country?' That's where the context comes in, sir."

Some of the congregants sneered at Leon like he'd just blasphemed.

False Flag - Brown

One of them said, "Yeah, and then they try to defend America by comparin' it to other countries."

"That's right."

"I know that's right."

"Well, when you try to make America resemble other countries—takin' our rights away and such," Leon said, "ain't it only fair that they compare it to those countries?"

Attitudes changed rather quickly, from polite hospitality for a visitor, to hostility toward an Uncle Tom. Body language, facial expressions and tones of voice all reflected this as the crowd in the foyer reacted to Leon's question—some verbally; some non-verbally.

"Hey, in case y'all missed it," Leon said, "the U.S.A. fought a war to end slavery. Slavery lasted about 80 years over here. Wanna compare that to how long it lasted anywhere else, includin' Africa? And take a guess who sold our African ancestors to the Europeans in the first place? Other black folks."

"Sounds like you get your information from the same source the white pastors do," the preacher said, smugly.

"That's right!"

"I know that's right!"

"You ain't nevah lie."

"Well what does **your** history book say?" Leon asked, and pushed his way outside.

Yeah: black lives matter, Leon thought. *But are we the only ones? Do Arab lives matter? Do Chinese lives matter?*

He stuck his hands in his pockets as he walked to his truck.

They were so convinced slavery in North America was the single most horrific phenomenon in world history...what about the slavery still going on around the world? Leon would bet everybody in that church bought clothes, and shoes, and electronics that were made by slave labor, without a second thought. They didn't even bother to look at the labels to see where it was made.

At Wal-Mart and most other stores it was nearly impossible to buy anything **not** manufactured by slave labor. Where was the outrage about **that**? People had it better in America than they could have it anywhere in the world, but all that mattered to them was what happened to black folks in the southern states from 1787 to 1865.

He climbed in his truck and tossed his Bible on the passenger seat.

Probably none of those people had ever set foot in a socialist or Muslim country, and had no clue what it was like to live under such a regime. But they were hell-bent on "fundamentally transforming"

False Flag - Brown

America into one of those hellholes.

How was it they went to church more than him, but he know the Ten Commandments better than they did? The first one they needed schooling on was: "thou shalt not covet." The Democratic Party would fall apart overnight if the black church obeyed that one. But all they could think about was how much they wanted to get in Whitey's wallet; how they wanted to shake down the One-Percenters.

"I'm oppressed. Buy me more stuff," he mocked, aloud, starting the engine.

The First Commandment, forbidding idolatry? They put their own blackness before God 24/7. The Commandment not to murder? They broke that one against their own children, except when they used them to get more entitlement money. "Thou shalt not steal?" Well, technically they got the government to do the stealing for them—so that made it okay. "Thou shalt not bear false witness?" Ferguson showed how seriously they took that one, didn't it? Religious blacks all over showed themselves to be just as dishonest as the "eye witnesses" to the Michael Brown shooting. They claimed to have seen pictures and video clips that didn't exist, and lied about what was on video that did exist, all to push a narrative that made America sound like the Confederacy.

Leon drove away shaking his head. He hadn't meant to cause a scene. But he thought he had finally found some folks who were different. Then they went pushing his buttons like all the rest.

There was so much more he should have said, and what he did say could have been said better. But ultimately it would have made no difference. Like Josh Rennenkampf once told him: there were certain people whose minds could never be changed by giving them information.

How could America survive, when so many wanted it destroyed, and so few wanted it preserved?

Once back home, Leon checked his news feeds again. The professional race-baiters were already in Amarillo stirring things up, and wild exaggerations were flying. According to one Facebook meme, when Delton Williams was pulled over, he asked the reason for the stop and was told, "We don't want your kind in our city."

Shades of Ferguson. It only served to desensitize average people to fiascoes like what happened in New York City around the same time, and Baltimore later on. Leon had watched the video and, so far as he was concerned, Eric Garner had been murdered by those cops for no reason. But they got away with it because they had badges and Garner didn't.

During that same time a story circulated about a representative from Timberland Boots insulting his black customers at a press conference. It was being passed around as legitimate news, but just sounded too over-

False Flag - Brown

the-top to Leon—especially the part about the boots being designed so men could walk from the construction site to the local Klan meeting. Family members and other black folks he knew called Leon naive and gullible for finding the story suspicious.

After a little bit of research online he discovered that the story was, indeed, a hoax. But none of his outraged acquaintances would believe him--even the ones who were intelligent when it came to other matters. He'd mulled the whole experience over since then. What it came down to was that most African-Americans just desperately wanted to believe everything that reinforced their victim mindset, and reject anything that didn't. No matter what.

Leon might have turned out the same way, but during his military career he had developed a different outlook. Sure, there were brothas who retained their ethnocentric worldview throughout their military service, but Leon had found that judging men by their character was more conducive to wise decision-making. Who would prove trustworthy when it counted most couldn't be determined by looking at skin color. Hadn't Martin Luther King himself said something to that effect?

Since leaving Fort Benning, there were times when Leon honestly didn't notice what color other people were. Well, he noticed, the same way you might notice somebody is bowlegged or has a tattoo.

It was others who forced him to start noticing again. When ignorant whites uttered racial slurs, it was hard not to notice. When welfare recipients and beneficiaries of race-based scholarships and hiring practices obsessed about how Whitey oppressed them, it was hard not to notice. When , it was hard not to notice was expected to support Obama because of his color, it was hard not to notice. Nearly all the brothas jumped on the big "O" bandwagon, for that reason alone.

It all made it really hard not to notice color.

When Leon first got back to the World, he experienced some of the normal stuff—white women clutching their purses tighter when he got too close; subdued hostility in looks and under-the-breath comments from rednecks; store clerks assuming him ignorant when they tried to explain something to him.

When dirtbags like the guy in the Nissan tried to bean him with a bottle, it was hard not to notice color.

And then there were people like Lachelle--a living stereotype of the lazy, good-for-nothing welfare princess. Well, she was useful for one thing. But that made the stereotype even uglier. Leon cringed, imagining the redneck in the Nissan pointing to her and saying, "See, Ah toljah how them thar negras act!"

The sad part was, Lachelle was far from unique. Flagstaff wasn't big enough to have much of a ghetto, like Valdosta or Atlanta. And yet folks like Lachelle caught the ghetto mindset seemingly by osmosis. Then there were the folks in church, who had the same exact mentality as the punks on the street...except they didn't cuss.

So if Rocco was right, America might fall apart from within for a number of reasons—one of them being racial animosity.

Where did Leon fit in the scheme of things? He sure wasn't on the side of the government and their badge-wearing gangsters. He kind of sympathized with the men who stood up to the government at Garber Ranch, and the Bundy Ranch before it. But those kind of people were almost all white—and all racists according to the media. Would such people even accept him? Could he ever trust them or feel comfortable if they did? Or was the only option for someone of his color to stick with his own—even though he didn't trust most of "his own" as far as he could throw them?

The most tempting answer was to just leave the country and watch it tear itself apart from afar. But the looming oppression (the **real** kind, this time) coming to the United States was *status quo* everywhere else. And America didn't have a monopoly on racial strife, either, as the professional victims would find out when they got what they were pushing for.

When America bit the dust, there would be no place to go.

False Flag - Brown

Arden Thatcher only knew his contact by the first name: Ted. He had never met the other guy with Ted today, but the guy carried himself like he had a lot of authority.

Arden met them at a doctor's office right beside a one of those pre-employment drug test labs, in a strip mall. He'd been in here once before, but never seen a doctor or nurse.

Ted said nothing when he saw Arden. He rose from behind the counter, opened the door on the side and waved him in.

Arden followed him down the hall past a couple exam rooms to a sort of small conference room with a table, chairs and not much else. He took a chair. Ted and the overweight old balding guy sat opposite him.

Arden fished out his lighter and pack of cigarettes, putting one between his lips. "You guys been spendin' a lot of time in Armadillo lately." He laughed to himself. "Y'all call this town Amarillo, but to me it's Armadillo."

"What do you think you're doing?" Ted demanded, pointing at the cigarette.

Arden froze, dismayed. "Smells like somebody's been smokin' in here already. I just thought..."

"It's a damn doctor's office, moron," the stranger growled.

Embarrassed, Arden put his smokes away. "Sorry."

Ted folded his hands on the table and fixed Arden with a hard stare. "Look, Arden, we don't have time to fool around. You screwed up the last two assignments."

"No, wait, Ted," Arden protested. "I didn't screw up at CBC Southwest Tactical. They just didn't like me for some reason. It wasn't my fault."

"Why didn't they like you, Thatcher?" asked the heavy bald guy.

Arden shrugged, face heating up. "I dunno. I didn't do nothin'."

"Then you said something," Ted accused. "It's you're mouth that gets you in trouble."

"I didn't say nothin'!" Arden insisted. "I did just like you said--asked to get some trainin' on their shootin' range. You know—start a business relationship like you said. I didn't say nothin' 'bout niggers or Jews or anything."

Fat Bald Guy leaned forward and said, "Alright, shut up. I don't want to hear excuses for why you failed, or denials **that** you failed. This is your last chance, Thatcher. You better get this one right, or we're done with you. Got it?"

"Yes sir," Arden said, burning with shame and desperation.

Ted dropped a folder on the table and opened it. He pushed it toward Arden, who pulled it the rest of the way toward himself. There were pages inside the folder full of digital images and text.

"These are the men you're gonna make friends with," Ted said.

Arden briefly scanned over the faces in the printed snapshots, relieved that they were all Caucasian "Is it a militia?"

Ted nodded. "A dangerous one, Arden. Call themselves the 'Free American Patriots, or F.A.P. They know all about the Zionist Occupation...**and they approve of it**. Take some time when you get home and read some of their social network comments; how they drool over Ben Carson and Walter Williams and Thomas Sowell and Mia Love. About how wonderful Israel is and how we should support Israel and how they just luuu-uuuv the Jews."

Arden bit his tongue because cussing probably wouldn't come across as professional to Ted and the other guy. And his future depended on controlling his tongue.

"In other words, Arden, these guys are traitors to the white race. Groups like this are going to help the Zionists take over. And you know what that means. You think there's too much mudsharking now? Just wait. They'll have the white race bred out of existence in 20 years." Ted pointed at himself and Fat Bald Guy. "And we won't be able to help you. We won't be around anymore. The Jews will replace us with nigger police."

Arden's mind flooded with visions. In one of them, a hulking black beast in a police uniform raped his mother.

Ted pointed at the folder. "We've got to find out what these guys are up to; who their friends are; what weapons they have; everything. And when the time comes, we'll need you to go into action."

"So listen real good, dumbass," Fat Bald Guy said, with a withering glare that made Arden avert his gaze. "To do that, they've got to trust you. That means you have to pretend. Get it, dumbass?"

Arden's face burned even hotter.

"You luuu-uuuv Israel," Ted sing-songed. "You're a patriotic American. You luuu-uuuv your little black, brown, red and yellow brothers as long as they love America. You're colorblind, see? I know it's disgusting to even pretend, but the survival of the white race depends on you making these Zionist stooges think you believe the same things they do."

Arden forced himself to nod. "I get it."

"You better give an Academy Award performance," Fat Bald Guy said. "Or you're done."

"You only criticize niggers and Spics when they disagree with what F.A.P believes," Ted said, pointing at the folder again. "And you're careful about what you say, even then."

"At no point," Fat Bald Guy said, "you listening to me? At no point, ever, do you take one of these scumbags into your confidence."

"You have to get them to take **you** into **their** confidence," Ted emphasized.

"You might get friendly with some of them," Fat Bald Guy said. "You might get where you think you can trust one of them."

"Don't ever trust anyone," Ted said, "except us."

"Your little pea-brain might play tricks on you," Fat Bald Guy went on. "Agents under deep cover have been known to start sympathizing with their enemies."

"Even hostages," Ted added. "Stockholm Syndrome. You heard of Patty Hearst? White girl. Good blood. Good, pure white family. Got kidnapped by some niggers and after a while started robbing banks for them."

"Stupid whore," Arden snarled. "Damned zebra, monkey-lovin'..."

"No, she was intelligent," Ted interrupted.

"She was educated," Fat Bald Guy said. "Unlike you."

Why did Fat Bald Guy keep calling him stupid? Arden's father always insulted him like that, too, whenever he was out of prison. Arden would have liked nothing more than to kill his father. But he had to be cool with this fat bald guy, or his days as a secret agent against the Zionist Occupational Government would be over.

I may not be book smart, Arden thought, but I'm street smart.

Ted didn't call him stupid. Maybe Ted could be convinced he wasn't. Arden could prove himself if he could infiltrate this nigger-loving Zionist militia and make them think he was one of them.

"So the point is," Fat Bald Guy said, "you might find some of these guys likable despite your differences. You may even come to think of them as friends. That's fine—in fact, it will reinforce your cover. But don't ever so much as peep about the Z.O.G."

"Or white purity," Ted added. "Or anything about Aryans. Don't let anything slip about mud people and don't even so much as use the word 'nigger'."

"Now, when this assignment is complete," Fat Bald Guy said, "assuming you don't jack it all up as usual, then if somebody sticks a microphone in your face...then and only then: feel free to tell them all about the kikes and the jungle bunnies and pure Aryan bloodlines. Mix in some 'America the beautiful' shit and mention the Constitution a few times. Just don't say anything about your work for us."

"Just like I told you in our first conversation," Ted said. "Never say anything about us or what we ask you to do. The survival of the Aryan race may very well depend on agents who don't blab what they know."

"I understand, Ted," Arden replied, with a determined look. "I won't let you down."

The office used by some of McMillan's boys had been a functioning mini-clinic at one time. The name on the sign and window decal even bore the name of an actual doctor--though the doctor worked for one of Lawrence Bertrand's organizations in another city.

Once Arden Thatcher had left, Bruce Shilling ("Ted") turned to Macmillan and said, "That business about saying what he really thinks if somebody puts a microphone in his face...that could backfire."

Macmillan shook his head. "No. That's why I specified 'when the assignment is complete, and not before'."

"This isn't exactly a rocket scientist we're dealing with here, sir," Shilling said. "What if he gets confused about when the assignment is complete?"

"Make sure he doesn't," Macmillan said. "With any luck, he won't be able to talk then, anyway. And if he is, we may have to Jack Ruby his ass."

That would be the safest option. Even dead, Thatcher would point to the enemy. His background had been sanitized to help in his efforts to infiltrate right-wing networks, but it was only a temporary cleaning. All the information needed on him would read like an open book if and when the time came.

Shilling swallowed his resentment. He'd been handling informants for years successfully and didn't appreciate this "personal attention" Macmillan was giving. Yes, Thatcher was dumber than a box of rocks, which made infiltration very difficult. But when a good fit was found for him, his weak mind would prove perfect for the mission, and pay enormous dividends. Macmillan poking his nose in and telling Shilling how to do his job could only complicate matters.

But Macmillan was a hard-charger to begin with, and was evidently under pressure from the money men.

"Who you got next?" Macmillan asked, lighting a cigarette.

Shilling didn't need to check his notes. Instead, he lit up, too. "My 11 o'clock is another closeted Aryan activist. But she's not quite as stupid."

"Is she the Neo-Nazi chick we paid with a boob job?"

Shilling laughed. "Yeah, and it's paying off, too."

"What's she going to ask for next--a face lift?"

False Flag - Brown

"No, she's already good there, and knows it," Shilling said. "I'm guessing she'll want money for clothes and jewelry."

"I can't wait to see this rack. She any good in bed?" Macmillan asked.

Shilling flashed a wolfish grin. "She knows what she's doing, all right. We've got video archived."

"Hell with video." Macmillan checked his watch. "Eleven, you say?" He walked over to the restroom, closed the door behind him, pulled a plastic baggie out of his pocket and popped one of the blue pills inside it. "*Sieg heil*," he mumbled. "I'll be ready to salute *der Fuhrer* when you get here, *Fraulein*."

False Flag - Brown

Joe Tasper no longer lived in a house. He had begun his own scrap-hauling business, dumped Crystal, and moved into an apartment on the other side of town.

He was having a decent day. He had one more stop, to pick up an old washing machine, then should be able to get to the scrap yard before it closed. He drove through an upper-middle-class residential district, enjoying the fresh air and sunshine.

To get to the customer's house, he had to turn right at the next street. He pulled into the turning lane, behind a slow-moving Honda. Once behind it, the Honda slowed even more, and finally came to a complete stop in the lane, before reaching the intersection.

"What the...?" Joe had dealt with too many idiotic drivers, and had given up on figuring them out. They could sit there and brainfart all they wanted to, but he had somewhere to be.

Joe checked his mirrors, swung into the thru-lane and accelerated to get around the Honda. Then, from the right turn lane, the Honda driver made a left-handed U-turn right into him.

Two older women were in the Honda. The driver cried and blubbered, insisting she had never been in an accident and accusing him of tailgating her.

Police showed up on the scene eventually. Joe cringed, but there was no way they could blame him for this one.

Back when he lived in the 'hood, Joe's home had been burglarized. Some fatass donut-eater came by to fill out a report, but refused to take fingerprints. Same deal when Joe's car window was smashed out with a cinder block and his custom sound system was stolen. The message sunk in over the years: cops had no interest in serving, protecting, or catching bad guys. Their purpose was to shake down normal people just trying to make an honest living, who minded their own business.

Cops were lazy, stupid parasites—petty bureaucrats who were drunk on the power of their badges. Still, there was no way they could screw this up, was there? The woman had made a left-handed U-turn from a right turn lane without even checking for traffic.

After spending about an hour in his cruiser, the cop cited both the woman and Joe for the accident.

Joe refused to sign the citation, at first, but the cop threatened to throw him in jail if he didn't.

He signed, while fantasizing about killing the officer with multiple

False Flag - Brown

gunshots to his ignorant face, and bulging belly.

False Flag - Brown

Most individuals with good horse sense would be careful not to attract police attention with an AK47 and live ammo in the trunk, even though the weapon was a semiauto-only version—perfectly legal.

Takoda Scarred Wolf had more good horse sense than people assumed. But he also had a huge whopping lifetime prescription of *Fuqitol*.

He averaged 140 miles-per-hour on the Interstate, except when his radar/laser detector warned him of speed traps. When it fell silent, he went back to streaking through traffic like it was standing still. This brought him through Arizona, New Mexico, and Texas without molestation.

This had been a good day. The Shootout course had been a real challenge. He had missed a lot of targets, but knew he would get better with more practice. The course was great for reflexes, but unlike a video game you had to combine reflexes with the real techniques and weaponry you would need in a firefight.

The other thing that impressed him was the obvious camaraderie between Carlos, Leon and Rocco. You could just tell they'd been through stuff together, though there was no tangible point of evidence to prove it was there.

Takoda knew that bonds like that were forged in combat. But the only men he knew well who'd experienced combat were his father and his great uncle. Well, and Gunther, now.

Everyone who knew him assumed Takoda was antisocial. Looking back at his own behavior he could see why people would think that. But though he was a loner in many ways, he had always longed for that kind of brotherhood that warriors had. At times he considered the desire silly, and didn't like admitting he had it. But at times like this it was hard not to think about.

Psychologists said that degree of close friendship only came from shared trauma (like combat), or from family relation.

Takoda had family. Good family. His two brothers were honorable. Why was he not close with them like that?

He had to admit that the biggest reason was probably his own behavior and attitude. Though everything he'd told Gunther that one night at their father's house was true, Takoda was still in the wrong. Sure, Gunther had lessons to learn, but some things took care of themselves.

Looking at that altercation honestly, Takoda admitted he harbored

False Flag - Brown

resentment because his father had chosen to take Gunther along with him to Indonesia. Takoda had been left behind when his dad needed men he could count on and, though he'd never admit it, it made Takoda feel like he wasn't good enough. It reminded him of all the times he felt slighted growing up, when it seemed his parents favored Gunther over him. And that case of butthurt led him to act like a first-class jerk sometimes.

He needed to patch up relations with his family. He needed to dial down his *Fuqitol* dosage.

He'd even shunned little brother Carl, though Carl had done nothing wrong and had been left behind just like him.

Carl's birthday was coming up in a few months. Maybe Takoda should take him to CBC Southwest Tactical for the occasion. Dad's old war buddies could put them through the paces. They'd make a day of it. Carl would love it and maybe it would be the first step of their journey toward the brotherhood they should have had all along.

Maybe Takoda should invite Gunther, too. But he was almost certain that wouldn't go over well.

How could he fix what he'd broken?

He slowed down approaching Oklahoma City, and took I-35 South, getting back on the gas after clearing the city limits.

Takoda now lived east of the rez, by himself.

He tore through the Shawnee Trust Land to reach his place, because it was a more direct route and traffic was lighter. By this time he was on rural highways and had slowed considerably, but was still blasting along at triple digits when traffic didn't slow him down.

The radar detector went from silent to full alert in a split second. He instinctively backed off the gas, but the full L.E.D. meter meant he was already clocked.

The Tribal Police must have instant-on radar, now.

In the rear view mirror, far distant, he saw a patrol car swing out on the road with lights flashing.

Takoda took stock of distance and traffic, and put the hammer down.

His LS7 Chevy small block snarled with hunger for speed. He hadn't done much to the internals of the aluminum V8 besides installing a healthier camshaft, and porting/polishing the heads. But the twin turbo system made an already impressive powertrain thrust like a moon rocket. The suspension and drivetrain were up to the task of keeping that power planted, too. And the light composite body slipped through the wind like a bullet.

The speedometer and tach needles swung hard to the right, but Takoda did little more than glance at his instrument panel. At the speed he was doing now, his life depended on seeing developments on the road miles in advance.

***

Officer Rachel White Bird had just clocked an S.U.V. at 16 miles over the limit and was about to go after it when she heard the mechanical snarl growing in volume. Already following the S.U.V. with her gaze, she saw a low, dark shape bearing down from the opposite direction.

Holy crap, but it was **moving**!

She aimed the radar gun and triggered the instant-on. The vehicle blasted by with an ear-shattering roar. It was green but she didn't get a good look at it.

The readout showed 97 MPH.

She set the radar gun back in its mount and switched it to scan. The speed of the vehicle was climbing higher, fast. She put the cruiser in gear and floored the accelerator, tearing grass and spitting dirt as she peeled onto the pavement, toggling her lights.

Officer White Bird only caught a fleeting glimpse of the green vehicle. It had a swoopy shape like maybe a Ferrari or something. It could be somebody visiting the rez, but she knew of only one local who had a green sports car: Takoda Scarred Wolf.

This could be a big break.

The patrol car hit 100, but the perp was still pulling away--just a small shape in the distance. White Bird kept the pedal mashed and continued to accelerate. 105, 110, 115...

The perp was still losing her! She reached for the radio mike but fumbled around, scared to concentrate on anything but the road at this speed—now 120. Finally she got the call in, unable to accurately identify the vehicle—much less read the plates. The desk sergeant told her to maintain pursuit until they could get more assets in on the chase.

130. The patrol car felt strangely light, like it might lift off the road at any minute. She was terrified. Was this the "rush" that she heard her male counterparts discussing now and then? They could keep it.

At 130, the perp just continued to pull away. The green object was almost too small on the horizon to see, now.

The border of the Tribal Trust Land was coming up in just a few miles, and her jurisdiction ended. And frankly, she wasn't going to catch that car if she had a thousand miles to do it.

She radioed the Pottawatomie County Sheriff's dispatcher to warn them. They could set up a road block to catch the perp. But though the County was tough on drunk drivers and other violations, they didn't make a big effort to nab speeders.

False Flag - Brown

Besides, even if it was Takoda and they could catch him, another force having him by the short hairs didn't give her the leverage she needed. Especially when Takoda's own father ran the show, there.

She would have to find another way.

False Flag - Brown

24

Y MINUS TWO

ABSENTEE SHAWNEE TRUST LAND, OKLAHOMA

Officer Rachel White Bird didn't have an invitation to the party, but she showed up anyway.

She could only speculate about who talked to the Chief of the Tribal Police, or what all was said. But the Chief had taken her to the side; sworn her to secrecy; and gave her the assignment to get what she could on the Scarred Wolf family.

He wouldn't tell her why, though she had heard the rumors about a murdered police officer overseas. Word was, however, that the murder was an attempted frame.

Rachel asked for parameters and the Chief told her to make friends with one of the Scarred Wolves if she could, or find a reason to arrest one of them if not. Once one of those toeholds had been achieved, they could cross the next bridge.

Rachel was technically off duty. She dressed like she almost never did: tight skirt, girly blouse and her hair down. She didn't have a definite plan--just decided to exploit whatever developed.

The celebration was at Tommy's house. Gunther and Carl had built a kennel in back to lock the dogs in so they wouldn't go crazy or scare visitors.

The front yard was treated as a parking lot during normal circumstances. The only difference about this occasion was the number of vehicles parked there.

Neighbors and friends from around the rez came by, of course. Uncle Jay was the first guest to arrive and even Vince's widow, Betty, made an appearance. Frank, an old buddy from Fifth Group, brought a keg, which might not have been such a great idea with the rampant alcoholism in the area. But how could there be a party in these times without at least beer?

Leon had checked with Tommy before bringing Shotgun. She went by to snoop around the kennel, driving Tommy's dogs insane for a few minutes, but after that she followed Leon around pretty much everywhere he went. Leon and Tommy shook hands and slapped backs, exchanged a few words, then Tommy got pulled away by someone else. That would happen a lot before the night was over.

Leon had just filled his first plastic cup with beer when Rocco arrived. Leon wandered over to greet him. Rocco climbed out of the driver's seat of the GMC Yukon, and a beautiful shortie got out of the passenger side.

Cavarra, you old dog, Leon thought. But then he was introduced.

"Hey Cannonball," Rocco said, shaking his hand. "This is my daughter, Jasmine. She's spending a couple weeks with me. Jasmine, this is Leon."

"Oh, okay," Leon said, shaking Jasmine's hand. "Nice to meet you."

Jasmine smiled and it was dazzling. "Nice to meet you, Leon."

"Hey, got something for you," Rocco said, sauntering back to the rear hatch. He opened it and pulled a scabbard out from under some blankets and other stuff. He handed it to Leon.

"Uh-oh," Leon said. "This what I think it is?"

"Happy birthday, Cannonball," Rocco said.

Leon zipped open the scabbard and pulled out the contents. It was a black anodized M21 in a polymer pistol grip stock. Leon worked the bolt and checked the chamber out of habit before turning it over in his hands to admire it. "Aw, man...I don't know what to say, Rocco. Did you put this together?"

Rocco nodded. "I've been meaning to do it for years, but it kinda' got buried under other projects in my shop. I found it again when I was packing for the move. Did a little grinding, filing and sanding before the stock would fit, but it fits good now."

"This thing is the truth, Rocco. Thanks, man." Leon had thought about buying a chassis for an M14 (the sniper version of which—the M21—had become his favorite rifle), but balked at spending that much money for something that shouldn't even cost a quarter of the asking price.

Then something Rocco said sunk in. "Wait a minute...packin' for a move? Where you movin'?"

"Arizona," Rocco said.

A rumbling sound caught their attention. A red-and-white Camaro pulled up into the yard and shut down. The driver's door opened and a average-sized Hispanic man climbed out.

Rocco and Cannonball recognized him at the same time. "Bojado!"

Carlos Bojado squinted at the two guys calling to him. He hadn't seen them face-to-face since that boat ride back from North Africa, but he recognized them on sight. Campbell hadn't aged a day, despite all the years. More of Cavarra's black hair had turned white, and his weathered face made him look more like a Mafia don now than a Mafia enforcer. And who was the little hottie standing near them? She was drop-dead gorgeous.

Carlos walked over for handshakes and backslaps. The babe was

False Flag - Brown

Cavarra's daughter, it turned out.

"I heard you went back in the Corps," Rocco said.

Carlos conffirmed that he had.

After the <u>Sudan mission</u>, Carlos gave serious thought to what he wanted to do. Initially he went back in because the economy sucked; he wanted three squares a day; the Marine Corps wanted him back at his previous rank; and he wanted to see more action.

He did see action. And when it was time to get out again, the economy was even worse.

It kept getting worse, so he kept signing on the dotted line. Finally he decided to just finish out his 20 years and get a pension, in case the economy never recovered.

"I did some contract work over in Iraq," Campbell told him. "Tried to look you up a couple times, but never found your unit."

"They had me in Ass-Crackistan by then," Carlos explained.

"It's good to see you again," Cavarra said.

"Yeah, same for me," Carlos replied.

"We got all the survivin' Retreads together, man," Campbell said. "Except Mac, this time."

"He's with SSI too, no?" Carlos asked.

"Vice-Prez," Campbell confirmed, nodding.

Carlos had kept in touch somewhat with the other "Retreads" via email and social networks. He was retired now, unable to find decent work, and had time on his hands. When he heard Tommy Scarred Wolf had run for office and won, he just had to make the party.

The three of them sipped beer and caught up a bit.

The party was underway when Joshua Rennenkampf arrived, and dusk was giving way to darkness. Off to the side of the house a bonfire was blazing. Suspended over the fire by a crude brick structure was a rectangle of iron grating, which somebody was loading up with burgers and chicken breasts. Josh chuckled as he switched off his radios and got out. Tommy couldn't just use a back yard gas or charcoal grill like anybody else. Nope, the *dinky-dau* redskin had to have meat cooked over a wood fire in the open air.

Josh walked toward the house, but saw somebody he recognized grabbing something out of the trunk of a wicked-looking brown '04 Mustang. When the lean young man with pronounced Shawnee features straightened up, he glanced to the rear and saw Josh.

"Yo, Rennenkampf," he said with what passed for a smile on the Scarred Wolf men.

"Gunther!" Josh closed the distance and shook his hand. "How it is, hero?"

"It's all legit, man. What you been up to?"

Josh had only known Tommy's firstborn for a short time, but considered him a stand-up guy.

"Maintaining an even strain. How's the pilot deal going?"

"I'm certified now," Gunther said. "Trying to get a job flying freight."

Josh slapped his shoulder. "Wow. Congrats, man. That didn't take you long. You must've kicked ass."

Gunther shrugged. "I'm not playing around. I want out of that stupid casino like yesterday."

"Well, I hope you get the freight job. You gotta take me for a ride some time."

"You and everybody else here," Gunther said, gesturing in a circle, with a hiccuping sound that passed for laughter.

"There's a lot of folks here," observed Josh, taking in all the vehicles parked in the area.

"Rocco and Cannonball showed," Gunther said. "Some other guys Dad knew from the service. Plus family, friends, and a whole lot of folks from around the rez."

"How's Tommy taking the crowd?"

Gunther laughed for real this time. "You know Dad—he'd probably rather be swimming in the Everglades."

Josh grinned, remembering how much Tommy hated swimming. "Where is he, anyway?"

"Over by the fire," Gunther said, pointing. "I think Jennifer's still in the house helping Mom with side dishes."

Josh wasn't going to ask about Jennifer, but Gunther knew they were into each other and was cool with it. Tommy knew; but wasn't always as cool with it.

"Thanks. You need help with anything?"

Gunther shook his head. "Naw. Go grab a beer or soda and just enjoy yourself."

"My, what a civilized host you are." Josh winked, tipped an imaginary hat, and made his way to the fire.

Even in a crowd like this with noise and movement all over the place, you still couldn't sneak up on the Scarred Wolves. Tommy turned to spot him before Josh reached the fire.

"Baby Face!" Uncle Jay called out, while flipping ground chuck patties on the makeshift grill.

"Jungle Walk!" Tommy greeted. "I was hoping you could make it."

"Why?" Josh asked, warily. Did Tommy intend to "have a talk" with him about his niece? Josh dreaded that conversation. He now wanted to patch things up with his old friend and mentor, but Jennifer made everything complicated.

Tommy squinted his obsidian eyes at him. "Whaddya mean, why? 'Cause I haven't seen you for a while."

"Oh." Josh felt relief, then guilt for being defensive. "Hey, congrats on the victory, Tommy. I'm happy for you."

"Thanks," Tommy said, slapping his shoulder, then waved toward his uncle. "You remember Uncle Jay?"

"Wazzup, Uncle Jay?" Josh greeted.

Jay Scarred Wolf, with his 1st Air Cavalry Division hat on, as usual, saluted with his spatula. "Fighting soldiers from the sky..." he sang. "Fearless men...who jump and die..."

"Oh, blow it out your schnoz," Tommy said.

Laughing at his own joke, Jay said, "I heard you Green Berets are sooo-ooo bad, there's 35 ways you can kill somebody with your bare hands."

"Pick a number, leg," Tommy retorted.

"Gee, that's the first time I heard that one," Josh groaned.

"Jay sets them up; Tommy knocks them down," said a big outlaw biker-looking bear of a man with a beer in one massive paw.

"Griz!" Josh cried, and embraced his old buddy, who nearly crushed him.

"I been hearing about you," Griz said. "Heard you live in an old missile silo, shoot down drones to pass the time and count black helicopters instead of sheep."

"Close enough," Josh replied. "But Tommy said I couldn't wear my tinfoil hat if I wanted to come to his party."

"Joshua is a good man. He scares many, because he sees what they don't want to see."

The words were spoken by somebody with a whistling old gravel voice and a stilted accent. Josh peered over the flames but couldn't make out who said it.

Tommy and Jay shared an arched-eyebrow look, then Tommy placed his hand on Josh's back and steered him around the fire.

"We're all bolo," Josh said. "This fire has ruined our night vision."

Tommy chuckled. "You know you're a grunt when you close one eye to open the fridge at night."

"Grunt, hell," Josh said with an exaggerated scornful look. "I'm an A-Team commando."

They stopped in front of a decrepit-looking old Shawnee man in a wheelchair with a patch over one eye and a deformed hand missing three fingers. "I don't think you ever met Michael Fastwater." Tommy now addressed the old cripple. "Grandfather, this is my friend Joshua. We knew each other in Special Forces."

Fastwater nodded acknowledgment His piercing gaze made Josh squirm. His still features in the fire light made him look kind of spooky.

"A warrior brother," Fastwater said, as if a juror reading a verdict. "That's what you are."

Confused, Josh's gaze bounced between Tommy and the old man. "Um, does he...have we...?"

"Nope," Tommy said. "Pretty sure you haven't met." Under his breath he added, "Just smile and nod. He does this kind of stuff all the time."

"You two have faced death together," Fastwater said. "Good friends. Brothers. You need to put aside your differences. It's more important now than ever."

Fastwater didn't have the nervous tics or laughter or banal chatter Josh associated with most lunatics. But he sure was digging into some personal stuff. Normally Josh would assume he was just going off information given in confidence. But Tommy had never been one to "bare his soul" to another human being, so either the old man made some lucky guesses, or he'd received the information some other way.

"Michael was a marine in the Pacific," Uncle Jay said. "He's the reason most of us just can't bring ourselves to buy Japanese cars."

Josh examined the old man in the wheelchair and realized he must have lost his eye and hand in defense of their country. "It's an honor to meet you, Mr. Fastwater. Thank you for your service."

Fastwater nodded slightly and blinked his one eye. "*Semper Fi*," he said.

"Are you a medicine man?" Josh asked him.

Tommy and Uncle Jay laughed. Before Fastwater could reply, somebody called out, "Where's the *dinky-dau* redskin?"

Everyone turned to the sound. Rocco, Cannonball, another guy, and a gorgeous young woman had arrived on the periphery of the crowd around the fire. They all peered into the mixture of darkness and patterns of flickering light.

Uncle Jay waved his spatula up in the air, then pointed to his nephew. "You're surrounded by redskins; but the *dinky-dau* Injun is over here."

The newcomers wandered over. Once close enough, they recognized their friends and greetings were exchanged with jokes and insults. Josh was introduced to Carlos and Cavarra's daughter, Jasmine. The three men didn't go back as far with Tommy as Josh did, so introductions were made between them and Uncle Jay. And Michael Fastwater.

With a misanthropic nature, Josh wasn't normally interested enough in other people to observe them closely. But he noticed looks flashing

False Flag - Brown

between Carlos and Jasmine which were easy to read even for a dumb hermit like Josh: they had only just met, but there was a strong attraction already.

Tommy noticed it but didn't mention it, either. He turned to Josh and, with some resignation, said, "Jenny's in the kitchen with Linda. She's been waiting for you to get here."

Josh made eye contact with Tommy and again felt waves of guilt for being a judgmental prick over the years. And for not giving Tommy the benefit of the doubt on certain matters, the way one would for a friend.

Just a bit self-consciously, Josh gave him a quick man-hug and said, "Thanks, Chief."

Tommy turned to shoot the breeze with his other friends while Josh headed for the house.

The house was crowded, too, though the population here was mostly female. When Josh stepped inside the front door, a brief silence fell over the din of overlapping chatter as a party of Shawnee women turned to stare at him. Tommy's wife, Linda, stepped out of the kitchen with a dish towel in her hands and a curious expression. She brightened when she saw Josh, ran over to him and seized him in a warm embrace. "Joshua! Oh my gosh!"

She was a small woman, pretty, but with that matronly pear shape which came after multiple childbirths. Josh hugged her back. She had always been like a big sister to him, and he remembered that now. He missed her.

"Thank you for coming," she said, pulling back. "Does Tommy know you're here?"

"Yeah. I swung by the fire and said hi."

She asked him how Uncle Jay was doing on the grill and he began to answer when Jennifer emerged from the kitchen.

Tommy's niece was built nicely, had a pretty face, and radiant brown eyes that Josh would never get tired of looking at. A smile spread over her face when she saw him. She walked over and addressed Linda first. "All that's left to do is add the tomatoes to the salad...and the potatoes should be ready in ten minutes."

"We have it covered," Linda told her niece with a motherly smile. "You two go ahead."

Jennifer stepped close and inclined her head up to study Josh's face with a grin of her own.

"How are you?" he asked, as Linda went back to the kitchen.

"I'm blessed," she replied. "You?"

He steered her toward the door with his hand on her lower back. "I'm living the dream."

False Flag - Brown

Once outside he led her by the hand into the dark, away from the house and the noise and all the people.

"I miss you," she said, squeezing his hand.

"Yeah? Well, when you gonna come visit me?"

She made a humming noise, then leaned her head against his arm as they walked. "I have a long weekend coming up."

"Sounds good," he said.

"You know, I graduate this year."

"Yeah, I figured."

"It's kind of scary all the sudden," she said. "Don't know where I'll go afterwards or even if I can get a job, degree or not."

"It's rough out there," he said. "Only gonna get rougher."

"You're such a bright little ray of sunshine," she said with a laugh. "You really know how to alleviate a girl's insecurities."

He stopped and pulled her against him. Her lips were ready and willing.

"Did that help?" he asked, afterwards.

She opened her eyes. He nearly drowned in them at this range. "I feel a little better." She pulled his head back down to hers.

Carl found Tommy at the fire, listening to his friends and Uncle Jay talk and joke.

"Hey Dad, you know where Takoda is?" Carl asked.

"He's around here somewhere," Tommy said. "I heard his Corvette pull in a while ago. Haven't heard it leave. Why?"

"He said he'd tune my carburetor," Carl said.

"Son, don't worry about the dirt bike tonight, okay? Just hang out and be sociable. That's probably what your brothers are doing. At least they're supposed to."

"But Dad, you heard how rough it's running..."

"Oh, I heard alright," Tommy said. "Everybody for 50 miles hears that thing when you ride it. Don't start it tonight, Son. We won't be able to hear ourselves think over that racket. It's bad enough when your brothers start **their** engines."

Carl chewed his lip briefly. "Well, if you see him can you tell him I'm looking for him? Maybe he can look at it after the party."

Tommy sighed and nodded, while Carl wandered away from all the boring old folks.

Gunther brought the bags of hamburger buns to Uncle Jay, who directed him to set them on the fold-up picnic table a few yards from the fire. Gunther figured he might as well bring out the condiment jars so

135

people could spread it on right there, and so made his way back toward the house. On his way he nearly bumped into a woman he vaguely recognized. He excused himself and began to step around, but she smiled and greeted him as if they were old pals.

"Sorry," he said, "but you'll have to jog my memory how we know each other."

"I used to work with your father," she replied, extending her hand. "I'm Rachel."

She had some Shawnee features and was moderately attractive. Gunther shook her hand.

"Where did you work with him?" he asked.

"The Tribal Police," she replied.

"Oh, okay. Well, glad you could make it."

"Thanks," she said. "I was so happy to hear your dad won. Pretty sick, huh? You must be so proud."

"Yeah. Everybody who knows him is. But then I was proud of him even before this sheriff thing."

Rachel nodded, the grin still plastered on her face. "I wish I could have heard that speech. I heard it was really truth."

"It probably wasn't much as far as speeches go," Gunther said. "I think people liked it because he didn't try the normal BS. He just mentioned some of what's wrong in the county, and what he'd try to do if he was running the show. He was just honest—which usually doesn't score many political points with folks who matter. He's more surprised than anybody that he won."

"Oh, we all knew he'd win," she said.

Gunther tilted his head and studied her face closely. "From what I understand, your boss doesn't like him much."

"Oh, that's not true. Where'd you hear that?"

"From everybody who knows both of them," Gunther said. "Except you, I guess."

"Oh, everybody knows Tommy's a hero," she said.

"Well, anyway, nice to see you. I gotta go get some stuff."

She maintained the smile, but it dimmed with disappointment somewhat as she nodded, gave him a wave and proceeded toward the fire. Gunther wondered why she addressed him with such familiarity, when they just barely knew each other.

He didn't notice that she disappeared behind a Minivan and never reemerged on her way to the fire.

As Gunther turned around from there, he saw Susan Pyrch approaching him.

Susan was a knockout, by Shawnee or any other standards. Possibly even better looking than Jasmine Cavarra. Susan was mixed, and all the most physically attractive qualities of the different races seemed to be consolidated in the little diva. Nevertheless, Gunther had to suppress a groaning eye-roll when he saw her.

"Hi Gunther."

"Hi," he said.

"Surprised to see me?"

"A little."

"You never did withdraw the invitation," she said. "So I thought I still might be welcome."

He forced a polite smile. "You are. Thanks for coming. Mom and Jenny and your mom were all in the house last I saw. I'm heading there now if you want to come along. I know Jenny will be happy to see you." He sidestepped her to continue toward the house, assuming she would fall in step beside him.

"Are you not happy to see me?" she asked, standing still.

He stopped, frowned, sighed and turned. "Not tonight, Susan. Okay?"

She blinked her eyes and a tear rolled down from one of them. "Can't we at least talk? I promise I won't be a shrew this time."

Gunther stifled a second sigh and backed up to lean against the bed of a pickup truck. She drew close to him but before she could touch him or say anything, he said, "It was your idea to see other people. You said you wanted space and all that. Well, I'm giving you space."

"But I changed my mind," she said, in a pleading tone.

"You should quit changing your mind and stick to a decision for once."

She flinched. "That was a mean thing to say."

"Just being honest."

"No you're not," she said, more tears streaming, now. "This isn't about that. You're mad because I talked to that investigator. That's what this is about!"

"You want to go there, Susan? You really want to go there?"

"Go ahead!" she snapped. "We might as well! Is that a threat? Am I supposed to be scared? Are you going to slap me around or something?"

He pushed away from the pickup and began to walk away but she jumped forward to grab his arm. "Don't walk away from me, Gunther. Please."

He could have brushed her off easily, but he decided maybe she did deserve a discussion at least. He leaned back against the truck and she moved in to embrace him, but he grabbed her by the shoulders and held her at bay.

Like Jennifer, she didn't normally wear jewelry. But he noticed she

False Flag - Brown

was wearing it now. Takoda would say the reason must be because she was ovulating. Maybe he was right. She seemed borderline hysterical and that definitely could be something menstrual.

"I told you not to give them anything, Susan."

"What was I supposed to say?" she demanded. "They knew about the boat trip. They knew we'd been kidnapped. And they knew that we came back here the same time as you and your father."

"They didn't know who else was in on the rescue," he reminded her, "until you told them."

"So what, Gunther? It's not like I said they did anything wrong. I think they should all get medals for what they did. And I didn't even know their real names, anyway!"

"You gave them descriptions, Susan. And I bet you would have given them names and addresses if you'd known them. In fact, you **did** give them **my** name."

"They already talked to the other girls," Susan said. "They'd know if I was holding something back, and I'd be in big trouble. Should I have lied to federal...whoever they were?"

"That's a classic interrogation trick, Susan: to make you think other witnesses have already spilled the beans so you'd better do it, too. My dad told you that's what they would do."

"Well I'm sorry, but I wasn't raised by a war hero and I never learned this 'death before dishonor' code you seem to have."

"You better check that snarky tone when you talk about my father," Gunther said.

"What was I supposed to do?"

"What me and Jenny did," he snapped. "Keep your mouth shut. Play ignorant if you have to. Ask them if you're suspected of a crime. If not, then ask if you're free to go. Keep asking until they give you a straight answer."

"Jeez, Gunther—you're the one who told me about the NDAA. They could just say I'm a terrorist and lock me up for the rest of my life without a trial."

She was right about that one, so he didn't retort.

"I don't see why it's all got to be such a big important secret," she continued, encouraged by his silence. "You act like you're Spiderman and I just revealed your secret identity or something!"

Gunther took in and let out a deep breath. "You weren't there for everything that went down. Somebody tried to kill my dad and Uncle Vince. When that didn't work, they framed them for murder. They did eventually kill Uncle Vince. Any day now somebody might try to assassinate my dad again, or bring that murder rap back here and

138

False Flag - Brown

indefinitely detain him for that. When you opened your big mouth, you put everybody at risk for the same kind of thing. Everybody who went with him to bring you back."

Susan raised her hands. "Hey, I have nothing against your father. And of course I'm grateful to everybody who went with him. But do you even realize how paranoid you sound?"

This time when Gunther walked away, he didn't let her stop him.

"And that's why I didn't want to have this talk," he said, not caring if she heard him or not.

Still listening at her spot behind the Minivan, Rachel White Bird was sure some of what she'd just heard must be valuable. After Gunther and Susan had gone away in different directions, Rachel went over to where the crowd was concentrated, near the fire.

The beer flowed steadily. Rocco, Leon and Carlos found seats among the sycophantic core of the crowd, tightly orbiting Tommy, Uncle Jay and Michael Fastwater. Rocco got asked about his move to Arizona a few times, until finally some drunk opined that the economy in Arizona might wind up as bad as in California. This got a grumbling conversation started about the economy, and more questions were asked.

Carlos had his retirement check, which wasn't great, but would keep him from starving. Rocco had his pension, of course, but was also relocating his tactical shooting school and supply business. Leon anticipated returning to the Sandbox because not only was there work for him there, but it paid better than anything he'd be able to find back on the block, even if the economy wasn't wrecked beyond what anybody with a platform was willing to admit.

"I'll tell you what part of the private sector is booming," Tommy said. "Ammunition sales. Retail."

Rocco whistled. "Boy, don't I know it. It's hard to even find 22 Long Rifle these days, much less nine mil, .40 cal or any NATO rounds."

"Maybe I should start reloading," Carlos thought out loud. "I could sell that for some extra bucks. People would buy it, I bet."

"Reload your own ammo," Leon said. "Sell the virgin stuff. That's the smart way."

"There's a demand for sure," Tommy said, using tongs to transfer a chicken breast from the grill to his styrofoam plate.

"Don't you need a license or something to sell ammunition, though?" Jasmine asked. "I bet it's illegal."

"Everything's illegal, anymore," Uncle Jay said.

Rocco tapped Leon on the chest, backhanded. "You ever thought of

139

teaching people how to shoot, Cannonball?"

"What you mean? My own sniper school or sumpthin'?" Leon asked.

"It wouldn't have to be sniping," Rocco said. "But there's lots of guys who hunt or target shoot and are always looking for ways to improve accuracy."

"I thought that's what your school was for," Leon said, and the others snickered.

"I teach some different techniques," Cavarra replied, ignoring the laughter. "But I was never a sniper. I don't know all the sniper tricks."

Leon shot to his feet. "Hey! Did y'all hear that? I think Rocco just admitted I might know sumpthin' he don't!"

More people laughed, and harder. "Score one for the grunts," Uncle Jay remarked.

"Sit down, punk," Rocco said, still enduring the laughter and backslaps.

Leon resumed his seat, giving Rocco a playful push.

Carlos stopped laughing and said, "Wait. was that a job offer?"

Leon turned serious and studied the former SEAL Team commander. "Is that what that was, Rocco?"

"Could've been if you weren't such a jerk." He paused to make a face, then sobered again. "No, I mean, if you want to keep contracting, that's fine. But I was thinking about expanding the school a bit from what it was before. I've got customers--a lot of them from the area where I'm opening shop. I think I'll get more customers, too. Seems like somebody's always asking me about long range marksmanship. They see all these sniper movies out there, I guess, and think it looks fun."

"Fun, hell," Leon said. "Ain't one man in a thousand would want to do what a real sniper has to do."

"But you got to admit," Rocco said, "there are parts of it that are enjoyable. If you take all the fun parts, minimize the suck, and package it as really good training...what do you Army pukes call it again?"

"High speed," Tommy said.

"Right. Really high speed training. Civilians would eat it up. I've been thinking of other stuff that would be fun, but useful, too."

"Like what?" asked Carlos, with undivided attention.

Rocco shrugged. "Well, I'll probably set up a jungle walk. Everybody likes those. But if I had the money, I'd build something like that pop-up/moving target range you guys had in Fort Benning."

"Oh yeah," Leon said. "I went through that, waaayyy back in Infantry School. It was high speed."

Tommy nodded, finishing a mouthful of chicken meat. "Yeah it was."

Rocco addressed Tommy and Leon. "How much would you pay to be

False Flag - Brown

able to shoot there again? Or some place like it?"

Rachel White Bird drifted from clique to clique, listening in on portions of conversations. How many people recognized her she couldn't say, because most paid her no mind. She hadn't made any enemies on the rez, that she knew of. But she hadn't made a lot of friends, either.

When she reached the inner core surrounding Tommy Scarred Wolf, though, she parked for a while. There were a few men she just knew must be worth remembering. Judging by the way they interacted with Tommy, and some of what they said, she was pretty sure they were military men, too. She knew all about Jay Scarred Wolf, who served in Vietnam; and Michael Fastwater, the WWII veteran. Her boss knew that much. She needed to find out all she could about the strangers.

Carl hadn't been able to find Takoda yet. He put his search on hold when he heard the dogs fussing. They had finally quieted down a couple hours ago, so something must be stirring them up, now. He decided to check it out.

The whining and tentative barking fizzled out as the dogs heard and smelled him drawing near. Inside the chain-link structure he and Gunther erected for this occasion, they watched him with tails wagging, dancing in place or rearing up to lean their front paws on the chain link. When Carl reached them, he pressed his hands against the fencing so they could lick him. Whatever they'd seen or heard, it must not have been anything threatening.

He heard somebody cry out. It sounded like Susan Pyrch.

He had caught a glimpse of her earlier, and she looked upset. He knew she and Gunther had a fight a while back, and he hadn't seen much of her since. He assumed they must have broken up, but here she was at the party...so he wasn't sure what was going on.

Susan Pyrch was a smoking hot babe. Gunther must be crazy not to treat her like a queen.

Maybe she went off by herself to cry. Carl felt a pang of sympathy for her. He was just a kid to her, but maybe there was something he could do. He moved through the dark toward the sound he'd heard.

Now he could hear more noises. There was rustling of fabric, friction of something relatively heavy against the ground, wet glitching sounds and labored breathing in between, laced with whimpers almost too soft to perceive. It was all coming from somewhere behind the mound of the septic tank.

Carl had practiced moving silently since he was five years old. It was something he prided himself on, and proved he was a Shawnee warrior

141

(to himself, if nobody else). He closed the distance now without making a sound.

Just before Carl rounded the corner of the mound, he heard a whisper. "What are we doing?"

"Isn't it obvious?"

After some more of the wet sounds, Susan whispered, "I mean we shouldn't be doing this."

More wet sounds, and she whimpered.

"It doesn't...feel right..." she panted.

The other voice chuckled, "You're acting like it feels right."

"But he's here. He's on the other side of the house, for cr..." She interrupted herself with a gasp.

"I'm pretty sure he doesn't have X-Ray vision, Susan."

"But he...we only...it's not like...I mean we didn't actually..."

"You want me to stop?"

She moaned.

Carl recognized the second voice, but he advanced until he could see the two figures in the deep moon shadow behind the septic mound. His young mind would never forget the image of Takoda and Susan together in that instant.

He backed quietly around the mound, turned, and wandered quickly away.

His heart pounded. He felt all kinds of emotions at once. Most of all he felt dirty, and outraged.

He should tell Gunther. Susan was his girlfriend and he deserved to know. But he didn't want to snitch on Takoda, who was also his big brother. But whether Gunther and Susan were broken up or not, this was a shameful betrayal and Takoda deserved to be called out for it. Still, Carl didn't want to be a snitch. What was he supposed to do?

Linda had arrived at the fire. By now almost everyone had food and drinks. She yelled and waved to get everyone's attention, calling Gunther to join her. She held onto her husband's arm with one hand. She smiled broadly, but Tommy looked embarrassed.

"I just want to say something about my husband and my son," Linda called out. The crowd quieted to listen.

"Just in case you don't already know the reason for this celebration," Linda said, "Tommy won the election and will be the new sheriff!"

People clapped and cheered.

"I want everyone to know how proud of him I am," Linda went on. "And also, my oldest son, Gunther, has finished his hours, passed all his tests, and is now a certified, instrument-rated pilot!"

False Flag - Brown

More clapping; more cheering. Gunther looked as embarrassed as his father.

Linda had both of them by the arms, now. "Many years ago, this handsome guy I remember seeing in school and around the rez, he just disappeared. I was still in school. But he graduated... Anyway, I asked around about him, and found out Tommy had joined the US Army. So time went by; I graduated; I dated some boys..."

Several wolf-whistles sounded in the crowd, and everybody had a wisecrack.

"You asked around about me, eh?" Tommy asked, trying to be playful.

"Don't let it go to your head, Big Boy," she replied.

This inspired more drunken laughter and catcalls.

"I heard some more about Tommy from time to time," Linda continued, undaunted. "I found out he had joined the Green Berets."

Josh, Frank, Kurt and Griz barked their approval and Jenny hooted, but Uncle Jay, Rocco, Carlos and some others blew raspberries and made derogatory remarks.

Linda laughed but went on. "Well one day I got this call from Tommy. He was home on leave from Fort Bragg, North Carolina. I don't know how he got my number, and he never would tell me...but his brother was on the Tribal Police and I always wondered if that's how he found out."

People laughed, intoned comments and catcalled some more.

While Linda entertained the crowd, Rachel slipped away discreetly. She wanted to write some notes on the legal pad in her car before she forgot any details of what she'd learned. Someone might get suspicious if they saw her taking notes, but with everybody gathered around paying attention to Linda and Tommy, this was the perfect time.

Before reaching her car, Rachel saw somebody crossing her path heading toward the fire. She hadn't seen Tommy's youngest son very much, but enough to recognize him.

"Hi, Carl."

He didn't even turn his head to acknowledge her. "Hi."

"You're missing it," she said. "Your mom's talking about how her and your dad got together."

He grunted and kept walking.

Every bit the conversationalist as the other Scarred Wolf men.

Rachel unlocked her car door and slid inside, but didn't shut the door. She pondered Carl Scarred Wolf, who seemed in a trance. She heard the caged dogs yipping tentatively and her curiosity got the better of her.

False Flag - Brown

She stepped out, closed and re-locked the door. Carl had come from a direction that, when she traced it backwards, led behind the house to the approximate area the dogs were making noise.

Susan felt a little better now. Or did she? In a way, she felt worse.

In school she had occupied the highest strata of popularity and never considered the Scarred Wolf brothers in her league. Not the taciturn loner Gunther; and especially not the rowdy delinquent Takoda--who was younger than her, anyway.

But things had changed.

She tried to kiss some more, now that they were done. She wanted reassurance that what she'd done was justified and everything would be all right. Takoda kissed her back, perfunctorily, but began to dress and grew preoccupied with that.

She searched around for her own clothes in the dark, found her panties and slipped them on. "What do we do now?" she asked.

"I'm going to get a burger from Uncle Jay," he replied, "if there's any left."

"That's not what I mean."

"What do you mean, then?" he asked, with a casual attitude that gave her none of the reassurance she sought.

She wrapped her bra around her, backwards so that the fastener was in front where she could easily clasp it. "I don't know how to tell Gunther."

"Tell him what?" Takoda asked, pulling on his boots, his pants on already.

She spun the bra around her torso, loaded the cups and slipped her arms through the straps. "About us." Jeez, why was he so dumb all the sudden?

"What about us?"

It was like he was deliberately playing retarded to annoy her. She'd found his aloof nature attractive just a little while ago, but right now it tempted her to scream at him. She didn't like having to spell these things out. "That we're **together** now." She resisted the urge to add a "duh."

"Who said we're together, now?" Takoda asked. "We never said that."

"But..." Words failed her for a moment. "Takoda! What is this?"

Whatever he might have said in reply, it remained unsaid. The dogs began going crazy. Then Rachel White Bird appeared around the corner of the septic mound and stopped in her tracks, staring wide-eyed. "Oh, I'm sorry..." she blurted.

"White Bird," Takoda said, pulling his shirt on. "Who invited you?"

At first Susan played it cool. She finished dressing with a casual

144

False Flag - Brown

greeting to Rachel. Then once Susan finally excused herself and retreated, the shock and shame was too much for her. Susan's throat constricted; the tears flowed like water from a tap; and she felt nauseous. She lost it—a sobbing, wailing breakdown.

Takoda sauntered over to the fire and grabbed a burger, like nothing was amiss. His mother, father and older brother were collecting hugs, handshakes and general good will from the attendees gathered around. Evidently, Takoda had missed something. He thought of asking Carl what happened, but his little brother gave him a stony glance and walked away.

He'd never seen an expression like that on Carl before, directed at him. He was like Takoda's personal servant growing up, willing to do almost anything to please his big brother. Carl had been asking him to tune the carburetor on his bike for weeks, and Takoda still hadn't done it yet. But that hardly warranted icy hostility. Or did it?

Takoda stopped eating the burger after two bites. His stomach knotted on him. He didn't want to admit, even to himself, that it was guilt he felt. He headed for the garage to take a look at the dirt bike. He wouldn't fire it up tonight, but at least he could look at the spark plug and a few other parts.

Rachel returned to her car and scribbled notes furiously. Her instructions had implied getting dirt on the Scarred Wolf family if possible while winning what confidence and gathering what information she could. She'd done pretty well for one night's work.

Movement caught her eye and she looked up. It was Takoda walking by. She continued writing. A few minutes later, he passed going the opposite direction with a partially eaten burger on a styrofoam plate. She wrote on. A few minutes later, Susan staggered toward the fire, pretty face still shining with tears.

Rachel got out of the car. This might be a scene worth watching.

Rachel followed the young woman at a discrete distance, and saw Susan march right up to Gunther.

The garage door was open. Tommy's <u>Victory Hammer</u> sat near the work bench, while Carl's dirt bike leaned on its kickstand near the tool chest. Takoda had the spark plug out, examining the electrode and insulation as he chewed a mouthful of burger. Gunther arrived and stood in the doorway. Susan was a couple steps behind. Takoda looked up, then stood.

Gunther remained silent for a long moment, just staring at Takoda.

False Flag - Brown

Finally he said, "You're a real class act, aren't you, brother?" He spoke in Shawandasse, and coated the word "brother" with sardonic contempt.

Susan didn't speak Shawandasse--few people did, even among full-blooded Shawnee. But Tommy, Linda and their boys were all fluent.

"You still got her on a pedestal?" Takoda asked, in their indigenous language, chinning toward Susan. "I thought you nexted her."

"Oh, well I guess that makes it okay, then," Gunther said, feigning epiphany.

Takoda shrugged. "It is what it is."

"I've stuck up for you all your life," Gunther said, shaking his head. "At the casino; in school; even with Mom and Dad. I've actually got in fights when people called you a sociopath or a moron... because you're my brother. I never would have believed you'd do something like this."

Takoda's face remained perfectly blank, as all the Scarred Wolf men were naturally expert at.

"You know," Gunther said, "I just realized something about you: You've never apologized for anything in your whole life. Never once. I would think that this, at least, is something you'd be sorry about. But I'll die of old age before you could ever see that you were wrong about something."

"You're better off without her," Takoda said, pointing at Susan. "You think she's a special little snowflake, even now? Let me tell you about her: she's had the red carpet rolled out for her all her life. She's never had to work for anything. Everywhere she goes she gets special help and special attention that other people don't get. Teachers and all the guys who orbit her, and pervy old men—they all fawn over her and line up to make life easier for her. She got awarded letter grades at least two places higher than what she ever earned, and never had to do homework because there was no shortage of chumps willing to do it for her. You can bet money it's the same way for her in college."

"What is he saying about me?" Susan asked Gunther, who stood listening, dumbfounded.

"Everything has always just magically fallen into her lap," Takoda continued. "She's become convinced that it's because she's just so damn good. The world and everything in it is her entitlement—but listen to her talk about how oppressed she is, some time. How hard she's had to work, if you want a really good laugh. So nothing's ever good enough for her, and never will be. She deserves more simply because she exists. You think she was upset because you dumped her? Wake up! You're too naive to guess it, so I'll tell you: she's upset because you dumped her before she could dump you. You accidentally threw a wrench in her twisted psyche. She deserves more and better than you, bro, so how dare you act like you don't need her?"

False Flag - Brown

"How did this all become about her?" Gunther asked.

"See?" Takoda chortled, setting down the ratchet, stepping around the dirt bike and advancing toward Gunther as he spoke. "You're proving my point. You naturally blame it all on me, like she had nothing to do with it. She gets off scot-free, and smells like a rose. I must have mind-controlled her or something. It had to be that because God knows she can't be held responsible for anything negative. Hasn't it ever bothered you that she has no friends? Oh, she's got other girls who are jealous of her, and guys who want to bang her..."

"What's Jennifer?" Gunther interrupted. "Chopped liver?"

"Jennifer would try to make friends with a rattlesnake," Takoda said, laughing harshly. He stopped with only a few feet between them.

Their father, mother, and little brother all arrived in a hurry right then, with Jennifer and Josh right behind. Uncle Jay and Jennifer's mother brought up the rear, only a couple seconds behind them.

"You're spending a lot of time making her sound bad," Gunther said. "That's just a smokescreen for what somebody who claims to be my brother did."

"What's going on?" demanded Tommy, his gaze bouncing back and forth between his sons.

"Ask him," Gunther said, index finger aimed at a point between his brother's eyes.

Everyone's attention shifted to Takoda who, for a moment, was uncharacteristically speechless.

"Somebody better answer me," Tommy said, voice raising.

Takoda thrust his chin toward Susan. "Me and Head Cheerleader there, Miss College Beauty Queen, just finished having some fun together."

Linda gasped, hands flying up to cover her mouth.

Both boys wore blank expressions, but Tommy knew them well enough to read the fury underneath. Himself stunned, he willed himself to move and betrayed no emotion of his own as he stepped between the two dangerous young men. He had taught his sons how to fight and one of them might very well seriously hurt or kill the other if they threw down.

"I don't know what she's going to say now," Takoda continued, in English. "But it was consensual."

Susan turned and fled into the darkness, wailing like a siren. Now Jennifer's jaw fell slack. Josh surveyed the scene, wanting to escape from it himself, but standing ready in case Tommy needed help if it got physical.

Linda stepped forward and slapped Takoda hard across the face, voicing how shamed and crestfallen she was in nigh-unintelligible screeches.

Takoda made no move, his head held high with stubborn pride.

Jennifer moved forward and positioned herself to face Gunther. She touched his shoulders soothingly and made eye contact. Gunther's eyes had gone dead, which meant he was possibly microseconds away from extreme violence.

"Please, cousin," Jennifer said. "Don't do anything to him. Please."

Her words did seem to rinse some of the death out of Gunther's stare.

"Congratulations, Takoda," Gunther said, cold as a tombstone. "Some say that betrayal is the highest form of *coup* you can count." His gaze shifted to Jennifer. "I'm not going to touch him, cousin. He was right about one thing: Susan's obviously not worth it. But neither is he."

Gunther stepped back, turned around and stalked away into the dark. Everyone knew better than to go after him. Trying to comfort him or make him talk would only make him angrier.

Tommy turned to face Takoda square-on. "Aren't you just full of yourself? You showed us all, huh? What a big, proud badass you are."

Takoda held his head erect, but his gaze involuntarily lowered. The chink in his armor...the fallibility of his *Fuqitol* prescription...was that he couldn't now look his father in the eye.

Gunther's Mustang fired up with a powerful snarl. He didn't let it warm up like usual, instead ripping wide strips out of the turf with his rear tires, peeling out of there.

"If you weren't his brother, he would have killed you just now," Tommy stated in cold, terse Shawandasse. "If you weren't my son..."

Tommy never finished the sentence. His gaze raked over his middle child like two red-hot spikes. Finally he just shook his head and turned away. He wrapped his arm around his wife and led her from the garage. Gradually everyone else left, too.

Takoda stood there like a statue for a moment after everyone had left him, then tried to shake it off. That look of disappointment in his father there at the end cut him deeper than anything could have. But he wasn't going to admit that—not even to himself.

Ramp up the dosage in his *Fuqitol* prescription--that was the answer. He cleaned the spark plug and reinstalled it, then examined the magneto. It looked like the party was breaking up now anyway, so he started the dirt bike's loud, two-cycle engine and adjusted the fuel-air mixture.

Rachel White Bird didn't speak Shawandasse, so most of the yelling had just sounded like gibberish to her. But from her vantage point in her parked car she had seen the confrontation and could guess the gist of what was said. Surely there was some way what she'd just learned about the family could be put to use.

False Flag - Brown

25
D MINUS 50
LAS ANIMAS COUNTY, COLORADO

Jennifer Scarred Wolf was an early riser. Joshua Rennenkampf was not.

By the time Josh got up and dressed, her bed was made and she was nowhere to be found in the house. Josh peeked out the window and saw her Jeep was still there, so he figured she was out taking a walk or picking flowers or some of that other girly stuff she liked to do. It was one of the things he loved about her, come to think of it: she was so easy to please, even just nature made her happy.

Another thing he loved about her was that she didn't watch much TV. When she did, it was usually the Weather Channel. She'd sit and watch it like it was a fascinating interview or something.

Josh booted up his work station in the living room. He still had work to do on a couple of his contracts, but decided to get started on Tommy's request instead. This was the weekend, after all.

He had lost track of time when Jennifer came inside, shedding her jacket.

"Good morning," she greeted, cheerily. "Brrr. It's nippy up here in the mornings."

"Morning," he replied, taking a sip of coffee.

She pressed her small, cold hands against the back of his neck and he jumped at the icy sensation.

"Told you it was nippy," she said, laughing.

"You're such a brat in the mornings," he said, finding her cheer contagious despite himself. "Jeez, it's not that cold outside, but your hands are like icicles."

"Cold hands, warm heart," she sing-songed, sweetly.

"Where were you?"

"Oh, I played with the dogs a little," she said. "Brushed Indy down. I had to do **something** while you were sleeping your life away. I'll go make breakfast in a minute."

"Sounds good," he said, rubbing her hands in between his to warm them.

She sat in his lap and glanced at the monitor. "What's 'MK Ultra'?"

"Just one of the rabbit trails I followed, checking into something for your uncle."

Her expression turned thoughtful as she skimmed over some of the text on screen. "Monarch... *Montauk*... What is all this?"

Josh alt-tabbed to another window. "Oh, just some conspiracy stuff

False Flag - Brown

you probably don't want to hear about."

"Ah," she said, poking him in a ticklish spot. "Trying to find out whether I'm real or a lizard-person?"

"Oh, I know you're reptillian," he deadpanned. "Your hands just gave it away, you cold-blooded thang."

She frowned, started to speak a couple times, then hesitantly said, "I've been meaning to ask you something."

Josh sobered in an instant. He dreaded "the Talk," but knew, sooner or later, they were going to have it. Was now the time? They'd already had a couple Big Talks recently—surely he had earned a postponement?

They had the Religion Talk, wherein he had assured her he had no problem with her faith. He believed in God; just didn't know much about Him and never made an effort to know. He'd never read the Bible before meeting her, and still wasn't very keen on it, or going to church. But he suspected there was something to Christianity, or the pinkos wouldn't be so rabid in their efforts to smear it.

They had the Political Talk, wherein she acknowledged the Hegelian patterns he pointed out in economic and foreign policy over the last century; conceding it might be plausible that people in authority could conspire to frame their enemies and kill innocents just to accumulate more power for themselves and push an agenda that couldn't achieve popular support otherwise. She just didn't like to dwell on it, and he could certainly understand that.

The Talk that was still forthcoming was about their future together--if there was to be one.

"I've been thinking about how my dad and Uncle Tommy were framed for that murder in Indonesia," Jennifer said.

Relief flooded through Josh's brain, despite the sobering subject of her murdered father. "Yeah?"

"Uncle Tommy thought it must be because of what they were investigating before they left. He couldn't think of anything else it could be."

Josh nodded. "It implicated some powerful people in some pretty serious crimes. It went high, high up in the so-called Justice Department."

"Which fits just perfect in your conspiratorial worldview," she said, tweaking his nose playfully.

Josh shrugged. "Guilty as charged."

"Well, this unit, or secret team you found out about," Jennifer went on. "What did you call what they do? Black Ops? False...?" She frowned, trying to remember the term.

"False flags," Josh said.

False Flag - Brown

"False flag, right," Jennifer said. "Like the Gulf of Tonkin incident, or..."

"The Gulf of Tonkin was just a fabricated story," Josh said. "There was no actual operation. But it does fall under the same category as far as motive—if not execution."

"You said maybe even the JFK assassination," Jennifer reminded him.

"Well, Rocco Cavarra heard scuttlebutt about a secret team when he worked for Naval Intelligence, which may go back that far. It would make sense to me, but then every "lone nut" narrative makes me suspicious."

She tousled his hair. "No comment. But you said the reason they must be worried about the investigation is that they probably have another false flag planned."

Josh nodded.

"Well, did you change your mind?"

"No."

"Then why aren't you looking into that?"

Josh was surprised by the flow of this conversation. He was used to people he cared about trying to push his head into the sand, not deeper into his "tinfoil hat."

"I don't know," he said, shrugging.

"Don't you believe it's true?"

He nodded.

"Don't innocent people die whenever there's one of these false flags?"

"I don't know how many are always innocent," he said. "But yeah, people always die. That's the whole psychology behind false flags: they have to be shocking and tragic enough to illicit the desired response."

"Then aren't you morally obligated to do something about it?" she asked.

Josh sighed. "What's the point, Jennifer? I've been tipping at windmills for years. Nobody wants to believe what's going on. On the rare occasion they'll pay attention long enough for me to build a case and prove it to them, they just don't care enough to do anything but watch more TV. All it takes is a few hours of the idiot box and they forget everything except that I'm a hopeless whack-job. What's the point? I'm supposed to make people stop what's happening? You can't even get them to elect the lesser evil, anymore. Well...okay, the Bushes. Granted. But people are begging for what's coming, and they're gonna get it, good and hard. It doesn't matter what I do."

Still in his lap, she leaned back away from him a little. "So you're content to just hole up here like a hermit and let the world burn?"

"It wants to burn," he said.

False Flag - Brown

She pressed her hands against both sides of his face. "Joshua, I might not have believed all this stuff if I hadn't seen some of it over in that horrible place. I still wish I didn't believe it. But I think it's real; and I know you do. Maybe if you can at least leak word out to the right people...I don't know. But you have to at least try to do something. For me, if nobody else."

Why did she have to pierce him with those big puppy-dog eyes when making her hare-brained request?

But she was right, of course.

Josh wanted to adopt the attitude of so many people who disgusted him, and just ignore an impending disaster rather than take action to avoid it. But there were people out there who saw the danger--Jennifer, Tommy, Gunther, Cannonball...maybe a handful of others around the world. Maybe not.

Were five people worth risking his life for? Worth charging at another windmill?

Yes, they were.

"Tommy hasn't said anything about it for quite a while," Josh said.

"I'll ask him about it next time we talk," Jennifer said. "It surprises me he'd just let this go."

Josh sighed. "You're right, Boo. I'll start digging again."

She kissed him and got up to make breakfast.

False Flag - Brown

26
D MINUS 49
BOSTON, MASSACHUSSETS

McMillan's phone beeped first.

He stirred, groaning, and fumbled for the lamp switch. When it lit up, Jade Simmons rolled over and made a few groggy, profane remarks. Both had been enjoying deep sleep from post-coital exhaustion.

Macmillan took his glasses from the end table and slipped them on. Then, blinking repeatedly, focused on the backlit screen of his phone. "It's priority message from Bertrand," he said. "Encrypted."

"It better well be priority at this hour," Jade grumbled, throwing her forearm over her eyes.

Macmillan swung his feet over the edge of the mattress and lurched to his feet. He only had two minutes from the time stamp on the text message. He woke up his tablet and opened the correct page in his browser, then fished his keys out of the pants hanging over the chair back. At the two minute mark he copied the code on the display of his key fob, and entered it into the appropriate field on the web page. The code table appeared on screen, with which he was to decode the text message.

By now Jade's phone was beeping.

Macmillan began decoding, and in two minutes Jade was doing the same.

Even busy with her own message, she noticed when he had finished, and gave him a curious glance.

"We've got the city," he said. "And the probable venue."

When she finished her own, she nodded. "It's a go. This means the event is coming within a couple months."

Macmillan began pulling his clothes on. He'd start making calls once dressed, and have a meeting in his office at 0630. He and most of his key support elements would be operating exclusively out of Texas for a while.

Jade also dressed. "The suspense is over," she said. "Just not the waiting."

"Looks that way," he agreed, cheerily, pulling on his socks. "Do you have teams going active, too?"

Her eyes now adjusted, she switched on the main overhead lights. The interior of the hotel room now stood out in harsh clarity. "You know I can't talk about my little projects." She flashed him that smirk he found so sexy for some reason. "So are the facilities going to be big enough at Amarillo Station?"

False Flag - Brown

"I think we're going to need at least one more property to stage..." he began, then stopped himself.

She had done it again. After refusing to divulge her own ops, she had casually managed to make him confirm the location of his own.

That annoyed him for a couple reasons. One was the usual way she effortlessly wormed information out of him. The other was that she already suspected Amarillo was the city, and evidently knew something about his facilities there. He had no clue where any of her ops would be-- unless Amarillo was one of them. If it was, then maybe that's how she knew. But if it wasn't, then she was being told more than he was...

"Why do you think my place is Amarillo?" he asked, tying his shoes.

She shrugged. "Isn't it?"

"You're not answering the question," he said. "And quit giving me that non-disclosure bullshit."

"Didn't I warn you when we first met, Jason," she asked, "that Lawrence would try to set us against each other? You're playing into his hands. This doesn't need to be a competition. There's a reason why I have more access than you. Think of it this way: you are Plan A; I'm Plan B. It's just normal security protocol that you wouldn't have access to my work. But I need to know yours, in case I have to pick up where you left off."

Macmillan didn't like her answer, but he had too many items on the day's agenda to waste time pursuing it further.

Jade remained in the hotel room after Jason left. Checkout wasn't until noon, so she might as well take advantage. She sent messages to the handlers for the assets she had in Amarillo, Fort Worth, Oklahoma City, Phoenix, and elsewhere. Then she sipped at her coffee while scanning the CNN site.

She read about the latest school shooting, this one in good old California, and frowned. How many more atrocities had to take place before the neanderthal gun nuts in flyover country would finally give up the death-grip on their deadly phallic substitutes?

There was a photo and one-sentence bio of the shooter. Jade sighed.

She multitasked back to her daily planner and entered a note for herself to look over the most recent rejects who had washed out of training. Often they took to conditioning well enough for simple tasks, but physically or otherwise just couldn't hack the advanced training. Another batch of them were being sent back to China Lake in the coming week.

The handlers replied by the time she had skimmed through the top stories. She blasted them with an encrypted message revealing the venue

False Flag - Brown

for the activation protocol and mission briefings.

Out loud, she had told Jason the Event would take place within a few months. In reality, she had a much more precise understanding of the timetable. She knew within a few days when the Event would kick off.

POTAWATTOMIE COUNTY, OKLAHOMA

Terrance Handel got a signature on his clipboard, left the package with the customer and returned to his truck. As he finished logging the delivery, his ears picked up a high frequency whine. He knew right away it didn't come from the truck, his cellphone, the smart clipboard or any of the electronic equipment he carried around. It was just something his ears picked up every now and then for no apparent reason. He assumed it was just a very mild symptom of his hearing disorder. It wasn't painful, and was quickly forgotten.

He started the truck and continued his route.

Terrance had been assigned this rural route after years of delivering inside OK City. He knew it well enough now that he usually didn't need to use the GPS...except inside the reservation, simply because he didn't get that many deliveries there and so hadn't learned the roads well.

Normally, on the reservation, he delivered to the casino and that was about it, but lately he'd been getting deliveries and pickups from the police station and the homes of a couple managers at the casino. If it kept up, he'd know the roads there without the GPS, too.

Terrance went about his day like normal, listening to a local Top 40 station whenever in his truck. Normally he would hit the gym for a while after work, but as the day went on he thought more and more about just going home to chill. He worked hard, consistently, and deserved a break from the regimen. By the time he clocked out, the decision was made.

He prepared a microwave dinner in his apartment later, turned the TV on and sat down in front of it to eat. Normally he would spend the evening texting the girls on his dating rotation, but he didn't even feel like going through all that trouble tonight. He'd been getting plenty of sex, so there was no urgency.

He flipped through dozens of channels, trying to find something worth watching. He finally settled on a sitcom, because one of the actresses was pretty and thin, but had a nice rack.

A beer commercial came on, and he remembered he had a 12-pack in the fridge. He fetched three back to the coffee table, kicked his shoes off, propped his feet up, and went to work on the first beer. Now another commercial was showing exotic vacation spots around the world. Some

False Flag - Brown

credit card with travel points or something. It got him thinking about vacation time.

Terrance had five PTO days saved up at work. It seemed like he should have more. He knew he'd vacationed in Mexico last year; California the year before; and Appalachia the year before that. He knew because of records and receipts, but he couldn't remember a thing about those vacations.

To anyone else this might have been so weird it was disconcerting, but Terrance Handel had gaps in his long-term memory going way back to childhood and grudgingly accepted it as just one of those things.

He accepted it, but it still felt like he'd been robbed when he couldn't remember enjoying those vacations. Of course he'd likely been blitzed on vodka the whole time.

I'm not going to get drunk at all next time, he thought as he watched video footage of translucent blue surf, golden sand and sexy beach bunnies.

The first gap in his memory occurred in grade school, long before he'd ever had his first swig of vodka. He had trouble sitting still in class; blurted out questions or answers without raising his hand and waiting to be called on; and showed too much competitive behavior on the playground. His parents took him to doctors for a while, then he went back to school but was sent to see some grownup every day who asked all kinds of questions.

Terrance noticed the gaps when his mother would ask what he'd learned...and he couldn't remember anything he'd done all day, besides riding to and from school. He already had to swallow pills every night; and after the memory problems began he had to swallow even more.

He had plenty gaps from his time in the Marine Corps. And then it wasn't just days at a time—most of his enlistment was just a fog. He remembered random minutia from those years, and that was it. He mentioned it when the doctors screened him at the V.A. Hospital once he got back, and they told him it was most likely a psychological reaction to his PTSD. He didn't think he had PTSD. He didn't have flashbacks or freak out when he looked up at ceiling fans or any of that Hollywood stuff. He didn't remember **any** traumatic experiences. That was part of the point: he didn't remember much of anything.

But he sure had some medals and certificates when he got back to civilian life.

Now the gaps were back to a manageable level. So maybe he **had** seen something traumatic overseas and his subconscious just blocked it out.

The sitcom ended and the news came on. Terrance finished a beer and started another.

False Flag - Brown

The big story was about the investigation on the Delton Williams beating in Amarillo. Local blacks were convinced that they would be denied justice again. A reporter interviewed a young black woman with glasses and a hat turned sideways. On the screen toward the bottom, text read "Eye witness to the beating."

"These white cops pulled him over for no reason," the young woman said. "Just DWB. Drivin' While Black. With all the white drivers, they just look at the driver's license and let 'em go. But they surrounded this man's car from both sides. Drag him out on the street. Started beatin' him. They's laughin' and jokin' with each other while they beat him, too."

The sober-faced newscaster mentioned the scheduled date for the trial before moving on to the next story.

There was a school shooting in California. The owner of the Bar G ranch had recovered from his heart attack, but was now under investigation by the IRS. There was another college campus rape accusation. There was more tension between Israel and its neighbors, and threats were being made. The White House had given the Israeli prime minister an ultimatum about Jewish settlements in the occupied territories, but Jews were flooding into the small country from France, Germany and other parts of Europe. New settlements were popping up in the West Bank at a frenzied rate.

Then they got to a story that lightened the mood a little bit: an upcoming Woodstock-style festival being held out on the Nevada desert in the fall, called Autumn Rave.

Footage from the previous year's celebration was shown while the news anchor explained there would be music, dancing, motivational workshops and so on. It looked a lot like an updated Woodstock, by the images on screen.

It sounded kind of lame. Terrance wasn't into that scene. He wasn't even into music that much (though it was all right, he guessed).

A strange animation took place on screen as the anchorman kept talking: a mirror shattered, and in multiple shards of it the reflection of a butterfly appeared. The butterfly morphed into the Autumn Rave logo. Then the scene jumped back to last year's event footage.

There were several shots of young women with blurred or blacked-out video effects concealing what must be bared breasts. Even with strategic body parts concealed, Terrance grew aroused. They also interviewed some old dude who said his memory had been restored after participating in one of the workshops.

It wasn't lame, after all. He should spend his vacation at Autumn Rave. It might be life-changing.

False Flag - Brown

27
D MINUS 14
NSA DATA CENTER
CAMP WILLIAMS, UTAH

Justin arrived at his work station and noticed the room was mostly empty.

The department had processed all the intel from Chapanee Valley, finally, and were back to a normal schedule and the old routine. Most everyone could now take time off to catch up on sleep and life, or blow some of the overtime pay they'd made.

Barnes was there, though, and saluted him with a coffee cup.

Justin waved back, then walked to the break table and poured himself some coffee. The pot was nearly empty, so he did the right thing and started a new batch before getting to work.

After he logged in and took a look at the cases still needing profiles built, Barnes peeked his head over the divider.

"I had four different Priority Threes from the Chapanee."

Priority Three was high up on the risk chart.

"There were a lot of high-risks to be at one location," Justin said. He would probably never be friends with the motormouth Barnes, but he tried to be friendly and conversational with him at least once a day.

"That's because of their behavior patterns," Barnes said. "If you're a consistent voter, then all the sudden quit cold-turkey--like these guys did after the 2012 election--well, that'll shoot you right up past Priority Five and Four, even if all you've ever owned is a BB gun."

"I had one of those," Justin said, sipping his coffee, eyes scanning The List.

"A BB gun?"

"No. A priority Three."

"Those guys are flagged dangerous, because they've given up on the electoral process," Barnes went on, as if Justin had asked him to elaborate. "They've put on their tinfoil hats because now they're sure that the alien lizard-people have rigged the elections so there's no point in voting."

"No. Ya think?" Justin was unable to hold back the sarcasm.

"They're more disposed to use violence," Barnes said, with a defensive tone as if Justin had challenged his premise. "That's where DomTers come from. One place, anyway."

"You ever seen a Priority Two or One?" Justin asked.

"I've built a profile for a Two," Barnes said, brightening. "Every indicator somebody can have, plus he was blacked out. I mean, no social

159

media at all. Only used encrypted email. Minimal talk on the phone--and had a cellphone that can't be remotely activated. Didn't use credit or debit cards--cash only. When they saw upstairs what I was working on, I had like three guys in suits looking over my shoulder. I got emails from all over the Agency asking for the Google Earth files and whatever else I had on him. I'd bet money they took a closer look at his house within a matter of days."

"Ex-military, I guess," Justin said.

"Oh yeah; hardcorps. Had a Top Secret clearance, then went off his rocker. Got into that right-wing crap. Got out of the military short of retirement; quit talking to people. Probably got an arsenal and is hiding in a bunker somewhere with a gun in one hand, Bible in the other, waiting for the black helicopters."

"You ever seen a Priority One?" Justin asked.

"I've never worked on a profile for one," Barnes admitted. "But I've looked at some files."

"Really? Where?"

Justin was sure his co-worker's head tilted a little higher with pride. Presenting an opportunity to instruct had just made Barnes's day.

"You can access it from your desktop there," Barnes said, hanging his arm over the divider to point at the computer assigned to Justin. When you back out of the dashboard, right-click that little icon on the lower right, that looks like a grayed-out triangle. Click 'database' on the drop-down menu, then 'archives.' You should see a list of P-One-through-Nine."

Justin followed these instructions on the desktop as Barnes spoke. "Jeez, I would have never even known this was here."

"You don't surf around the network?"

"No," Justin replied. "How do you have time to find all this stuff?"

Barnes shrugged. "Sometimes I get bored on my breaks. Plus, you're new here. You weren't around back when we were having all that trouble with the dashboard, and the aggregator. Had some down-time then."

"Thanks, Barnes," Justin said, absently, opening a completed file in the P-Two archive.

"Sure," Barnes said. "Have fun. It's kinda' cool seeing profiles you worked on mixed in there with the other ones from around the country."

An hour had been spent before Justin knew it. It was fascinating, reading the profiles of the higher level DomTer threats in the NSA database.

He knew he should get to work, but he opened the P-One archive instead, purely out of curiosity. He wanted to see if he could isolate what flags made the difference between Priority One and Two threats.

False Flag - Brown

He noticed another hour had passed, and chastised himself for the butt-chewing he had probably earned goofing around. But the profile in front of him was just too fascinating to let go of. The DomTer was listed both as "white supremacist" and "Native American" for one thing. Justin was baffled by such an oxymoronic mistake, and wondered if the profile would still be considered Priority One if it was corrected. But the guy in question had plenty of other flags.

He was ex-Special Forces and a decorated veteran of Desert Storm. After that he served as "contractor-covert ops." He had dozens of other DomTer probables in his network, and, oddly enough, was now a county sheriff. Justin had never seen a profile quite like this one.

"Scarred Wolf, Tommy" was the name on the profile. That name sounded vaguely familiar.

It bothered Justin that anybody in this particular database should be familiar to him in any way.

False Flag - Brown

Tommy had borrowed a seasoned interrogation specialist from the metro force, who was used to dealing with young people. He questioned Zack at the county jail, and Dave, who was recovering from his gunshot wound, in the hospital.

Tommy, alone in his office, watched the recording of Dave's interrogation for the second time.

"Didn't you find it odd," the interrogation expert asked, "that Ms. Greeley needed to sacrifice animals, and a newborn baby?"

"It's all about energy," Dave said, in a groggy voice. "Patterns of energy. There's things you have to do to focus energy in the right time, at the right place."

"So Ms. Greeley did those things to the pigs, and the baby, because she needed energy?"

"Right," Dave said. "Exactly."

"Just to be clear," the interrogator said, "when you say 'energy,' you're not talking about electricity or something like that. Right?"

"Oh, no," Dave replied, and laughed drunkenly. "There are so many kinds of energy. Electricity is just one. Humans like electricity because they can harness it with machines, and circuitry...no. I mean mystical energy. Cosmic energy..."

"Dave, did you see how the baby was...what did you call it?"

"Released. But let me..."

"Focus, Dave. Did you see how the baby was released?"

"Wait. Wait. This is important. Because the whole universe is full of conflicting energy," Dave said. "It's everywhere. It's in this room with us, right now. This energy is dark, gloomy, because you're a simple man with an ugly job. But I've seen, you know, power, that...that's just, wonderful."

"The baby, Dave. I need you to focus on the baby."

"Oh the baby had very nice energy," Dave said. "It was clean and bright... I've seen mystical power that's just, you know, colors. Swirling colors. And then there's the energy when Ms. Greeley and I make love." He grinned and blinked his eyes. "Oh, it's so..."

"Dave, tell me who killed the baby. Start with the knife if you have to. Who had the knife?"

"Why do you want to focus on the one thing?" Dave asked, annoyed. "Simple man. Simple. I'm trying to describe the forest but you've got this hang-up for one tree."

The interrogator sighed and lit a cigarette. "If you'll just answer a few easy questions about the baby, Dave, I'll be glad to let you tell me about cosmic energy."

"You know that thing is poison, right?" Dave said, waving at the smoke. "And it's illegal to have in a hospital. I should call the nurse. Do you know I can see your energy get weaker, and dimmer, every time you inhale that poison?"

"I've got a deal with the nurses," the interrogator said with a perfect poker face. "But it's good that you can see and hear some of the things I can see and hear. You can see and smell the smoke, and you know you're in a hospital, and the hospital has rules. That means you could also see and smell the baby, and you knew you were in Ms. Greeley's basement, and that the police have rules. So let's talk about that, and leave the stuff about colored energy swirls for later."

"Energy doesn't all swirl," Dave said, laughing as if the cop was a dunce. "Like the gun. When that man shot me, the energy from the gun was sharp and straight and red. Then it burned white when it went into me. My body responded with blackness, to dull the sharp white pain. But the black energy almost drowned me. Then there was the sheriff. His deputies had, you know, nice auras. But his was blinding. It was, like, so bright..."

The interrogator exhaled a stream of smoke and wiped his face with his free hand. "Dave, I need you to tell me about the baby."

"It's connected to the blood," Dave said, in a confused voice. "Somehow, when you separate blood from a being, it releases the aura. And there's an intense energy surge, but it doesn't last long. Once the blood starts to cool and dry, the energy's gone."

"Alright, Dave. Blood's something I know about. Tell me about blood."

"There's going to be rivers of it!"

The boy's sudden passion took the interrogator by surprise. Tommy too, even though he'd watched the footage once already. Dave's nostrils flared and his eyes narrowed, His voice got huskier.

"There will be rivers of blood all through this renegade nation," Dave went on. "We're going to weed out the weak, and the naysayers, and the interlopers. You're worried about one worthless infant? We're going to release thousands! Millions! We're going to bring it all under control."

"Who's we?" the interrogator asked. "What are you talking about?"

"The black awakening," Dave said. "We're going to rise up and restore it all to the state of order it should have always been in." He turned his head to stare right into the camera. "You have no idea what's coming. You have no idea how to deal with it. You're too simple to ever imagine that it's true. And even if you did, you still couldn't stop us. I'm telling you the black awakening is coming, so you know beforehand, but there's nothing you can do about it!"

By that point the interrogator had completely lost control. Dave continued ranting until the recording was stopped.

Everyone who'd seen the interrogation wrote Dave off as insane. Dave did, in fact, have a prescription for some fairly serious bipolar and skitzo drugs. And yes, he was presently off his meds.

But Tommy didn't believe what he saw in that basement was the byproduct of insanity. Rose Greeley and the two teenage boys were no more crazy than Tommy was.

Tommy had never liked the knee-jerk tendency to classify horrific behavior as insane. Like Hitler, for instance: everyone assumed he was crazy. Tommy didn't. Hitler was egotistical, arrogant from his early successes, threw childish tantrums, made some self-defeating decisions...but underneath all of that, he was **evil**. Just pure evil.

Evil existed. Tommy knew that long before this bizarre case. And it was confirmed when he watched Dave's transformation from a spaced-out flaky kid into...into what? Something else, for sure.

As soon as the interrogator encouraged him to talk about blood...

It was like watching a metamorphosis. Dave's voice even changed. And toward the end the horny, easily-manipulated New Age boy was gone. In his place was some homicidal megalomaniac just awaiting a green light. And victims.

ABSENTEE SHAWNEE TRUST LAND, OKLAHOMA

When Tommy got home that night, he got in touch with Josh.

"Have you turned up anything?" Tommy asked.

"Oh yeah," Josh intoned. "Maybe more than you wanted."

"Well, go ahead. I got some time."

"Well first of all," Josh began, "there's a name for this kind of thing:'Satanic ritual abuse.' According to most of the Internet, it was never anything but hype, drummed up by Bible-thumping evangelicals using fear to increase church donations."

"If it says it on the Internet, then case closed," Tommy replied.

"Exactly," Josh said, laughing. "You sounded like me there for a second."

"I probably would have believed it was all hype too, once."

"But there's a lot more of it going on than you'll ever hear of through official channels," Josh said. "There's a preacher in the Midwest, for example, who deals with this stuff on a regular basis. Could be a kook just perpetrating a hoax, but people from all over the country call this guy for help, including some police departments."

False Flag - Brown

Tommy was tempted to call the guy himself, after what he'd seen happen to Dave.

"Anyway, I did some digging like you asked," Josh said. "I can't make blanket statements that cover all these cases everywhere, but I'm seeing a pattern for sure. Going back to the 1940s, there's a strong connection between these occultists and some government programs in the fringe sciences."

"Fringe sciences?" Tommy asked.

"Well...I shouldn't say government programs," Josh corrected himself. "There's been plenty of private sector work, too, at different universities. But the universities are subsidized...it all gets murky. Anyway, they experiment with weird, far-out stuff like remote viewing, automatic writing, astral projection..."

"There was a movie a few years ago," Tommy interjected, thoughtfully. "With George Clooney..."

"*Men Who Stare at Goats*," Josh said. "A comedy, I think. But what it was based on wasn't quite as ha-ha funny. That was about just one program among many, and famous mostly for its failure. Something else I found, though: It looks like there's been success in splitting personalities."

"Wait," Tommy said. "Are you saying somebody is **creating** psychological disorders?"

"Like I said, I can't tell you about every case there's ever been. But from what research I've done, Multiple Personality Disorder can be created in some of these experiments. And has been. I can send you links."

Tommy sighed. "No. My hands are full enough. This is looking like it's bigger than what I'm equipped to deal with, anyway."

"The evidence is mostly circumstantial," Josh said, "and I know it sounds far-fetched But it sure looks like there may be something to it."

"Thanks, Josh. But I might as well hand this off. It's over my pay grade."

"Hang on a minute, Tommy. You should hear this: The fringe science programs have changed their names a couple times, to sound more vague and innocuous. But some are still active. Technically, they're private sector, but the funding is from the Feds, laundered through various front companies. It's kind of surprising how easy it is to find some of the names associated with these pseudo-secret R&D programs. Some years ago a Professor Jade Simmons rose to the top of one of these labs. She got recruited into the Alphabets."

"The Alphabets" was what Josh called government agencies like the DHS, NSA, FBI, etc. He had his own paranoid conspiracy theory vernacular. Tommy was a little bothered that he himself now spoke it fluently from being around Josh so much.

"Guess who she works for now?" Josh asked.

"Who?"

"Your old friend, Lawrence Bertrand."

Tommy grew lightheaded for a moment. "Are you sure about that?"

"It sure looks that way, Chief."

Lawrence Bertrand had come under Tommy's sights back when Tommy himself was a Fed, unofficially investigating some major coverups he stumbled upon, ranging from sanctioned drug deals and gunwalking schemes, up to an infamous domestic terrorist incident.

"Guess what?" Josh continued. "He's not technically in the Justice Department anymore. He's pulling the strings in the DHS."

Tommy supposed it was only natural somebody like Bertrand would wind up in the Department of Homeland Security. With the so-called Patriot Act and the NDAA 2012, a mountain of Executive Orders and who-knew-what-else, a high-ranking criminal like him should now have even more latitude to obstruct and pervert justice, while receiving a princely salary to ostensibly **preserve** justice.

"I know you already think I'm half a lunatic," Josh said, "but can you think of any justification for having a mind control expert working for the DHS?"

"Her expertise is in mind control?"

"That was the subject of most of her experiments and papers," Josh said.

Tommy briefly hypothesized that maybe they wanted psychology experts so they could better interrogate terrorists, but nixed the idea quickly. It didn't take a high-level fringe science professor to get answers out of perps. That was something law enforcement could do well—and had for decades.

"There's different levels of mind control," Josh said. "The country's been subjected to the soft type for maybe 80 years."

"The 'soft' type is what," Tommy asked, "television?"

"Bingo--that's one for sure. There are different phases your brain goes through. Movies and television put the brain in the alpha phase. It's a trance state, no different from what a hypnotist tries to put you in. But TV can put some people there in seconds. Has to do with the flicker and stuff like that. So that's when your mind is most vulnerable to suggestion. Or 'optimal for programming,' in fringe science terms."

"And then they feed you subliminal messages?" Tommy suggested.

"They can. They've experimented with that. But they don't even need to be that sneaky. I mean, your defenses are already down when you

False Flag - Brown

watch a show. You **want** to suspend disbelief when you're looking to be entertained. And most everything you can watch on TV or see at the movies...or hear on the radio for that matter, or read in a book or a magazine...it's all just different angles from the same overall narrative. The most powerful computer is only as smart as the data you put into it. If everything the human brain receives through the eyes and ears reinforces the same worldview..."

"Which is why you guys wear tinfoil hats," Tommy said. "To protect you from brain waves."

"First time I heard that one," Josh replied, "I laughed so hard I fell off my duck-billed platypus. But that's just the soft stuff, for the unwashed masses. It explains why they vote the way they do--assuming elections are still legit, that is. The soft programming is based on 1930s vintage research on brain functions. Obviously the mind-benders have had a lot of time to get better at it. Imagine what they can do to somebody in an enclosed environment, with the use of drugs or some sort of direct electronic stimulus. I've heard they can embed complex messages in a simple high-pitched carrier frequency that your ears may or may not hear, but that your subconscious mind can decode."

"What are you suggesting?" Tommy asked. "Sleeper agents?"

"I'm not saying it's that," Josh said. "But it's got to make you wonder. The Pentagon has been interested in mind control and 'super soldiers' since the end of World War Two. Is it completely unreasonable to think the government might have made an effort...considering some of the other stuff they've wasted our tax dollars on?"

"You're wrong," Tommy said. "You're a **full** lunatic; not just half. Please don't start on that Internet theory about school shootings being staged."

"Okay," Josh said, with a tone of resigned dismissal in his voice. "Have you seen Jennifer since she got back?"

"No. Her and Linda went shopping yesterday, but I didn't get home until late. Want me to have her call you?"

"No, it's not that," Josh said. "She, um, kind of chewed me out for dropping the ball on your other investigation."

"She chewed you out?" Tommy asked, surprised. His niece was ultra-feminine and always gentle and respectful, even when she had reason to rock the boat.

"Well, by Jennifer standards it was chewing, I guess. Anyway, she's right. We really shouldn't let go of that deal. Especially if we're right, and there's another false flag in the hopper."

Tommy puffed his cheeks. "Yeah. I know. I got busy with all that's going on here...but I have no excuse. And now this new thing ties back to Bertrand. It's like fate is trying to tell me something."

False Flag - Brown

"Not many degrees of separation, are there?" Josh remarked. "Well, I mean I haven't found a direct link between Simmons and what happened at your crime scene there, but..."

"No," Tommy said. "And we don't want to go chasing rabbits off the main trail. Who knows how much time we have."

"The Shadow knows!" Josh declared in a nasal voice, followed by an attempt at a sinister laugh.

Tommy ignored the interjection. Josh had a tendency to crack jokes when the situation was grim. Well, a lot of the Sneaky Petes Tommy once worked with tended to do that. "Get whatever you can on Simmons. And see if you can find others who might be working for Bertrand. I'll do the same and we'll exchange notes as we go."

"Wow. Does that make me one of your deputies?"

"Yeah. Your badge is in the mail. Let's see if we can get any leads about what these people are up to. Just take precautions, Josh. These are heavy hitters and you don't want them tracing your hacks back to you."

"I'll be quiet as a little mouse, Chief."

"Thanks. And...um, how is it going with you and Jenny?"

"I haven't scared her away yet," Josh replied. "I'm as shocked as anybody about that."

"Look, Josh: I don't want this to get awkward. And she's an adult who can make her own decisions. I get that."

"What?" Josh asked, his tone suddenly defensive.

Tommy sighed. "I'm not implying you're not good enough for her, or anything. But you know how...tender-hearted she is. And it seems to me she's getting really serious about you."

"Are you telling me to break it off?"

"If you're not as serious as she is, then yeah. That's what I'm saying."

"What if I am, though?"

"Are you?"

"The truth is," Josh said, hesitantly, "she scares the hell out of me. It kinda' seems like I'm a bull and she's the china shop. Like maybe she deserves some really graceful pussycat instead, who's willing to give her all of what she wants."

Tommy chewed on his lip for a moment. He knew Josh had some issues because of what his first wife put him through. And Tommy wasn't comfortable even talking about relationships, so he was hesitant to offer advice. Nevertheless, he cleared his voice and said, "Look, Josh: women don't really want all the things they say that they want. It's not like you need to 'change your ways' or anything. She obviously likes you as you are. If you change, I can almost guarantee she'll start cooling down...regardless of whatever comes out of her mouth. I know you're a good man; **she** knows you're a good man. And **you** know she's a good woman. Just make up your mind if you want her. If you do, then it's simple. Go mostly by your instincts: protect her; provide for her; make babies with her...but some other stuff you need to go **against** your instincts: stay faithful to her; be patient with her; listen to her when she babbles about stuff that doesn't seem important; spend time with her; open doors for her; leave the toilet seat down."

"That last one would be really tough," Josh quipped, but he was too solemn to really pull off the humor.

"Forgive me if I'm not welcome up in your business," Tommy said. "But she's my niece. Jenny is family."

"Roger that, Chief. You gave me some stuff to think about. Thanks."

When they said their goodbyes and broke the connection, Tommy marveled at how, even with the world falling apart around them, the old mating game just couldn't be curtailed.

He needed to dig out his old notes on Bertrand, but put it off for the night. He was going to spend what time he had left today with Linda; listen to her babble about things that didn't seem important; and open a door for her if he got the chance.

False Flag - Brown

Rachel White Bird normally did her shopping in town, where prices were cheaper. On her way from the super Wal-Mart back toward the rez, she navigated the traffic on the business route, where the highway resembled a four-lane urban street.

She stopped at a light behind other traffic. When the light turned green she noticed, in between the cars, a young man on a dirt bike as he pulled a wheelie. He darted between traffic until he had clear lanes ahead, and sped away until stopped at the next light.

The dirt bike was not legal on public roads, and had no license plate. The young man wore no helmet. Plus he was speeding and driving unsafe. But not only was Rachel off-duty, she was outside her jurisdiction.

The light turned green and the rider popped another wheelie, his unbuttoned flannel shirt flapping behind him like a cape. His shock of black hair streamered behind him from the wind. When his front wheel came down he accelerated forward, leaving everyone behind. In between changing gears the loud high-pitched two-cycle engine screamed like a huge chainsaw echoing off the asphalt.

Rachel wove through traffic to get closer to the mad biker. Thanks to a couple more traffic lights, she was able to get close enough for a better look. He was dark and athletically built, with Shawnee features. He looked like the youngest Scarred Wolf boy: Carl.

Her assignment with the Scarred Wolf family hadn't panned out in the last two years. Rachel had thought, after the scene at the party, Susan Pyrch would be vulnerable enough to welcome a new friend, and Rachel could get inside that way. Rachel presented herself as that friend, but Susan already had a support network and was on the snobby side to begin with. That effort went nowhere.

Rachel then tried to befriend Gunther, who no doubt must have been vulnerable himself, after finding out his girlfriend cheated on him with his brother. But Gunther was suspicious from the start, and never showed an interest in her friendship.

His cousin Jennifer was friendly. But then, she was friendly with everyone. And Rachel wasn't able to get close enough to be in her confidence.

Takoda was just a bad seed, who apparently needed nobody at any time. But it was Takoda who inspired her to change her strategy and work it from another angle. She might not be able to win their confidence, but

False Flag - Brown

if she could get legal leverage on them somehow, maybe her boss could use that to squeeze information from one of them.

The potential for leverage was right in front of her face with the Scarred Wolf boys: their habitual unsafe driving. If she could bring one of them in and threaten them with jail time...well, it was a start, maybe. But Gunther was too cautious to be observed breaking the law. Takoda was observed on several occasions—at least, she felt certain it was him—but nobody could catch him.

As she followed the dirt bike toward the rez, it occurred to her that Carl might be the best entry point. Younger people were less guarded or jaded, and usually more open to new friendships as well. Or, from the other angle, they were more likely to get themselves into trouble and be desperate to get out of it.

She called the dispatcher and reported the Scarred Wolf boy, so they could send someone to intercept him.

Before crossing into the rez, Carl took the bike off road, the terrain features serving as ramps for him to take the bike bounding into the air, jump after jump. Rachel cursed and watched him disappear behind his own dust trail. They'd never catch him out on the plains. In fact, riding a dirt bike off road was not against the law either, so they couldn't do much even if they did catch him.

She would have to do her homework on Carl, and figure out where their paths could cross.

False Flag - Brown

30
D MINUS 42
LAS ANIMAS COUNTY, COLORADO

Josh wrapped up the latest I.T. consulting gig over the phone that morning. He spent some time working with the dogs, then rode up the mountain to check his traps.

Also, Jennifer had given him a book on edible plants of North America. He thought he recognized a couple types from the area, and took a detour to gather some. Snow covered the top half of the mountain, which made tracking animals easy, but identifying plants difficult.

He arrived back at the house in the afternoon. After taking care of chores, he did some online legwork for Tommy. In researching all he could find about Lawrence Bertrand, he came across another name: Jason Macmillan

Like Jade Simmons before him, Macmillan left his job to join the DHS...then effectively disappeared off the face of the Earth. His background was not in fringe science, but more traditional law enforcement—first state, then federal. As a Fed he'd been involved in some very shady operations.

The dogs began barking outside, then he heard a droning noise—an engine straining to pull a vehicle uphill on his private drive from the highway below. He changed seats and cued up his security camera feed. He toggled between the cameras and saw a subcompact creeping up his drive. There appeared to be only one person inside but he couldn't tell who it was.

He strapped on the shoulder rig for his sidearm, pulled his jacket over it, and yanked his Mini-14 off the rack before heading outside. He drifted into the woods to the back of his parking area, and took position at a hide which gave him a good view of the drive and parking area, while concealing him fairly well.

When the subcompact pulled up and stopped, he recognized Paul Tareen's daughter, Terry. She remained inside her car, though, staring warily at the two large pit bulls standing stiff-legged on either side of the car, watching her.

Josh broke from cover and strode toward the car, telling the dogs to stand down. Ragnarok and Valkyrie ran back to join him, then matched his pace, one on each flank. He had really hit the jackpot with these dogs. They responded to command very well with minimal training.

Seeing Josh, Terry got out of the car with a dimpled smile and a casserole pot. "Howdy, neighbor!" she called.

Josh slung the rifle around his back and said, "Hey, Terry. Never seen

False Flag - Brown

anyone in your family drive a car before. Thought you did everything on horseback."

She laughed and lifted up the ceramic casserole pot. "I couldn't figure out how to carry this on a horse."

When he reached her, he extended his hand to shake. She hugged him instead. It was a brief contact, but the message was received: she was interested in being more than a handshake kind of neighbor.

"What's that?" he asked, gesturing toward the dish.

"I made apple cobbler," she said, cheerily. "We couldn't finish all of it, so I thought you might like to, before it goes bad."

"Well thanks," he said. "That's real nice of you."

"You're welcome," she said, beaming. He felt guilty that this young, possibly innocent girl was so sprung for him.

"Well, come on inside," he said, waving toward his house. "Might as well visit a spell, since you took the trouble to drive over."

He led her inside. She asked polite questions and made polite comments about his dome home while looking around like a bumpkin in New York City.

Josh retrieved bowls and spoons from the kitchen. "Why don't you have some with me?"

"I guess I'll have a little bit," Terry said, grinning again.

She was a pretty girl, with a natural willowy figure, and more feminine than most of her generation. Her rustic upbringing by a gruff father and no-nonsense mother had gifted her with manners and a degree of humility despite her youthful confidence.

Maybe marriage could live up to the hype with a woman like this. He hoped she would find a man who appreciated what she brought to the table, and not some abusive jerk, alcoholic, or deadbeat.

They chatted as they ate the cobbler at his small table, and he again felt a pang of guilt about her attraction to him.

"Just out of curiosity," he asked, "does your family know you came over here?"

She nodded. "Yeah, why?"

"And they're okay with it?"

She laughed. "They're pretty sure you're not a serial killer, or we wouldn't have had you over for Independence Day."

"How do I know **you're** not a serial killer?" he asked.

She laughed some more. "Don't ever make me mad, or you might find out."

After a couple glances into his eyes, she said "Y'know, it's going to be dark soon. Do you think you can show me how to navigate by the stars?"

By country girl standards, Terry was coming at him with all guns

False Flag - Brown

blazing.

He had given her family a copy of the *Ranger's Handbook,* from which they could learn as much about using the stars as he could teach her. On the 4th of July at their house he had shown her family the basics of land navigation with a compass. He also answered a lot of questions about communications and military tactics, and discussed with Paul teaching them some more skills in the future. They ate a big meal cooked by Terry and her mother, and watched *American Sniper* on the flat screen, too.

"There's not all that much to it," he said, "but that's fine."

What cobbler they didn't finish went into a plastic container, which he stored in the fridge. Terry asked if she could wash the casserole pot and lid in his sink, and volunteered to wash the other dishes, too. He gladly consented, and they continued to chat as she did.

She slyly worked in a few probing questions about Jennifer. Josh answered honestly that he wasn't sure whether they would stay together, or even if they were still officially together right then. He wasn't seeing anyone else, and didn't think Jennifer was, but who could tell, regarding such things?

By the time Terry finished the dishes it was getting dark. They went outside and played with the dogs until it was dark enough to see the constellations clearly. He pointed out what she should be able to see on any clear night in the northern hemisphere, and how to judge direction by their position. The most important object to find was Polaris, the North Star, which was easily done after locating the Big Dipper.

As he pointed things out, she closed the distance until she was backed up against him. Her body language suggested that he should wrap her in his own body heat to fend off the cool evening air. Josh hadn't always been a hermit, so he knew what was going on. And the pleasance of her proximity was overcoming the guilt he'd felt earlier. She was only a few years younger than Jennifer, after all...

Their age difference didn't seem like such a big deal anymore. It was only thoughts of Jennifer that allowed him to keep his hands off Terry.

He said he had work to do, and sent her home. She bid goodbye with a smile that promised she would test his resolve again soon.

Despite himself, it was hard to concentrate on work that night. He went to bed with the idea that it really sucked being alone sometimes, and only then realized that Terry had been the victor in their friendly hormonal struggle.

The next night Josh finished the cobbler, and Jennifer called as he did. When she asked what he was doing he naively answered honestly, and the conversation quickly became an interrogation. Before it was

False Flag - Brown

finished, Jennifer found out where the cobbler came from, who delivered it, what happened afterwards and how long Terry visited that night. Having shown what he thought was respectable restraint, Josh answered her questions honestly, but was on the verge of telling her to mind her own business more than once.

Instead, he went the playful route and took every opportunity to crack jokes and poke fun.

He was tired of being in sexual limbo. He had been content with going Galt before meeting Jennifer, including the whole celibacy aspect. But she had awakened hungers in him which went unresolved for an extended period, and it was kind of satisfying making **her** squirm for a change.

Instead of getting pissy and hanging up in a huff, though, Jennifer said, "I'd like to come visit again this weekend."

Jennifer drove up Friday. She had an interview at a law office in town before coming to his house. He avoided obvious questions like, "Why do you want a job here when you live in Oklahoma?"

He suspected any such question would trigger an ambush she had planned, to instigate the Talk.

But he knew the Talk was inevitable, and probably this weekend, so he instigated it himself when they put Denver and Indy back in the stables after a ride.

It was time to let the other shoe drop. Maybe she would take the deal he was willing to offer. If so, great. More likely, she wouldn't. She could get on with her life and find the perfect supplicating church boy to marry, if that's what she wanted. Josh could go back to being a hermit, or have some fun with Terry once he got over Jennifer...or whatever. He just wanted to **know**, and cut his losses if it wasn't going to work out.

The Talk took them through the evening chores, back into the house, and finished on the couch.

"You've got expectations, right?" he asked, after they'd gone over the love motive extensively. She'd been claiming to be in love with him ever since Indonesia.

"Expectations?" she repeated. "What do you mean?"

He sighed, uncomfortable with these touchy-feely conversations about relationships and other daytime TV fodder. "I mean you want to get married. You've made that pretty obvious. So you must have certain expectations about how it's going to be. What do you expect a husband to bring to the table?"

"You make me sound so demanding," she said.

"**I've** got expectations," he said, shrugging.

False Flag - Brown

"Like what?"

"Fine, Jennifer: I'll go first: Outside of war, nuclear attack, or natural disaster, I'm not moving anywhere."

She almost smiled. "I wouldn't dream of asking you to leave this place."

Jennifer didn't like the cold, but she loved snow. When she visited he would often wake up to find her drinking a cup of coffee just staring out the window at the scenery, bundled up in blankets like an Eskimo even though it was warm in his house.

"Okay, good," he said. "But I'm the king of this castle. I have the last say and the bottom line on decisions, and I expect you to back me up, even if you disagree with me."

She flinched. "You expect me to just keep my mouth shut and do as I'm told?"

"I said king; not tyrant," he replied. "We can talk about stuff. You can tell me what you think. If I see you're right about something, then fine—we'll go with that. But if I listen to all your reasons and still decide on something else, you need to let it drop and not pitch a fit."

"That's not really fair," she said. "You could refuse to admit I'm right, and stick with your decision just to be stubborn."

He shrugged again. "If you can't trust me, then you got no business marrying me."

She mulled this over for a while. "I guess I'm not really against you being king of the castle. But I would expect to be queen."

"I have no problem with that," he said. "Just don't start thinking we're on a chess board."

"What else?" she asked, warily.

He hadn't expected to get past that one. He had been sure she would storm out calling him a sexist pig and plenty other names. Still, she hadn't explicitly agreed to the term, either. He decided not to press her on it right now, because he had plenty more he was sure would bring her claws out.

"I'm not gonna tolerate disrespect from you," he said. "I don't care how mad at me you are, or if you've had a bad day, or if I've done something really stupid. If you're my wife, then you give me respect, period. You can disagree with me or whatever without disrespecting me."

She nodded. Well, that was easier than expected, too.

"You have to put up with my lunacy, " he said. "Because I'll probably never change. My worldview isn't going to change; I'm not giving up my guns; I'm not going to get a national I.D. if it becomes mandatory; I'm not getting kitchen appliances with microchips for the smart grid; I'm not going to register or get permits for anything I already have a right to."

False Flag - Brown

"I've never called you a lunatic, Joshua. I just get scared sometimes because you dwell on gloom and doom stuff so much. I think I ought to get a gun of my own. Something like what Uncle Tommy has, but maybe doesn't kick as hard."

At that point Josh's goal began to transform from scaring Jennifer away as fast and decisively as possible, to seeing if there was actually a glimmer of hope they could be together long-term.

"My rule about cellphones stands," he added. "And anything else that can be used to spy on me. That's a deal-breaker."

This was it. No woman on Earth, once aware of cellular technology and social networks, would ever give them up. They would die first.

She sighed. "I know. What else?"

His jaw dropped. "Do you mean you agree?"

She nodded, frowning. "I'll go along with that. But there's got to be some kind of compromise we can both live with. For now: okay. Anything else?"

"W-well," he stammered, still off balance, "you're not allowed to kick me when I'm down."

"Okay."

He scratched his head. This had gone completely different than he had imagined. Normally he would suspect she was lying just to trap him, but she had proven honest to a fault so far. "I want sex," he said.

"That's part of marriage," she said, with a reserved laugh.

"Well," he licked dry lips, feeling awkward about all this, "I want it often, and I want...you know, passion. You can't just lay there like you're bored or being traumatized."

"I don't think I would be like that," she said.

"You can't be claiming headaches all the time, or you don't 'feel sexy,' or other excuses."

"What if I'm sick?" she asked, with an indignant sharpening of tone. "I'm still expected to...?"

"No, no," he interrupted, shaking his head. "Legitimate reasons are one thing. But you can't use sex as a weapon. It's not a training tool for you to withhold as punishment or give as a reward. It's just something we do. And if you're not gonna enjoy it...if you're not gonna give it a good ol' college try, then I really don't want to go through the trouble. What's the point of us sharing a bed?"

Jennifer chewed on her lip for a moment, then said, "I've got some expectations, if you're done."

"I think those are the big ones," he said, feeling dazed. "If we can agree on those, we can work out the rest."

"Okay," she said. "If I'm going to be your wife, then we have to find a good church somewhere around here, and I expect you to go with me."

This was no surprise. "I can do that. Sundays and Wednesdays?"

"Probably," she said. "We can take a day off now and then. But we might get invited to extra things I want to go to."

"I'd be willing to do that," he said.

She looked relieved. "Also, I'd like you to keep an open mind about it."

"About Christianity?" he asked.

She nodded. "Just give it the benefit of honest consideration, the way you've done with other things you believe."

He shrugged. It seemed like a fair compromise.

"And I would raise our kids to believe in God," she added quickly. "To read the Bible, and believe what's in it."

"You can't force people to believe something, Jennifer. I'm living proof of that."

"That's not what I'm saying," she said, putting her hand on his. "I'm saying I'm going to teach my kids the truth as I see it. When they get old enough, they'll make up their own minds just like we do. But they'll at least have the benefit of the option."

"I'll go along with that," he said.

"You won't try to contradict what I teach them?"

"No, but while we're on the subject of kids..."

"Hold that thought, please," she said, pointing an index finger in the air. "We'll get to that in a minute."

"Okay," he said. "Go for it."

"I won't tolerate abuse," she said. "That's a deal breaker for me."

"That's no prob...wait a minute. Define 'abuse.' Does it include when you don't get your way, or you don't like something I say?"

"You can't hit me," she clarified. "Ever. Or choke me or...manhandle me..."

He waved his hands and shook his head. "Physical rough stuff. I wouldn't ever do that to you."

"But just like you don't want to be disrespected," she added, "you can't be verbally abusive, either."

"What's verbal abuse? Define that."

"I'm not talking about arguments..."

"You mean sarcasm?" he asked. "Because I use sarcasm all the time, even when I'm not upset."

"Sometimes," she said, twisting her lips as if searching for the right words. "Any kind of character assassination directed at me. Anything meant to demean or defame or belittle me."

"Okay."

"I expect faithfulness," she said. "If you're my husband, there can't be any other woman."

"Give me sex on a regular basis and I won't **want** any other women," he said, a bit defensive.

"Joshua, I'm serious. I can't tell you how serious I am about this."

He squeezed her hand. "Same thing on the flip side, though. You have to be faithful, too. No exceptions, no excuses."

"You don't have to worry about that," she said. "Believe me: I've had opportunities."

"I'm on board. But it's a two-way street."

"And just for the record," she said. "Once I'm married, I plan to give my husband all the sex he can handle."

Josh said nothing, but his mind sure was noisy right then.

"I'd like to have three children," she continued. "Maybe more."

"Hmm. Who decides if more and how many more?" Josh asked.

"Something we'd have to agree on. Would you give me at least three?"

Josh thought about it. "Yeah. But what if I decided no more, and you still wanted more?"

She took a deep breath. "If I couldn't convince you, then I guess I'd have to respect your wishes."

He couldn't believe how this was going.

"But we can't argue in front of the kids," she said. "We have to work out disagreements in private, and present a united front to the family."

"Fair enough," Josh said. "And you can teach them Bible stuff, but I'm gonna teach them to shoot, hunt, trap and prep."

She seemed to look a little less worried the further along the conversation went.

"I know you love your privacy," she said, "but I want to be able to have family over."

"Tommy and Linda are welcome here any time," Josh said, with a magnanimous gesture. "Same with Gunther and Carl. And Uncle Jay for that matter. I'm just not so sure about Takoda, though."

"Me neither, right now," Jennifer said. "But what about my mother?"

"If she minds her manners, we can do that."

And we should go there to visit them sometimes, too," Jennifer said. "And you'll have to be sociable."

"Life of the party—that's me."

"And I'll work as a legal assistant; or at whatever job I can find, if you want me to," she continued. "But when we have our first baby, I'm done. I stay home and raise our children after that."

"You mean you don't want to build a career first, and wait until your

30s to start popping them out?"

She shook her head.

He was stunned. He knew Jennifer marched to a different drum, but had no idea she was this divergent from the feminist norm. "Well...how soon do you want to start popping them out?"

"We can spend a year or two just enjoying each other," she said. "But I don't want to wait any longer than that."

"Done. And you don't have to get a job at all if you don't want, baby or not. I make enough consulting to keep the bills paid here."

She cracked a smile. "Done? Does that mean my terms sound acceptable?"

They did. In fact, he was getting excited. Truth be told, she had him at "all the sex you can handle."

With the big concerns dealt with, they moved on to smaller stuff. He felt even better about the whole thing when he found out she didn't want some huge dog-and-pony show of a ceremony. It seemed she understood that the marriage would be more important than the wedding.

As the exchange of terms lightened up and wound down, she snickered a little and said, "You know, I guess you could say what we're both insisting on is an old pre-war, maybe even Puritan, marriage."

"Welcome to the new frontier," he quipped, kissing her hand. "The new counter-culture."

"Well, except for your doomsday prepping, anyway," she said.

Josh snapped his fingers. "Hey, wait right there. I got something for you."

He left her on the couch, went back into his workshop, found what he wanted on the bench next to the soldering iron, and returned to the living room with the customized phone.

"I was saving this for your birthday, but it's ready now." He handed it to her and she stared curiously at it. "I modified it. It's safe to use here at the house or wherever. And you don't need a warranty plan from the carrier. If it breaks, **I'll** fix it."

She turned it on, eyes lighting up before the screen did. "Does it have Internet?"

"Of course," he said, laughing. "It's rooted. You get not only wi-fi but 4G, free. Texting. A few aps. But you can't trust all the aps out there, so you have to check with me before you download anything."

She threw her arms around him and squeezed with surprising strength for her size.

He slapped her on the thigh and stood. "Go get dressed up."

"What?" she asked, tearing her gaze away from the phone to look at him. "Why?"

False Flag - Brown

"I'm taking you to a restaurant in town," he replied. "There's a question I want to ask you there."

False Flag - Brown

31
D MINUS 37
AMARILLO, TEXAS

Joe Tasper eked out a living hauling scrap for a couple years. After the Feds raided his brother's house, and during the subsequent fruitless lawsuit, his brother offered him a job at his sporting goods store in the 'hood. It was a good opportunity for a steady paycheck, some benefits and even paid vacation, and Joe jumped on it.

Usually Joe's brother relied on a delivery service to bring his stock, but with taxes strangling his profits a little more every year, he was cutting corners wherever he could. That's why Joe was driving a box truck packed with free weights, stair-steppers and other heavy stuff that day.

The speed limit was 65, but two cars, one in each lane, traveled at about 60. Joe couldn't get around them because they were side-by-side. Joe changed to the fast lane and crowded the driver in front of him. After a minute or so, that car sped up and passed the other. Joe pushed on the gas to pass both of them.

The timing stunk, because now he was traveling uphill and the truck labored to pull its heavy load. And for whatever reason, now that she was no longer blocking traffic, the other driver found her own accelerator, matching Joe's speed.

Joe sighed and gave it more gas to get around her. The car sped up to remain abreast of him. Joe mashed the pedal to the floor and the burdened motor strained to pull the truck faster. Finally he began to make headway. The car lost pace gradually, but Joe had lost patience to get around it. As the hill crested, the box truck finally found its stride.

Joe widened the gap by a few car lengths and let off the gas. Rolling downhill now, there was no longer a problem. He signaled and switched back to the right lane, letting the truck coast. Once the road leveled out again, gravity would bleed off his momentum and he would just hold it steady when it slowed to the speed limit.

He just wanted to do the speed limit.

Colored lights flashed, nearly scaring the piss out of him. He checked his mirrors and cussed.

Just a couple months ago he'd been pulled over and ticketed for not wearing a seatbelt. That was it: no other reason; just a seatbelt. He hadn't been speeding; hadn't failed to stop at a sign; run a red light; used his cellphone; nothing. Just didn't have a seatbelt on. Over $200 for that.

He made the mistake of asking the cop (who had "To Serve and

False Flag - Brown

Protect" written on his prowl car doors) who exactly was being protected and from what. The cop came back with some rehearsed line about a "click-it or ticket" policy."

Joe pointed out he was driving safely; not endangering anyone.

You were endangering yourself, the cop informed him.

I choose not to press charges, Joe had replied.

The cop turned nasty and threatened him at that point. No surprise there. Why should they have to justify their extortion when they could just hide behind a badge?

The raid on his brother's house came to mind. The Feds were hoping to bust John on some sort of weapons charge, evidently, because they stormed the house at three a.m. when everyone was sound asleep, on a no-knock warrant, and busted into the gun safe before tearing the place apart looking for anything else they could bust him for. Carrie, Joe's seven year old niece, was in her bedroom when one of the masked, armed agents stormed in, tossed the room and stomped Carrie's baby kitten dead right in front of her.

They found nothing illegal. They also made no apology or paid for any of the damage they had caused. The damage done to Carrie's young mind might never be undone.

Cops were the enemy, whether federal, state or local. They had proven as much time and again.

Joe pulled over and got his papers ready. The two cars that had been blocking the lanes a few minutes ago whizzed by, and he cussed them as they went off on their merry ignorant way.

This cop went through the usual bullshit about how he was so concerned for people's safety; what you were doing was dangerous; if I really wanted to be a jerk I could blah blah blah.

Joe just sat there and said nothing. He handed his papers over mechanically and only answered with "yes" and "no." It was no use reasoning with these revenue men. Their whole purpose was to interfere with honest people's livelihood, confiscate their hard-earned wages and work with the insurance companies to make living even more expensive.

After the self-important prick bid goodbye in that practiced phony polite way, Joe grumbled under his breath, "Every dog has his day, pig. One day I might just have mine."

False Flag - Brown

Brigadier General Clayton P. Vine, USMC (retired), spent most of his free time reading through his personal library of military history. He'd been too busy to read the books he collected when on active duty, but after life came to a screeching halt, his biggest challenge was finding distractions to keep him occupied.

He went for a run every morning and went bicycling with his wife most afternoons. He played golf ever so often, but wasn't a fanatic about the game. What he found most interesting was studying US Marine deployments in Vietnam, Korea, and the Pacific during WWII. It seemed there was a limitless supply of books about the Second World War, which filled his schedule nicely.

It took effort, day after day, to avoid becoming bitter about how he'd been sacked.

Vine routinely went online to research something specific mentioned in a book. A couple times he tried searching for information on other officers who were forced into retirement for the same reason he had been. As a side effect of these searches, he met other retired commanders online.

One officer he got to know through email had resigned his commission way back in 2009 over Obama's illegitimacy. "Birthers" had always made Vine uncomfortable, but the man buried Vine with information about the self-declared "foreign student" status, the multiple fake social security numbers, the obviously fraudulent birth certificate, and the ongoing coverups. Vine still believed that what a man **did** was more important than where he came from. For Vine, the birther arguments simply added evidence of a consistent hostility toward the law by the highest officials in the land.

Of course, that was all old news, now. Maybe it mattered, but few people could be convinced it mattered. And really, it was too late anyway. If the Bill Clinton legacy was any indication, Obama's record would be completely whitewashed by those who wrote the history. And succeeding presidents would get worse and worse until...

Another former officer Vine met online had been sacked as he had, and for the same reason.

In Vine's dialog with these men, both mentioned something called "Oathkeepers." Vine grew curious, and did some research on the organization.

Before his career ended, Vine would have dismissed the Oathkeepers as a group of malcontents with nothing better to do. But when it came right down to it, Vine had been purged from the Corps for the very reason that he refused to violate his oath.

His curiosity got the better of him, so one evening he attended a meeting.

The group met in a rented storefront at a strip mall. Less than a dozen people showed up. When the meeting came to order, first time attendees were asked to stand up and introduce themselves. Vine and a couple others did.

The meeting was dull and Vine regretted coming. They talked about petitions and delegates and calling Congressmen and getting out the word about this and that.

The one good thing about civilian life was that Vine no longer had to sit through tedious meetings if he didn't want to. So he wouldn't be coming back.

But out of politeness, Vine remained seated until the meeting broke up.

On his way to the door, two men intercepted him. They were both maybe 10-15 years younger than Vine. One had a high-and-tight haircut like his, and popped bubblegum. The other had a more lax civilian haircut and a cocky sneer carved permanently into his face. Both wore huge wristwatches.

The gum chewing man extended his hand first. "*Semper Fi*, sir. Glad you came out tonight. My name's Wade Haugen." He tapped the arm of the other man. "This here's Gordo Puttcamp."

Vine grinned and shook Haugen's hand. "*Semper Fi*. Pilots, right? And you're obviously in the Corps."

"**Was**, sir," Haugen replied. "But you're right. I flew Harriers. This clown here was Air Force. I don't even know what kind of garbage they call aircraft in that outfit."

They exchanged *bona fides*, and a few more friendly wisecracks.

Puttcamp extended his hand. "Nice to meet you, sir. Even if you served in the wrong branch."

Vine shook his hand and chuckled. He could relate to these men.

"See," Haugen said, elbowing Puttcamp. "Why do you say 'served'? That's like a dead giveaway you weren't in the Corps."

"You say that as if it's not a compliment," Puttcamp said.

"Anyway, sir," Haugen said, "what brings you by?"

"Curiosity," Vine said. "And I'm sure you men are accomplishing good things here. I just don't think it's for me."

The two pilots exchanged a look, as if something they'd previously speculated on had just been confirmed.

False Flag - Brown

"We were gonna go grab a beer," Haugen said. "If you don't have somewhere else to be, sir, how 'bout you knock one back with us?"

That sounded great to Vine. He didn't normally hang out in bars, but these two kind of reminded him of his marines. And he really missed his marines.

They took over a table at a sports bar a few stores down the strip mall, and had some generic conversation before Haugen asked about Vine's retirement.

Vine thought about the mealy-mouthed civilian errand boy and his threat, and almost immediately decided, "Screw him and the dog he rode in on." He told the former jet jocks plainly about his sacking, and why it happened.

The pilots exchanged another look, frowning this time.

"I've been hearing that's going on," Haugen said, "but took it with a grain of salt, because there's a whole lot of cockeyed scuttlebutt getting mixed into what's happening."

"Aliens," Puttcamp said, bugging his eyes out. "Lizard people. Fake moon landings. Elvis lives!"

Haugen ignored his friend and said, "I wondered if it was a coincidence. The timing of your retirement, I mean. What exactly was the acid test, if you don't mind me asking?"

"The little civilian *pogue* beat all around the bush," Vine said. "Getting him to just come out and say it was like pulling teeth. So I asked him myself: 'You want to make sure I'm willing to have my boys open fire on American citizens, right?' He finally said yes, that was the $64,000 Question."

Haugen whistled, then turned to Puttcamp. "Here it is, man. Straight from a reliable source."

Vine didn't mention the blackmail, because he was more ashamed than ever of what happened in Japan.

"To be honest, sir," Puttcamp said, solemnly, "we don't care much for the activist stuff at the Oathkeeper meetings either. What makes it worthwhile; the reason we go; is networking."

Vine squinted at him. "Networking?"

"Making contacts," Haugen said. "Like we did with you, tonight. You got skills. We got skills. There might come a day when we need to pool our skills. I don't know much about infantry tactics like you do. But I **do** know something about close air support. See what I'm saying?"

Vine wasn't sure he understood. Maybe he didn't want to understand. "We're civilians now," he said. "Our skill-pooling days are over."

Haugen contorted his face into a pained expression and popped

False Flag - Brown

another bubble in his gum.

"Humor us for a minute, General," Puttcamp said. "You're right—we're civilians. Now think back to when they retired you. The condition they gave you for your continued service was your willingness to wage war on who?"

"Civilians," Vine said, quietly. "American civilians."

"We're all Americans, right?" Puttcamp asked, exchanging glances with the other two men. "Right? Next question: do you like the idea of, say, a regiment of US Marines coming after you with guns blazing?"

Vine took a swig of beer but said nothing.

"Or U.S. Army troops, for that matter," Puttcamp said.

"Bring 'em on," Haugen cracked, making a muscle.

"Or an armored division," Puttcamp suggested.

Haugen shrugged. "Well, I guess if they ran over me with a few tanks, it might slow me down."

"Here's the point, General Vine," Puttcamp went on. "If they're firing senior field commanders who refuse to make war on American citizens, might it be within the realm of possibility that somebody is planning to make war against American citizens?"

Vine was silent for a while.

What other answer could there be?

Vine feared that answer from the day of the errand boy's visit. He didn't want to deal with it. So he ignored it. But now there it was, staring him right in the face.

The pilots nodded at each other again. "We've been where you're at, sir," Haugen said. "We didn't want to believe what's happened to our country, either. I still wish it was all a bad dream or a crackpot theory."

"The Oathkeepers are mostly on the fence, too," Puttcamp said. "They don't want to believe the signs all around them. They're clutching at straws. They're hoping all this paper-shuffling they do is going to turn everything around and make it right again. God bless 'em. It's too little and probably at least 40 years too late, but you gotta admire them for their optimism."

Puttcamp knocked back some more beer before continuing. "But see, their hearts are in the right place. And when they've got no more straws to clutch at anymore and their brains acknowledge reality...we're gonna need them. They have skills, too. They're veterans and cops with the integrity to honor the oath they took."

"You're talking revolution," Vine said, in a gruff voice many senior military men used to mask their own fear.

"Technically, no," Haugen said. "The revolutionaries are in Washington, and the State Capitol, and City Hall. The revolution's been going on for a century, waged from the other side. Quietly, while we've been asleep. But there's no way to pull off the final stage of it without making a whole lot of noise. That's why they've been positioning their forces so quietly for so long, to make it happen sudden and all across the front, with minimal resistance."

The last time Vine had heard talk anything like this, it was from his father. It all sounded more crazy than he wanted to believe it could be; yet the evidence was all over the place. "Then you're talking civil war," he said.

"Maybe," Haugen said. "I guess it depends if enough people like us can pull ourselves away from our big screen TVs long enough to fight."

"Technically," Puttcamp interjected, "everybody's probably gonna lose their TV reception for a while. And other luxuries. And plenty of necessities, come to think of it."

Haugen rolled his eyes. "My point was, there may be no significant resistance if we're all too busy with bread and circuses. In our case, beer and videogames; or porn and social networks. Whatever." He now directed his attention back to Vine. "I hate to admit it, but Air Farce here is probably right: when the dollar collapses, there'll be chaos for a while, and they'll let us learn what discomfort is **really** like before they come in with the solution they've wanted to give us all along. We'll be starving, freezing, killing each other over a scrap of food, until the brain-dead survivors, who've been raised by the idiot box and government schools, **beg** for martial law, regulated distribution of resources, civilian disarmament...the whole nine yards."

"Conspiracy theory," Vine said, thoughtfully. "That's what you're talking about."

"You can believe it's all happening by accident and coincidence if it helps you sleep better," Puttcamp said with a shrug. "But it's happening, for whatever reason."

"I read on the Internet about FEMA internment camps," Vine said. "It just sounds like fearmongering to me."

"A lot of the rumors floating around **are**, sir," Haugen said, with a nod toward Puttcamp. "Mix in enough silly garbage about space aliens and the Elders of Zion, and it discredits everybody who doubts this is all coincidence, doesn't it? Almost like somebody **wants** to discredit whistleblowers, maybe?"

"I don't know if all the stories about FEMA are true," Puttcamp said. "But I know some stuff happened after Hurricane Katrina that wasn't legal, and those involved still aren't allowed to talk about it. And I've flown over some facilities that sure look a lot like internment camps...that weren't charted on any map I've seen."

Vine stared at the label on his beer bottle. "Men, I've read history, so I know about what happened in Russia, and Germany, and China. But this is America."

"What you're saying is that it can't happen here, right?" Puttcamp challenged.

Vine set the bottle down a little too forcefully, so that it made a loud thud. "Damn right."

"You'd be right, if this was 50 years ago," Haugen said. "Even 30 years ago. But hell sir, it's no longer a question of if it **can** happen here. It's happening."

"We've got checks and balances against centralized power," Vine said. "We've got rights protected in the Constitution, that every public servant has to swear an oath to uphold..."

His words trailed off, and he never finished the thought.

Neither pilot stated the obvious. They didn't have to. Vine wasn't stupid; just...willfully ignorant.

False Flag - Brown

Joshua spent a week with the Scarred Wolf family, partly so he could be there to give them the news personally, a week before he and Jennifer tied the knot.

Jennifer's friends and relatives had mixed reactions about her engagement to Josh. It surprised most of them, who assumed Josh wasn't right for her.

Michael Fastwater wasn't surprised. He also seemed to be the most pleased by the news. Gunther was happy for both of them, while Takoda only shook his head and made a scoffing noise.

A natural, accomplished multitasker, Jennifer set about planning the wedding without letting it distract her from enjoying family. At Josh's insistence they wouldn't acquire a marriage license from the state. They would have a small ceremony in the church Jennifer had been attending for years, and would make sure the local paper printed it in the announcement section. Of course there would be pictures and videos posted online, too. Since it was a simple affair, not much notice was required. The preacher scheduled their nuptials for later in the week, after he'd counseled them. Most of Jennifer's planning involved her change of residence.

Tommy found it hard to take much time off, with one of his deputies still on medical leave. another one on vacation, and a heavy workload. Josh joined him at the office for a few days in a row, and they pooled their efforts to fill in the gaps on Lawrence Bertrand, the people working under him, and what he might be planning.

Josh had the ninja hacking skills and Tommy had the official channels and investigative experience. They were careful to avoid the official channels as much as possible, in order not to be compromised, but the detective brain came in handy.

There was too much information, and not enough. There were multiple possibilities for false flag operations but little specific poop to narrow it down to any helpful degree.

"Maybe they're not even planning something," Tommy said, yawning, after a frustrating number of hours fishing around for a clue. "I'm stumped. How could they have ever been truly afraid of me finding out their plans? We haven't uncovered anything better than what's already on the World Wide Web."

"Depends what part of the World Wide Web," Josh replied, standing to stretch. "Most of what's out there is disinformation."

False Flag - Brown

"Well, it sure looks like they've overestimated me," Tommy said. "If they're even..." He exhaled a big breath and stood to stretch, himself. He wanted to believe there were no malevolent efforts to do harm to him or the country. But there was that little matter of the assassination attempt; and being framed for a cop-killing overseas; and the murder of his brother. There was no choice but to believe it. Tommy didn't aspire to self-delusion.

"I appreciate all the work you've been doing on this, Josh," Tommy said. "We might as well call it a day. How 'bout I buy you a burger before we head home?"

"Sounds good to me," Josh replied, hands against his stomach. "You're a slave-driver."

Tommy shut down his work computers, touched base with the dispatcher, and checked on a few other matters. Then they walked out to the parking lot together.

Tommy playfully body-checked his old friend as they walked. "Big day for you coming up, huh?"

"Yeah. Uh-oh. Is this the speech where you threaten me?"

"I wouldn't be much of an uncle if I didn't, right?"

"Well," Josh said, with a slight grin, "if I ever did hurt Jennifer, I'd hope you **would** kill me. Or scalp me, or something."

Tommy shook his head and simply said, "I know you'll take care of her, *nijenina*. Even Michael Fastwater is in your corner. He thinks you're just what she needs. That you'll protect her and give her children and all that stuff."

"And keep her in line?" Josh quipped.

Tommy, only half-joking, said, "I think it's **her** that'll keep **you** in line."

"Good one, Chief."

Instead of getting in his Blazer, Tommy leaned against it. "How long have you believed this conspiracy stuff?"

Josh stopped and faced his friend. "Since before my tour in Iraq was over. Why?"

"It's just that most conspiracy nuts can't shut up about it," Tommy said.

"I was that way for a while," Josh said.

"I'd call you 'high-functioning' if I was a shrink. You don't even talk about it much."

"Thanks," Josh said, sarcastically. "I only talk about it if I have to. You're used to the idealists, right? Who think they can save the world if only they can wake people up?"

"You don't want to wake people up?" Tommy asked.

False Flag - Brown

"Sure. I'd love to wake them up. I'd also like to ride a flying unicorn to the land of Oz and have a weekend pass in the Emerald City. People don't want to be woken up, Tommy. They consider you the enemy when you try."

"So, because they call you crazy, you just give up?"

"That's not the gist of it, by a long shot," Josh replied. "They call you crazy or stupid or whatever. You show them the patterns of history. Just coincidence, they say. You show them the consistent patterns of foreign and domestic policy, and who is responsible for it. They either think it's ushering us toward utopia, or it's all coincidence, accidentally brought about by misguided, well-intentioned dummies. So you show them evidence of what those 'dummies' are doing behind the scenes to make it all happen; they call you crazy and dismiss it as just silly harmless games played by the rich and powerful. And you're stupid and crazy for assuming it's more than just coincidence when what those people want to happen actually happens, consistently. So you show them quotes from the insiders, revealing their motives, their intentions, and sometimes their methods. They laugh you off and call you stupid and crazy for taking it seriously. You point out that stuff you warned them about years ago has happened, or is happening. They get mad at you for believing it happened for the reasons you said it would. Then, the ultimate smack-down: you find that rare person, who's not deranged, but has opened their eyes and sees what's going on...and they tell you it's wrong to prepare for what's coming, or to take action against it."

Tommy studied his friend's eyes for a moment. They didn't have the youthful light in them they used to, though he still looked very young, otherwise.

"What's the point?" Josh asked. "I don't particularly enjoy beating my head against a rock. It's easier to deceive someone than to convince them they've been deceived."

"Mark Twain," Tommy said, with a half-hearted grin.

"You like that one? Here's another one: 'repeat a lie often and loud enough, and it becomes the truth.' I can't compete with years, decades of programming."

"See, when you say stuff like that, you sound like the typical tinfoil hat type."

Josh shrugged. "I know. Trigger warnings and all that, right? From my perspective, though, when I see otherwise reasonably intelligent people cling so desperately to irrational assumptions in order to dismiss evidence right in front of their face...to me it smacks of conditioning."

"I can't deny what happened to me and Vince," Tommy said. "I just don't believe in this big, overarching plot to take over the world, by the Bilderbergers or whoever."

False Flag - Brown

"I rest my case."

"No, hang on," Tommy said. "I don't buy the official story that Oswald acted alone. The official story about *Benghazi* is ludicrous. I get that."

"No, Tommy. The official story is right. Just ask the people responsible—they'll tell ya. Ask the people in bed with those responsible—they'll tell ya, too. You tinfoil asshat."

"Politicians don't think past the next election," Tommy said, ignoring Josh's sarcasm. "Conspiracies, by their very nature, have to be very short-lived. Most criminals can't even keep a secret, when their freedom depends on them keeping their mouths shut. The more people involved, and the longer it goes on, the more likely it is that somebody will talk, or slip up."

"Somebody like David Rockefeller?" Josh suggested. "Or Carroll Quigley? Edward Mandell House? Walter Cronkite? Hillary Clinton? Want me to keep going? You mean people who talked or slipped up like **that**?"

Tommy almost, instinctively, dismissed anything those people might have said as grandiose posing and braggadocio by blue bloods in exclusive country clubs or sophomoric secret fraternities. In other words: a silly, harmless game being acted out by the rich and powerful.

"I'm not gonna call you crazy or stupid," Tommy said. "I just don't buy this James Bond SPECTRE business."

"And why is that?"

"You believe this conspiracy really got underway in 1913, right? When the Federal Reserve Act and Income Tax got pushed through while most of Congress was gone on Christmas leave."

"That was the big turning point in America," Josh said. "But it goes back much farther. To before the French Revolution."

"It's just far-fetched that so many people would invest themselves in this plan, and try to keep it secret, for so long," Tommy said, shrugging.

"I have an even more far-fetched scenario," Josh said. "Let's say that generations of adults, all around the world, of different nationalities, religions, or tribal affiliations, who speak different languages, and who mostly have never even met or heard of each other, all carry out an unspoken agreement with fanatic uniformity to perpetuate some kind of deception. Let's make it something really ridiculous. Let's say the lie they all commit to spreading and maintaining is that a magical fat man from the North Pole uses flying reindeer to deliver presents to good little children all over the planet at the stroke of Midnight once a year; and that all those toys are contained in one sack that he slings over his shoulder."

Tommy frowned and didn't answer right away. "You can't compare a

False Flag - Brown

harmless children's fable to a plot to enslave the entire world."

"I'm not comparing the fable itself," Josh said. "Just the conspiracy to hoodwink a whole class of people gullible enough to fall for it."

"Whatever. You know what I mean."

"So the capacity for generations of insiders to maintain a lie doesn't bother you," Josh said. "The part you can't believe is that people would ever use that capacity for something that might **harm** others. Because people are basically good. They never act out of contempt, arrogance or self-interest. And they certainly wouldn't dream of doing harm to someone else. Especially powerful people. The more powerful they get, the more sterling their character. And they wouldn't be allowed to become rich or powerful in the first place if they weren't nice, honest, transparent people to begin with, who indulge only in 'harmless' behavior. Is that consistent with what you've learned about human nature as a cop?"

Tommy sighed. "I forgot what a sarcastic prick you are. Feel better? Let's go eat."

Josh turned to his own car. "Hey, you got me started. You asked for it."

"Yeah," Tommy said, climbing in his car. "I did."

Despite the seemingly fruitless investigative work, Josh enjoyed himself during the vacation more than he had since farther back than he could remember.

Then the Big Day arrived.

The wedding was a mixture of Christian teaching and Shawnee customs. Jennifer had enlisted the help of her mother and Linda, and had sewn costumes of bleached doeskin for herself, Josh and some of the witnesses. Tommy and Linda still had theirs from long ago, and Tommy still fit in his. Linda's needed sone alteration around the hips.

During the ceremony the grinning bridal party danced for the blank-faced groomsmen, each woman singling out her male counterpart for a flirtatious retro-twerk.

Josh had always been attracted to Jennifer's mind and disposition. And she was attractive enough physically, too. He sometimes thought of her as a short, Native American <u>Princess Leia</u>...only **she** would politely suggest that Luke Skywalker blow a hole in the garbage chute so they could jump in and escape the Death Star's garrison of Storm Troopers, instead of yanking the blaster out of his hands to do it herself.

But that day, with her hair down and fixed just right, her curves showing through the beaded doeskin shift, and wearing a radiant smile, her beauty was stunning. He was crazy about her, and supposed it was safe now to admit it to Jennifer...and himself.

The reception was small and quick, but everyone seemed to have a good time--even Takoda, though his relationship to his family was still strained. Jennifer's mother cried, and got her daughter crying for a while, too; but overall it was a happy send-off.

The honeymoon was one of many odd compromises that the couple made to get things done quickly and efficiently. They drove separately in order to haul all of Jennifer's belongings to Colorado in one trip. But they stopped at a hotel along the way and spent a couple nights there.

The first day back on the mountain was spent getting Jennifer settled in the house. Right away she began to implement a redecoration scheme. But Josh didn't mind, because she jumped in with both feet on tasks like cleaning, cooking, and food rotation. For the first time he understood that old saying he'd heard somewhere: "A man can build a house; but it takes a woman to make it a home."

She seemed to be happy, and was making him happy. He hoped it lasted.

MIAMI, FLORIDA

Lawrencel Bertrand had his choice of who to play golf with, right up to the President's handlers. It was important that he made such appearances now and then, but he preferred playing with those of a lower rank. It let him concentrate more on the game, and the lower castes did all the sweating.

There were other factors, too. The press was always hanging around the President, for instance. It's not that Bertrand was worried about them reporting anything he might say, but it just made sense not to have certain conversations with them around. One of them might tip some cool ones at a local watering hole, and tell tales out of school. There were too many leaks already.

Also, he didn't like kowtowing to the trained, polished little Crack Addict in Chief. They got their marching orders from the same source, through most of the same channels and the pathetic creep could never hack it anywhere true leadership was more important than image and speech-giving.

Bertrand scored a birdie on the third hole and removed his gloves, sitting in the cart to admire the blue sky. There was a nasty winter coming and for some people it was already here. But in Florida the birds were singing, the sun was warm, the grass was green and golf was never interrupted.

His cellphone rang and he checked the caller I.D. It was from his shop at the Data Center. "This is Director Bertrand. What is it?"

The underling introduced himself and said, "Sorry to bother you, sir, but just thought you'd want to know this. There's been some concentrated activity directed toward sensitive information over the last couple days. No breaches into our secure sites...unless they're good enough to do it without detection. But there've been a lot of searches related to subjects that concern unlisted assets, as well as yourself."

That was not surprising by itself. Bloggers were always snooping around. It was routine to identify them and build a profile; but the only immediate action to be taken was by the Nerd Squad...it wasn't his problem.

"And?"

"And we're not going to be able to build a profile on the surfer I'm telling you about, sir. He's managed to send us on a wild goose chase. Whatever I.P. he actually searched from has been effectively cloaked."

"Hmm. That is noteworthy," Bertrand said.

"I hope you know, sir, that there are several hackers out there who can mask their I.P., and we don't disturb you about them. But this one is trolling for information that's close to home. I'm not sure what I can do about it, if anything, so I thought at least you ought to know about it."

"You did the right thing," Bertrand said. "That's good initiative on your part. Don't be afraid to call me on things like this."

He asked to be read a list of the search terms used, and sites visited. He thanked his subordinate again and hung up.

On the cart ride to the next hole, Bertrand mulled this over. He couldn't be sure who was poking around through his back yard, but he couldn't help thinking of that damned elusive Indian from Oklahoma. He probably should have done what it takes to finish him, blowback or not.

It was a little harder to blunt public sympathy when the target wasn't white. But only a little. He could still be implicated in something. Or maybe an accident could be arranged. The bigger problem was that the redskin nuisance had run for sheriff, and won. Now Chief Fly-in-the-Ointment was higher profile, and any corrective action would invite too much scrutiny from the rogue elements out there.

More and more were listening to the rogue elements. It made business tricky and sticky.

Plus, the Indian had seemingly settled down, content to mind his own business. Maybe he still was, and somebody else was snooping. The Indian hadn't been asking questions or otherwise investigating through official channels. He'd been very careful in that regard, in fact.

False Flag - Brown

Bertrand had reasoned that, so long as the Indian behaved himself, he wouldn't need to be dealt with until the gloves came off for everybody. But news like what he heard from the Data Center made loose ends bother Bertrand even more than normal.

And quiet and well-behaved or not, the Indian was a loose end.

Bertrand had never completely let go of Tommy Scarred Wolf. He had people who talked to people, who had the Chief of the Tribal Police working an angle on him. But absolutely nothing had come of that, so far. It was time to be a little more diligent.

False Flag - Brown

34
D MINUS 21
RICHMOND, VIRGINIA

DeAngelo Jeffries maintained a steady connection with Jake McCallum since meeting him in the hospital overseas. He stopped by to visit when possible, called every couple weeks and emailed in between. From what he heard, McCallum was doing a great job and the shooters on his team liked him. He served no-knock warrant after no-knock warrant, making several collars and confiscating some nice hardware.

Today DeAngelo had to put on a different face. He couldn't come at this like a buddy. And he couldn't do it in their usual casual venue over chicken wings and beer, either. He had McCallum meet him at an office in the local substation.

"What's up?" Mac asked when he got there and folded his massive frame into the chair beside DeAngelo's desk.

"We got problems," DeAngelo said. He didn't affect the Ebonics or ghetto accent this time. That didn't fit the frame he built for this meeting.

"I didn't squeeze you for information when we first met. I was easy on you; accepted the song you sang after getting your story straight with the white girl. That's coming back to bite me, now."

Mac scratched his cheek. "How so?"

"Your war buddy, Scarred Wolf, is involved in something we can't ignore."

Mac looked skeptical. DeAngelo had to work this carefully.

The girls had been questioned about everything that happened in Indonesia and on the boat ride back. They were confused about the whole deal and their memories jumbled--normal for a traumatic experience when you've been drugged and raped. So they couldn't provide much detail and they weren't even sure about the names of all Scarred Wolf's accomplices. Questioning the son, Gunther, and the niece, Jenny, had been futile. They acted like they didn't remember much, either. But it was just an act.

The interrogations went nowhere. But the other girls remembered just enough of the interactions between accomplices to give DeAngelo an angle.

He had to play it just right or Mac would clam up, too.

"How long has he been affiliated with hate groups?" DeAngelo asked.

"Hate groups?"

"Like white supremacists. That kind of thing."

Mac grimaced at him. "I don't know where you're getting that. First of all, Tommy's not white. Kind of disqualifies him, don't you think?"

False Flag - Brown

"You don't understand, Mac. He hangs out with those kind of people."

Mac's eyebrows furrowed, and DeAngelo saw the flicker of doubt he hoped for.

"And at least one of those kind of people were with you and him in Indonesia," DeAngelo went on. "Weren't they?"

"Tell me what's going on, DeAngelo."

DeAngelo leaned back in his chair and waited for a moment, so that he'd appear to be considering whether or not to share what he said next. "One of Scarred Wolf's gun nut buddies is active in an Aryan Nation cell. They've been collecting explosives. Enough to kill a lot of people. There's reason to suspect they're going to do just that if we don't get a handle on them quick."

Mac looked part skeptical, part horrified. "Are you sure about this?"

DeAngelo feigned anger. "Look, man, I'd expect that kind of shit from a white man. Don't go there, Mac. This is brother-to-brother. I don't snow you; you don't snow me."

Mac sighed. "There is one guy. Right-wing whack-job. I never did figure out how a redneck like that could be friends with Tommy."

"I doubt if he's really a friend," DeAngelo said. "Who can say how these sick minds work. What's his name?"

Mac sighed again. "Rennenkampf. First name Josh or John or something like that."

DeAngelo jotted something down in his notepad. "What's his connection to Scarred Wolf?"

"They were in Fifth Group together. Same A-Team."

"That's Fifth Special Forces Group?"

Mac nodded.

Still writing, DeAngelo asked, "Got anything else on him? Address? Phone number? email?"

Mac shook his head. "I think he lives in the mountains somewhere, but don't know for sure. If he ever said more, I don't remember."

"Why in the mountains, do you think?"

"Well, his call sign was 'Mountain Man.' On the radio. Doesn't mean anything, I guess."

"Who else went with you?" DeAngelo knew six men touched ground inside Indonesia, including Scarred Wolf's son and brother who was killed. He had a good idea who the rest of them were, but his superiors needed confirmation and they needed whatever other information they could get.

Mac shook his head. "Rennenkampf is the one. If anybody is involved in DomTer stuff, it would be him."

"We need to know everything," DeAngelo said. "You might be right.

False Flag - Brown

That's fine. If so, that's great. But that's not your call, Mac. You were in Delta—you know intelligence gathering doesn't work like that. Don't strain our friendship just because you want to avoid looking like a snitch."

Threatening their relationship was a gamble. He needed Mac a lot more than Mac needed him. But big gambles were sometimes necessary on the road to change.

Mac thought it over and DeAngelo let him have a few seconds. He would browbeat a man of lesser intelligence and not give him time to think. But Mac might balk at a hard sell. DeAngelo would just give him a nudge or two, let Mac ponder the guy he already didn't trust, and basically let him talk himself into giving the others up.

"Suppose Scarred Wolf is clean, Mac. In that case, do you really want him at risk from this psycho? Or the others might get blindsided, if they're clean."

Mac continued to mull it over.

"With what's happening out there to our people," DeAngelo said, with an expansive gesture meant to include the entire country, "and what's about to happen in Amarillo when that verdict comes in...you know they're gonna let those white bastards walk. With all that, and worse, building up every day, you really want to let the White Man get away with another one?"

After a few cycles of nudge-and-wait, Mac talked. When he finished, DeAngelo was confident he had spilled all he knew.

False Flag - Brown

35
D MINUS 20
LAS ANIMAS COUNTY, COLORADO

Joshua did his best to be sociable at the little church down the road Jennifer had found. When visitors were asked to stand up, he did so. Jennifer teased him for blushing, afterwards.

Josh sat through the singing, and the announcements, and the praying, and was able to pay attention to the sermon. Then toward the end, the preacher said something so stupid it was shocking. Josh turned right and left to observe the reactions of the people in the congregation.

After the service was over and they were driving home, Jennifer asked him, "So, what did you think?"

"Next," Josh replied, simply.

"What does that mean?" she asked, frowning.

"It means let's try a different one next week."

She studied him for a moment, then asked, "What was it you didn't like?"

"That preacher's dirty," he said.

"Dirty? Why do you say that?"

"He's either dirty or stupid. And he seems to be fairly intelligent."

She stared at him, awaiting further explanation.

"You didn't catch his little plug for <u>government control of the Internet</u>?"

"Oh," she said. "Well, Joshua..."

"Well, nothing. You see how he appealed to emotion there, saying how he didn't like the idea of teenagers being able to look at porn? Oh sure, **that's** what it's really about. And who would dare challenge him after framing it that way? Who wants to be accused of supporting pornography for teenagers?"

"Pornography is a huge problem," Jennifer said. "Have you seen the statistics?"

"Give me a break," Josh said. "You guys really believe that giving the government control over who can say what means that it's gonna be Christian-friendly censorship? The government's got control over plenty of other stuff already—how's that working out for you? Pornography's the last thing they're worried about."

"I guess that **was** a little manipulative," Jennifer admitted, "framing it that way."

"The Internet is the one leak they just haven't been able to plug," Josh said. "Too many whistles are getting blown in alternative media, so they have to shut it down. That's what it's about, period. And you're either

201

really stupid if you fall for this smokescreen about porn, or you approve of what they're trying to do, so you're regurgitating their lies."

"Still, calling him 'dirty' is kind of harsh," Jennifer said.

"It is what it is," Josh said. "Did Jesus help spread deception for the Romans, to keep his tax-exempt status? 'Cause if he did, that's not a god I'm gonna follow."

"Okay. We'll try another church next time."

"Why does it have to be in a fancy building, anyway?" Josh asked.

"You thought the building was fancy?" Jennifer asked. "I didn't."

"Well, why all the formality, is what I'm asking. Is that the way Jesus wanted you to do church?"

Jennifer thought about this for a few moments. "Actually, the church was underground for the first couple centuries, I guess. A lot of Christians were martyred, so they met in secret, kind of. Like they have to do in China, or the Muslim countries. You've seen the fish symbol everywhere, right?"

Josh nodded, sneering. "Yeah. Some real asshole drivers put it on their cars."

"Language, please," she admonished. "Anyway, you know where that came from?"

"Didn't Jesus tell his first followers to become fishers of men?"

"Good!" she said, smiling. "That's right. But also, when you ran into somebody on the road in the Roman Empire, but didn't know if you could speak freely with them, you would draw half of that fish symbol in the dirt with your foot while you talked. If they drew the other half of it, then you knew it was a fellow believer, and you could trust them."

"Sounds Masonic," Josh said. "Secret gestures and handshakes and all that."

"Well, it wasn't Masonic. It was way before the Free Masons. And it was to keep themselves and their families from getting fed to the lions— not to keep secrets or ace job interviews or win court cases."

"Funny you should bring this up," Josh said. "You know you're gonna have to go underground again, right?"

"They'd never crack down on the Church in America," Jennifer said. "People here would go crazy."

"They have to be subtle and gradual about everything in America," Josh said, thumbing over his shoulder. "The frog is already boiling, though. But anyway, just like in the Soviet Union, they'll give organized religion a pass. Guys like that preacher back there who sell out and do as they're told—they'll be allowed to go on, so long as they toe the line. If you want the real deal, though, you're gonna have to break free of the formal structure."

False Flag - Brown

"That's your answer for everything, Joshua."

"From what you just told me, it was the answer for the folks Jesus taught, too."

They fell silent. Joshua pondered the fish symbol identification. As someone for whom communication was a preoccupation for most of his life, it fascinated him.

He genuinely believed that Christianity would have to go underground again, or be thoroghly corrupted—just like genuine patriotism.

What would the equivalent of that "challenge and password" be in modern times?

False Flag - Brown

36
D MINUS 13
AMARILLO, TEXAS

To Ken Fowler, it seemed the whole world was waiting for the verdict on the trial of Delton Williams's killers. And everybody had an opinion on how it would go. Ken kept the store open but tuned to a cable news channel a half hour before the verdict was scheduled to be announced.

Ken had gotten out of the cable business two years before. He used his savings to open a store that sold cellphones, tablets and accessories. He managed to save enough because he was frugal; worked overtime whenever it was available; had no expensive habits; was unmarried with no kids; and avoided long-term relationships.

He opened the store not quite in the hood, but in the inner city, because he couldn't afford rent in a fancy suburban strip mall. It turned out to be as good a place for that business as anywhere else. Plenty of college aged kids rented cheap apartments in the area, and even hood rats just had to have the latest gadget. Taxes and regulations made it hard to turn a profit for any small business, but Ken chose the right product to sell, and he remained frugal.

A couple doors down from him was a sporting goods store, which seemed to do good business for such an urban environment. And as outdoorsy as the neckbeards and their treehugger girlfriends were who patronized the place, they couldn't live without the latest technological doo-dad, either. Ken got some decent overflow business from there.

Today, however, business was light. It might be best to close early to plywood over the windows and front door before the verdict was announced. His store was a few miles away from where Delton Williams was beaten, but riots could spread.

***

Surrounding the Amarillo Courthouse, and other government buildings, was a small army of police. They wore body armor, combat helmets and ballistic glasses. They bore pistols, shotguns, carbines or grenade launchers for tear gas shells. They were backed by MRAP vehicles, some mounted with water cannons. It was a scene that just didn't look right in America.

Jurors, attorneys, city government officials and other V.I.P.s exited the Courthouse inside the thick blue lines. They got in their vehicles surrounded by phalanxes of cops and blew town before the news broke, some with police escort.

False Flag - Brown

There was no snow on the ground in Amarillo, but it was chilly. In the 'hood most everyone stayed indoors watching the TV. No shouting, cussing, woofer bumping or sirens echoed through the streets. Almost nobody could be seen outdoors, hanging out or wandering in the alleys. Some of the drunks even sobered up for the occasion.

It wasn't coincidence or osmosis that had the inner city all on the same sheet of music. Their marching orders had come by committee. From the veiled, non-committal statements by the Attorney General down to the blatant declarations of the Panthers, Crips and community organizers of various affiliations (most of whom came in from out of town for the occasion), people who were normally at each other's throats sat prepared to spring into collective action when the verdict was announced.

The talking heads on television announced that the police involved in the fatal beating had been acquitted. Thousands of doors banged open at once and people flooded into the streets, shouting their rage. They wielded sticks, bats, pipes, knives...and some had guns. This wasn't going down like it had in the past. Whitey wasn't going to get away with it this time.

***

John Tasper had covered the windows of his sporting goods store with plywood, but for now he kept the front door propped open. He stood outside the door so he could observe down the street in both directions. He hoped there would be no riots. In fact, he hoped the cops involved in the beating all went to prison, because he saw the videos of what they did to Delton Williams. But if they beat the rap, as cops usually did, he at least hoped that the riots wouldn't spread to this area.

The verdict was announced, and the cops beat the rap.

He decided he should stay at the store just in case. And he should carry his loaded Browning 9mm...just in case.

He found it curious that with all the police mobilized and geared up like they were ready to do battle with ISIS or something, that absolutely none of them were in this business district. Looking up and down the empty street, John figured somebody could fly through there at 120 miles-per-hour and not have to worry about getting pulled over on a night like this.

Somebody called to him from across the street. "Hey, you hear anything yet about which way the mobs are going?" It was the guy from the cellphone store, who also appeared to be packing heat.

False Flag - Brown

Most of the stores John could see were boarded up, like his. A couple of them had "BLACK OWNED" spraypainted across the plywood. This was one situation where John couldn't blame people for playing the race card—if they had it to play.

"No—nothing," John replied. "The news shows are all still filming around the courthouse."

The other man walked out into the middle of the street and took a long stare in both directions. "I guess it's early yet."

John walked out to take a look from the center of the empty street, himself. With the sun setting, the landscape was tinted orange. John thought the scene looked like something from a zombie movie—right before the zombies attacked. "They only just announced the verdict."

The man extended his hand. "Ken Fowler."

John shook it. "John Tasper. Nice to meet you."

"It'd be nice under other circumstances, right?"

They shared a chuckle.

"Never seen the city like this," John said. "It's like a ghost town."

"Not for long, I'm afraid," Ken replied, and pursed his lips.

"You think they'll come this way?" John asked.

"They are going every way," announced a voice with an Indian accent. Ken and John turned their heads toward the sound and saw a short, dark man heading their way from the cafe on Ken's side of the street. John had never eaten there, being a little wary of any Asian food—even from India.

"They are leaving their neighborhoods and going in every direction," the Indian man said, when he reached them.

"How do you know this?" Ken asked.

"The local access channel is reporting it," the man replied. "It does not look random at all. It looks rather organized."

"Oh shit," Ken said.

The Indian extended his hand. "I am Nihar. I own the Calcutta Cafe."

They shook his hand and introduced themselves. Nihar looked at John's Browning and Ken's Glock. "This is like the wild west out here. Are you going to shoot somebody?"

John frowned. "I hope nobody has to. I'm hoping the most I'll have to do is scare somebody into leaving my store alone. With any luck, maybe they'll just pass this area by."

"You don't have a gun?" Ken asked Nihar, who shook his head.

"Then you really ought to get home," John said. "Stay with your family. Nothing good can come out of you being here."

"My family is with me," Nihar said, pointing back to the cafe.

"Are you crazy?" John asked. "You need to get them out of here right now!"

Nihar's eyes were wide. He looked on the verge of panic. "But...if I lose my cafe, I lose everything."

"You being here ain't gonna change whether you lose it or not," Ken said, "if you can't defend it."

Another man joined them, from the clothing store. He at least had a stun gun and some mace. They stood talking in the middle of the street.

All of them urged Nihar to take his family and evacuate while the streets were still clear. They made no promises, but told him they would try to keep rioters away from his business if possible.

They all stopped talking when an explosion sounded in the distance.

"What was that?"

"A gunshot?"

"Maybe something just got blown up," Ken said. "Rioters set places on fire when there's nothing left to steal."

"Maybe it's the cops," the clothing store owner suggested, hopefully. "Maybe they're moving out to stop the riot. That could have been a flash-bang or something."

John turned to Nihar. "This might be your last chance to get your family somewhere safe."

Nihar thought this over for a moment, then nodded. Finally he returned to his cafe. Minutes later they heard a car engine start from behind the cafe, and the vehicle sped away.

"You might should do that, too," John said, to the clothing store owner.

"Really?" The man hoisted his stun gun. "You don't think I can keep them away with this?"

They never answered. All of them heard it at once. The source of the noise was so distant, it had gone unnoticed for a while. When a car alarm went off, though, they suddenly noticed the din growing underneath it, composed of glass breaking, smashing noises, and hundreds of enraged voices.

"Good luck," Ken said, turning to go back to his store.

John bid him and the other guy the same, and went back to his store, shutting and locking the door behind him.

His phone rang. The caller ID showed it was his wife. She was probably worried and just checking on him. He answered, and was immediately taken aback by her hysterical demeanor.

"I got a call from Janice," she said. "They're tearing her neighbor's house down!"

"Who is?" he asked.

"The rioters! Her neighbor had a flag in his front yard, and still has

False Flag - Brown

those bumper stickers on his car. They broke his door down! Janice hears screaming from inside the house! John, he's got a wife and kids in there!"

John swallowed. "Just keep calm, okay?"

"Keep calm? John, she says they're headed this way! I hear gunshots down the street!"

Icy fingers tickled down John's back. He had assumed the riots would be limited to business districts as they had been in the past. The agitators stirring them up were uniformly socialist, and it only made sense they would try to focus the mob's anger on "capitalists." This time they were spilling over through residential neighborhoods?

John had moved his family after the Feds raided his house. Too many bad memories for the wife and kids. Plus, living closer to the store meant a shorter commute and therefore less gas money; and his mortgage and utilities were less expensive in the city than in the suburbs. They lived in a mixed neighborhood where there didn't seem to be that much racial strife. It certainly didn't seem to be a likely target for rioters.

"Alright, let's not take any chances," John said. "Take the kids, throw some blankets and pillows in the car, bring some snacks, and come here to the store. Park in back and you'll all stay here with me tonight."

"Will we be safe there?" she asked, voice quavering.

"I've got the windows boarded up," he said. "I've got the Browning. I need you to load the Sig/Saur and keep it in your purse. Take all the other guns and put them in the trunk. Okay?"

"Okay," she said.

"Come straight here," he said. "Don't stop for anything."

***

The mobs bypassed most of the houses in residential areas at first. Exceptions were made for homes which appeared to be occupied by the enemy. Indicators of enemy occupation included signs like one that said "Land of the Free; Home of the Brave," or bumper stickers like an old one on some honky's car that said "Real Scandals. Phony President." Confusion ensued when some driveways with stickered cars were identified as being part of the wrong house. But once a window was smashed or a door broken down, nothing inside the house was off-limits, whether the enemy lived there or not.

In the mixed neighborhoods, white and Hispanic families mostly stayed indoors. There was good reason to be afraid. Some houses were being set on fire. Other houses had armed occupants who chased away the mob. In a couple cases, the mob called their bluff and shots were fired.

False Flag - Brown

White residents called friends and family, panicked and exaggerating about the scope of the violence. What was in actuality a few houses and occasional gunshots became the neighborhood burning down and a firefight on the streets after they finished telling the story. The recipients of those phone calls made calls of their own, each adding their own exaggeration or embellishment until fear blotted out whatever sanity there had been before the verdict.

On Polk Street young men began appearing outside by twos and threes. They wore pointy-toed boots and cowboy hats. They congregated into ever-growing clusters, expressing their opinions about what "them niggers" were doing to the white folks of Amarillo, and what they might try when they reached here.

It didn't take long for them to form a mob of their own, and start heading toward the riots, to teach them coons a lesson about who was really tough. Others heard the white mob outside and came out to join them, bringing whatever weapons they could find. One of the charismatic, spontaneous leaders summed up the sentiment of the mob at large: "It's time to settle this nigger problem Texas-style."

***

John's wife arrived behind the store with their kids and some provisions just before the mob got there. John went out the back door and saw the mob bearing down on them, as his wife threw open the car door and got out, eyes nearly bugging out of her head.

John paused to put a reassuring hand on her shoulder. "You did good. But keep it together. Get everything in the store, right now. I'm going to keep them away from you. Just get everything out of the car and into the store as fast as you can, okay?"

She nodded, wiped tears from her eyes and grabbed an armload of bags from the car, telling their kids to do the same. John went to the rear of the car, positioning himself between his family and the advancing rioters.

The angry black faces were close enough to distinguish, now, lit by the lamp posts over on the street. The foremost ranks of the mob broke into a run, frenzied at the sight of live meat. Heart pounding like a jackhammer, John pulled the Browning, hoping he'd only have to fire a warning shot to give his family some time.

When the front runners saw that John had a pistol they slowed to a stop, and almost got trampled by those behind them. John checked over his shoulder and saw his son hauling an armload of guns from the trunk. His wife and daughter were already inside.

False Flag - Brown

"How much more is in the car?" John asked.

"I think that's all of it, Dad."

His son was obviously scared, but was still working like a trouper, while his sister and mother were safe inside.

"Good job, son. Get in there but don't shut the door yet. I'll be right behind you."

His son complied. John backed up, shutting his wife's trunk and car door as he passed. He didn't bother locking it—that would just cause the rioters to bust the windows in. All that was left in the car was the stereo. If they only stole that, maybe the damage would be minimal.

John backed toward the open door. He was going to make it. The rioters were leery of his Browning. He would be able to get inside and lock the door before they reached him, even if they began running again. Then he saw a young guy covered with gang tatts push from behind to the front rank, holding a gun.

John felt the blow as he heard the crack of the shot. Searing pain creased his arm and side. He fell back and would have gone down, but hit the door instead. The corner of the steel door split his scalp and hurt like blazes. He got his bearings and lurched inside, pulling the door shut and locking both the knob and the deadbolt.

His wife screamed. His daughter was crying. He heard the mob outside get closer--both the ones in back he'd just escaped from and the much larger group on the street in front. Hard objects banged off the steel door. He heard glass breaking--they were smashing the windows in his wife's car anyway.

He touched the throbbing painful spot on his head and his hand came back bloody. He pulled at his shirt to see what all damage the bullet had done to him. His phone began ringing.

"See who that is, will you, son? I don't want to get it bloody."

John's wife got ahold of herself at the mention of blood. Then she saw it, and crossed the store to get the first aid kit.

Their son pulled the phone from its holster and checked the caller I.D. "It's Uncle Joe."

John sat on the floor, trying to gather his wits. His wife brought the first aid kit, and began working to stop the bleeding.

Something hit the steel door so hard and so heavy, it shook the whole wall. It had to be a human body, John thought. He was thankful that the door opened outward, so that it was secure by both the jamb and the deadbolt.

His wife took the phone and answered it.

***

False Flag - Brown

Joe Tasper had been down sick with the flu for the last couple days. The fever was bad and he'd spent almost every hour of those two days in bed. He still felt horrible, but at one point remembered the last conversation with his brother. John had said something about the possibility of a riot if the verdict didn't go against the cops.

Joe turned on his television and saw that the verdict had been announced already. And there were, indeed, riots.

He called his brother, who would probably be keeping vigil at the store.

His sister in law answered. In a shrill, hitching, sobbing voice she blurted out a long monologue with almost no space in between words. The gist of it was that the whole family was at the store; rioters were outside the store trying to get in; and John had been shot. In the background he could hear pounding on the doors of the store, and his niece crying.

Where were the cops, Joe wanted to know. He'd seen hordes of them on the news, armored and geared up.

His sister in law didn't know where the police were, but they sure weren't outside breaking up the riot.

With a surge of adrenalin, Joe got dressed in a hurry. The danger his brother was in cut through the fog of his fever. He grabbed boxes of shells, his 12 gauge Mossberg from the closet, wrapped it in a blanket and ran down the outside stairs to his truck.

His apartment was in the suburbs. It was doubtful the riots would reach his neighborhood on foot. So ordinarily he would be safe if he just stayed put. Instead, he had to run toward the trouble. The sound of his terrified niece crying in the background haunted him. She'd been through enough already as a little girl.

His brother was shot, but he didn't know how serious the wound was. John's wife said something about trying to stop the bleeding, and that sounded bad. It was doubtful an ambulance would risk the rioters to get to him.

And what if they managed to break in? Or what if they set the store on fire with John and his family inside?

Traffic was light that evening and it got lighter as he drew closer to the city proper. What traffic there was headed the opposite way. People were getting the hell out of Dodge. Joe put the hammer down and negotiated the roads just as fast as he could safely go.

Less than seven miles from the store, a cop car pulled out of a speed trap behind him with lights flashing.

He couldn't believe this. Just could not believe it. Hundreds of cops

False Flag - Brown

surrounded City Hall and the Courthouse, protecting the fat cats while people like his brother were under siege, but this guy had nothing better to do than hand out speeding tickets.

He kept going. If the pig wanted to follow him right into the riot, maybe he'd have no choice but to do his job.

The cop gave chase for over a mile.

Joe would have run the stoplight, but a fire engine, ladder truck and ambulance crossed his path at the intersection, sirens and horns wailing. They weren't heading in the direction of the store. At least they were on their way to help **somebody**. Joe hit the brakes, hard.

When he came to a stop, the police car rolled in front of him at an angle, parking so that it cut him off.

***

Officer Cleveland Parker adjusted his belt when he stepped outside his cruiser, and turned his big Mag-Lite on, his other hand unflapping his holster. He clocked this fool doing over twice the legal speed limit. It was too bad the jails were going to be full of brothers soon, because he'd love to throw this white boy in the slammer.

Then again, maybe this pink toe was more than a speeder. He was driving toward the trouble instead of away from it, so unless he was crazy or on drugs, he must be up to no good. Either way, Cleveland would make sure he lost his license.

The pickup truck's headlights switched to high beams, impairing his vision. This clown thought he was cute. Cleveland liked to blast a pulled-over vehicle with his own high beams, and add the side spot for good measure. Then when he reached the driver's window, he liked to blind them with the Mag-Lite. He didn't appreciate this punk using his techniques.

"Turn off those lights and shut off your engine!" he commanded, pulling his pistol. Oh, he was going to ruin this fool's life, for sure.

Those were the last coherent thoughts Cleveland Parker would ever have. The pickup's door swung open, and less than a second later most of Cleveland's head disintegrated in a hail of buckshot.

***

Joe Tasper and his pickup truck were gone by the time the Polk Street boys passed the scene of the traffic stop. So were Cleveland Parker's sidearm, his burner piece, the riot gun from the car, all his ammo, and his ballistic vest. The Polk Street Boys found the lifeless uniformed black

False Flag - Brown

body on the street next to the car, and stripped it of valuables without so much as a pause to consider what might have happened. If any of them appreciated the irony, it was lost in the mobthink

One of them got behind the wheel. Others piled in until the car was full. Others hopped on the hood, trunk and fenders, whooping rebel yells and cattle calls. The overloaded cruiser now led the mob toward the riots. One of the young men in the front seat got on the police radio, laughing, and made many comments about the "headless nigger cop." He hoped there would be plenty more dead cops before the night was over, because they were obviously useless.

***

Willie Mae Harris had sore feet. She wasn't used to walking so far.

She and many other women of various ages had followed the advanced party of looters at a safe distance. Her son Rick was up there, and she tried to keep track of him. Her daughter Shirolle and grandchild Antwoshae were in the same group as her. She lost track of the rest of her household along the way, but hopefully they'd be able to find some good stuff. In any case, her, Rick, Shirolle and Antwoshae would grab all they could carry.

She heard a gunshot from the alley behind a boarded-up store. The skittish crowd recoiled at the sound, but realized the action was happening elsewhere and kept going.

Rick turned around, eyes searching the group of women behind him. "Mama?"

"Go on up there!" Willie Mae called to him, pointing to the side of the street opposite where the gunshot came from. "Try them stores over there! Act like you got some sense, boy. Damn!"

Rick couldn't hear her over all the noise, but understood by her gesture where he should go. He pushed to the other side of the street.

A big commotion went on up ahead. Willie Mae asked the folks on either side of her what was going on. In time word was passed along from the front: there was a clothing store up there with some nice, expensive name brands.

The forward progress of the looting party slowed and stopped now that it reached a prime resource conglomeration. Willie Mae and her peeps went forward until they saw a swarm of young men working to tear the plywood shielding off a store front.

The plywood came down with a ripping sound and a chorus of victorious profanity. Glass shattered as the young men smashed out the windows and flooded into the store.

False Flag - Brown

Willie Mae grabbed Shirolle and pushed her forward, then gestured for Antwoshae to go with her. Willie brought up the rear. She was jostled around and nearly crushed a few times by others, but managed to avoid cutting herself stepping inside the shattered store front window.

Something was happening in the center of the store. Racks were knocked over as a group of maybe nine young brothas swarmed on something or somebody, kicking and beating on it with their weapons. Word was passed back that some white fool used a stun gun on one brotha, and sprayed Mace at another. Willie Mae turned to the shelves while others were distracted by the violent beating.

Antwoshae found some nice sneakers, and Shirolle some designer shoes. Willie was only able to get a suit before everything was picked clean, and almost lost that to a young brotha with a knife before he took a better look and decided he didn't like the suit. She didn't have a chance to check the size, but was sure she could sell it if it didn't fit somebody in her house.

Something else buzzed through the crowd, and people evacuated the clothing store, trampling others in their haste. She spotted Rick and grabbed his arm. "Where they all goin'?"

Rick bent down to speak in her ear. "There a store we done passed already. Got cellphones and stuff, Moms."

"Well get over there," Willie said. "I'll catch up. Get me one of them iPhones and a few chargers."

***

Ken Fowler used his outside security cameras to watch the developments outside. At first the mob passed his store by. It looked like he and the "BLACK OWNED" stores might survive.

He shook his head, biting back the rage, as the rioters got inside the clothing store. His video feeds, with only the street lamps for lighting, didn't pick out enough detail to see faces. It looked like a solid mass of black cancer out there.

Then they came back toward his store.

Fear and anger made him feel weak and energetic at the same time. He took a position behind one of his merchandise counters, pulled his Glock and waited to see what happened.

They went after his door. They beat on it with hard implements. Ken's blood ran cold as he heard the plywood cracking over the din of cussing, yelling voices.

Ken had gone the extra mile securing the plywood, and they had a lot more trouble with it than they were expecting. Still, sliver by sliver, they hacked and ripped it away. Finally the plywood shielding was gone. An electric charge wrapped around Ken's brain and vibrated in his teeth. If he hadn't urinated earlier, he probably would have pissed his pants right then.

The glass panel of the door exploded inward when a salvo of bricks hit it. A dark body appeared in the opening, silhouetted by the glow of the street lights.

No lights were on inside the store. Ken leaned over the counter in the darkness, took aim, and fired.

The body fell backwards. Another figure appeared in the opening, stooping over the first. Ken dropped it with another shot. Over the ringing in his ears, Ken noticed the pitch and volume of the crowd noise change. Then, incredibly, another figure appeared in the opening, yelling something at him like, "Yo, man, hold up! Hold up, in there!"

Ken fired again, and that figure went down. There was a pause in the attack, and Ken couldn't tell what was going on. He changed magazines and pushed jacketed hollow points into the first mag during the lull.

Some kind of activity blurred just outside the door but Ken had no clear shot at anything.

Something pounded on the steel back door, but he was fairly sure they couldn't break that one down.

A hand appeared in the front doorway, holding a bottle with a rag stuffed in the neck. The rag was burning. A brick came flying in from the street, but instead of sailing inside and hurting Ken or anything in the store, it hit the bottle before the hand could chuck it inside. Liquid flame burst outward and a torch-like apparition tumbled out onto the street, screaming. Ken might have laughed if he wasn't so scared.

Somebody else appeared in the door, fired two quick shots with a small caliber pistol, and dodged back out of sight before Ken could draw a bead on him. The shots were wild, coming nowhere near him, but they provoked him to action. If he didn't do something, it was only a matter of time before somebody with a gun or another Molotov Cocktail got lucky.

Ken gritted his teeth, climbed over the counter and marched to the door. This close he could see more than he had from further back. He brought the Glock up level, taking aim at one of the figures...

The guy with the small caliber pistol appeared again, sticking his gun inside the door for another wild shot. Ken grabbed his wrist and yanked hard. the skinny man smacked into the door frame and staggered to regain his balance and pull back. Ken shoved the Glock's muzzle into the guy's chest and fired. The man flew backwards and landed like a limp rag doll on the street. A chorus of shouts erupted in the immediate area.

Ears ringing and blood thumping in his temples, Ken stepped through the door. He pivoted left and fired into a big man up close. The man went

False Flag - Brown

down. He pivoted right and fired at a muscular kid running away, and missed.

The area cleared as looters saw him, saw the gun, realized what he was doing with it, and ran.

Ken surveyed the destruction all around him, wrought by these urban savages. The anger burned hotter than the fear at this point. He shot at a couple who didn't run (or didn't run fast enough) and that convinced the rest they should clear away from this particular area with a quickness.

"You better get your black ass away from my store," he bellowed, "before I put a cap in it!"

***

Joe Tasper drove down the street and saw it clogged with people up ahead. The people he saw had bats, pipes, and other weapons. Joe floored the gas. Some of the rioters thought they could intimidate the driver of the Chevy truck into stopping. For some reason they didn't believe the driver was willing to run them over.

When the pickup rammed one of them, who went down and underneath, causing the vehicle to bounce roughly as the tires ran over the body, reality sank in. Cussing and screaming, they cleared the street as the truck bore down on them.

The crowd parted before Joe like the Red Sea before Moses. He slid to a stop right in front of the sporting goods store and threw the door open. He stepped out slinging the Mossberg around his back and pumping a shell into the breach of the police riot gun. He gave the looters no time to debate if he was as merciless on foot as he was behind the wheel, by blowing the nearest man right off his feet.

Some whirled and ran. Others backed away, then turned and ran. Joe fired into their backs for good measure. The shot had a good spread at that range and a couple of them yelped and went tumbling.

Joe posted himself in front of the door, screaming obscenities at the looters in his raw, scratchy voice. Somewhere in his fever-fogged mind he knew the cops were going to come for him eventually. He would kill every single one of them he could. They wouldn't take him alive. If he didn't have his brother's family to worry about, he would go find some cops right now.

***

The mob decided to move on, hoping to find some easier prey farther out. In just a few blocks they crossed paths with the white mob from Polk

False Flag - Brown

Street. A rumble ensued.

The organizers of the various black rioting and looting forces remained in touch via cellphones. Some of their followers wanted to unleash their surprise weapons on the gang of rednecks. Their leaders insisted they save the big stuff for the po-po.

***

When the police finally did move out to suppress the riots, they dealt with the rumble-in-progress first. It was a shock to see that one of their cars had been captured. It meant the rumors were probably true about one of their own getting killed already.

And that pissed them off. They brought up an MRAP with a water cannon, and put some tear gas into the convulsing mass of humanity as well, but were more than happy to deal out deadly force on an individual basis to the young men who wanted to continue fighting. They would justify it all in the paperwork later.

There was solidarity among the boys in blue. There would be no whistle-blowing on each other.

But the looters in the melee with the Polk Street gang were only one faction. Other mobs were wreaking havoc in other parts of the city. When the cops finally engaged them, they ran into automatic weapons and rocket launchers. If the rioters had known anything about tactics, they would have killed hundreds--not just dozens--of Amarillo's Finest.

***

Two veterans, Jimmy and Bill, called their network of like-minded friends and gathered together at Bill's house. All of them brought pistols and rifles; a few of them brought shotguns as well. They wore urban camouflage pattern fatigues, ballistic armor, including helmets for some, and mostly standardized load-bearing equipment. They had a brief operations order regarding a roadblock at a nearby major intersection.

Rioters had barricaded the streets to stop traffic and attack commuters, dragging them from their vehicles. Rumors flew that they were killing and raping; but all the militia men agreed that they were certainly robbing and beating people at the very least. They remembered what happened to Reginald Denny in the Los Angeles riots a couple decades before.

Bill had an extended cargo van which was beige with several primer gray patches. They removed the license plate. The men piled into it and Bill drove them to a parking lot two blocks from the intersection in

217

False Flag - Brown

question.

They performed a last minute commo check with their radios. Three of the older, less mobile men were left to guard the van, forming a triangular perimeter. The rest of them formed two fireteams and moved in bounding overwatch toward the objective.

They hadn't traveled far when they sighted rioters, still half a block from the intersection. Bill had everyone find cover and assigned sectors of fire while making sure rear and flank security was covered.

They opened up on the mob.

Rioters dropped by twos and threes, some not dead, but screaming from debilitating wounds. The surprise factor was strong, and many rioters were rendered inoperable before any who were still able attempted to return fire. Those who did were ineffective at that range (about 200 meters), and were dispatched quickly when they failed to find adequate cover.

In a matter of minutes, the survivors chose flight over fight, and an avenue to the intersection was partially cleared.

Bill led his squad forward. They encountered some hostile fire from the flanks but were prepared for it. The enemy had nothing like their mobile discipline or volume of accurate fire, and were cut down or scared off.

Still with no casualties, the militia squad forged ahead until they had eyes on the intersection. A firefight ensued, and the ambush force was swept away in less than 10 minutes after about a 40% casualty rate and ineffective return fire at best.

The militia established a perimeter to protect their two volunteers who cleared the dumpsters, park benches and other debris of the makeshift roadblock out of the intersection. They remained in their perimeter for nearly 15 minutes, engaging a few probing attacks by armed but poorly disciplined rioters, while Jimmy took his medical bag around to do what he could for the still-living victims who had been dragged from their vehicles and beaten, raped and/or shot. The squad then tactically withdrew back to the cargo van.

Before Bill joined the rest at the van, something caught his eye. He pushed his helmet back and detoured by a building that was still smoking from the fire that had left it a ruined skeleton. The whole area looked like a war zone. In front of the building was a small flagpole. The rope used to raise and lower the flag had been cut and the flag was gone. He took a look around the area, not expecting to see it, but he did.

The flag had been tossed at a rain gutter, but hadn't fallen completely in. He slung his rifle, walked over and picked it up. It was partially torn, and apparently somebody tried to burn it, too. For whatever reason the fire died before it was completely consumed. Bill held the flag in both

False Flag - Brown

hands, examining the damage and pondering the symbolic meaning of it.

He remembered back to when he first enlisted, years ago. The officer who swore him in with several others had warned them that if they disrespected Old Glory in any way, he would tie them to a chair and feed it to them stripe-by-stripe; star-by-star. He wondered what that officer would say about this.

Any garment or bedding or other item made of similar fabric with the same level of damage, Bill would have written off as not worth keeping. This flag could never be repaired to a reasonable facsimile of what it was supposed to be. Even so, Bill folded the tattered remnant as best he could and stuffed it in his cargo pocket. Then he jogged back to the van where his friends stared at him as if he had a screw loose.

They debated among themselves whether or not to go clear some more of the roadblocks in the city, but came to the consensus that they best not push their luck. They loaded back in the van and sped off by a different route to Bill's house, where they would remain geared-up but wait to see if the situation got worse or better.

False Flag - Brown

Rocco and Carlos were already there when Leon arrived at the office in the morning. The television was on and both his partners were standing in the lobby watching it.

On the screen was a scene of a police water cannon hosing down looters in Amarillo.

"...Violence shows no sign of stopping any time soon," announced a female voice over the riot footage. "Once again, it has been confirmed that the Governor has activated the National Guard, and the first troops should be arriving within the hour. In Washington, the President held a special press conference for the developments in west Texas."

The scene changed to the press conference, where the chief figurehead of the western world issued some carefully crafted statements built around the words "tragedy," "crisis," and "hate."

Leon set his fag bag down and said, "You called it, Rocco. It's goin' down just like you said."

"Did you hear about the other ones?" Carlos asked. "There's copycat riots already today in Detroit, New Orleans and Los Angeles."

"I heard sumpthin' about Atlanta on the radio, comin' in," Leon said.

"So far they're only classifying that one as a demonstration," Rocco said.

"The body count so far is 26 cops dead, and they don't know how many regular people," Carlos said.

Leon whistled. "That just in Amarillo, or all the riots together?"

"Just Amarillo," Rocco said, gravely.

Leon watched the screen with them for a few more minutes, then went to put his stuff away. He joined them for coffee as usual.

They sat around the table with grim faces, with no attempts at humor this morning.

"That one customer already called in to cancel his appointment," Carlos said.

"Nice of him to tell us," Rocco said, sipping some coffee. "This might turn out to be a dead day, amigos. Most folks are probably waiting to see what happens. The kind of folks who give us business will most likely hole up and load their magazines while they wait to find out if martial law is around the corner."

"How far do you think this will go?" Leon asked.

Rocco shrugged. "There's no way to tell. It's already gone further than Kent State, or Watts, or Ferguson."

False Flag - Brown

Cavarra's cell beeped to announce a text message. He slipped on his glasses and looked at the screen. His countenance transformed from grim to perplexed.

"Everything okay, Rocco?" Carlos asked.

Cavarra stood from the table, with a far away look.

"Rocco...?" Leon asked.

"Listen guys," Cavarra said, hesitantly, as if busy thinking something over and only limited brain power was available to speak. "Something came up. I've gotta go. I won't be back in today, but I'll try to call you tonight to check in."

"What's up, man?" Leon asked. "Is it bad? You need some help? Carlos can mind the store if you need me to..."

Rocco showed them his palm and forced a smile. "It's not necessarily bad. Just something personal. Can't really talk about it now, but I'll fill you in when I get back."

"Come on, *Papi*," Carlos protested. "You know you can tell us, right?"

"I know," Rocco said. "And I will. Just for right now, I gotta go. You two hold down the fort. If nobody shows by 1300, it would be a good day to service the chains on the Shootout targets."

Rocco got his trash packed and was gone within five minutes, leaving his friends to ponder who the text might be from and what it might mean.

From the television a female voice with all the practiced inflections and intonations standard for electronic media was saying, "Willie Mae Harris, a mother of nine, was marching in the demonstration with two of her children."

A teary-eyed, overweight, middleaged black woman appeared on the screen, with a white hand from off-screen holding a microphone in front of her mouth. "We was walkin' past these stores, just carryin' signs. 'Cause what happened to Delton is just wrong. And we got to the part of the street where these stores is, and this white man came runnin' out of his store with a gun. And he just started shootin' at us."

The scene changed to the jailhouse, and the affected female voiceover continued. "A local store owner, Kenneth Fowler of Amarillo, has been charged with multiple murders during the demonstration. The district attorney says he will prosecute according to the new hate crime legislation, since it is evident from witness testimony that his killing spree was racially motivated."

"Gringos are going crazy," Carlos said.

"They ain't no worse than my people," Leon said, sadly. "Or yours."

"Rocco was right, no? All those people were just waiting for an excuse to do something like this."

False Flag - Brown

"Hey, man," Leon asked, fishing for a cheerful distraction, "does Rocco know about you and his daughter?"

"Nothing to know," Carlos said, shrugging. "We never did anything."

"It looked to me like you were gonna hook up," Leon said.

"She was into me," Carlos said. "But she's in Sacramento and I'm here. Probably for the best, anyway. It would be weird being with Rocco's daughter, no?"

"I know that old fart would skin you alive if you pumped-and-dumped her," Leon said, snickering.

"No, I got too much respect for him to do that," Carlos said.

About an hour later, Carlos was pulling routine maintenance outside, while Leon went over the books inside, when a vehicle pulled into the parking lot. Leon looked out the window and saw a silver Lexus, with a trailing dust cloud just settling. The huge black man who got out had lost significant muscle mass since Leon last saw him, but still resembled Eddie Murphy's big brother on stilts and steroids. Leon went out to meet him.

"Big Jake!" Leon called out, happy to see his old buddy.

Mac's gaze fell on Leon, recognition flashed, and he returned the smile.

Something seemed kind of off about that smile, though. Maybe because of how they parted ways last time.

"Yo, Cannonball! I'm surprised you're out of bed this early, man."

Leon stopped when he was close enough to rub skin.

"What's up, Mac? Thought you was workin' for The Man, now?"

"I still am," Mac said. "That contracting gig got much too crazy about the time I left. And it's crazier than ever, now."

It was getting pretty crazy back on the block, too, Leon thought, but he'd been dwelling on that non-stop for long enough already. "Good to see you. What brings you this way?"

Mac looked around and took a big breath of the clean Western air. "Was out this way, more or less. Hadn't seen you in a while. Wanted to check this place out."

"Man, you just missed Rocco," Leon said. "He took off a while ago. Says he's not gonna be back today. How long you in town for?"

"Oh. That's too bad," Mac said.

There was something off about the way he said that, too.

"Where did he go?"

"Leon shrugged. "Didn't say, man."

Mac checked his watch. "I only got a couple hours, but had to swing by, my brotha."

"That's legit," Leon said. "I might as well give you a tour, while you're here."

"Yeah, man. Sure enough."

They walked at a leisurely pace toward the office, side-by-side. Leon noticed Mac had a slight limp. "How's your knee?"

"It sucks, to be honest," Mac replied. "Can't do half the stuff I used to."

"Hey, Mac," Leon said, extending his hand to slap skin again. "I hope I didn't leave you in a pinch when I quit SSI."

Mac made a dismissive face. "Naw, man. You snipers are a dime a dozen over there. Forget it."

"I was just worried about Tommy," Leon explained, anyway. "Plus, it was time for a break. That whole gig in Indonesia, on the boats and stuff. That was pretty hairy."

"Hairy? Hairy?" Mac teased. "You sound just like your white buddies."

Leon chuckled. But "hairy" was an expression exclusive to Rocco, among their mutual friends. He wondered why Mac attributed it as a white thing.

They entered the building and Leon let Mac glance around the lobby and counter before he took him in the back where the workshop was. Mac scanned the room keenly, as if memorizing what he saw.

"What's all that?" Mac asked, pointing to some equipment on a workbench in the corner.

"That's the reloadin' bench," Leon replied. "They're bustin' heads with ammo prices these days. We save a whole lot of money this way."

"You sell reloaded ammunition?" Mac asked, surprised.

"Naw. We sell the virgin stuff by the box, same as ever'body. We do this for ourselves. I learned to do it, too. Got my M21 zeroed to my own loads. It's almost all I use."

Mac nodded toward a Mini-30 in the vise. "What's that there?"

"Just where we modify; put accessories on. Like that."

"Convert to select fire?" Mac asked.

Leon felt a bit insulted. "C'mon, man. We ain't stupid. These days you can get locked up for nothin'. We don't do anything we **know** will give The Man an excuse. We put on foldin' stocks, bayonet lugs, stuff like that."

"Got to be careful," Mac warned. "All that might be banned again, soon."

"That's right, **you work** for The Man. Tell me Mac, why they so upset about bayonet lugs? There ever been a bayonet used in a drive-by, or a school shootin', or anything else they keep tellin' us is why they gotta take semiautos away?"

False Flag - Brown

Mac frowned. "It's not so much the things that have already happened, but what **could** happen. The kind of weapons that have bayonet lugs are not what you take to go duck hunting."

"What's duck huntin' got to do with anything?"

"It's a legitimate purpose to own a gun," Mac answered.

"This week it is, anyway," Leon said. "But the Constitution don't say nothin' 'bout duck huntin', Mac. It's about keepin' a militia armed. You can't point to a better militia weapon, than a semiauto rifle with a good stock that can take a bayonet."

Mac shook his head, the frown deepening. "You got the wrong idea of what the Second Amendment is for. It's so we can have a National Guard; not so some ignorant cracker and his inbred cousins Bubba and Billy-Bob can go play soldier."

Leon let that one go and wrapped up the inside tour. He led Mac outside to show him the cool stuff. They found Carlos collecting brass on the Jungle Walk.

"Look who!" Carlos greeted, standing. "Big Jake!"

They shook hands. "Bojado!" Mac said. "A civilian again, huh?"

"Ooh-rah," Carlos replied.

They chopped it up for a few minutes before Leon and Mac moved on. Carlos invited him to stay for lunch and he'd buy the pizza. Mac politely declined.

As Leon showed him the Western Shootout Course, Mac asked, "You ever feel isolated out here, Leon?"

"What'ya mean?" Leon replied.

Mac shrugged. "You know: out here in Shitkicker Central, the only black face around..."

Leon rubbed his scalp and stared thoughtfully into the woods beyond the course. "Yeah. There's some bad stuff comin' down, from what I can tell. Sometimes it's like I'm already stuck in the middle."

Mac shook his head sadly. "See, when I heard you was moving out to this Clint Eastwood country, I knew it was a bad idea."

This confused Leon for a minute. "Naw, man—it's not because I'm here. It's bad ever'where."

"At least you'd have some support with your own people, though."

"My own people? You mean my folks back in Valdosta?" Leon now shook his head. "I wouldn't get no support from them. They'd only want me around as long as they got some kinda' benefit, anyway."

"Not them, necessarily. The black community in general."

Leon flashed him a sour grimace. "You serious, man? You want me to trust the 'hood rats to watch my back? Maybe I never graduated college, but I ain't stupid, Mac. Nearly any nigga on the continent would sell me

224

out for beer money, or a damn bag of weed. They'd do it to you, too. Where you been, man? Under a rock?"

"That's ghetto trash," Mac said. "What about cats like me? You know I'd have your back."

"Yeah, that's my best bet. So at least I got Rocco and Carlos close by, if sumpthin' goes down."

Mac frowned, shaking his head again. "Hey, I got nothing against Cavarra. Or Bojado. We all ate some of the same sand. They're good soldiers and all that, when you're talking about <u>first or second generation war</u>. But we're facing something different, here."

Leon scrutinized the big man's face. He took a moment to speak; then did so slowly. "Jake, man, I don't know what you're drivin' at. Seems like you're tellin' me I can't trust my friends. I'm tellin' you they're just about the only people I **can** trust. Rocco, Tommy, Carlos—they proved themselves to me, man."

"What side you think they'd be on if we all lived in Amarillo?" Mac challenged. "Because Amarillo might be coming to a theater near you, my brotha."

Leon took his time answering, again. "So what you're sayin' is, Rocco is the enemy 'cause he white. Carlos is the enemy 'cause he Mexican. And I should go march with some punk-ass thievin' gang bangers 'cause we the same color. That what **you** plannin' to do? Man, what they been doin' to your mind?"

"My mind is fine."

Leon shook his head. "You got out of Delta 'cause of what the politicians did to you guys in Somalia. Can't you see it's even worse, now? And this tribal attitude, man. I can't believe you're tryin' to make me doubt Chief, and Rocco, after all we been through together."

"I'm just saying," Mac said, "there's a lot of people who aren't necessarily your enemies right now, who'll end up on the opposite side of you when things get busy. Hey, it's great that you can coexist and all that. I'm just trying to get you to think smart, Leon. Think about the future. You don't know everything I know. It's about to get uglier than you could dream, my brotha."

"What is it that you know?" Leon asked, voice tinged with irritation.

"I can't tell you everything," Mac said. "But for instance, that white boy who went into Sumatra with us—Rennenkampf?"

Leon nodded. "Yeah, Josh. What about 'im?"

"He's Aryan Nations, Leon. He's into some subversive shit. And I'm telling you, Cavarra talks almost just like him."

"That is so weak," Leon said. "Josh is Tommy's best friend. He just married Jennifer, man."

False Flag - Brown

Mac never lost a beat. "I don't know how those sick people think. They make some kind of exceptions for Indians. And don't think you know everything about Tommy, either."

"What's that s'posed to mean?"

"He believes in that cockamamie shadow conspiracy shit. Just like the white supremacy groups."

Leon couldn't believe how Mac was characterizing everything. "First of all, news flash: Tommy's not white. That sorta' disqualifies him, don'tcha think?"

"He hangs around those kind of people," Mac reasoned, oblivious to the *deja vu* and irony of the role reversal from his conversation with DeAngelo.

"Man," Leon said. "You a conspiracy theorist, too. Why you down on them for that?"

Mac raised his eyebrows. "Me? A conspiracy theorist?"

"You're damn skippy. The only difference is, you think the conspiracy is only against black people. There's a whole forest a' problems out there, but that's the only tree you see or care about."

The two men had become tight while contracting together in Iraq. There was a lot Leon admired about Mac, but friction began growing between them ever since 2008 and the campaign to put Barack Hussein Obama in the White House.

Leon didn't care for either of the presidential candidates in any election he was old enough to vote in. And he didn't appreciate being expected to vote a certain way just because he was born with brown skin. Mac and everybody else **did** vote and think and talk the way they were expected to, but acted like it was their own idea.

Having a black president could have been a great vindication, if it was somebody who tried to do the right thing...or at least had a clue what the right thing was. But nobody Leon knew in "the black community" saw things the way he did.

Mac once opined that even if Obama were to walk on water or raise the dead, white folks would still break bad on him.

Leon thought that the opposite was true—that Obama could rape a nun or strangle a baby on national TV, and his followers would either ignore it or find a way to justify it.

The two friends had reached an impasse.

Politics really came down to something very simple: How a person voted and what they believed depended on whether they loved or hated America. Nobody in politics yet had the courage or integrity to admit that they hated America, and a lot of regular people still weren't willing to admit it even to themselves. But that was the issue at its ugly, naked core.

False Flag - Brown

When you hate something, you try to destroy it. If you can't destroy it outright, you try to "fundamentally transform" it. Any lies, betrayals and deception are justified when you hate it enough. At least half of the people enjoying her benefits hated America passionately. It was a lot like spoiled rich kids who had nothing but contempt for the supplicating parents who pampered them.

Leon respected Mac despite their differences; but he also respected his other friends. Neither Tommy, Rocco, or even Josh Rennenkampf had ever done him wrong. He received no special treatment from them, which he also appreciated. Some people automatically tried to coddle Leon because he was black, which had always irked him. He preferred to be judged by conduct and performance, by the same standards everyone else was. His friends did that. Rocco and Carlos did that. Tommy and Josh did that.

There just didn't seem to be much to discuss with Mac anymore. In a matter of minutes, their friendship was strained to the breaking point.

After Mac left, Carlos noticed something was bothering Leon, and asked what was wrong. Leon couldn't answer honestly. Mac had planted seeds of doubt and despite himself, Leon now wondered how much he could really trust anyone.

227

False Flag - Brown

The newlyweds worked with the dogs for at least an hour every day. Josh wanted to make sure they would take commands from Jennifer as well as him. After spending a couple hours with them that day, Jennifer had to get in out of the cold.

It was a winter wonderland all over the mountain, already.

They took their boots off by the door and Josh shed his coat, since it was comfortably warm inside. Jennifer kept hers on, and went to the kitchen to heat up water for some herbal tea while Josh hung their boots and his coat and hat on the crude rack by the door, consisting of thick pipes protruding from the wall. He then sat at the desktop he used for normal productivity and web surfing.

He checked his news feeds. The situation in Amarillo sounded bad. Plus there were copycat riots in other cities. Only time would tell how bad those might get.

Police suspected that a lot of the cop killings were being perpetrated by the same shooter, who dispensed head shots with a scattergun. For the mainstream media pundits the most tragic aspect of the whole affair was that some mysterious vigilante group had used "military weapons and tactics" to gun down an unknown number of "African-American demonstrators" at a major intersection.

Hispanics were getting into the riots as well, with big numbers in the southern cities. This was the third world "nation within a nation" created by executive amnesty, doing what it was designed to do—not only bleeding the taxpayers dry, but beginning to spill their blood literally as well. At the rate they were still flowing unchecked into the country, they would have the numerical advantage on the streets soon.

Another story was almost buried, about a skirmish on the border between a rancher and some drug runners from Mexico. It remained to be seen whether authorities in his state would do their job, or intervene on the side of the invaders. If they did their job, they'd come under the guns of the Feds. The world had become a place where it was dangerous to do the right thing.

Islamic whack-jobs had just murdered some more infidels in Syria. Whack-jobs that had been funded and armed by Washington.

Some of Josh's fellow crackpots were speculating about the latest school shooting. The wildest theory was that actors had been hired to play the victims' parents. The "evidence" for this was a flimsy stretch at best. Josh thought such theories were only truly useful as straw men, to

False Flag - Brown

discredit alternate media as a whole.

Jennifer, with her coat finally off, arrived at his side with a steaming cup in each hand. She placed them on the desk and sat in his lap. "What happened to the world while we were outside?"

"I'm reading about it, now," he said, giving her a back massage while leaning sideways to view the monitor around her.

"Oh, that feels good," she purred. "What's going on in Amarillo?"

"It stinks. The police had plenty of warning, and had riot squads there standing ready from before the verdict. But they weren't sent into the troubled areas until hours after the looting and riots started."

"What? Why? Are they that incompetent?"

"It's not incompetence," Josh said. "It's calculated. We've seen this over and over. The cops take their orders from somebody who thought this would be a great opportunity to demonstrate why militarized police are necessary. Give the sheep a taste of chaos, and they'll bleat for more order."

Jennifer made a sad noise and pulled her hair behind one ear. "It's kind of hard not to think that cops hate the blacks, when they do things like this."

"There's more to it than that," Josh said, scrolling down to read more of the page he was on. "Divide and conquer. Easiest way to divide is along racial lines. Political differences aren't enough. If right-wingers were really as dangerous as they say we are, they wouldn't have to do this. But they need to set off some loose cannons in a powderkeg, and this is how to do it. They spent the last 20, 30 years packing the powderkeg, and priming the cannons, and now it looks like they're trying to touch it off."

"It's all so unnecessary," Jennifer lamented, instinctively pushing fingernails to teeth. "Different races can get along fine. We're proof of that. It's these agitators and race-baiters trying to stir up racial strife."

"They're part of it," Josh said, pulling her hand away from her mouth. "Quit biting your fingernails."

She craned her neck to make a face at him.

"You're right," he said, lifting the mug to his lips, blowing on the surface of the hot liquid. "It's unnecessary. But somebody more influential than us wants a race war, and every day it looks more and more like they'll get one."

"Well..." she began, but didn't complete her thought.

Josh took a sip of tea. Too hot. He put it down.

He recognized the almost musical sound of that one word. Jennifer didn't gloat or throw I-told-you-sos in your face. She simply sang, "We-ell," then never finished the sentence.

False Flag - Brown

"Let me guess," he said, cynically, "the Bible predicted this would happen."

She sighed and took a sip from her own cup, then said, "It does. I just didn't want to believe it. When Jesus said 'nation will rise against nation, and kingdom against kingdom'...well, the word translated 'nation' is ethnos. Sound familiar?"

"Ethnic," Josh said, blowing on his tea again. "Ethnicity. Interesting, professor."

She twisted in his lap until she was sideways and could make eye contact. Her brows were knitted into a frown he didn't see on her very often. "What are we going to do, Joshua? What do people like us do, if that's really what it means?"

He pulled her to him and kissed her forehead. "We stay up here out of everybody's way. We survive."

"What about your neighbors?" she asked. "Or other people nearby?"

"The ones I know just want to be left alone," he told her. "They're not into 'white power' or anything stupid like that. But whatever; I'm not gonna let anybody hurt you."

She hugged him tight. "I'm worried about my mother. Uncle Tommy and Aunt Linda. The Shawnee are outnumbered on every side. Whites, blacks, Mexicans...anybody may go after them."

"I feel sorry for anybody who goes after Tommy," Josh said, only half-joking.

"I'm serious," she said.

He rubbed her neck soothingly. "If and when it comes to that, they're welcome to come up here. We got high ground and can watch each others' backs."

She remained on his lap for a few minutes, then took her tea and stood up. "I'm going to figure out what we're eating," she announced, cheerily. "Any special requests?"

This was something else he loved about her: how quickly she bounced back when she was obviously troubled. "I like everything you've made, baby. Your lemon chicken was the bomb—we can have the leftovers if you don't feel like making a new dish."

She glanced at the time display on the computer. "We've got time. I might as well rustle something up."

He watched her hips rock as she walked away. She tossed her hair glancing over her shoulder and busted him, grinning and giving him a wink as she disappeared into the kitchen.

Life was good for him these days. Josh wondered how long that would last.

He spent the next couple hours doing his normal work, took some

False Flag - Brown

time to watch a movie with Jennifer on the big screen, then did some more cyber-legwork for Tommy.

False Flag - Brown

Cavarra knew the sender as soon as he read the text:

"Keep a stiff upper lip."

It took him way back to when his kids were young. He taught his son some contingency plans for various situations. In one of them, in case his mother was going crazy, or one of her boyfriends did, or a burglar or kidnapper or whatever was in the house, if Cavarra was away and they were speaking on the phone, he would say, "I think I've got a migraine."

His son was not a headache person, and he certainly didn't get migraines. Cavarra would then decide where his son should go to wait if he could escape from whoever it was.

"Keep a stiff upper lip," meant Cavarra wanted him to wait to be picked up at a specific lifeguard tower on the beach.

In Leucadia, California.

His son needed to meet him, in person.

All during the long drive, Cavarra speculated about the reason. His son didn't check in with him all that often. But he still knew his son, and knew he wouldn't ask for a face-to-face out of the blue unless there was a good reason, and it concerned something that couldn't be discussed over the phone or email. His son had never served in the Armed Forces, but Cavarra had passed down an OpSec (operational security) mindset from an early age.

Officially, his son worked as a "market analyst" for an Internet Service Provider, but Cavarra knew better. Heck, he'd been the one to put in a word for his son with Cavarra's old spook contacts. Straight-laced agents with dark glasses went around questioning the boy's old teachers, coaches, friends, neighbors and employers. There was no mystery about what line of work Cavarra's son was in.

Which meant something awfully hairy must be going down.

Cavarra listened mostly to music on his satellite radio during the drive, but tuned to the news channel periodically to get the latest on the riots.

Rioters from the black neighborhoods had set up crude roadblocks at key intersections in a few cities, and had yanked many a white commuter out of their vehicles to be robbed, assaulted and/or killed. A grocery store owner who became a victim of looters on the first night now had armed guards at every door and was "racially profiling" all potential customers.

False Flag - Brown

Technically he was actually "class profiling," refusing to accept food stamps for anything, from anyone. But non-whites who were turned away at the doors were confident in their assumption that it was racial. The store came under siege first by a Hispanic mob, then the police.

The National Guard was on the scene in Amarillo, now. Clashes between whites and blacks in the street had died down, but impromptu roadblocks went up hastily, vehicles were attacked, and the cutthroat mobs dispersed faster than police could coordinate and arrive in force. People quit reporting for work at their jobs in the city, fearful of attack and aware the police couldn't protect them. Business was drying up fast, too, for the stores not destroyed in the riots. Neither commuters, customers, nor truckdrivers delivering supplies wanted to risk running the gauntlet.

There was an outbreak of arson all over, now, and police were being ambushed and killed when hunting down the riot organizers, despite the presence of the National Guard.

Some were demanding answers from the mayor and police commissioner as to why the riot squads weren't deployed right away on the day of the verdict. Blame was shuffled around like a hot potato as politicians passed the buck. Even the pundits Cavarra somewhat respected wanted to assume incompetence was behind it all—not intentional, criminal dereliction of duty.

Cavarra hoped the governor didn't order house-to-house searches for weapons. Texans might not stand for it. Amarillo was not Boston.

D MINUS 10
LEUCADIA, CALIFORNIA

Cavarra reached the beach that evening. It was cool enough by southern California standards that the sands were mostly deserted. Rocco got turned around a few times trying to remember how to get to the right lifeguard seat. He felt a pang of sadness realizing how long it had been since the last time he brought his kids here. He missed them. Especially the young, innocent versions of them. The older he got, the more he wished he could go back and spend more quality time as a dad.

After a few minutes he realized that the lifeguard station he remembered was no longer there. A more modern tower stood in its place.

As Cavarra approached it, there was movement to his right. A tall, athletic figure rose from where it had been sitting in the midst of some scrub brush on the sand near a 50-gallon barrel used for a trash can. In one hand was a partly emptied six-pack.

False Flag - Brown

There was enough light that evening for Cavarra to recognize him. He was still handsome, and in good shape, but was unshaven, disheveled and looked as though he'd drunk more alcohol than he was used to.

Justin wasn't a hugger. They shook hands. "Hi, Dad."

"How long you been out here?" Cavarra asked.

"Couple hours. Didn't want to risk missing you. Let's walk down by the surf, huh?"

They walked side-by-side toward where the cold breakers were crashing.

"You got a cellphone or any other electronic devices, Dad?"

"In the car," Cavarra said, smiling at the irony of his son questioning him about potential security risks.

"Want a beer?"

"Sure," Cavarra said, and took one. "How you been, Justin? Don't hear much from you anymore."

"Not much reason to hear from me," Justin replied. "Usually."

Upon reaching the surf, they turned to walk parallel with it. This was a good location for Justin to pick (if only it wasn't so far from both of them, now). The crash of waves would render it unlikely anyone with a long-range microphone could make out their conversation.

"Look, Dad, I know you're in Arizona now. I'm quite a ways from here, too. I couldn't risk long distance comms. This was the safest meet I could think of. I'll be in deep *caca* if anyone guesses what I'm doing. I took a couple vacation days; said I wanted to hook up with a girl I met online. I actually did meet with her earlier; and will again tomorrow, just to make it look real, in case."

"I'm warmed by your sacrifice," Cavarra quipped. "I hope she's not too ugly."

Justin ignored the joke. "I'm not for sure if you know what I do, Dad."

"I've got an idea."

Justin nodded. "I kinda' figured you put in a good word for me with your old contacts. Don't know I would have made it otherwise."

Cavarra shrugged. "All the good words in the world wouldn't get you hired, unless they saw talent."

"Technically, I work for the NSA," Justin said. "But my paycheck comes from the DHS. I hear that the NSA is going to hand over all its domestic work to the Department eventually, anyway—so it'll all be less confusing."

Cavarra nodded. "It's a tangled web, isn't it?"

"I don't know what you called it in the Navy," Justin said, "but what I do is compile data as intelligence is gathered. We use it to build profiles."

Cavarra raised an eyebrow. "Really? On who?"

False Flag - Brown

"DomTers," Justin said. "Domestic terrorists. Well, **potential** terrorists, anyway."

Cavarra was hoping the profiles would be of ISIS or Muslim Brotherhood operatives, double agents from Russia, China, North Korea, or some sort of external threat. But he feared it would be this. "Ah, the fabled 'List'."

"Not so fabled, Dad."

"Yeah, I know," Cavarra said, taking a swig of beer. "Once upon a time it really was just a paranoid theory. At some point fiction became fact. I know by the time of Janet Reno, at the latest, it was reality. Well, I mean I guess it goes back to J. Edgar Hoover. But Hoover was actually after folks who **hated** this country and wanted to bring it down. Now everything's upside-down and backwards."

"Since we got these new servers," Justin said, "you wouldn't believe how long The List got."

Cavarra grabbed his son's shoulder. "I know we didn't see eye-to-eye on everything, son. And you're pissed off at me for a lot of reasons. I get that. But this business they've got you involved in—it's wrong, Justin."

"Just wait," Justin said, polishing off his own beer. "So I get curious and look at some of the top level DomTer risk profiles the other day. I come across this one, and the name sounds familiar. He's ex-military, SpecOps, so I wonder if maybe I heard the name from you. But he was Army, not Navy."

"What's his name?" Cavarra asked.

"Last name is Scarred Wolf. I take it he's Native American."

Cavarra felt a cold sensation spread all through his body. "Oh my God."

"Wait, Dad." Justin held up his index finger, then opened another beer and took a long pull. "I try to open the profiles in his network. They're grayed out for some reason. But this chick works right next to me. Always talking my ear off. So I flirt with her a bit. Long story short, I memorized all her logins and passwords looking over her shoulder, because she blabs for so long she gets automatically logged out all the time. One night when she's gone, I log into her computer. It allows me to click on the grayed-out profiles."

"And my name came up on The List," Cavarra said, solemnly.

Justin nodded and chugged some more beer. "I don't know who wrote the program or how, but it must have recognized the match in our last name, and locked me out of the accomplice list. Now I'm wondering why they even cleared me for this job. But everything's growing so fast; procedures and protocols are being developed on the fly. We must have just partially slipped through the cracks on the user side."

False Flag - Brown

"It won't last," Cavarra said. "They'll make the connection sooner or later."

"Oh, they'll probably figure it out inside a week," Justin said. "The Internal Security bots will report that somebody viewed your profiles. It won't take a detective to figure out I'm the one. I'm toast, one way or the other."

Cavarra said, "Thanks for telling me, son. I guess it shouldn't surprise us."

"It was a surprise to me," Justin said, "to put it mildly."

Cavarra stopped, turning to stand facing the ocean. Justin faced out with him.

"I was never into politics," Justin said. "This job was a rush, in some ways. We get intelligence by way of some really cool technology. The things I consider at work...my next performance review, where I might be, how much I might be getting paid 10 years from now if I do a good job here...that's as far as I thought about what I'm doing. Remember that movie, *Jack Ryan*? That's me, briefing the president one day, I thought. Anyway, if my bosses say all these people are potential revolutionaries or whatever, they must be right. That's above my pay grade and the ones who decide have more information than I do."

Justin gulped some more beer. "Then I find out my dad is on The List."

"Domestic terrorist," Cavarra muttered, thoughtfully. "That's me, alright. Technically, that should qualify me to be the mentor of a presidential candidate. I could ghost write the autobiography of a 25 year-old nobody ever heard of, for a five-figure advance."

Justin squinted. "Huh?"

"Bill Ayers—commie terrorist that ran the Weather Underground. He ghost-wrote *Dreams From My Father*. Nevermind."

They watched moonlight flash on the waves for a moment.

"We've had our differences," Justin said, slurring his words just a bit. "But I know my dad is not a terrorist—domestic or any other kind. So I seriously doubt this Tommy Scarred Wolf dude is a terrorist threat, either."

"Well, you're right again," Cavarra said.

"You spent your life serving this country," Justin said. "You risked dying for it I don't know how many times. You sacrificed everything, including your family..."

Cavarra winced at this last item. It was true: his family fell apart because he was too busy commanding a SEAL Team. He took an early retirement to patch it up, but by then it was too late to save it.

"I know you loved us, despite what Mom says," Justin admitted, and belched. "And I know you're nobody's terrorist."

Cavarra took a deep breath, and let it out. "I still love my country. But the country's been hijacked. Now good is evil and evil is good. Patriots are terrorists and traitors are heroes."

For a while they just stood there, staring out to sea. Waves rolled in by relentless ranks, broke on the shoreline, only to be replaced by the next rank. The aftermath of each crash sent dying shock waves of water up the beach to lick at their feet. Cavarra could feel the sand being eroded out from underneath him with each succeeding wave, sinking him deeper. If he stood in the same spot long enough, they might bury him alive.

What a way to go.

"I'm glad you see that, Justin," he finally said. "That I loved you and your sister, I mean. And your mom, while I could."

Justin belched again and finished off his present beer. "I need to drain the lizard."

"You're right about them figuring it out, too," Cavarra said. "The transition wasn't complete when you first got hired, so I probably wasn't on The List, then. But sooner rather than later, they're gonna connect you to me, and you'll get the axe, for starters."

"Yeah," Justin agreed.

"As far as they're concerned, you're the enemy, too. You need to tell me everything you know about your department; their assets; how they operate; and what they have on me and my friends."

Justin nodded, and trudged away to take a leak.

False Flag - Brown

D MINUS NINE

ABSENTEE SHAWNEE TRUST LAND, OKLAHOMA

Gunther checked his heading by compass, and gave the hand-arm signal to move out. The night was cool and dark, but everyone's eyes were adjusted. They recognized the signal and filed after him out of the O.R.P. (objective rally point).

Each member of the patrol carried an AK, and a full load of 7.62X39 Warsaw Pact ammo. Gunther, on point, turned to check their intervals en route and saw the Saxton brothers were too bunched-up, again. He signaled for them to spread, and continued on.

He led them to the ambush site and stopped to direct them into position, man-by-man, counting heads as he went. A wide ditch simulated a road for this exercise. Their mission was to bushwhack a small supply convoy.

They didn't go by-the-book. They almost never did. For this mission, Gunther had Maurice Swope and Ralph White Feather carry out a sub-unit task which involved running a heavy length of steel cable across the roadway at a steep angle. On a real road it could be anchored between two telephone poles, if no big trees were handy. The lead vehicle would be pulled aside by the angling cable, into one of the poles. This method had been inspired by a proposed S.O.P. on a long-vanished website.

Little brother Carl's sub-unit task was to rig explosives on that pole to disable the engine, plus driver and gunner with any luck. The older guys, plus Jason Lone Tree and the Saxton brothers, pulled security during this time. The latter would serve as crew for a belt-fed weapon, should they ever acquire one.

Their noise discipline was excellent, as usual. The only hiccups came in handling the cumbersome coil of cable. Gunther thought it took entirely too long to string it.

There was nobody playing opfor (opposing force) so after a few minutes in position, Gunther coached them through actions on the objective. After all gear was secured, they fell back into a column-of-ducks and Gunther led them back to the LD (line of departure) by a different route.

Tommy shadowed them through the entire exercise, noting mistakes and weaknesses for later correction. Overall, it was an encouraging performance. Gunther had evidently kept the Shawnee Militia well-regulated and it showed in the execution of this drill. He led them well, too.

False Flag - Brown

Drilling the men was just another part of Tommy's life to be placed on hold when he took on cleaning up the mess the previous sheriffs had made of the office and the county.

He rested a little easier knowing that Gunther had stepped up to fill his shoes. Takoda hadn't participated in a drill for over a year, which was disappointing. But some of the older guys were now attending regularly and seemed to be taking it seriously.

Peaks and valleys, Tommy mused.

At the after-action review (A.A.R.), Gunther did a good job debriefing the unit. Tommy wouldn't have classified Gunther (or himself, for that matter) as a "natural leader," but he was a strong leader—natural or not. He had caught most of the mistakes made and chose wisely which to correct on the spot and which to deal with afterwards. The A.A.R. was perhaps similar to watching a head coach like Marv Levy or Joe Gibbs address his team after a close victory--giving credit where due but pointing out that there was room for improvement.

When done reviewing, Gunther turned it over to his father. Tommy was careful not to step on Gunther's toes. He spent twice as much time reemphasizing what Gunther said than he did adding additional corrections.

Afterwards it evolved into a bull session, as it usually did. Tommy was okay with this. They were citizen soldiers after all; not professionals. And some of them never saw each other except during a drill, so it was an opportunity to bond. Basic human psychology was at work, too. They were all thinking men, or they wouldn't participate at all. Each had opinions, and wanted to share them.

Tommy usually did a lot more listening than talking during these times, and this night was no exception.

Maurice Swope wondered aloud how relevant the exercise was. He couldn't think of a scenario in which a convoy would come through the rez. Several of his comrades jumped on that one and he rather deserved the scorn for popping off without thinking it through.

Gunther, quite the armchair military historian for the last couple years, then explained that interdiction was really the best offensive option in the strategic toolbox of an unorganized resistance movement against a large, well-supplied occupational force; and guerrilla units would live or die by the hasty ambush.

Ralph asked him who he envisioned as an occupational force, which initiated a debate about the current political situation.

Tommy often marveled at the cognitive dissonance of his people, and even a couple men in the Shawnee Militia suffered from it. On the one hand they constantly rehashed the record of betrayals by the federal government, and believed it would one day come after them again,

False Flag - Brown

perhaps to finish the genocide it failed to complete in the 1800s. They saw the increasingly tyrannical behavior of urban police as confirmation that such a holocaust was forthcoming. And yet, at the same time, they believed that the answer to nearly every problem was to give more power to the government.

Tommy finally spoke up. "Don't fall for the cover story. The issue isn't race; it's about control. The white man isn't your enemy, necessarily. Neither are Hispanics or blacks. All this racial identity *zeitgeist* is just a divide-and-conquer gambit. Sure, if the Neo-Nazis come here looking for a fight, we'll give them one. But that doesn't mean we welcome the Federal Gestapo with open arms, either. The enemy of our enemy is **not** necessarily our friend. That's stupid, infantile logic and it's why so many of the nations lost their lands and live on reservations now. We were so worried about petty squabbles and blood feuds with other tribes and clans, we made deals with the devil. Don't let the devil tell you who your enemy is this time. We can figure it out for ourselves."

A few of the braves vocalized their agreement with enthusiastic whoops or grunts.

"That's the **white** devil you mean, right?" Charlie Drake asked, and the others laughed.

Tommy received a text from Josh on his way home, declaring an urgent need for a secure chat ASAP.

Once they were connected, Josh wasted no time.

"I think the false flag is going down in Amarillo."

False Flag - Brown

Sitting at his computer desk, Tommy searched and clicked as he talked with Josh, to look at the same information his friend used to make his deduction.

"It's official," Josh said. "The announcement for this convention was made this morning. Now look at that roster of speakers. Anything seem odd to you?"

"Just tell me what's odd," Tommy said.

"It's supposed to be a big Utopian summit to smooth over race relations and find common ground and bind cultural wounds and ride unicorns farting rainbows," Josh explained, "right? And it's being held right there at the most infamous scene of racial strife in recent memory. Wouldn't you expect a lineup of the usual suspects—a bunch of communists and Black Muslims masquerading as civil rights champions —with maybe a token NeoCon speaker mixed in?"

"I guess," Tommy said. "That does sound like the kind of balance they usually give public forums."

"Look at these guys," Josh said. "What's their political affiliation? These speakers have been calling out the establishment for drone assassinations; indefinite detention without trial; using the IRS and FCC to crack down on dissenters. Where are all the lefties?"

"Could it be the pendulum is swinging the other way?" Tommy suggested.

"The pendulum is a myth, Tommy. No such thing. There's a Hegelian ratchet. This is just being efficient. These guys are a nuisance to the narrative; but being black they can't be silenced with the usual race card tactics. So silence them permanently, and frame another faction of your enemies."

"I don't buy it," Tommy said. "I've heard of some of these guys. Some of them are in Congress. But they're not a big enough threat to justify an operation of this scale."

"Pay attention, Chief," Josh said. "That's not the goal. It's just the gravy. The side benefit. They want justification for what they're about to do. If they can get rid of a thorn in their side at the same time...why not? And I guarantee you, after the fact, the politics of the victims won't come up—only their race. The politics of the patsy will come up though, at every opportunity, so that everyone of like mind will become racist by association."

Tommy read over the page which described the upcoming summit.

False Flag - Brown

The underlying theme was, "Whatever our color, we all love our children." Echoes of Martin Luther King's "I have a dream" speech. And a huge multicultural children's choir would be performing at the event. Tommy closed his eyes and pictured a dead, bloody child being cradled by a crying mother, or paramedic, or DHS agent. As loopy as Josh sounded so far, Tommy knew such an image would be enough for most people to cheer on whatever legislation Congress presented as a countermeasure.

"Macmillan just expanded his Amarillo station," Josh said. "He's been practically camped out down there. And Jade Simmons? Over the last few months she's visited Amarillo 20 times more than any other destination. You think she's just really, really interested in the Delton Williams business? Now look at the proposed venue for the summit."

Josh sent him a jpg file. Tommy opened it and studied the picture of an outdoor football stadium. He looked at it with a tactical eye. "Not an ideal spot for a bombing."

"You could kill plenty with the right kind of bomb," Josh said. "But they don't need a bomb this time. They've already got the Patriot Act and NDAA 2012, etc. *ad nauseum*. Bombs are *passe*, though I guess explosives could play a small part."

Tommy enlarged the picture.

"Look at the surrounding terrain," Josh said. "Yeah, you can post police snipers in a few locations, but what a crappy field of fire they'd have. Meanwhile, if you're a shooter for the other team, you've got all the options you could want. Huge avenues into the stadium from four directions, not counting going under and through the bleachers. Plenty of cover, including 15,000 or more other human bodies. No matter where you post security, they can be taken out with ease after just a little bit of recon."

"Do you know who's tasked with security?" Tommy asked.

"Yeah, and it's perfect: the county sheriff. When his security detail is compromised, and proves completely ineffectual, add yet another excuse to finish federalizing all law enforcement. You probably know from your own dealings with the Feds that they don't care much for guys like you who have jurisdiction but are accountable to the people. Too many sheriffs around the country have been interfering in their plans."

"This is Texas," Tommy reminded him. "Chances are a lot of people in the crowd will be armed, and just might return fire if something goes down."

"Again, perfect," Josh said. "Whoever does this is geared up with the new armor, that can stop rifle rounds...which Congress is also trying to ban, by-the-way. These Texans try to play hero, shoot back, wind up causing collateral damage and still don't stop the bad guys...it works like a charm. Pro-gun people been saying for years that hijackings and school shootings and the like would go down much differently if some of the victims were armed. This will be a case study for negating that argument. Armed civilians just make everything worse, see?"

Josh sent another file, which flashed in icon form at the bottom bar on Tommy's screen.

"I just sent you an update to the stadium's calendar," Josh said. "This summit is supposedly a spur-of-the-moment deal, inspired by the awful violence of the riots, blah blah blah. The summit organizers booked the stadium for this event weeks before the verdict was announced. Maybe not a smoking gun. But I find the timing interesting."

Tommy looked over the document and sighed. "Still pretty thin, Joshua. Seems like more of a hunch than a lead."

"Okay," Josh said. "You might be right. Maybe it's nothing. But you wanted me to look for potential targets, and this looks better than anything else right now."

"Explain more on the no-bomb aspect," Tommy said.

"They need a really big atrocity committed with 'assault weapons'," Josh explained. "The school shootings just haven't been getting it done for them. They need something big, and organized. I wouldn't be surprised if one or more of the shooters has a select-fire receiver from a 3D printer, either. They've got to find an excuse to shut that technology down. And it won't be a lone nut this time, I'm betting. Look for an entire unit, with right-wing militia *bona fides*. A whole squad or two of 'lone nuts,' who've assembled peacefully to plan this whole thing; have taken advantage of free speech to learn their deadly skills over the Internet or whatever; who used some kind of secure communication to recruit and coordinate; who took advantage of freedom of mobility to cross state lines, for some dastardly reason...let's see, what else? Oh, they're motivated partially by a hateful ideology hiding behind freedom of religion, of course. Who knows: maybe it'll turn out there's documented evidence that they failed to meet their daily quota of network news, too." Josh paused to utter a scoffing chuckle. "Maybe that's too tall of an order. But you can bet that 'hate speech' from alternative media sources will be cited as motivation so often that people will hear the talking points echo in their sleep."

Tommy thanked Josh for the research and opinions, and spent the next hour mulling it over.

It sounded like paranoid lunacy, of course. Josh was good for that, when you got him talking. But Tommy had come across some loony stuff in the past that just happened to be true.

And while he could come up with a rational explanation for everything Josh told him, something about this summit in Amarillo did

False Flag - Brown

smell wrong. Lawrence Bertrand had organized false flags in the past. Two people working directly for him had been spending a lot of time in Amarillo. A supposedly last-minute organized event had been planned well in advance...

Tommy wanted more tangible proof. But with Bertrand and his stooges operating in secret, could there ever be much more to go on?

Tommy was so deep in thought, he jumped when his cellphone beeped.

A text message came in from an unknown phone. It had call signs once used by himself and Rocco Cavarra, and a brevity code from their last mission which meant "Rendezvous last rally point ASAP."

Where had he and Rocco last met?

It had been after the victory party. Tommy had taken his friends out to one of his deer stands so Leon could zero his new rifle. They had a good time, but Tommy didn't enjoy it as much as he would have, after the debacle Takoda engineered at the party.

Tommy didn't have encrypted commo with Rocco like he did for Josh. But he needed to know how soon to expect him. This cloak-and-dagger stuff was a pain in the 4th point.

He finally texted back: "Text again two hours out."

The reply came back: "Wilco."

False Flag - Brown

42
D MINUS EIGHT
ABSENTEE SHAWNEE TRUST LAND, OKLAHOMA

They met at the deer stand the next day. Rocco introduced Tommy to his son, Justin, who shared the same information he'd given his father.

Tommy questioned Justin, to get a feel for the big picture. Then he merely sat in silence for a while, pondering the madness of it all.

"Rennenkampf is up toward the top of The List with us," Rocco said. "And some of my friends, too."

Tommy snorted out what could pass for a cynical laugh. Josh Rennenkampf had been operating for years under the assumption that a list like this existed somewhere. It was just another one of his paranoid, tinfoil hat quirks.

"Just because I'm paranoid doesn't mean they're not out to get me," Joshua often said, poking fun at himself while never quite letting go of his fringe lunatic beliefs.

"You remember our conversation about false flags," Tommy said, locking eyes with Rocco. "And the secret teams that have been operating possibly as far back as the JFK assassination?"

Rocco nodded. "The 'tier zero' units; like the ones we ran into in Sumatra."

"Yeah," Tommy said. "Josh thinks he may have found their next target."

"I'm listening," Rocco said.

Tommy shared Josh's theory about the race relations summit. Rocco listened and worked his jaw for a bit afterwards. "So the purpose of this convention is to find common ground," he mused aloud. "Meet halfway. Extend the olive branch; whatever. So then the right-wing boogeyman shows up and proves himself just as evil and dangerous as we've been told all along. The implied message is that the 'good guys' tried to compromise with the 'bad guys,' but there is no compromising with them. It's fatal to try. In other words, what nobody on TV's got the balls to admit about Islam... is what they're gonna try to pin on the liberty movement here at home."

"So you don't think it's far-fetched?" Tommy asked.

"I didn't say that," Rocco replied. "But we've seen a lot of far-fetched scenarios play out in recent history, and they multiply at a geometric rate. Fast and Furious; *Benghazi*; using the IRS to shut down political opponents; stealing elections with massive voter fraud; trading five top terrorist leaders for one turncoat deserter; bypassing Congress to implement a *de facto* invasion; getting caught red-handed making deals with your Russian bedfellows to compromise national security; all Hillary's emails magically disappear from every server...those are all pretty far-fetched And not anybody who matters was ever held accountable for any of it. Nixon was guilty of what—conspiring to cover up a petty burglary? But now the same press that crucified him **participates** in the coverups. It's ludicrous. But people are conditioned to accept the ludicrous, and only be truly suspicious of people who question the official story. Maybe Rennenkampf is just shooting in the dark. We won't know for sure until after the fact."

"Right," Tommy said. "Exactly."

Rocco waved toward his son. "Justin's been working on the other side. He's never seen things the way I do. What do you think, son? Is this beyond the scope of possibility?"

Justin took a long time to answer. Finally, he said, "Since I found out my father is considered an enemy of the state, I've been thinking a lot about what I've seen and heard, and what I've been taught. There's like this...atmosphere. It's like we're working toward something really ambitious, and it's going to kick off at any time. Nobody says it out loud, but you get that impression, you know? There's a sea change coming, and we have to be ready, because it's going to be crazy for a while, but we're going to do great things and be heroes before it's all done. That's the atmosphere of the world I live in."

"You're saying it's not a ridiculous theory, then," Tommy said.

Justin shrugged. "I can't give concrete evidence. But it's like we're expected to be able to do whatever is necessary, even if it seems kind of fishy. I can see this Amarillo scenario being true. To be honest, I could have seen myself playing a part. Of course they take pains to compartmentalize everybody in the Department. I'd have never known the full story. But even if I knew that we were selling a hoax, and innocent people would die, I'm sure I'd tell what lies I had to, and break a few rules, to make sure my part of it went without a hitch."

Tommy grimaced. "Why?"

Justin shrugged. "Eggs and omelet, I guess. I've never bothered much with politics. It's kinda' like *Who Wants to be a Millionaire*, where you base a decision on what the audience thinks. Most people think the government and news networks are honest and have good intentions. The majority must be right, right? Plus I work for the guys doing this. They're smart people. They think all these misfits clinging to guns and religion are dangerous; ergo: they **are** dangerous. Putting these dangerous people where they can't hurt anybody must be worth telling a few lies, breaking a few rules..."

"Killing a few innocents?" Tommy asked.

Justin shrugged again and stared at his feet. "Right."

False Flag - Brown

Rocco thrust he hands in his pockets and paced. "People just don't ask questions. We forgot how to ask questions."

"Thanks for your honesty, Justin," Tommy said.

"When is this convention supposed to be?" Rocco asked.

"Next Saturday," Tommy said.

Rocco sighed. "Let's say Rennenkampf is wrong about the false flag. Say he's just chasing after the wind on that." Rocco pointed at his son. "The stinking secret police have us at the top of a watch list of domestic terrorists, Tommy. They've got lists of our friends and family. They've got our credit card numbers; our utility bills; they're watching our bank accounts, email and Internet activity. They've got aerial spy footage of where we live and work. How long do we have before they take action on this intelligence?"

Tommy shook his head. "Maybe 20 years. Maybe five minutes. I don't know."

Rocco continued to pace, his boots stirring up tiny clouds of dust on the prairie floor. "I'd like to know where you're at mentally, Chief. Are you entertaining the possibility that they never intend to act on it? Maybe they collected it just out of curiosity and only keep it in case they need to help you if you lock your keys in your car or something?"

"No," Tommy said, quietly.

Rocco stopped pacing. "Then my next question is: are you going to just pretend it doesn't exist until they kick in your door at zero-dark-thirty some morning? If not, what are you willing to do about this?"

Tommy remained silent for a while, then said, "This involves more people than just us right here. Maybe the first thing we should do is bring them into the loop."

D MINUS SIX
LAS ANIMAS COUNTY, COLORADO

A special operations veteran had friends...and then he had **friends**.

It was a brotherhood of sorts that many never completely dropped out of, even after throwing boots over the wire. "*Nijenina*" was the word Tommy Scarred Wolf used to describe the men in this unorthodox fraternity.

For a true member of the brotherhood, a man would drop whatever he was doing and travel around the world to help a brother in trouble. When a brother called you out of the blue and said your presence was urgently required at, say, some remote area near the San Isabel Forest, you went. You delayed plans, called in sick, pissed off the wife or girlfriend; and it had better doom-well be something of utmost importance. But you went.

False Flag - Brown

Men began arriving at Josh and Jenny's mountain home the next day, and straggled in from all over for the next 24 hours. The hosts made room for them as best they could and Jenny ensured everyone ate well.

Josh, Tommy and Cavarra were present, of course. Also Leon, Carlos and Justin. Rocco's old SEAL buddies Butch, Jorge and Tony showed up. Josh's friend Griz, plus some other 5th Group friends of Tommy's, Kurt and Frank, joined them. Phil Jenkins, who the surviving Retreads knew from the Sudan mission, was the final partner in crime.

Cavarra had briefly considered inviting Mac, but Leon talked him out of it.

Mac's attitude bothered Leon. He didn't trust him. Mac was different now. Or maybe it was the world that was different.

Rocco gave them the sitrep (situation report), calling Justin and Josh to brief them on specifics. News of The List didn't make anyone happy, but neither did it surprise most of them. The reactions to Josh's theory about the false flag were more varied.

They all agreed on the gist of the national situation: the news media was nothing but an Orwellian propaganda machine, attempting to distract or confuse when it wasn't lying outright. It suppressed more news than it reported. The government, meanwhile, was pretty blatant about their intentions, for anyone paying attention who hadn't been brainwashed by the media. To the ruling establishment, Public Enemy Number One was the American people. Occupants of the Oval Office gave strategic military secrets to the Red Chinese and the Russians without batting an eye.

It was an armed populace that could move around freely and say, publish, or learn anything it wanted to that **really** worried those trusted with the reins of power.

*Coup de tat*s were easy in other countries. But in the USA, obstacles to consolidation of power had been purposely built into the structure of government.

Those safeguards had been gradually dismantled over the last century. Many observers assumed the process had been a random sequence of steps that just happened push all in the same direction purely by coincidence. People like Josh Rennenkampf believed the fundamental transformation was by design.

If the direction of the country was not set by benevolent altruists with strong parental instincts who just happened to consistently violate their oaths of office by accident; but by people willing to lie, steal and scheme in order to achieve their own goals by whatever means necessary, then the most formidable obstacle to the course-setters was the will of the people.

False Flag - Brown

Americans took their freedoms for granted, but most would prefer to keep them. They would prefer to live comfortably, avoid war, and be governed by representatives accountable to them. And some of them resisted infringement on their right to keep arms. History had proven, time and time again, that crisis was required to make Americans surrender portions of their political inheritance.

If the coincidence theorists were the true tinfoil hat camp, then it only made sense that crises would be manufactured when there wasn't one handy to exploit. There was at least one more major crisis needed before the will of the people could be neutralized once and for all.

While each of the men gathered at the Rennenkampf place had experienced enough of human nature to realize that people do tend to conspire when they know there is strong opposition to their ambitions; for some reason they had trouble believing that authority figures shared that human tendency. That was one of the points raised in a marathon debate among the former operators.

That presumption sounded ridiculous when summarized in simple terms, and tempers flared.

Tommy and Cavarra shared some details of their encounter with a "tier zero" team overseas. Cavarra went on to repeat some scuttlebutt he heard when assigned to the NSA headquarters at Fort Meade, about a Black Ops department specifically assigned to develop false flags.

The final consensus was that a false flag in Amarillo was possible, but unlikely.

Jennifer wasn't present, having left the testosterone-flooded living room to give them privacy, but Josh brought up the point that she had made: that if such an event was possible, they should at least plan for the possibility.

"I see the false flag as the easier thing to deal with," Cavarra told everyone. "Whether it's real or not, just get the stadium cleared. Call in a bomb threat or something. If the attack does come, the victims are evacuated beforehand."

A few men nodded agreement.

"As for The List, a cyber attack is the way to go," Rocco continued. "Josh is a pretty good hacker. I'll let him take over, here."

Josh stood and turned to face the men scattered around his living room. He pointed to Justin. "I've been finding out what I can about the Data Center. What I want to do is wipe their database. I mean totally clean out all the info they're holding, and jack it up so bad they'll have to start from scratch."

Leon folded his arms across his chest. "Won't that wipe out legitimate data along with the illegal stuff? I mean, they collect poop on foreign powers, too, and real terrorists."

"I don't know if you've noticed," Josh said, dryly, "but nobody in Washington has shown any interest in stopping **actual** threats to our national security. Whistleblowers and guys like us are the only ones they consider dangerous. So what good is that intelligence if they never intend to use it anyway?"

"We've been over this before," Rocco said. "We should move along."

"Anyway," Josh continued, "I don't think I can hack in from the outside, as it stands. Or it might take me years to do it, and who knows how much time we have. With Justin's help from the inside I think we can install a back door through all the security of his facility. I'm developing a really destructive blended threat which should be able to infect all the databases and even the software, working its way into every intranet linked to it."

"Won't their protection detect the virus and destroy it?" asked Tony.

"That's why I need Justin to open the back door," Josh said. "I'll have to disable their security, without them knowing it, before I can upload the worm." He cleared his throat and paused for a moment. "I don't want to bore you with a bunch of geek talk, so let's leave it at that for now. But there's something else I'd like to do. Justin's bosses have access to the Emergency Alert Service. That means they can override programming any time. All programming. I think while I'm in there, doing this, I should use that to send a message to every TV on every cable system about what's going on."

A few of the men laughed, or whooped. They obviously liked this idea.

"That's really gonna piss them off," Frank said.

"Ya think?" Butch replied, sarcastically. "They might put us on a list or something, huh?"

"It's a big turd burger any way you look at it," Tommy said. "The Gestapo will go on pretending they'll live-and-let-live for as long as we swallow it. They're coming after us sooner or later. Our choice is to wait until it's too late, or do something about it while we still have time."

Griz, the big, bearded man who looked like a viking without the funny hat, said, "I like it. Wake the sheeple out of their boob-tube trance if you can. Maybe some of them will stay awake afterwards. It's worth a try."

A few men grunted agreement.

"Does anybody think we should **not** try to hijack the signal if we can?" Cavarra asked.

Nobody spoke.

False Flag - Brown

"Okay," Josh said. "Now with all I need to tweak once Justin opens the back door, it's not something I can do with a laptop at Starbucks. I need a hardwired connection into the Data Center that can move a whole lot of information fast. And I'm probably going to need a few hours to do this, because I'll need to tweak some software on the fly, once I see what it is. Also, there are some things I can't accomplish remotely. Someone has to physically be there to push certain buttons."

"If that's the case, maybe we should just break into the Data Center itself," Carlos said.

"The Center itself was built on Camp Williams," Rocco said. "The Utah National Guard is all around the place, and there's a Special Forces Group there, as well. We could probably break in. Some of us might even make it out. But to stay there long enough to give Josh the time he needs? Too much can be brought down on top of us. That's a suicide mission."

"But information does flow in and out of the Data Center," Josh said. "And they don't rely solely on microwave towers. The country at large may be completely vulnerable to an E.M.P. attack, but the NSA wants to be able to continue spying on us even if the grids go down. So they've got some hardened satellite installations here and there. I think I can get in from one of those. I need you guys to help me get in, and cover me while I work."

"What about the false flag?" Griz asked. "I mean, I know it might not be real. But what if it is?"

Tommy stood and turned to address everyone. "He's right. I'm gonna take a few people with me to Amarillo before the convention starts, just in case an anonymous phone call isn't enough."

"We've decided that both operations should be simultaneous," Cavarra said. "If the false flag is real, then at least some of the Feds' resources will be tied up in that, which could give us some extra time."

"This substation, or satellite facility, or whatever it is," Butch said, "It'll be guarded too, won't it?"

Cavarra nodded, grimly. "Yeah. I was honest with you. I never said 'there's good news and bad news.' There's only bad news...and slightly less bad news."

False Flag - Brown

Terrance Handel parked his car in the roped-off area in the desert which served as a parking lot. There were thousands of cars already parked there, though the festival didn't officially kick off until that afternoon. He took an extra day of vacation so he could make the drive and still be early for the commencement ceremony.

So far he hadn't done any drinking. So far there were no more gaps in his memory. He rewound back through the last couple days...yup: he remembered every mundane detail.

Terrance pulled his backpack out of the car, locked the doors and wandered over in the direction of the signs, banners and pole-mounted loudspeakers. The pack was heavily loaded and despite his upper body strength, lifting it and getting it on his back took some effort.

It was perhaps a half mile walk before he reached other human beings. Banners and pennants flapped in the desert breeze everywhere—rainbow banners, yin-and-yang, the U.N. flag, several flags with yellow stars on either red or red-and-blue fields, plus banners bearing the portraits of Mao Tse Teung, Che Guevara and Barack Obama.

Tents were erected in many different groupings. Some people were still setting up their tents. There were more middleaged and elderly than Terrance would have preferred; but they at least were outnumbered by people closer to his age, including some bangable chicks.

Portable toilets were already in place. Plenty of booths and kiosks littered the landscape. Long tables were stacked with merchandise in a flea market type plaza. All this lined the borders of the festival area. In the middle was a large, bare clearing, surrounding a shaded stage with enormous amplifiers all around it. The stage was high, on top of what must be a sound-deadening shelter for the generators, and it extended out in an ornate design, like some ancient temple from Rome, Greece. or Egypt.

After having a look around, Terrance located the hottest babe still putting up a tent, with an open space adjacent, and dropped his backpack there. He approached the girl (a petite blonde with tanned and toned legs, and high-sitting C-cup breasts) smiled and introduced himself.

She smiled back. "I'm Kari."

"Looks like we're going to be neighbors," Terrance said.

He offered to help her finish staking out her tent. She accepted. The small talk went well as they worked together, then her boyfriend arrived with a plastic ice chest. She introduced them.

False Flag - Brown

Terrance had been hoping Kari was alone or had come with girlfriends. Now he regretted choosing this spot.

There had been another chick with space to camp next to her. She had D-cup breasts and a small waist, but her hips were kind of wide. He should probably have picked her anyway. But likely somebody else had already claimed that spot by now. Besides, he really didn't want to have to lift that backpack again today.

Kari's tent was all set minutes after her boyfriend arrived. Terrance pulled his own tent out of his pack and began unrolling it.

Kari stooped and took hold of Terrance's backpack, as if to move it. She grunted and let go, standing and rubbing her lower back. "Oh my god. Nice to see you packed light."

"It's good where it is," Terrance said.

"Did you go to Burning Man?" Kari asked, squatting opposite him to assist in stretching out his tent.

"No," Terrance said. "This is the first thing like this I've gone to."

"What made you decide to come?" the boyfriend asked.

"I don't know," Terrance replied. "Just wanted to see something memorable, I guess."

"Well, you will," Kari said. "If it's anything like last year, or like Solstice Slam, you'll never forget the experience. I wish I could just stay out here all year 'round."

Terrance assembled the fiberglass poles and stuck one through the loops sewn into the tent seams. "Speaking of forgetting, I heard one of the workshops here is about restoring memory."

"Why? You have Alzheimer's?" the boyfriend asked. It seemed he felt a little threatened by the attention Kari payed Terrance, and was looking for an opportunity to insult him.

"Oh, they have so many workshops," Kari said. "Memory loss; healthy eating; meditation; sexual healing...there's something for everybody. And the music...it's like, so incredible."

"Something for everybody?" Terrance replied, skeptically. He flexed the first pole into position, the fittings sewn to the tent floor holding it bowed. "I kind of doubt that."

"No, really," the boyfriend said. "They even have groups for fascist pigs here."

Kari gave her boyfriend a look, then said, "Yeah. One of the groups is called *Shinar* Soldiers and *Montauk* Marines. It's for people who've been a part of the military industrial complex, but who love the Earth and care about people around the world. You look kind of military, to me. Are you?"

"Used to be," Terrance said. As soon as he heard the name of the group, he felt compelled to check it out. Just as he couldn't explain why he wanted to spend his vacation out in the desert with a bunch of treehuggers, he couldn't explain why he wanted to drop in on the "*Shinar* Soldiers and *Montauk* Marines." But he knew he was going to do it.

False Flag - Brown

The police were unable to track down the vigilante group in the chaos, but acting on tips they did bring in Kenneth Fowler—a man accused of hate crimes against the demonstrators.

While Fowler was locked in jail awaiting trial, a small group of counter-demonstrators showed up outside the courthouse. They carried signs with messages like "HATE CRIME=THOUGHT CRIME," "STOP THE DISCRIMINATION," and "RAPE & MURDER OK, BUT SELF-DEFENSE IS PUNISHED."

With so many police around, this was the safest area in the city. The little counter-demonstration attracted the attention of everyone but the news media, and people wandered closer to see what the gathering was about.

A white woman with a pixie hairdo, a belly protruding farther out than her breasts, and a hard sneer, read a few of the signs and called out "Go home, you pathetic scum! Your racist martyr is in jail where he belongs!"

A couple of the counter-demonstrators responded. More individuals wandered over, and joined the sneering woman. The counter-demonstrators were called racist and all the usual names. They countered by asking what race had to do with the issue, which they saw as a right to property and self-defense.

While the white folks went back and forth, Tareyton Daniels swaggered over to see what was up. Tareyton was six foot three and built like a bouncer. He only had two tattoos on his dark brown skin--both portraits. One was of Malcolm X; the other of Muhammed Ali. One of his front teeth was gold. Both his ears were pierced. He wore a gold watch that was part of what he looted during the initial riots, and carried brass knuckles he traded food stamps to acquire, along with a bag of weed.

Tareyton never laughed because he found nothing funny. The most amusing thing in life was pain.

Other people's pain.

His favorite color was black. His favorite team was the Panthers. His favorite pastime was the Knockout Game.

He came up on the demonstration and read the signs, but didn't understand what they meant. He listened to the white folks without signs taunt the white folks who did have signs for a few minutes. Then he

False Flag - Brown

understood that the ones with the signs were against the riots.

They were against black people.

Tareyton Daniels didn't play that. He was about to show those crackers what year it was.

Tareyton shoved the butch white chick out of the way to get to a 40-something man holding a sign.

"'Scuse me, man. Check this out," he said, and cold-cocked the guy with a blow right behind the ear.

The old white fool went down, banging his head on the pavement. He wasn't getting up any time soon.

Some pink toe started yelling like a bitch, "Police! Call the police!"

An old white woman with a sign got up in his grill, but he knocked her out with one punch to the face. He bore down on the little bitch yelling for the police, grabbing him by the arm...

Something hit the back of Tareyton's knees, causing them to buckle. Then something crashed into the side of his head.

Tareyton staggered back a few steps before his vision cleared. There before him stood a skinny little white fool with his dukes up like he wanted to throw down. It must have been him that kicked him in the back of the knees and walloped him in the head. Furious, Tareyton stalked toward him and swung a roundhouse at his head.

White Boy ducked under the punch, hit Tareyton hard in the gut twice, then his little white fist clipped Tareyton's mouth.

"C'mon you big chickenshit!" the pink toe jeered. "You're not up against a woman or an old man, now!"

Tareyton touched his lips and his fingers came away bloody. He slipped on the brass knuckles and charged the little pink toe fool. The punk could fight. But Tareyton outweighed him by at least 80 pounds. He would get him on the ground where he could use his weight...

Unfortunately for Tareyton and the others opposing the demonstrators, not every curious passerby was on their side of the issue. A few more pink toes showed up wearing cowboy hats, boots, and big ugly belt buckles. They weren't interested in peaceful resolution or involving the police. They not only went to work on Tareyton, but on the males in the anti-protest contingent.

As people of color came upon the scene, they saw one of their own getting a beating, and that was all the stimulus needed. Fists, elbows and knees flew in a brutal, growing melee, while the counter-demonstrators evacuated their injured compatriots out of the area.

Cops moved in to break it up, but not with enough numbers. The belligerents were more frenzied than the police were prepared for, and the cops got swallowed by the churning violence. Both sides were like

False Flag - Brown

rabid dogs, ready to die before they backed down.

More people joined in. More cops joined in. Word spread through the streets. A camera crew for a news affiliate finally took notice. They went live with the rumble in the background while an attractive reporter gave the landmark report of her career, describing how a right-wing mob had attacked peaceful black demonstrators.

***

Meldrick Jones hadn't joined in the looting and vandalism of the last several days. Not because he wasn't on board with defying the oppression by the white devil. It was because...well, there was just something undignified about walking the streets in a mob, burning, looting and fighting. Meldrick couldn't picture a Denzel Washington character in a movie doing any of that, so he didn't do it. If brotha Denzel was above it, then Meldrick was above it.

He hadn't seen his neighbor, Cleveland, since before the riots started. But Ms. Harris, two houses down, had been on TV.

Meldrick was the sales manager for a furniture store downtown. He hadn't been to work for days because the store had been looted and burned. Most likely it was out of business for good. He had spent the afternoons since then calling around his network to find another job, but there were no openings at a level commensurate with his expertise.

The low-hanging fruit was just to go on welfare. But Denzel wouldn't go on welfare. That brotha would find a title and position worthy of his swag even in the midst of a zombie apocalypse.

The looters showed how undignified they were, by putting a brotha out of a job. Sure, some rich old white fool owned the furniture store, but the looters should have checked first, to make sure there were no black employees working there.

Well, at least the riots had left Meldrick's neighborhood alone.

Until now.

A commotion outside got Meldrick's curiosity up. He stepped through his front door to check it out.

Down the street a house was on fire. Hundreds of men were on the streets, yelling, throwing rocks, smashing car windows and mirrors. Even at this distance, it was obvious they were all Hispanic.

Meldrick's wife and daughter joined him on the front lawn. "What's going on?" his wife asked.

Meldrick didn't answer.

"This must be *La Raza*," his daughter said. "I kept hearing about them when school was in session, from the Mexicans."

257

False Flag - Brown

She hadn't left the house for days, because all the schools were closed. Teachers and bus drivers feared for their lives and didn't want to risk the commute, even with the National Guard securing the roads.

"*La Raza*?" Meldrick's wife repeated. "Why are they tearing up **our** neighborhood? They should be down around Polk Street or somewhere, burning white people's houses."

"Baby," Meldrick said, "go inside and call the police."

She put hands on hips and shifted her head from side-to-side as she said, "Nigga, it's the po-po who started all this from jump, in case you forgot. How you gonna ask them to come save a black neighborhood? Far as they're concerned, we might as well be part of the ghetto."

He grabbed her by the shoulder and said, "Well call the National Guard, then. Just call 911 and tell 'em what's goin' down."

A chubby young man with a Mohawk, who had just demolished a mailbox with a sledgehammer, glanced down the cul-de-sac and spotted Meldrick's wife and daughter. He turned to his nearest comrades, thumping them on the chest and pointing down the street at the two females. Those men turned to alert others.

This was bad.

"Get inside! Now!" Meldrick pushed them both through the front door. His wife turned back to protest, but saw a wave of Hispanic men begin to advance toward her house and changed her mind. She found a phone and dialed 911.

"I can't get through!" she cried. "It's like the switchboard is jammed!"

Meldrick followed them inside, closed and locked the door.

His daughter tuned the TV to a news broadcast which showed a street battle taking place down by the courthouse.

"Looks like the police are busy," she said.

Pounding began on the front door. Meldrick wondered how long the lock could hold.

A rock smashed through the living room window. The females screamed. Meldrick searched around desperately for a weapon. All he could find was a statue of an African warrior. He gripped it as he would a club, trying hard to think.

What would a Denzel character do in a situation like this?

***

The buses weren't running and it was too dangerous to walk the streets nearly anywhere in Amarillo. Entire residential neighborhoods were burnt down, and swarms of refugees seeking shelter from the cold broke into whatever buildings were left unguarded. Anyone brave or stupid enough to walk the streets unarmed got robbed, usually by violent methods. The stolen money went to buy food and drugs, when such could be found.

Arden Thatcher drove his Toyota to the suburbs and waited in the Wal-Mart parking lot until the plain blue S.U.V. with tinted windows parked next to him. Arden exited his pickup, opened the passenger door of the S.U.V. and quickly slipped in. Ted was behind the wheel. The engine was still running.

Ted shifted into gear and took off.

"You been watchin' what's goin' on?" Arden asked, exuberantly. "We been kickin' those niggers' asses all over town."

"Yeah? How about you?" Ted asked. "You been involved?"

Arden shrugged, losing some of his zeal. "Just a little bit. Nothin' serious; you know. And nobody in the F.A.P. knows anything 'bout it."

"You sure?" Ted asked, turning from the road ahead to flash him a sharp, measuring look.

"Oh yeah. I swear to god, Ted."

"Listen Arden, this is very important: did anyone from F.A.P. contact you since the riots started?"

"Yeah."

"Tell me about that conversation."

Arden adjusted the seat, leaned back and gazed at the roof of the vehicle for a moment. "Well, they asked if I was alright, and I was like, 'yeah.' Then they was like, 'are you in any danger? Are the rioters gettin' close?' And I was like, 'no, they know better than to come anywhere near Polk Street.' So they was like, 'keep your powder dry, and your bugout bag handy, and keep an ear out. Call us if anything happens that you know about.' That was pretty much it."

"Do you know anything about a squad-sized militia unit that shot up one of the rioters' roadblocks?" Ted asked, steering into a freeway on-ramp.

Arden giggled. "Hell yeah! I heard they shot up over a hunnert niggers over there. They went coon huntin', is what they did!"

"Do you know who did it? Anybody in the Free American Patriots talk about it?"

Arden shook his head.

"Has anyone in F.A.P. told you to bug out; or said that they're bugging out?"

Arden shrugged. "No, not to me. I mean, but they're all thinkin' it might come to that, if the police or the National Guard start searchin' house-by-house."

Ted pulled onto the highway and accelerated to flow-of-traffic speed.

False Flag - Brown

"All right. Now listen, Arden. Pay real close attention."

Arden did as he was told.

"It's going down," Ted said. "You've screwed up over and over. But you've got a chance to redeem yourself. You just have to do exactly what you're told. You ready?"

"I'm ready," Arden said, eagerly. This was it? He finally had a chance to prove himself, then.

"First thing you're gonna do is call your squad leader in the unit. With me so far?"

Arden nodded.

"You're gonna give him the code phrase for everyone to link up at the oil rig. Don't say anything else. Just that and hang up."

"Oh," Arden said. "So how am I gettin' to the oil rig? You're takin' me?"

"You're not going there. **They** are. We're gonna nail them to the wall, finally."

Arden cried a rebel yell.

Ted cringed, rubbed his ear and shot an angry glance at him. "Don't do that again. Now listen: I'm taking you somewhere to meet some guys. They're going to give you some gear and a weapon."

""Wow. Really? 'Cause I didn't bring mine. I didn't know I'd need one tonight."

"That's alright. We got you covered. But you just keep your mouth shut and your ears open. Do as you're told and don't say anything unless one of the men on the team asks you a question."

"I'm gonna be on a team?" Arden asked, hopeful.

"Yup. And if you do exactly what you're told, you'll get to shoot some niggers before it's all over."

Traffic thinned out as they headed out of town.

Arden phoned his contact, and gave the appropriate code phrase.

***

Members of the Free American Patriots grabbed their bugout bags and headed for the designated rendezvous at an abandoned oil rig outside Amarillo. Most of them were half-expecting this call. It seemed the world around them was coming apart.

They were all paying attention. They all believed that the times were grim. They all answered the call.

They gathered, performed a head count and realized that Arden Thatcher, who made the call, was the only member absent.

Federal agents were waiting for them.

False Flag - Brown

Everyone had left their weapons in their vehicles, so nobody had the ability to resist when the Feds sprang the trap.

False Flag - Brown

Carl's dad called a meeting of the Shawnee Militia the night he got back, and nearly all the active members showed up. Even Takoda.

Tommy told them he needed volunteers to go with him out of state Friday and not return until Saturday evening at the earliest. All the older members begged off at that point. Tommy thanked and dismissed them. To the young men who remained, Tommy warned them the mission would be either boring or dangerous, and gave them the opportunity to decline.

Nobody did.

For Carl's part, he would gladly endure some boredom if it meant a possibility of excitement or doing something useful. With the exception of his father and oldest brother, none of them had ever done anything but train. This was something real.

All except Carl were old enough to join the conventional Armed Forces. But plenty of men throughout history had gone to war even younger than him.

Tommy explained that what he needed them for was lookout duty. There was a convention at a football stadium in Amarillo on Saturday; and a possibility of some sort of terrorist attack taking place, there. They would place an anonymous bomb threat call to get the stadium evacuated. But just in case, Tommy wanted men placed strategically around the place, on the lookout for anything suspicious.

They would all have radios to keep in constant contact. They would also all be armed. This was Race Riot Central, after all, and anything could happen.

Carl kept cool on the outside that week, but inside he was chomping at the bit. He almost didn't hang out with his friends like usual, but Ray kept pressuring him.

It was hard to turn Ray down. Normally the gang just played videogames at Ray White Bird's house. But lately Ray's older sister Rachel had been kicking it with them a lot, and she seemed to like Carl.

Carl didn't normally pay much attention to adults outside his family, but he did enjoy Rachel's attention. She had moved out years before and Ray said she almost never visited before she discovered her little brother's friendship with Carl. His friends noticed what was going on and said she was into Carl. They made conspiratorial comments about how older girls were experienced and knew how to show a good time. Carl wasn't a natural with women, like Takoda was, so he didn't know how to escalate, much less close the deal. Besides, he wasn't even positive she had romantic aspirations. He'd be a real ass if he tried to put the moves on when all she had in mind was friendship.

With his big day coming up, Carl still didn't want to blow off his friends. And he didn't want to miss the chance to see Rachel. So he decided to just drop by, briefly, Friday afternoon before meeting his brothers for the Amarillo trip.

***

Rachel White Bird had quite a stroke of luck with the youngest Scarred Wolf boy, since he was buddies with her own kid brother. She used the connection to get close to Carl.

Rachel didn't get a lot of romantic attention from men her own age and older. Some of them treated her like "one of the guys," which is what she once thought she wanted. It turned out she didn't enjoy her status all that much. She would have preferred the romantic attention of some high-status men, but they chased after prissy missies. They were probably intimidated by a strong, independent woman like her with a take-charge attitude. But somebody as young and obviously inexperienced as Carl Scarred Wolf had not yet been jaded, or scared, or whatever most men's problem was these days.

She kind of liked Carl—he was smart, intense, and as modest as a teenage boy could be. That made it easier to get to know him. And as she came to know him better, she found more of his buttons to push. She just about had him figured out.

Close enough, anyway.

Carl arrived that afternoon with Ray's other videogame junkie pals, but he didn't remove his jacket, and shied away when she tried to take it off him.

"I'm not staying long," he said.

"What's up?" Ray asked.

"Just got something else going on tonight," Carl said. "I can't hang out this time."

The other boys probed him for details, but Carl was evasive. Finally Ray convinced him to come down to the basement for a minute. He just **had** to show him the latest weapon or something in one of his stupid games. Carl went down, as did all the boys.

Knowing he would have to come back upstairs to leave, Rachel remained in the kitchen. She poured a mixture of whiskey and soda in two plastic cups, and waited.

When Carl returned, he waved, smiled, and made as if to walk right

False Flag - Brown

by and exit.

"Come here," she said.

He altered course and joined her where she leaned against the kitchen counter.

"You were kind of rude," she said. "Didn't even say hi. Acted like you don't know me."

"Sorry," he said. "I didn't mean to be rude."

She reached out to comb his hair with her fingers. It wasn't any more unkempt than usual, but she pretended it was so she had an excuse to touch him. Today she wore tight shorts and a tight halter top that exposed her stomach. It was not the time of year to dress that way; and Rachel didn't dress that way even in the hottest days of summer. But she showed as much skin as possible when around Carl. And she touched him as much as possible during conversation.

"So where are you going tonight?" she asked.

He shrugged. "Just got other plans, is all."

She feigned jealousy. "You must have a new girlfriend."

"No," he said, with an uncomfortable laugh. "Nothing like that."

"Then what **is** it like?"

"Why are you so interested?" he asked.

She shrugged. "I'm not."

For some time now she'd been trying to make him tell her what exactly occurred during the outings he went on with his father, brothers and some other men from the rez. So easy to manipulate in some ways, he was a stone wall when it came to that subject. She saw the same stubbornness in him now and it irked her.

She lifted the drinks and handed the stronger one to him. "One for the road, then." She drank from hers, maintaining eye contact over the rim of the cup.

"Thanks," he said, and took a swallow.

His face scrunched up. He coughed. She was afraid he'd spew the mouthful out, but he'd already swallowed it. "What the...?" he rasped.

She giggled. "What's the matter, Carl?"

He set the cup down, giving her a bewildered look. "I didn't know you drank."

"Not much. Oh, come on—have a drink with me."

"Sorry," he said. "I mean, thanks and everything, but no."

"Oh, all right," she said, nodding with a disapproving frown. "That whole thing about Indians not being able to hold their liquor. Your parents probably don't allow you to drink, either."

His brow furrowed. His pride was wounded by her implying he needed parental permission.

False Flag - Brown

As she hoped.

"It's not that," he said. "I just gotta go."

"I understand," she said, dismissively. drinking some more from her own cup. "You still live with your parents. Their house; their rules."

She saw his jaw jut out a bit. He grabbed the cup and chugged two big gulps. He set the cup down, wiped his mouth and said, "See you later." Then he went through the door and was gone.

Rachel pulled out her cell and dialed the number most recent in her call history. A male voice greeted her, "Yeah, what's up?"

"He's coming your way," she said.

Outside, Carl's engine cranked to life, and he sped away. A few seconds later she heard the siren peal.

Rachel dumped the remaining contents of both cups down the sink, then marched to the bathroom to change into her normal clothes.

False Flag - Brown

46
D MINUS ONE
TEXAS PANHANDLE

Ted pulled over at a rest stop and blindfolded Arden, before continuing the journey. He dropped Arden off somewhere where it was really quiet. Ted introduced Arden to somebody named "Stallion One." There were other men present who went by the names Stallion Two through Stallion Eight.

Arden heard Ted drive away.

Arden asked if he could remove the blindfold.

Stallion One said, "No. Not until I say."

"Oh."

"We're gonna let you get some sleep in a minute," Stallion One said. "Tomorrow I'll go over the plan with you and we'll do some rehearsals. But I want to get something straight with you right now. You listening?"

"Yes sir."

"You don't ever mention us or Ted to anyone, got it?"

"Sure. Yeah. Don't worry 'bout that."

"Even should you get captured," Stallion One said, "you can talk about F.A.P. You can talk about ZOG. Say anything you want about the Aryan race or whatever. But you never, **ever** mention us."

"You think I'll get captured?" Arden asked.

"Maybe. This is a dangerous mission, after all. But keep quiet about us, and we'll mount a rescue mission. If you talk, we'll make sure there are 20 big niggers waiting for you every time you go to the prison shower, hoping you'll drop the soap."

"Not me," Arden vowed. "Hell, no. I swear."

"Good," Stallion One said. "Now I've heard you screwed the pooch a few times already. Tomorrow is your big chance to put all of that behind you."

"I won't let you down," Arden said. "Ted said you're gonna give me a weapon?"

"That's right. And if you do everything as you're told, you'll get to use it all you want. There will be targets all over the place, and nobody is off limits but my squad, and Viper Squad."

Arden licked his lips. He wished he could remove the blindfold, see who he was talking to and where he was. But he was going completely by the book this time. Ted had given him another chance and he dared not blow it. From what he'd just heard, the first reward for his obedience was coming tomorrow.

False Flag - Brown

Arden spent the night in a dark room much like a prison cell, with a cot, a toilet, and not much else.

In the morning a man in a woodland-camouflage uniform and a khaki balaclava, with dark sunglasses, let him out of the cell. He brought Arden into a small kitchen and tossed him an MRE, telling him to eat it quickly.

After Arden was done, the man in woodland cammies brought him outside. Arden saw he'd spent the night in a simple, block-like stucco building in the middle of the desert. On the hood of a nondescript dark blue S.U.V. was a balsa wood model of a football stadium. Other men gathered around, dressed just like the one who woke him up.

Arden recognized the voice of Stallion One, muffled slightly behind his balaclava "You'll get your weapon and gear a little later. For now, it's time to learn what we're going to do today."

"Have you ever wanted to kill people and get away with it?" one of the masked men asked. Before Arden could answer, the same voice laughed and said, "Today your dream comes true, boy."

False Flag - Brown

Tommy waited as long as he dared for Carl to show up. It wasn't like his youngest to flake out. But it was well after midnight and still no sign of him.

Last time he'd spoken to him, Carl was raring to go, so this was disturbing. Tommy, Gunther and Takoda asked and called around everywhere they could think of, but ran out of time. Linda assured her husband she would track him down via Carl's friends.

Meanwhile, they had to go.

They traveled in a convoy. Tommy wanted enough vehicles with him so they could all get back even if something happened to one or two cars. Takoda's 'Vette could only take one other passenger and some gear in the trunk, but it and Gunther's hot rod Mustang offered blazing speed, should that be needed at some point. Tommy drove his Blazer; John and Mike Saxton took John's old Dodge Ram pickup; Ralph drove a Ford Explorer while Jason braved the cold on a motorcycle and Maurice took his economy car.

They drove through the night hours, when there was less traffic. They moved a little slower than flow-of-traffic, with the fast machines bringing up the rear.

Tommy had nothing but worries. The most recently added worry was about Carl. Tommy couldn't even call Linda to see if she'd heard anything because he'd forbidden anyone to bring cellphones on this trip. Including himself.

Then there was the mission. If Josh was wrong about the attack, then half a weekend and a bunch of gas money was wasted. But that was still much preferable to the alternative.

Whether the attack was real or not, there was still the matter of all the weapons and ammo they were hauling. None of it was illegal, but legality had been proven not to matter over and over again in recent years. What mattered most was affiliation. Most parts of the country were ruled by men; not by law. Tommy ran his own county by what was right and legal, but he was in a rapidly shrinking minority. If the wrong person found out about what the Shawnee Militia was hauling and where they were going, they could be up a creek with no paddle. Given Tommy had some powerful enemies, he could be killed or locked away forever, and a plausible excuse concocted for public consumption...which would never be questioned by enough people to matter.

Having planned for gas stops, the convoy arrived in town Saturday

False Flag - Brown

morning.

The city looked a little like a ghost town. Parts of it resembled a war zone. Even in the suburbs many businesses were closed and few people ventured outside. In the city proper fire swept the streets, leaving what looked like a red coal carpet from a distance.

D-DAY, H MINUS SEVEN
AMARILLO, TEXAS

After treating everyone to breakfast at a truck stop outside town, and giving them some time to relax for a while, Tommy conducted another radio check. Their convoy drove to an isolated spot on a side road where he had everyone load and strap on sidearms. He checked them for concealment. When satisfied, they mounted up again and rolled into town.

Tommy led the Shawnee Militia into the empty parking lot of a closed grocery store inside town and had everybody get out for a pow-wow. He put Gunther in charge and told them he'd be back in a couple hours. While they were waiting, they should see about buying a pre-paid cellphone for a burner. Cash-only, he emphasized.

Tommy took Takoda with him for a recon into the city.

National Guard troops could be seen outside certain businesses that were still open. Tommy had mixed emotions about them not stopping vehicles for inspection. Checking his road map frequently, Tommy scouted a few different routes to and from the stadium. But he stopped when he could see it in the distance—never actually driving past it or up to it.

When Tommy spotted a bored-looking cluster of soldiers at a freeway on-ramp, he pulled over and shut off the engine.

"What's up?" Takoda asked, looking a little unnerved at the prospect of parking so close to the Guardsmen.

"Hand me that bag, there," Tommy said, pointing to a plastic grocery sack on the floor just in front of the passenger seat.

Takoda handed it to his father, who opened it. Inside was a black hat with gold piping and letters, with a 5th SFG emblem on the front. The hat was wrapped around a pack of cigarettes.

Takoda grimaced, confused. "When did you start smoking?"

"I haven't," Tommy replied. "That right there is legal tender on a deployment. It's an ice-breaker, if nothing else. At least when it comes to soldiers."

"Isn't that the hat Mom bought you, like, eight years ago?"

Tommy nodded. "Looks like it's finally time to wear it." He shook the hat, pushed it into shape from the inside with his hand, then dropped it onto his head. He shoved the cigarette pack into his breast pocket and opened the door. Takoda began to get out with him, but Tommy said, "Stay here and watch the truck."

Takoda watched his father approach the Guardsmen, hands in pockets, with the easy stride of a bumpkin. The weekend soldiers converged to face him, wary at first. They listened to him, though. Tommy was not a verbose man, but he talked at length, gesturing casually and sparingly with his hands. One of the Guardsmen replied, then another. Tommy talked some more, drawing another soldier into the conversation. The discussion went on. More of them replied. Takoda watched, with interest, the back-and-forth pattern play out.

One of the Guardsmen gestured toward Tommy's chest. Tommy produced the pack of cigarettes and shook one out for the man to grab. Three others indicated interest, and Tommy obliged all takers. The guardsmen lit up and Takoda saw their posture relax as they blew streams of smoke into the air. After a few minutes, a couple of the soldiers were doing a lot of the talking. And laughing.

Takoda knew his father had a lot of skills, but this was one he hadn't been aware of.

The soldiers shared anecdotes with Tommy, who turned to follow their pointing gestures with his gaze, then ask follow-up questions. When he finally turned to leave the Guardsmen, a couple of them shook his hand, while the rest waved or chin-thrust a goodbye.

Tommy climbed back in the truck, started it, and U-turned back the way he'd come. It took him a minute to acknowledge Takoda's stare.

"What?"

"You're quite a huckster, Dad. I haven't seen you glad-hand like that, even when you ran for sheriff."

Tommy shrugged, putting the hat and cigarettes back in the bag. "I still like soldiers. Even in the National Guard. And there's a certain way to go about talking to soldiers you just met. You can get a lot more out of a talk when they know you're one of them, than you can by pulling rank or acting ignorant. They can smell it when you don't know the drill, and when you don't know soldiers, or soldiering."

Takoda thought about why Tommy chose him to ride along. Most likely, it was to ensure he didn't start trouble among the others in Tommy's absence. Meanwhile, Gunther was the trustworthy one, who he left in charge. That stung, but in all honesty Takoda couldn't blame him.

"Learn anything?" Takoda asked.

"Some white store owner got arrested, charged with hate crimes," Tommy said. "White people showed up to protest. Black people showed up to demonstrate...you can imagine how that turned out."

False Flag - Brown

"Like a mad bull lost its way."

"The National Guard isn't stopping vehicles to search," Tommy said. "Neither are the local cops, who are on the defense and pretty busy with other stuff. The No-Gos are guarding businesses, hospitals, major intersections and freeway ramps. Those guys weren't there to stop cars, but to make sure nobody sets up a roadblock to shake down travelers."

"Has that been happening?" Takoda asked.

"Sounds like it. The first couple days people got raped or beaten to death. And everybody's talking about a vigilante group that shot it out with some of the looters and really brought smoke."

Takoda watched the wounded cityscape slide by out the window. "It looks like the zombie apocalypse has swept through this city, or something."

"Blacks and whites have quieted down some," Tommy said. "Some think they've had enough. The Mexicans are just getting started, though. They're fresh, and organized. Yesterday they looted four different drug stores that the No-Gos didn't have the manpower to secure."

"I'm sure they took all the pharmaceuticals," Takoda said.

"They weren't after the Ace Bandages. Anyway, the violence seems to be isolated to a few neighborhoods now, even though the whole city is afraid to come outside or answer their doors."

"How about the football stadium?" Takoda asked.

"That whole area's been relatively untouched. Might be the safest place in Amarillo."

"Well, maybe not, though."

"Right."

They returned to the parking lot where Gunther and the others waited.

Ralph had obtained a burner phone with cash and gave it to Tommy, who paid him back on the spot. They checked their radios again. Tommy assigned buddy teams and went over a loose plan of action that could be modified on the go as needed. Then they mounted up and the convoy moved out for the stadium.

False Flag - Brown

48
D MINUS ONE
ABSENTEE SHAWNEE TRIBAL POLICE OFFICE -
POTAWATTOMIE COUNTY, OKLAHOMA

Rachel, two fellow officers of the Tribal Police, and the Chief himself watched the young man through the one-way glass.

Carl Scarred Wolf leaned back in his chair, arms folded and eyes closed. He was motionless, like a statue.

"He looks entirely too comfortable," the Chief said, annoyed. "Is he sleeping?"

"He's not legally drunk according to the breathalyzer," Officer Muroc said. "And he's got his lips clamped. He wants a lawyer and a phone call, and that's all he's saying."

The Chief glared angrily at Muroc. "Have you forgotten how to be a team player? He's legally drunk so long as I say he is!"

Muroc shrugged apologetically.

"He chugged it down kind of fast," Rachel said. "Maybe we just need to wait for the alcohol to settle or something, then test him again." She didn't understand how Carl could blow any less than a Two, with as much liquor as she poured into his drink. But then he hadn't drunk it all. And maybe she hadn't mixed it well. If only she'd had more time, but he'd been in such a hurry to leave...

The Chief paced, scowling. "A teenage boy!" he growled at Muroc. "You can't even intimidate a teenage boy into talking." He now directed his attention to Rachel. "I was going to save you for later, White Bird, but you'd better go in now. I need something, quick. I have no doubt some crybaby will go over my head if we hold him much longer without some kind of reason."

She was no longer showing a bunch of skin, but Rachel was the only one present not in uniform. "I've done well with him so far," Rachel said, striding to the door.

"Be smart," the Chief said. "Remember your training. Make the little prick give us something."

When Rachel entered the room where Carl sat, she wore an expression of concerned distress.

Carl opened his eyes when she entered. He watched her, but said nothing. He betrayed no emotion whatsoever, either. She had no clue what he was thinking, and that irritated her. *The inscrutable stone face, just like his father. Just like all the Scarred Wolf men.*

Well, she couldn't display her true emotions, either. "Carl?" She rushed to sit down opposite him and reached across the table to touch his hand sympathetically. "I heard what happened. Are you alright?"

"I'm in jail, Officer White Bird. You tell me."

"Carl, I'm so sorry," she said, trying to convey warm sincerity through her eyes.

He stared back blankly and asked, "Is it normal in the Tribal Police to bring a DWI into the interrogation room?"

"W-what?" Rachel stammered. Muroc was right—he wasn't intimidated. He was thinking too clearly for someone who was supposed to be scared. And drunk.

"You heard me," he said. "I was never read my rights. I haven't been allowed my phone call. And nobody gave me a sobriety test, unless you count the breathalyzer. And the arresting officer wouldn't let me look at the readout. What are you people trying to pull?"

"Carl, please," Rachel said, putting a tremor of hurt into her voice. "I'm off-duty tonight. I'm not here as a cop; I'm here as your friend."

The stone face flexed for a moment, into what might be a smile. A cruel, sardonic smile. "Right. Were you on or off-duty when you gave me that drink?"

"What is **that** supposed to mean?" she demanded.

Carl shrugged. "I guess it's just coincidence that your buddies were waiting for me after you tried to get me drunk."

The problem was, the apple didn't fall far from the tree. Sheriff Scarred Wolf's son knew too much about cops and how they worked.

Rachel's exasperation was real when she let it out in a deep sigh. She didn't have the leverage she needed, but the Chief was watching through the one-way glass. She had to play the hand as best she could, now that he was in custody. "Listen, Carl, I don't think you appreciate what kind of trouble you're in. If you did you wouldn't be sleeping, in here."

Was that a smirk? Was he smirking at her?

She forged ahead. "I'm here to do what I can for you, but your attitude isn't helping at all. I heard you're being uncooperative. You don't want to piss people off, in your predicament, Carl. I can try to work something out with my boss. Maybe get them to go easy on you. But you have to be cooperative. That's the way this works. You want something from them, you have to give them what they want."

Carl turned his head to the side and spat on the floor. "I want my phone call. That's the law, whether I give you anything or not."

Watching and listening in the next room, the Chief cussed. "Little bastard thinks he's a real tough guy."

That whole family was bad news. Tommy and Vince's parents were alcoholics. Vince made a decent detective for a while, but toward the end he got in the habit of snooping around where he shouldn't. Tommy was a lot like him. Sure, he kept his nose clean, but he had some dangerous ideas and habits.

It wasn't clear what Tommy was into, but the Feds had classified him as a person of interest. They wouldn't do that without a reason.

Frankly, it was sickening how people on the rez were so enamored with the "Green Beret war hero." Tommy Scarred Wolf didn't impress the Chief, and neither did his miscreant sons.

They were bad seeds, all of them. Takoda was the worst--practically an anarchist since elementary school when he set off a homemade bomb inside a dumpster just for kicks. But the older and younger brothers thought they were Billy Badass, too.

He might have to let Carl go. But before he did, he would check with his contact in Homeland Security just in case they had any bright ideas.

False Flag - Brown

Justin Cavarra approached the entrance to his building, glancing briefly at the security cameras. He hoped he didn't look as nervous as he felt.

His I.D. badge got him in the outside door. The security team ushered him through the full body scanners.

His heart raced like a NASCAR engine while he was scanned. No flash drives or CDs came in or out of his work area. The only personal items employees were allowed to bring in, in fact, were their car keys and Agency-issued cellphone. The phones did not have the capability to record audio or video, and no access to any kind of app store.

Josh had disassembled a custom flash drive, hiding the plastic shell in Justin's car alarm key fob, and the storage section inside the cellphone, where it was effectively hidden between metal components.

If this was discovered, the security team would converge on him, and he would be locked away somewhere, never to see the light of day again.

The guards eyed him sharply as he went through the scanners, their gaze bouncing between him and their monitors. Justin told himself that it was just his guilty conscience that made them appear more suspicious than usual.

He made it through without tripping any alerts, and proceeded to the next door. Even as the retina scan and palm print reader unlocked this door for him, he felt like half a dozen eyeballs were burning holes into his back.

He had to use palm print and retina scan for two more doors before he made it to his cubicle.

Barnes was there, but not Frawley and Tench. The two girls put in less hours per week than anyone else. They never worked weekends even when everyone else was required to, so Justin knew they would be gone by the time he arrived. He had volunteered for the graveyard shift also so that Barnes would be leaving after only two hours of overlap.

Justin folded his jacket, setting it on the desk right in front of the computer in Frawley's cubicle. He then navigated the rows of cubicles to the coffee pot, just like normal. Barnes intercepted him there.

"Burning a late one, huh?" Barnes asked.

"Yeah," Justin said, shrugging. "They always want a couple people in here at any given hour, in case something Top Priority comes up. They ask me every week if I'm willing. I figure if nobody ever volunteers, they'll make it mandatory."

"I know your girlfriends would bitch and moan about **that**," Barnes said, laughing, nodding toward the cubicles of Tench and Frawley. "Well, you're young, and this is one place where overtime is always available. Might as well put in the hours and make the money while you can, before you start a family."

Justin smiled, not so much in agreement, but just as a polite way of acknowledging the comment. He pulled a white styrofoam cup off the stack and poured coffee into it.

"But you young guys don't really get married, do you?" Barnes remarked, conversationally. "Why buy the cow, when you can get the milk free and all that."

"It's not even that, really," Justin said. "You'd have to be a masochist to share a roof with one of these women today."

Barnes laughed again. "Well, we didn't have all the videogames and stuff when I was younger, so we needed something to do on the rainy days." He gave the kind of eyebrow wiggle older guys used when making sexual innuendo. They almost had to, because if an eavesdropper heard them utter any kind of "dongle" joke, they could lose their jobs.

"You been keeping up with the news?" Barnes asked.

"A little," Justin replied. "Sounds like there's a little war going on down on the border."

"What's up with these ranchers?" Barnes asked, shaking his head. "First that old Chapanee troublemaker; now this guy starts shooting Mexicans. He gets locked up, but more rednecks take his place."

Justin bit his tongue. To display any flavor of rogue thinking would invite attention that Justin didn't want.

Recently he'd become a lot more skeptical about the official story concerning any matter. How many times were the people on the border supposed to let the drug gangs from Mexico cut their fences, kill their cows, and steal from them? Their ranches were their livelihoods--the difference between their families starving or living. But you weren't supposed to question the narrative, and certain kinds of people were always the designated victims, no matter what. American ranchers didn't qualify as worthy of sympathy.

Justin wanted Barnes to just shut up and leave him alone, but he forced himself to be friendly. "That stuff in Amarillo is crazy, too."

"Oh my gosh," Barnes said. "They just won't stop. And people are saying Detroit might even turn out worse."

Justin let the conversation run its course, then they both ambled back to their cubicles.

The two hours dragged painfully. Justin had crazy thoughts that

False Flag - Brown

maybe the Agency could read his mind and knew what he was going to try even before he did it. He was so distracted he bumbled slowly through his work, making more stupid mistakes than he ever had.

Oh well. After tonight, this job is over.

Assuming that he could make it out of Camp Williams after his work was done that night, what in the world would his life be like afterwards?

He kept coming back to that question. But whatever doom he was bringing on himself, so be it. He might have issues with his father, but his father was **not** a terrorist. Whoever classified him as one was pure evil. Justin's eyes were open now. If the country was hellbent on becoming some kind of dictatorship, then he accepted his marginalization as an enemy of the state.

He'd just like to stay alive for as long as possible.

Finally, Barnes shut down his computer and prepared to leave, but stopped by Justin's cubicle one more time to discuss another news item—something about the economy, but Justin's mind wasn't in the conversation.

When Barnes left, Justin went to Frawley's computer and booted it. As the operating system loaded, he removed the cover from the key fob and cellphone. Stuck to the backing of the key fob cover was a small strip of black tape. Justin peeled that off and stuck it over the lights on the desktop which indicated the power was on. Now if anybody walked by Frawley's cubicle, it wouldn't be obvious the machine was running.

Next he assembled the sections of the flash drive. By then, it was time to enter the first password.

When he was fully logged into Frawley's computer, he stood and bent over to get behind the case and insert the flash drive in a USB slot hidden from normal view between the cubicle wall and the back of the desktop.

Justin had helped Josh design the blended threat.

Straightening from his hunched-over position, he found the appropriate drive on the "HDD Manager" app and initiated the program. He then shut the monitor off and returned to his cubicle.

He booted up his own work station and listened to the pounding of his heart. He resumed work on a profile he'd started before, but his mind wasn't in it.

Since his job here was gone after tonight, and he'd probably never get paid for it, he spent his time goofing around, using the tools unique to his occupation to look at the dirty laundry of well-known people. It was interesting that most "conservative" celebrities rated only a Level Five Threat or lower. A couple of them had been downgraded in recent times, while others were never as high up The List as some would guess.

He wondered why that might be, and decided that they must be compromised in some way. If only their devoted followers knew.

Justin didn't need coffee that night. Fear had him on edge. Goofing around was a needed distraction, but in the back of his mind he knew that Security could barge through the door at any moment and haul him away.

He continued to remind himself that if he didn't risk it now, his dad and other people like him would be hauled away later.

False Flag - Brown

Driving Jorge's elongated RV, Phil Jenkins dropped them off at an isolated spot in the woods. He drove away as they moved into the treeline with weapons and gear.

Everything that might rattle had been taped down prior to insertion, but they made last minute adjustments inside the woodline while Griz distributed the silencers. Josh and Butch had night vision goggles, Leon had a thermal imaging attachment for his scope, but most of the others saved the weight and space for other items.

Cavarra was the designated leader. He formed his volunteers into two fireteams. They moved out in a column-of-ducks with their sniper, Leon, in the middle, and Josh, humping all the high-tech stuff, right behind him. They wore old infrared camouflage over their normal outfits, and ski masks or balaclavas under their patrol caps or boonie hats. They carried a variety of rifles. Griz had an M4 slung around his broad back over his patrol pack. An M60 machinegun was slung around his front.

They didn't like starting the operation in daylight, but they were timing it so that Josh could cut into the broadcast during prime time, if possible.

Snow was predicted to start falling later that evening, but for now the forest was only cold and dry. It was early in the year for the first snow, but then it was supposed to be a bad winter, after all.

All of them were past their prime, but moving quickly and quietly through the bush was second nature to them. They made good time and reached the security fence in less than two hours.

The fence was surrounded by a firebreak, leaving no trees handy. Each of them had been humping components of a crude tower they now erected beside the fence. Gloves remained on, so no fingerprints were left. They filled sandbags on the spot to anchor down the outside legs of the structure as a counterbalance to the beam extending from the inside, over the edge of the fence. It was unlikely there were live patrols to worry about, but there might be remote listening devices, so the raiding party kept strict noise discipline while they worked. They had rehearsed this drill enough back at Rennenkampf's place that everyone knew what to do.

Griz, easily the heaviest of all of them, was first to climb up, after temporarily handing off the M60 to a lighter man. Four of the others added their weight to the sandbags for counterbalance. As Griz crawled out on the beam, it bowed to a degree that made everyone nervous. But

False Flag - Brown

the beam held. He stuck his boot in the loop on the end of the rope and visually checked to ensure the belay men had the other end before he put his weight on it. The belay men eased their braking grip on the rope and, with the dull rubbing sound of well-oiled pulleys, Griz was lowered to the ground inside the fence.

The next man climbed up, and the process was repeated. The machinegun was lowered down to Griz by itself.

They crossed over from heaviest man to lightest, with Carlos being the last man outside the fence. As he climbed the tower, he switched on the detonators for the thermite charges attached at various points of the structure. Before climbing all the way out on the beam, he pulled the rope out of all but the last pulley and dropped the end down to his comrades inside the fence. Once they had it secured, he crawled out, dropped to a hanging position, put his foot in the loop and was lowered to join them.

They pulled the rope the rest of the way through the pulley and coiled it up, giving it to Cannonball. Butch took the point and they moved out again. The little fence-crossing exercise had gone so smoothly, they were beginning to get stoked. Exhilaration took some of the sting off the oppressive gravity of what they were doing.

Less than another seven klicks and they had eyes-on-target. They hunkered down to observe for a while, then Carlos, Frank and Kurt separated from the main group to conduct a painstaking recon in a semicircle around the objective.

The area surrounded by fence was large, but the building sat relatively close to the stretch of fencing where the gate was.

The place did seem to be manned by only a skeleton force. There was a single guard at the shack by the gate, and another one in a booth by the main building's entrance. Aside from that, the facility seemed to rely mostly on cameras for its security. Another big part of the security scheme was the fact that nobody should know about this place because it didn't officially exist.

Judging by the bored stagnation of the sleepy guards, the infiltration hadn't been detected.

The recon patrol returned to the O.R.P. and briefed Rocco on what they'd found.

Rocco sent Tony, Butch and Jorge to the guard shack by the gate; Josh, Kurt and Frank to the guard booth by the building; Leon, Carlos and Griz around the back of the building. Everyone settled in behind what concealment was available, and waited.

Except Kurt, Frank, and Josh. At a snail's pace, so their movement was almost unnoticeable, they crept forward until they surrounded the guard booth, Josh closest to the main building's entrance.

False Flag - Brown

They waited some more, wound tight as steel traps.

The man in the guard shack radioed the guard in the booth, "Alright, I'm freezing my ass off. Tell Bob to come out and relieve me. I need to take a piss and get some coffee."

"Roger that," replied the guard in the booth, who then used the intercom to relay the request inside the building.

Butch broke squelch three times. Rocco and the others heard it in their radio earpieces. Gloved fingers slid toward safeties. Josh quietly pulled himself into the Ready Scat and leveled his silenced P91 at the door. The standing order was "commence on contact."

The door swung open and a man appeared in the opening, pulling a hat onto his head. Josh sprang from his position while firing.

With a subsonic .40 round through the silencer, the loudest sound was the metallic snick of the P91 bolt sliding back. The shot hit the man center-mass. He wasn't wearing armor, and the bullet deflected off a rib right into the corner of his heart.

Josh reached him before he fell, grabbing him by the collar and adding to his forward momentum with a hard yank that sent him sprawling belly-down on the cold ground. In the same fluid motion Josh caught the door before it closed, and slipped inside.

When Josh made his move, Frank rose to his feet, threw the booth door open and shot the guard point blank. Over by the gate, Butch did the same to the other guard.

At the same time, Rocco remotely triggered the thermites back at their fence-breach point. The sky lit up with a white-hot flash as the structure burned and melted.

The noise of the action was barely audible around the back of the building, but the men there saw the flash and glow of the demolition in the distance, back by the fence. Griz and Carlos gave Leon a boost up the wall. Leon's hands clamped onto the edge of the roof. Lean, hard muscles uncoiled, hoisting him up over the side with his weapons and gear. Once topside, he slipped the looped end of the rope over a vent pipe, held it there with one boot and dropped the rope over the side.

Carlos used the rope to climb up and join him, followed by Rocco.

The three guards on the ground were double-tapped, searched, and relieved of weapons, ammo, and everything else of possible use. Everyone had brought .40 caliber sidearms on this mission, knowing that was the round of choice for DHS personnel, so spare ammo was on site.

Jorge climbed up onto the roof also, while Kurt and Frank moved up to cover Tony, Butch and Griz, who opened the gate and slipped outside the fence.

False Flag - Brown

Inside the building was only one more person. When he saw Josh he reached for something and had to be shot.

His fingers had almost touched an alarm button.

Josh sat down at the computer the man had been using, first, to disable the timeout function and hack the passwords. Then he guided himself on a tour of the control room, figuring out where everything was.

Rocco's voice sounded in his earpiece. "Mountain Man, This is Sea Dog, over."

"Five by five, Sea Dog. Inside secure. Going to work, now."

Josh let out a deep breath and sat at the computer again, removing his patrol pack to extract the laptop. The task ahead of him was overwhelming. He reminded himself to think of it as dozens of smaller obstacles, and just take them out one-by-one.

Rocco got a head count over the radio. No casualties. Now they just had to secure the place and hope Josh could get the job done quickly. Quicker than the opfor could react, hopefully.

False Flag - Brown

Tommy led his convoy to the area where the stadium sat, but ordered his men to spread their vehicles out, toward the outside, rather than all park clustered together in the lot. He assigned them places to post themselves on foot, as well. Each of them packed a pistol under their jackets, with a handheld radio in their pocket.

The stadium filled up nearly an hour before the Summit was scheduled to start. The racial mix of the crowds seemed pretty even. Tommy used the burner phone to call in an anonymous tip about a terrorist attack, 20 minutes before start time.

He waited for the deputies on site to begin clearing the place out. Maybe someone would make an announcement through the sound system.

After five minutes there was still no flurry of activity. Had he called the right number? The person he spoke to identified themselves as working for the sheriff's office, and acknowledged his message. He checked the number anyway.

Yup. He had called the sheriff's office.

Tommy walked over to the bleachers and stood where he could casually observe the nearest deputies. Maybe they were figuring out the best way to evacuate.

Nope. It looked like business-as usual.

Maybe they hadn't taken the threat seriously.

Why would you not take such a threat seriously, in times like this? The TSA was molesting little old ladies at airports hoping to find a terrorist threat, for crying out loud. And with all the violence around Amarillo lately...

After 10 minutes, Tommy was annoyed. Well, he had planned for "just in case" contingencies.

He took a deep breath and punched a different number into the burner phone. He placed his thumb over the "send" button and thrust the phone in his jacket pocket. After waiting a few minutes, he pushed the button.

The explosive with the cellular detonator he stashed in the garbage can behind the goal post on the opposite end of the field from where the stage sat was a small one, designed more for noise than damage. And it delivered noise, as well as busting open the plastic trash can and sending garbage everywhere.

Everyone jumped, including the deputies. Scads of people pointed at the shower of garbage falling back to Earth. The crowd noise surged.

False Flag - Brown

Maybe a hundred women screamed. People stood from their seats in the bleachers, and from the folding chairs on the field. Some made to leave. A couple deputies ran toward the explosion; others looked to each other in confusion, speaking into their radios for instruction.

Some white guy in a suit charged out on the stage and grabbed a microphone. His voice blared over the P.A. system.

"Ladies and gentlemen, please keep your seats. There is nothing to worry about. The fireworks were just a tasteless idea of somebody's sick prank. I assure you that law enforcement is looking into the matter and whoever did this will be caught. There's no need to panic. Security is very tight. The best thing to do is remain in your seats and don't let hateful people disrupt what we're trying to do here."

Tommy's blood ran cold. "Oh, shit."

He checked the time. The Summit began in one minute.

He range-walked toward the parking lot. When he got to where the portable toilets were between him and observers back at the stadium, he keyed his radio. "Okay guys, stay sharp. Heads on a swivel. This could turn out to be something."

Somebody spoke again over the P.A. system, then the children's choir began singing.

"Ron," Tommy transmitted, "I'm coming over to relieve you. I want you to post yourself at the far side of the parking lot, where the road comes in."

"Roger that," Ralph replied, over the radio.

Tommy made his way for the corner building outside the stadium nearest the parking lot. He saw Ralph running for the drive feeding the lot.

The fix was in, Tommy realized. The guy Tommy spoke to on the phone was in on it...or whoever should have relayed the message of the bomb threat. And the guy who told the crowd to ignore the trash can explosion was in on it...or whoever put him up to that speech. Somebody wanted a bunch of people packed in here, and it wasn't because of concern over race relations.

The children's choir finished their first song, and an adult voice came over the P.A., greeting everyone and verbalizing some ideals that most of those gathered believed in, judging by the applause.

"Hey Tim," Ralph's voice said, through the radio. (Everyone had been given temporary pseudonyms for the mission. "Tim" was Tommy's.) "This looks like it could be something. Two rental trucks coming down the drive toward me."

Tommy whirled and launched into a sprint to get around the outbuilding. "Stop them! I'll be right there!"

False Flag - Brown

Tommy rounded the corner of the building and raced for the parking lot. He spotted the rental trucks on the drive. Ralph stood blocking the entrance to the parking lot, waving for them to stop.

They didn't stop.

Ralph waved more dramatically. The trucks veered around him, bouncing off-road, and continued on, circumventing the parking lot.

Running at full speed, Tommy was still too far to do anything. But he got a look into the truck cabs at a distance as they lurched past. There were two figures in each cab, wearing woodland camouflage and masks. They were bulky with ballistic armor.

Tommy shouted into his radio. "This is it! Guns up! Guns up! Two rental trucks headed toward the stadium! Don't let them get their back doors open!"

H-HOUR

Takoda had been standing among the crowd of outliers to the side of the bleachers, but he wandered away from the stadium so that the deputies wouldn't find his radio suspicious should he have to use it. As his father's words were crackling from the radio speaker, the two trucks in question bore down on him from the general direction of the entrance road.

Takoda moved out of the way, prepared to grab the mirror bracket of the lead truck as it went by, and swing up onto the running board. But the trucks slowed to a stop before they reached him. The passenger door of the lead truck swung open and somebody got out.

The figure was masked, with a boonie hat. He was dressed in a camouflage uniform partially covered by ballistic armor, knee and elbow pads. A Heckler & Koch G3 or HK41 was slung around his back.

The masked man hustled around to the back of the truck where he began to unlatch the garage-style sliding door. Takoda hit him hard from the blind side before he got it unlatched. The attack was part open-hand strike to the jaw, part tackle. They went to the ground. The man was bigger than Takoda; possibly stronger. But even had he not been restricted by his bulky outfit, and on queer street from the blow to his jaw, he probably wouldn't have lasted much longer. Takoda's knee drove hard into his crotch. His elbow slammed the masked face twice. He finished him off with a neck crank that caused an audible pop.

It was over in just seconds.

Takoda looked up to see a girl with a smartphone taking pictures of him and the dead guy. Her eyes were wide, her mouth twisted in horror at the savagery she'd just witnessed. Takoda rolled to his feet and snatched the cellphone out of her hands without missing a beat, on his way to the driver side of the cab.

Behind him the Saxton brothers converged on the cab of the second truck.

Takoda pocketed the phone and pulled his pistol. The girl screamed, but he barely noticed. He yanked open the driver side door, stepped up and clouted the driver in the masked face with the gun butt.

The stunned man fumbled for his own handgun but Takoda seized his wrist and struck him again. He pushed up into the cab, plowing the driver sideways onto the bench seat where Takoda pistol-whipped him unconscious. A hasty search of the man's gear revealed many items of interest. Takoda rolled the man sideways, pulled his arms behind his back and used his own zip-cuffs to tie his wrists together. He zip-cuffed his ankles to the steering wheel for good measure.

When the driver of the second truck saw the Saxton brothers level pistols at the cab, he threw it back in gear, hit the gas and jerked the wheel. The truck U-turned, shredding the turf with it's rear dual tires, and sped back in the direction it came from.

"Tim! Ron!" Takoda called over the radio. "The second truck is coming your way. These guys are armed, masked and armored."

Maurice arrived, breathing hard from the run from where he'd been posted. Takoda, stripping the rifle and magazines off the man with the broken neck, said, "Search these guys and take anything that might be useful." He found a flash-bang and a tear gas grenade. As he stripped items, he handed them to the Saxton brothers.

Maurice began searching the driver, glancing nervously over his shoulder. "The cops are gonna come over here any minute to see what's up."

"Good," Takoda said. "Be gone by then. But if they aren't curious about this truck by the time you're done, fire a shot or two into the engine compartment to get their attention. In fact, do that anyway. Use the captured weapon."

Tommy was already in the parking lot by then, running for his Blazer. He had radioed Ralph to give pursuit as soon as he learned of the escape attempt. By the time the rental truck reached the drive, Ralph was in his Explorer starting it up. He took off after the rental, switching from his walkie-talkie to the CB on his dash to let the others know he was in pursuit.

Gunther was on the other side of the stadium. When he heard what was going on, and that one of the trucks was retreating, he ran for the

False Flag - Brown

parking lot, yelling for Jason to come with him. A shot rang out on the other side. There were screams and yells. People saw Gunther running away and decided he had a good idea.

A new voice came over the P.A. and instructed everyone to sit tight. But after a small bomb in a trash can, two rental trucks that had come racing toward the stadium, and now a gunshot , people were motivated into a mass exodus toward the parking lot.

Gunther hoped nobody got trampled. He reached his Mustang, jumped in, twisted his key in the ignition and the engine roared to life. By the time he put it in gear, though, people were rushing past in front and all around him. He tapped the horn and eased forward. At the parking lot exit, he saw his father's Blazer swing onto the road and speed away. He grabbed his CB mike. "Ron, this is Gus. You have 'em in sight?"

"Roger that," Ralph replied. "They're heading...oh shit, they just ran a red light!"

"Run it if you have to," Tommy's voice advised urgently. "Don't let it get away. I'm behind, trying to catch you. Keep us advised of what turns they make."

Gunther could only move at a snail's pace, with all the pedestrians in his way. He gritted his teeth, inching forward, trying to get the message across that they should let him get by. Every second counted now, and he was forced to waste them by the hundreds in this parking lot, He grew a little more insistent on the gas pedal.

Some fat chick stopped right in front of him, turning back to talk to another person. Gunther nudged her with his bumper. She turned to face him, cussing a blue streak and pounding her flabby fist on his hood. Gunther grew angrier by the second. He gunned the engine, not allowing the car to move more than a couple inches—it was a feint—but the hopped-up engine snarled menacingly. The woman backed off a few steps, mouth frozen in mid-obscenity.

Gunther cranked the wheel to get around her and lurched forward. Then some skinny white jackass with a neckbeard jumped in front of him and stood there, refusing to move, with a self-righteous expression on his face.

Gunther was furious, now. He opened his door and stepped outside, pulling his pistol and leveling it at the neckbeard. "Get out of my way RIGHT NOW!!"

The self-righteous expression vanished like Lois Lerner's emails. So did the dude himself.

Finally, Gunther got the Mustang rolling. People pointed and cussed, but they stayed out of his way.

False Flag - Brown

Once Takoda reached his Corvette and got it fired up, pedestrians got in **his** way, too. He mashed down on the horn and moved ahead, bumping people out of the way who didn't get the message fast enough. The passenger side of the front bumper clipped one of them, snapping his kneecap and sending him ass-over-teakettle. After that, they ran to clear the lane for him.

The Saxton brothers reached their truck and didn't even bother trying to make it through the parking lot, plunging immediately off-road and tearing off across open ground for the exit drive. Jason did the same with his motorcycle. By the time Maurice dumped his armload of loot in the passenger seat and got his own car started, pedestrians were clogging the lanes again. People were also starting up their own cars and adding to the big logjam. Maurice was parked close to the exit, but it still took him precious minutes to get out of there. He had to watch Takoda's 'Vette, Jason on the bike, then the Saxton brothers cross ahead of him.

Gunther tore out of the stadium drive onto the street, laying rubber as his V8 overpowered the traction of his tires. A light turned red ahead of him. He slowed down, but there was no cross traffic close enough to be a threat. He stomped the gas and ran the red light with gusto, heading in the direction of Ralph's last reported location.

Behind him Takoda's 'Vette never slowed down for the 8th Avenue light. It turned green by coincidence as he blasted through the intersection. He gained on Gunther quickly because he never broke stride.

Up ahead the street teed off to the left and right. "Which way on 10th?" Gunther asked.

"Go right," Tommy replied.

Gunther took the corner hard, with Takoda on his tail. "Then what?"

There was no answer at first. "What's after the right on 10th?" he asked, again.

"Left on Manhattan," Ralph answered.

"We just passed Manhattan!" Takoda said.

Gunther cussed and slowed to make the next left on Nelson. He didn't know this town, had no GPS, and couldn't spare the time to look at his road atlas.

He powered through the left turn and mashed the go-pedal briefly before it was time to make another left on 11th. When he got around that corner and accelerated, he had to stand on the brakes almost immediately when two cowboys crossed the street in front of him.

Literal cowboys. On horses.

False Flag - Brown

Gunther pounded the steering wheel. Takoda sounded his horn behind him. Finally the riders were across. Gunther polished the asphalt digging out, and hung a right on Manhattan without lifting throttle.

Manhattan fed into Quarter Horse Drive and, after scaring some cross traffic on Tee Anchor, they could soon see the freeway ahead.

The rental truck had a head start of who-knew-how-many-miles by the time the Scarred Wolf brothers hit the freeway on-ramp. Gunther rolled on the gas and the Mustang dug out around the curve, thrusting him against the side of the bucket seat from the G-force. He was already climbing beyond 110 when he shot out onto Interstate 40.

Then he put the hammer down.

Takoda's 'Vette blasted out the ramp into the lane behind him. They ripped past traffic like it was going the other way.

Gunther turned up the volume on his CB so he could hear it over the throaty growl of his V8's performance exhaust system. Ralph reported the mile marker where the rental truck now was.

Some ignorant broad, who evidently didn't know how to check a rear-view mirror, cut him off. He mashed on the horn while slowing rapidly, and kept it mashed until she got out of his way. Takoda closed the distance.

"Come on, boys," Tommy's voice called, over the radio. "We need you up here. If these guys pull over and unload, we'll be outgunned."

"We'll be right there, Chief," Takoda replied, with that cocky tone of voice that really annoyed Gunther sometimes.

When he had an open fast lane again, Gunther dropped the hammer once more. The Mustang shot forward, speedometer needle swinging past 140 in a matter of seconds. Takoda settled into a drafting position behind him and they continued accelerating past 160.

Ralph called out the mile marker, which told them they were finally closing the gap.

They wouldn't have stopped, had a cop tried to pull them over. But there seemed to be no cops on the road near the city.

Ralph called them to report that the rental truck was taking an exit.

"They're looking for a place with no witnesses," Tommy radioed. "We're gonna need backup ASAP."

With two open lanes for a significant stretch, Takoda swung out for a slingshot pass and took the lead.

They were already rolling north of 180 MPH. Gunther shook his head, but focused on the road as he nosed up to draft the 'Vette.

Takoda came up on the exit quickly, stabbing repeatedly at the brakes to bleed off speed. Gunther did the same, downshifting. Still, they took the exit at about three times the suggested velocity. In minutes they had their father's Blazer in sight.

The gap began to close between all the vehicles.

The rental truck turned onto a dirt road, the top-heavy rig nearly tipping over in the corner. The Explorer and Blazer swung onto the road right on its tail.

Takoda fish-tailed onto the road, barely able to keep from sliding into the ditch. Gunther backed way off, to avoid getting pelted by gravel.

The three trucks were kicking up a tremendous dust cloud.

The road was not very wide—you wouldn't want to encounter a semi with an oversize load on it. But Takoda swung out to pass on the left. Gunther gritted his teeth, stomped the gas and passed on the right shoulder, the outside half of his fat tires hanging in the air over the ditch. With the thick dust cloud his visibility was minimal. If a mailbox or something appeared out of the dust, he was done.

American V8s blasting a throaty battle cry, the two street machines zung by all three vehicles before the driver of the rental truck understood what was happening.

With clean, clear air ahead, Gunther and Takoda now merged toward the center of the road and slowed down. The rental truck driver instinctively slowed to avoid rear-ending them, at first. Then he must have realized that rear-ending them wouldn't be such a bad thing, and floored the gas.

The Scarred Wolf brothers surged ahead to avoid the ramming attempt. Gunther realized this wasn't such a good idea. The truck outweighed either car by a ton or more.

A high-pitched scream rose above all the other noise. Jason Lone Tree slung past the rental truck and between the Scarred Wolf brothers on his motorcycle.

John Saxton's voice came over the CB. "Make a hole! We can stop him!"

Tommy and Ralph let the Dodge Ram pass. It rolled up behind the rental truck. Sunglasses on and hair flying in the wind, Mike Saxton stood up through the passenger window and shouldered the captured HK41. He aimed through the dust at the rental truck's rear tires and opened fire.

The rifle wasn't zeroed for him, and standing offhand while speeding over a bumpy road with a face full of dust was not an ideal firing position, but he got the tire in three shots. Another two rounds and both the dual tires on the passenger rear lost air.

John backed the Ram off as the rental truck began to swerve out of control. The driver over-compensated for the squirrelly handling and the truck veered into the ditch.

False Flag - Brown

Everyone stopped where they were, except Jason, who wheeled his bike around and rode back to park behind the Mustang. He jumped off the bike and ran to the wreck, pulling his sidearm.

The truck was tilted against the bank of the ditch, the passenger side mirror torn off and the passenger door trapped shut against the earth by the weight of the vehicle. The dust was still rising from where the truck slid to a halt.

Jason had the driver side covered.

Gunther popped his trunk, grabbed his rifle, locked-and-loaded. Takoda followed suit. They stalked up to the truck. Takoda kept his rifle trained on the windshield while Gunther joined Jason at the driver door.

"We've got you covered from the front and side," Gunther called to whoever was inside the cab. "We'll give you five seconds to open the door and come out with your hands empty. We have the means to make you come out if you want to be stupid."

The men in the cargo hold of the truck cussed and scuffled around, but there was no way for them to get out. The truck was not meant for passengers, so the garage-style retracting door on the "box" could only be opened from outside.

Tommy, Ralph White Feather and John Saxton dug out their personal rifles. They peered back through the billows of dust at the sound of a four-cylinder engine approaching, until they realized that Maurice Swope had finally caught up.

The driver door clicked open and a gloved hand pushed against gravity to hold it open as the driver climbed out, followed by the shotgun passenger. Both kept their hands visible and empty.

Takoda sidled around to help cover them. Gunther chinned toward Jason's pistol. "Put that away and get ready to search them. Just like we trained."

Jason holstered his sidearm.

"Drop," Gunther told his captives. "Belly-down, hands behind your backs."

The two masked, armored men complied.

Following Gunther's instructions, Jason zip-cuffed and searched them, pulling out weapons, radios, armor and knives. He rolled them onto their backs and continued. Takoda slung his rifle around his back and assisted with the search.

"No wallet or I.D.," Jason announced, when done.

Tommy walked up and kneeled beside one of the captives.

Jason climbed inside the truck cab and emerged with another HK41 and spare magazines.

Tommy opened a breast pocket on the driver. Embroidered onto the underside of the flap was the symbol of a knife piercing a globe. The knife was stylized so that, with long quillions angling back, it resembled a broken cross, or a peace symbol without the circle.

Tommy slipped the Buck knife out of his pocket, opened it and sliced off the pocket flap. He pointed with his knife at the other captive. "Check the other guy for this."

Takoda ripped the other man's breast pocket flap off his uniform. It had the same symbol. "What is that?" he asked.

"Proof Joshua was right," Gunther replied. "He was right about everything."

Tommy stood and waved toward the captives. "Get them up and bring them around back."

At the back of the truck the captives were positioned in front of the door. Tommy divided his men into two teams and had each team spread out and drop to the prone with rifles aimed at the back of the truck.

"You men inside the truck," Tommy called out, "there's only one way out of there. We've got you covered with a perfect enfilade. We will light you up if you so much as fart when we open this door. Lay all your weapons down--rifles, pistols, whatever you have. We're gonna open the door a crack for starters. When we do, start sliding your weapons out through the crack. When every last weapon is pushed outside, you can open the door the rest of the way and come out with your hands behind your heads. If we see any weapon of any kind still in your possession, we open fire."

Tommy waited, then added, "If you heard and understood, then somebody in there needs to sound off."

"Yeah, we heard," an echoing voice answered from inside. "We got it."

"Good," Tommy said. "Now stand by."

Tommy walked back to his men, and had a brief, whispered conversation with each one: Jason and Mike, armed with the enemy HK41s, were to initiate fire if the shooters in the truck tried anything funny. Only if they were unable to handle the situation themselves were the others to join in. And then it was imperative that they police up all their spent brass afterwards. It would be easy to identify their own casings, since the H&K brass was distinctly dented on ejection. Tommy reminded them that the shooters in the truck were likely armored up, so they should direct fire at unprotected body parts.

Tommy went back up to where the two captives stood facing the back of the truck. He stepped right behind the one on the right. "There's over half a dozen rifles covering you," Tommy said, softly. "I strongly advise you not to do anything stupid." He zip-cuffed the man's right wrist to the back of his belt, then cut the cuff holding his two hands together, so that the left one was free. "Open the latch and lift the door up just a crack," Tommy said, in his ear. "Then step back and stand right here again."

Tommy backpedaled quickly and took cover behind the berm of the ditch.

The guy with one free hand stepped forward, tentatively. He put his hand on the latch and paused.

"Guys, it's me, Brad," he announced, in a quavering voice. "They've got guns on me. They're having me unlatch the door. It's me. Alright?"

He swiveled the lock tab out of the way, then pulled on the steel latch hook until it rasped free of the embedded post in the steel floor. He grabbed the handle and pushed, lifting the door some three inches.

Before he could step back, somebody inside grabbed the bottom edge of the door and yanked upward.

False Flag - Brown

Tony called in the alert seconds before the engine noise could be heard on the approach road.

"Whoever it is," Rocco replied, "you know what we gotta do."

"Roger that."

All the veterans felt the pucker factor. If there had ever been a way to avoid a shooting war with the government, it was gone now.

A SWAT-style van bounced up toward the road toward the gate.

***

The Quick Reaction Force was cold, tired, and would rather be back in their bunks. Most of them napped on the way. They assumed some security guard fell asleep at his radio, or some kind of equipment malfunction had kept him from checking in. Nothing happening at this little podunk commo station in the middle of nowhere could be more than an excuse to waste their time.

The Force leader asked his driver where they were and tried one more time to establish secure contact.

No answer.

The van bounced and jostled down the rough backroad toward the station, multiplying the misery of the men who had to urinate. When the fenced-off compound finally appeared in the headlights, and the van slowed approaching the gate, the Force leader found it curious that no guard was visible in the shack.

***

When the SWAT van rolled over the spot where the mines were placed, Butch triggered them. Fire shot up from the ground and ripped through the bottom of the van.

The rear doors opened and wounded men staggered out in a shocked daze.

Griz opened up with the M60, chewing the agents to pieces and sweeping fire across the length of the vehicle. Butch and Tony added their fire to his from the side, while Frank and Kurt opened up from the front. They ceased fire after a minute had elapsed, waiting to see if anything moved. Then Butch moved in for search and double-tap duty.

False Flag - Brown

Atop the roof Leon watched the actions on the objective through his scope, then felt something small, cold and wet touch his neck. He looked away from the ambush site toward his more immediate surroundings and saw snowflakes falling. Darkness was falling, too.

"Here comes the hawk. This's that snowfall we heard about."

Cavarra remained focused on the ambush, scanning with binoculars. "Well, it's gonna hit the fan, now. We drew first blood." He keyed his radio. "Mountain Man, this is Sea Dog, over."

H-HOUR

Inside the little building, Josh was sweating bullets. It seemed he had very little to show for his efforts so far, and the cacophony of small arms fire outside just now emphasized the time crunch he was under to get results.

Josh was good with code and programming, but he wasn't up to speed on all the software in use, here. He had a whole lot of tweaking to do; but it took an expert to perform the tweaks without FUBARing the whole deal. He felt like Tarzan trying to teach himself brain surgery with a dying Klingon cut open on a tree limb while hungry leopards climbed up the tree after him.

Rocco came on the radio.

"This is Mountain Man," Josh replied. "Over."

"We had our first visitors just now. The ice is broken. Give me a sitrep, over."

Josh took a deep breath. "All good. Making progress. Just give me time and we'll be golden."

"Roger. Out."

Well, at least Cavarra was an experienced leader. Sometimes you had to give the proverbial kick in the 4th point to get subordinates to move faster. But it was not a good idea to pile up extra pressure on somebody who needed all their brain power focused on a highly technical task— that was just counterproductive to time-efficient work.

The lives of all the men outside were effectively in Josh's hands, now. He hated cliches, but one of the more macho slogans he'd seen on too many PT shirts really applied now: "Failure is not an option."

False Flag - Brown

Many actions played out in the short seconds after the agent inside the cargo hold threw the door all the way open. The door retracted into its coil at the top of the truck box with spring-loaded speed. Shooters were revealed in the truck, aiming their weapons outward. They opened fire even before the door had risen all the way clear.

After being in the dark cargo hold for so long, the bright outdoor daylight washed out their vision. Their fire was random and largely ineffective. But they did manage to cut down their own comrades, whom Tommy had placed facing the door without their body armor.

Jason and Mike opened up with the HKs, firing rapidly but efficiently, just as Tommy had trained them to do for the last few years. When they couldn't manage a head shot, they dropped to the shoulders, arms, groin or legs. The captured rifles were sighted for someone else, but at this short range they could hardly miss. The 7.62 NATO rounds took the crowded Tier Zero operators in enfilade, and only one of them managed to make it out of the truck, when Jason's magazine went dry.

"Get some!" Takoda yelled, and cut the man down.

All the shooters were down, now. Undoubtedly some were dead.

"Cease fire!" Tommy commanded. He pointed to Ralph and Maurice. "Sling your rifles. Get in there and search. No double-taps. Cover each other and toss out all the weapons first." He turned back toward Takoda. "Police up all your brass. Don't leave a single casing here." To everyone he said, "Keep your gloves on at all times. Loddy-doddy everybody."

The Shawnee Militia had never practiced this exact drill, but they followed their War Chief's orders and did what needed to be done with minimal bungling. They showed the discipline Tommy demanded of them in training.

Weapons were taken, first. All but one had HK41 rifles and 9mm Berettas. There was also a homemade rocket launcher.

Then wrists were zip-cuffed. Masks were removed from the shooters, as they were dragged out of the truck onto the road. The dead were separated from the wounded. Then each was meticulously searched.

Gunther took initiative to handle pocket flap-cutting detail, then passed out the knife-and-globe emblems to the others as *coup* trophies.

When Takoda had accounted for all his spent casings, he remembered the smartphone he had confiscated. He took pictures and video of the truck and men, careful not to show the faces of his comrades.

"How about that?" Maurice remarked. "Eight of them; eight of us."

False Flag - Brown

"They never had a chance with odds like that," Takoda bragged.

Gunther turned to face his brother. "We could have had all of them if you'd just taken the other truck."

Takoda flinched. "What was I supposed to do—have somebody leave their car back there, so we'd have to go back for it now? With law enforcement from all over the country swarming that stadium, probably."

Gunther chinned toward Mike Saxton. "He could have driven it. Now that's eight more goons free to pull another job somewhere, thanks to you. But all you could think of was not letting me catch this truck before you did."

Takoda's nostrils flared and his voice dripped with scorn. "Hey, I let you be the great leader, Tecumseh. That's why we missed our turn and almost **didn't** catch this truck."

"Okay, knock it off," Tommy ordered.

Gunther swallowed the retort on his tongue, with reluctance.

"Based on their reactions back there," Tommy said, with a tone meant to calm everyone down, "I think most of the deputies are honest. They weren't part of this."

"What about the bozo on the microphone?" John Saxton asked. "Telling everybody to just stay there?"

Tommy nodded. "You're right. There are people in high places who were in on it. Somebody involved in the event, there. Somebody in the sheriff's office who managed to get my warning ignored. But my point is, enough deputies on site are clean, the insiders might not be able to make those other shooters disappear."

"Oh, this'll get swept under the rug, all right," Gunther declared, bitterly. "None of those deputies have their own news network or TV show. All we're gonna hear about is Oprah's new diet or Brad Pitt's new girlfriend..."

"Brad Pitt's got another new girlfriend?" Maurice asked.

The others groaned and told him to shut up.

Tommy considered what Gunther said, and saw a lot of truth in it.

They were fortunate that the riots had scared enough people around Amarillo into staying indoors, as so far, this bloody encounter hadn't been observed by any curious citizens. But their good fortune couldn't hold forever. Since time was of the essence, Tommy directed his efforts back to the task at hand.

Besides weapons and ammo, the items found in the search were all piled next to the man who had carried them. Not surprisingly, none of the men had a wallet or any sort of identification on them.

Except one.

Tommy stooped beside that one, who was wounded in the leg and shoulder. He also wore a different style of uniform and had no embroidered emblem inside the pocket flap. Tommy opened the wallet and extracted the driver's license, then motioned for Takoda to come over. He bounced his eyes from the smartphone, to the wounded shooter, then to his son's face.

Takoda got the message and began video recording.

"Arden Thatcher," Tommy said, reading aloud from the driver's license. "You ever watch *Sesame Street*, Arden?"

Thatcher opened his eyes and focused on Tommy. "What?"

"*Sesame Street*," Tommy said. "They had some catchy music on that show. Remember this song: 'One of these kids is not like the others; one of these kids just don't belong.' Remember that?"

Thatcher's expression of intense pain contorted into one of confusion. He stared as if Tommy had three heads.

Tommy tried to sing the tune. "'One of these kids is not like the others; guess before my song is done.' Still don't recall that song?"

Thatcher shook his head, still slack-jawed.

"'And now my song is done'," Tommy finished. "You don't know what you are, do you Arden Thatcher?"

"Whaddya mean, 'what I am'?" Thatcher replied, with a thick drawl. He squinted his eyes, studying the faces of his captors.

"You're the patsy, dude," Tommy said. He wiggled the license and waved around at the other shooters laid out in a row. "You're the only one here with I.D. And did you ever wonder why your uniform looks different from everyone else's? And the armor you were wearing is old stuff that won't stop a rifle round, like theirs will."

Thatcher winced from some surge of pain in a wound. Through gritted teeth, he asked, "What are you—Mexicans?"

"Never mind us," Tommy said, smoothly. "This is **your** 15 minutes of fame, Arden." He inclined his head toward the stack of confiscated weapons. "You were the one with the makeshift bazooka, right?"

Arden's mouth twisted, but he said nothing.

"I think I know what the plan was," Tommy said. "The six of you...well, seven, counting the guy riding up front...you unass the truck, fire and maneuver into the stadium, shooting up everyone you see. And you fire homemade antipersonnel rockets into the crowd, or the group on the stage, or the children's choir. Maximum damage. Between you and these guys, and the other truckload of shooters, the body count could have been in the hundreds, right? It'd be a real turkey shoot after you wiped out the deputies and the crowd panicked. Tripping and climbing all over each other to get away. Sitting ducks. When their ammo runs low, they maneuver back to the truck and the getaway driver takes them back

False Flag - Brown

to where they came from. Job well done. Am I right?"

One of the wounded shooters near Thatcher spoke up. "Keep your mouth shut, Thatcher!"

Gunther stepped up to loom over the shooter, hanging his rifle down so that the muzzle hovered above his eye. "What's this? You wanna talk, tough guy? Wait your turn and we'll give you a chance."

The shooter choked down his anger and pain, catching his lip between his teeth.

"With your off-color uniform, you were easy to spot," Tommy told Thatcher. "Most likely they were gonna shoot you and leave you behind. With a single shot rocket launcher, it's not likely you could return fire effectively, even if you figured out what they were up to."

"Your accent isn't Mexican," Thatcher said. "Damn prairie niggers. What are you supposed to be?" His eyes shifted to the side, toward the shooter who spoke, as he licked his lips. Tommy got the strange impression Thatcher was seeking approval.

Tommy nodded toward the Saxton brothers and pointed toward the other end of the wrecked truck. "I should've done this before. Let's take him somewhere where we can talk in private."

The two husky young men hauled Thatcher up. He howled in pain. They ignored the cry and dragged him around to the front, where they dropped him unceremoniously to the ground again, like a sack of potatoes. Thatcher screamed.

"Shut up," John Saxton said.

Tommy slapped Takoda on the shoulder. "On me. Keep recording." He turned to the others. "One man watches the prisoners at all times. Everybody else puts weapons and gear away. Get ready to *di di mau*. Take the captured stuff, too. Don't worry about who gets what—we'll divvy it up later."

Gunther, the second-in-command, clapped Jason on the collar. "You have the least to pack away. Watch 'em and I'll have somebody relieve you in a minute."

Jason nodded while the others got busy packing up.

"Leave some of their ordnance," Tommy advised over his shoulder, walking to where Thatcher had been deposited. "I saw willie-pete in the pile. Leave two of them."

When Tommy reached Thatcher, he squatted next to him. "You think those guys are your buddies, Thatcher? You think they're too morally forthright to shoot you in the back?"

Thatcher groaned, tears spilling from his eyes. "Please...please, give me something for the pain. There's a first aid kit in the truck..."

"I'm disappointed in you, Thatcher," Tommy said. "You must not know much about 'prairie niggers.' Injuns are masters at torture. You never heard that? I want your pain to get worse; not better. I can guarantee you won't get any medicine if you don't cooperate. Well, that's not true. You'll get medicine. Heap bad medicine, paleface. Savvy?"

Thatcher groaned and sobbed.

"But before I was so rudely interrupted," Tommy said, "I was explaining how those guys threw you under the bus. Now maybe, just maybe, they wouldn't have killed you. Maybe they'd have just wounded you and left you for the cops. But who knows: maybe it would have turned out different. Maybe when news broke about the attack and they put police sketches on every TV set in the country, lo and behold, it just so happens they've already got the lone nut—you—in custody. The official story might be something like: you were pulled over for driving a car without a license plate and some heroic state trooper arrested you when he saw you had a loaded weapon, which you conveniently failed to use when he stopped you."

"P-please..." Thatcher murmured.

"You're getting weaker, huh?" Tommy asked. "You're bleeding out. Running out of time. We gotta pick up the pace here. See, now either way, they leave you holding the bag. The second scenario is one they've done before. It might be the worst option for you. They'll lock you away for years where nobody can see what they do to you, while you're on Death Row. Waterboarding is nothing compared to what an outfit like this can do to you. When the public gets a look at you again, you'll confess to whatever they want you to."

Thatcher groaned.

"I don't have all the high-tech stuff they do," Tommy said. "All I've got is pain. But pain works pretty good. You've got maybe 10 more minutes to live if we don't do something to stop the bleeding. That's more than enough time for me to make you talk. I can cause a whole lot of pain in that time. You **will** talk, Thatcher."

Thatcher turned his tear-blurred gaze directly at the phone's camera and cried, "Long live the Aryan race! You can't stop us! We're gonna bring down the Zionist Occupational Government!"

"That's good for starters," Tommy said. "Now tell us all about these guys you're with."

The threat of increased pain and the fear of bleeding to death was enough to make thatcher spill everything he knew. Which wasn't as helpful as Tommy hoped.

By the time the interrogation was done, everything was stashed in the vehicles and they were ready to go.

Dusk was settling in when Tommy had everyone gather around.

False Flag - Brown

His eyes were dead.

Gunther and Takoda had only seen their father's eyes go dead a few times in their life. It was a very, very ominous sign. He was notorious for always having his emotions in check. Now there was cold fury ready to explode out of him like a neutron bomb.

**

Gunther remembered the time when he was eight and his father took the family to the movies. Afterwards, Tommy went to get the car while Linda, pregnant with Carl, waited with Gunther and Takoda outside the rear exit of the theater. Two young white men, for whatever reason, zeroed in on the quiet family minding its own business. They mostly just insulted Gunther's mother, but they grabbed parts of her body, too. Gunther was too young to know what it all meant, but he remembered it bothered him bad enough to speak up against the white men.

Takoda sensed something, too. Barely as tall as the men's knees, the six-year-old threw himself at one of them. Up to then the white men had been content with verbal insults and the occasional sexual grope.

Tommy pulled up with the car just as one of the white men pushed Takoda, who fell backwards and smacked his head against the theater wall.

However many yards away he was, and looking through the car window, Gunther saw his dad's eyes go dead.

Gunther didn't remember how Tommy got from the car to the sidewalk. What he remembered was the white men trying to play the whole thing off as a joke...but even so, with a "what are you gonna do about it" attitude.

In the blink of an eye one of the men was on the ground clutching his throat, making a loud, labored rasping sound. Gunther only saw a blur in place of his father's hands and feet. Blood sprayed from the second man's nose. Then he doubled over. Then his head flew back, a tooth flying from his mouth. He staggered back and fell against the same wall Takoda hit. Tommy was there as he bounced back from the wall. Tommy added to his momentum, flipping him through the air to land hard beside his friend.

The image burned in Gunther's mind was of Tommy gripping each man by a fist full of hair, slamming their heads into the concrete sidewalk. Linda screamed over and over again that they should get Takoda to the hospital. At first Tommy didn't seem to hear. He was in some kind of trance-like rage. But finally he looked up to see his pregnant wife with his child in her arms, and he let go of the men. He swept pregnant Linda, Takoda and all, into his arms and carried them to the car.

301

False Flag - Brown

***

Tommy spoke in a measured monotone, but there was the trace of a tremor in his voice.

"I want all of you to understand something," he said, dead black eyes piercing each man like twin lasers. "We are at war. The war may be cold for most of the country, but it's now hot for us."

His hard, black gaze swept over them again. All of them found it jolting to meet it.

"In the rules of war, a civilized army treats prisoners of war with what mercy and dignity is possible. Wounded P.O.W.s get hospital treatment. You don't just torture or kill prisoners in cold blood."

Ralph White Feather nodded.

"The rules are different," Tommy continued, "when it comes to spies and traitors, during wartime." His jaw flexed and his nostrils flared.

"This is war," he said. "These men are traitors. Enemy agents. They waived their claim to the rights of captured soldiers when they decided to become the secret enemies of their neighbors."

He turned to look at the prisoners, then turned back. "I've done more talking than I want to, today, already. Everybody in your vehicles. Get them turned around and ready to go; and don't look back this way. One of you who doesn't have a weak stomach take that camera my son has, and record what the living ones are gonna say. I apologize for what you're going to see."

"I'll do it," Takoda volunteered.

Tommy shook his head. "Anybody else? I'd rather it not be one of my sons."

"Hup, Chief," John Saxton said, holding his hand out for the smartphone.

The wounded men were bleeding out, but Tommy made good use of the time at hand. The Tier Zero operators were hard, professional killers, but they had their limits like anyone else. One of them broke right about the time the stars appeared in the darkening sky.

Tommy got some information confirmed, and a whole lot more that was news to him.

When it was time to roll, Tommy took the phone and sent John back to his truck. Tommy took the two incendiary grenades and pulled the pins.

He didn't look back as the heat of the flames reached his nape on the way back to his vehicle. The blazing white-orange light behind him cast

302

False Flag - Brown

weird flickering shadows far down the dirt road.

He sent a text to Josh's burner phone, followed by a series of multimedia messages.

The convoy started up and moved out, assuming radio silence.

False Flag - Brown

H PLUS ONE
DHS COMMUNICATION SUBSTATION
MEDICINE BOW NATIONAL FOREST, WYOMING

Josh's gaze bounced between the screen of his laptop and the DHS computer monitor. The back door into the Data Center was open, and he was close to getting access to their secure intranet via the department Justin worked in.

"Sea Dog to Mountain Man," Rocco said, in his earpiece.

"This is Mountain Man, over."

"They're stepping it up. It's about to get hot. Over?"

"Roger that. Can't go yet. Need a little more time."

After a pause, Rocco said, "We'll give you what we can. Make this worth it, over."

Josh licked his upper lip, tasting salty sweat. "Wilco, Sea Dog."

He felt a vibration in his pocket. He pulled out his burner phone. He'd brought it along and turned it on once the building was secure. He mainly brought it in case Jennifer had an emergency of some kind. His own life was on the line right now, but he was armed and had guys covering his back and flanks. Jennifer was all by herself and he was more worried about what could happen to her in his absence, as silly as that was.

A text message came in from a number he didn't recognize.

Only Jennifer and Tommy knew the number to this phone. He opened the message.

Outside the sun had set and the landscape was dusted with snow. It was cold enough for the white flakes to stick, and the snowfall didn't show any sign of slowing down soon. The men shivered in their positions, but not just because of the cold.

In the distance they could hear the beating of rotorblades in the air.

"Beach Bum, this is Sea Dog," Rocco said, watching the dim sky.

"This is Beach Bum," Tony's voice answered in his earpiece. "I copy, over?"

"Three if by air," Cavarra said. "Time for Paul Revere to ride. Contingency Charlie. Over?"

"Roger. Out."

From his position on the roof, Rocco saw his buddies below rise from their positions and redeploy with quiet haste.

Rocco Cavarra hoped the opfor still hadn't guessed what was going on. If one of the approaching choppers was an Apache or even a Cobra, they didn't have a prayer. A gunship was the Angel of Death, if you didn't have serious antiaircraft assets. And the necessity of traveling relatively light had precluded them from bringing any robust surface-to-air weapons.

The shape of three helicopters appeared in the gloomy night sky amidst the clouds of falling snow.

"Oh shit," Jorge muttered.

Everyone else said something similar.

"Are those the black choppers we used to hear so much about?" Carlos wondered aloud. "Hard to tell at night."

"I think they're more like dark green," Leon said. "But whatever."

Whatever indeed, Cavarra thought.

Two of the choppers hung back. The small, bubble-shaped aircraft came on.

"Little Bird," Frank identified, from below.

The AH6 Little Bird passed at an angle to the building, about 800 meters out. It buzzed the mortally wounded SWAT van.

The two other choppers split up, moving in half-circles to hover about a klick out on opposite sides of the building.

"Sea Dog to all friendlies," Cavarra said. "Anybody got eyes on those other two birds? Over."

"Negative, Sea Dog," Butch replied. "Our view is blocked by the trees down here. Over."

Cavarra watched through the binoculars, but it was difficult to be sure what he was seeing through the snow.

"I got 'em," Leon said. "Blackhawks."

Rocco glanced at the sniper, who was peering through the scope on his M21.

"They're inserting troops," Leon said. "I see rappelling lines."

A chill slithered down Rocco's spine. A unit that inserted into the woods, by rope no less, was not just a gang of door-kickers.

"Fast rope?" Carlos asked.

Leon squinted through the scope sight. "I don't think so. But I can't tell for sure."

So maybe it wasn't Rangers, or anybody trained by them. Law enforcement units from all over the world had been sending their elite teams to the Air Assault school at Fort Campbell for decades, though. If these guys had been trained by the 101st instead of the Rangers, that wasn't exactly news to jump and cheer about. Air mobile infantry—by whatever name—would at least be trained to deal with a stand-up fight.

"Mountain Man, this is Sea Dog. Over."

"Go ahead Sea Dog," Josh replied.

"Be advised that there are boots on the ground. Opfor has air cover and ground troops, closing in from two sides. If you don't wrap this up in the next few minutes, we'll be trapped."

"Good copy, Sea Dog. Will advise. Out."

No, Rocco thought. *Wrong answer. You're supposed to say you're all done down there and we can get out of Dodge.*

The AH6 soared toward the building, switching on a bright search beam that swept the ground.

"We're out of time," Jorge said.

"Yo, Rocco," Leon said. "What you want to do about this chopper?"

"If one of us gets caught in that light," Rocco said, "the jig us up. We'll have to pour it on with all we've got." As if to emphasize his point, he loaded a 40mm shell in the grenade launcher custom mounted under his *Galil.*

"Let me try for the tail rotor," Leon said, changing magazines.

"What you got?" Carlos asked, chinning toward the M21.

"Steel core armor piercing," Leon said, working the bolt to eject the standard round and load one from the new magazine.

Rocco chewed his lip. With anybody else, the answer would be hell no. They would sit still, attract no attention and hope that spotlight never found one of them. But with Cannonball it was worth a shot. Literally.

"Go for it," Rocco said.

"Y'all get down from this roof," Leon said. "If I don't get him fast, he's gonna light us up."

"Bullshit," Carlos said. "You go, I go."

"Well, the Marines have spoken," Jorge said.

Despite the situation, Rocco smiled. Jorge was right to mock. But Carlos was right, too. "You can go, Jorge. Link up with Butch and Tony."

"Screw that," Jorge said. "Marines don't have a monopoly on crazy. Neither do...what the hell are you again, Cannonball? Army?"

Leon set his elevation, achieved his cheek weld to the polymer stock and, assuming it was time for silly bravado, quoted, "I'm the 82nd Airborne, and this is as far as the bastards are goin'."

The Little Bird came in slow, searchlight sweeping the compound carefully.

Leon had a sight picture head-on. When the AH6 turned at an oblique angle to him, he tickled the trigger.

The M21 bucked in his grip and the .308 round flew downrange into the spinning blur of the tail rotor.

He didn't wait, but squeezed off another round when his crosshairs aligned again. Then another. And another.

It was obvious when the Little Bird pilot realized he was taking fire, since the aircraft jerked and wobbled before nosing down and banking left. The chopper's minigun opened up with a ripping sound like chain lightning at close range.

Josh jumped at the horrendous noise from outside, and realized Rocco was not exaggerating.

He instinctively shot to his feet, reaching for his rifle...

Then he forced himself to sit back down and put fingers to keyboard. If he didn't finish this, then whatever happened out there was all for nothing.

All components of the blended threat seemed to be working. Justin, who was pretty good with hacking, himself, had helped Josh design them. The worm should be corrupting The List, and other files at the Data Center, already. Within a couple hours The List should be completely unusable. So technically, Josh could program the little video he put together to loop over the Emergency Alert Service, and they could exfiltrate.

But Tommy had sent him some footage that was the smoking gun of all smoking guns—much better than his own little subversive video production. Josh just had to finish removing everything incriminating to Tommy and the boys out of the audio and video, string it together, add some explanatory text titles, save the file, upload it, and feed it out.

He knew it was getting busy outside, but he had to take the time. There would never be a chance to do this ever again.

The minigun burst flew off into the trees, as the pilot neither had his gun oriented toward a target, nor had he even identified any targets. It was a dumb reaction, but understandable for a pilot who had never been shot at before.

At the burst of the minigun, Rocco and the others lit him up, The spotlight popped and went out. The chopper wobbled wildly. This new heavy fire was directed at the cockpit and the pilot was even less happy about that.

When the chopper had initially banked left, it went broadside to Leon's position. Leon poured round after round into the tail rotor.

At first it seemed as if Leon's work had been ineffective. But after the Little Bird had made about 150 meters of its escape, the tail slewed around wildly as three of the vertical blades fragmented.

The chopper spun in wilder and wilder circles. The pilot disengaged the turbine too late and it went careening into the trees. It was a spectacular crash.

"You da man, Cannonball," Rocco said.

Leon changed magazines again. "At least they got no close air support, now."

"Mechanic, this is Bone Crusher," Frank called, over the radio. "We all owe you a beer. If we make it out of here, that is. Out."

Others sounded off similar sentiments.

"Alright," Rocco cut in. "Guns up. We're expecting visitors, still."

Everything grew deathly quiet. The Blackhawks spooled up and beat away until they could no longer be seen or heard.

The snow continued to fall.

False Flag - Brown

Jennifer sat on the couch, with the big screen TV on. This weekend was the only time since she'd known him that Josh encouraged her to watch TV.

She knew Josh didn't let the dogs in the house because he didn't want them to get soft. But she was alone, worried and scared. So they were inside with her, enjoying the warmth of the dome home.

She jumped in her seat when an electronic buzz sounded, and the image on the television went black.

White text began a slow crawl across the blank screen:

"Earlier today thousands of people gathered for a conference at the Dick Bivens Stadium in Amarillo, Texas. The event was scheduled as an alleged response to the ongoing violence in that small city..."

Jennifer's jaw dropped lower and lower as she watched. The text spelled out the whole crazy conspiracy story, soon accompanied by still pictures and video footage. The footage was carefully edited to avoid showing certain faces, or sometimes blurred out the faces instead. Most voices were distorted, too. But even with the shaking of the cheap camera being used, she recognized two rental trucks and some heavily armed, masked military-looking men.

The scrolling text continued, now in a horizontal tickertape across the bottom of the screen as the scene jumped to where one of the rental trucks was wrecked, and several of the military men were lying wounded or dead, and unmasked. There was a short clip of some wounded kid prattling on about the mysterious men he was captured with. The text identified him as "the intended patsy."

There was a much longer clip of one of the military men being tortured by a something happening off-screen (the camera was medium-close on his face). The clip picked up just as the man was beginning to confess. He named names and spilled the beans about the false flag operation.

Jennifer wanted time to process what she'd just seen, but then the short video looped to the beginning and played again. She grabbed her phone and called her mother. People needed to see this.

GREENWICH, CONNETTICUT

Lawrence Bertrand sat in the half lotus, meditating on circular shapes, with his eyes closed, as he chanted.

False Flag - Brown

Many of his equals disdained Yoga as something for the useful idiots to practice. Why keep driving a Volkswagen when you had access to a Maserati? They had access to far more powerful techniques than twisting your body around on a rubber mat. But Bertrand found Yoga soothing, and healthy.

As he moved into the cobra position, the door to his meditation room opened and the butler appeared, holding Bertrand's phone, looking apologetic.

"So sorry to interrupt, sir," the butler said. "But someone is ringing you quite relentlessly. I feared there might be some sort of emergency."

"Set it down in front of me and leave the room," Bertrand said.

The butler did as instructed.

Bertrand frowned. He could understand how those at lower levels would be excited by the event in Texas, but there was simply no justification for anyone who had his contact information to be bothering him.

Less than 30 seconds after the door shut behind his butler, the phone rang again. He sagged fully to the floor, grabbed the phone and rolled to his side, scowling after checking the caller I.D.

He took the call. "Yes? No, I'm not watching television. You know I don't... WHAT?!?"

He hadn't risen off the mat that fast in 30 years. He stomped to the nearest room with a TV set and turned it on.

Just a few seconds into the video clip, blood boiled up into the skin of his face, flushing him with rage.

BOSTON, MASSACHUSSETTS

Jason Macmillan had arranged to be out of town on the day of the event, so he didn't have to put on a surprised act for his wife, in-laws and neighbors. Jade was able to get away as well, so they spent the night before, and most of that day, together in a nice hotel suite.

They had champaign chilled for the occasion as they waited for the first breaking news reports.

What he saw made him physically ill, like he'd been kicked hard in the stomach. Jade gave out a little cry and held her hands against her mouth.

Both their phones blew up less than a minute after the first loop had played. Macmillan ignored the incoming calls and dialed his team leaders.

He got a recording that the networks were down.

He dialed his contacts in the Potter and Randall County Sheriff's offices.

He got a recording that the networks were down.

"If networks are down, how the hell is my phone ringing off the hook?" he shouted.

"Switchboards are jammed because everyone's calling somebody about this," Jade said, pointing at the TV.

A call came in from Bertrand's number. Macmillan had to take it. Bertrand greeted him with a caustic stream of profanity.

"That's one of your shooters blowing OpSec all to hell on national TV!" Bertrand screamed.

"Yes sir," Macmillan replied, trying not to vomit. "He does look like one of mine."

"Looks like? Looks like? You idiot, he's naming names! What are you doing over there? How is it even possible you could screw this up so royally?"

"Sir, I followed every security proto..."

"You moron!" Bertrand interrupted. "Now I find out one of our repeater facilities has been hijacked! Haven't any of you incompetent buffoons figured out that they're using the E.A.S. from that very substation to do this?"

"Sir, I haven't heard anything about that," Macmillan said. "I'm not in charge of..."

"They're pumping this out on every channel! Every damned channel, Macmillan! What else has been compromised?"

"I have no idea sir."

"Well of course you have no idea! I shouldn't be surprised at that."

Macmillan suffered a dry heave, but managed to hold it back.

Bertrand took an audible breath and composed himself somewhat. "This is that redskin sheriff behind this. It's got to be. He pulled a stunt like this in Indonesia. This has his fingerprints all over it. One team all K.I.A. for all we know, and the other one in custody of a sheriff's department! This may require more damage control than the press can give us...assuming they can ever take the airwaves back from that son of a bitch!"

Macmillan heaved again. Jade, in a heated conversation on her own phone, shot him an annoyed glance.

"You listen to me, Macmillan," Bertrand said. "I want that Scarred Wolf bastard. You hear me? You've utterly destroyed all our other work. Your only job now is this: You take him down. His family. His friends. Anybody he knew in Special Forces. Take them alive or dead; do it quietly if you can, but do it!"

"Yes sir."

False Flag - Brown

"Now since your informant spilled his guts on national TV...in fact the little worm is still doing it! Over and over and over..."

"Yes sir."

"Since he's talking, we've got more damage control to do."

"Like what, sir?"

"Like the group you had him infiltrate, genius."

"Right. Of course, sir."

"Well we can't very well tell the world **they** did it **now**, can we?"

"No sir."

"Well, assuming you didn't let them go with all-expenses-paid vacations to Disney World or the French Riviera or something, which wouldn't surprise me at this point, I'm hoping you have them secured somewhere."

"Yes sir. I do."

"Well bravo, Macmillan You managed to keep somebody in custody. Next I'll teach you how to tie your shoes all by yourself. Now make them go away. We'll figure out who can do the PR for us on that later."

"Go away?" Macmillan replied. "Oh. The F.A.P. group."

"No, the New England Patriots, genius. Those two tasks are your job, now. So get moving on them. Now let me talk to Jade."

"Um...Jade...?"

"Oh really, Macmillan You think I don't know exactly where you are at any moment? Maybe you assumed you were her first? It's what she does. She'd fornicate with a boa constrictor if she thought she could mess with its head in the process."

McMillan's dry heaves became wet. He spilled the contents of his stomach all over the carpet.

"What was that? Bertrand demanded. "What are you doing? Give the phone to Jade, now."

Macmillan held the phone out toward her. At first she waved him away in disgust. When he explained who was calling, she set her phone aside and took his.

"Yes sir," she said. "They're ready. I can have the first wave of cells operational tonight. All of them can be active within a couple days. ...Well, for security reasons. ...Yes, I understand. Yes, it's a disaster. ...We will. I'll have good news for you in a very short amount of time, sir. ...All right. ...I already have that target allocated to one of my cells. ...That's fine. If Jason gets it done first, I'll just have them move on to the next target. ...Very good, sir. Yes, my phone is on. The switchboards must be jammed. ...Understood. Goodbye."

She tossed the phone back toward where Macmillan lay on the floor clutching his stomach.

False Flag - Brown

"All I can say, Jason," Jade said with a cold, severe expression, "is you better take care of this Scarred Wolf character."

Macmillan nodded, trying to get his breathing under control. This was the worst day of his entire life. And getting sick about it in front of Jade just added humiliation on top of it. "Scarred Wolf is going down. I guarantee it."

"Oh, he's going down," Jade promised. "But trust me: it will go much better for you if I don't wind up cleaning up this mess. My guys will be on this in very short order. You don't have much time to get to him first."

"Can't you...?" he began to plead, but stopped himself. He looked weak enough already.

"No," she answered anyway, sneering. "I suppose you have a profile for him and his potential accomplices?" She tossed her hair, gathered her purse and overnight bag, then headed for the door. "Nevermind. I'll get it straight from the Data Center."

The door slammed behind her. Macmillan rose to all fours and resumed throwing up.

PHOENIX, ARIZONA

Mac took a seat on the passenger side of the communication van cab and waited for his tablet to connect to the 4G network so he could fill out the necessary forms. He watched his agents lead a man, woman and teenaged boy in handcuffs out of the vinyl-sided house. Another agent escorted a younger girl over to their liason who dealt with children. Once the perps were hauled away for booking, his agents went back inside and began bringing out the weapons, ammunition, accessories and other equipment.

Once again, nothing was found that was officially illegal yet, but Mac's superiors had changed the policy. Now arrests were to be made and property confiscated whenever his team rolled out, and somebody else would worry about what was legal.

Agent Samuels spotted Mac and walked up to stand outside the passenger window, which Mac then rolled down. The agent removed his helmet and balaclava.

"What's up, Samuels? Please tell me you didn't stomp any cats to death in there."

Samuels grinned. "Nope. Shot the dog, though."

"Why?"

Samuels shrugged. "It was barking at us."

Mac groaned. "That's what dogs do, man. It's a family pet. It's naturally protective of its owners."

False Flag - Brown

"Hey, boss, it's bureau-wide policy. What's the big deal?"

Unfortunately, Samuels was right. Policy was that barking constituted aggressive behavior. And aggressive behavior from a dog justified deadly force. "Look," Mac said, "I know we've got clearance to do it. That doesn't mean we have to do it every time. Every single dog in the world is going to bark when strangers bust in a house and scare the owners."

Samuels shrugged again. "Hey, this guy had some nice stuff. You should see the computers and..."

"The computer goes into evidence," Mac interrupted.

"Well I've got dibs on the flat screen with the surround sound," Samuels said.

Mac straightened his posture in the seat. "I'm tired of telling you guys that I won't have you stealing from the crime scene."

Samuels scowled. "What's your problem, Mac? How come we're the only unit that doesn't get the normal side perks? You're not impressing anybody with this boy scout shit, and meanwhile somebody else is gonna have their pick of the loot while we get nothing."

"I don't have a problem," Mac growled. "But I'm about to give **you** one if your insubordinate attitude isn't adjusted real quick. Got it? Now finish what needs to be done and get back in the van."

Samuels whirled and huffed away.

"Mac!" the comm tech called from the back of the van. "You're gonna want to come back and take a look at this!"

Mac sighed, opened the door and got out. He walked around to the back of the van and climbed in. The tech had a live TV broadcast on one of his monitors.

"The game was on," the tech said. "Then the broadcast was interrupted."

Mac stared in disbelief at the little screen. After watching the video for the third time, he had his tech check other channels. This pirate broadcast was on every station.

Mac knew, as a federal agent in charge of a unit, he should be on the phone volunteering to go where needed. But he felt paralyzed.

He hadn't been this stunned when he watched the passenger jets hit the Twin Towers on TV.

Either this was an extremely elaborate hoax by fanatic right-wing whack-jobs or...

Or what?

False Flag - Brown

56
H PLUS TWO
DHS COMMUNICATION SUBSTATION
MEDICINE BOW NATIONAL FOREST, WYOMING

Cavarra and the others stowed their anti-infrared overgarments and replaced them with winter camouflage. The landscape was painted white, and snow was still falling steady.

The quiet before the proverbial storm set in.

Storm was an apt description for what was coming, Cavarra thought. But the scope of it was on a far, far greater scale than the impending firefight. Barring some kind of miracle, it was going to tear the whole country apart.

What would happen to Jasmine? What would happen to Justin? They didn't have the training to survive what was on the way. It would be up to him to get them to some kind of safe place.

The storm was threatening his very life today. For them he had to get some shelter, while America burned away.

The shooters moving in from the north side tripped one of the booby traps.

Safeties clicked off, on the roof and below. Cavarra adjusted his grenade launcher sights according to his distance estimation of where he saw the flash, and fired a shell.

A minute later and a booby trap went off to the south.

Gotta love bouncing Betties, Cavarra thought. That made for two UH60-fulls of troops, minus maybe two or more now. He *bloop*ed off another grenade into that general area.

On the ground, Butch scanned the northern approaches with night vision goggles. He spotted the opfor.

"This is Surf Rat," Butch said softly over the radio. "Enemy in sight. Looks like a squad of six men."

Hearts beat fast and everyone forced themselves to breath slow and steady.

The opfor moved in two wedge formations in bounding overwatch, again suggesting that they'd received combat training from some kind of US ground forces.

Butch watched them advance. He carefully laid his rifle down in front of him and grabbed a clacker in each hand. Soon even the men without night vision could see the approaching squad in the gloom. When they were 50 meters out, Butch squeezed both clackers.

The Claymores blew and the opfor went down. Griz opened up with

315

False Flag - Brown

the M60, raking them with grazing fire.

Butch and Tony sought targets for their rifles, and tried to make every shot count. Above them Carlos and Jorge did the same.

On the south side Kurt scanned the terrain with Josh's NVGs, watching for the enemy approach. Atop the roof Leon also faced south. They waited for minutes after the northern front went hot, and still didn't see the other element.

Leon left his position and crawled over the snow-covered roof to the west side, wondering if maybe the other squad had decided to circle around or something. Just as he began scanning with his scope, Kurt's voice came over the radio.

"This is Shortstop. Got 'em. Enemy in sight. Squad of seven, slow and cautious. Your sector, Bone Crusher. Out."

"Roger that, Shortstop," Frank said. "Standing by for visual. Out."

Leon crawled back to the south edge.

Before the enemy squad got within range of the Claymores, though, they halted and dropped.

What was going on with that squad?

The leader must be skittish. It was probable nobody had expected this level of organized resistance—surely he was in radio contact with the other squad leader and knew they were getting chewed up. He was probably trying to decide what to do. He could skirt the perimeter and try to attack from another direction. He could continue skirting until he linked up with the other squad. Or he could retreat back in the woods and live to fight another day.

Cavarra hoped he would choose the latter option.

The northern squad was pinned down, maybe with half or more wounded. The biggest problem for the time being was the southern squad.

H PLUS THREE

"Sea Dog, this is Mountain Man. Over?"

Rocco keyed his mike. "This is Sea Dog, over."

"It's a wrap. Leaving party favors now. Ready for exfil, over."

Cavarra could have jumped for joy. He instructed Josh to link up with Kurt and Frank on the south side when he finished planting booby traps and came outside.

While Josh got into position below, Rocco keyed the radio. "Sea Dog to all hands: Prepare to move out on my command. Everyone on the south side: the opfor can't make up their mind whether to fish or cut bait.

False Flag - Brown

We're gonna give them incentive to back off in less than three mikes."

The "wilco" replies came in from the individuals one by one. Then Griz said, "Sea Dog, Judge Dredd, over."

"Go ahead Judge Dredd," Cavarra replied. "Over."

"Enemy pinned on this side," Griz said. "How 'bout I bring some rock & roll to the southern concert? Over."

"Make it happen," Rocco said.

Once Griz was in position behind a tree trunk on the south side of the building, Rocco broadcast, "Sea Dog to all hands. Initiate on my 203 splash. Out."

Rocco sighted the M203 at where the enemy squad still lay in the snow. They were little more than dark shapes on the white earth to his eyes. But that was good enough for a grenade.

Rocco fired. The shell arced in and exploded in the midst of the dormant squad.

Leon's crosshairs already rested on his first target. He squeezed off a round. The prone figure winced with the impact. Leon acquired his next target and tickled the trigger.

Griz cut loose the M60 upon the impact of the grenade shell, peppering the area with six-round bursts. He couldn't make out individual targets at this range from ground level in the dim light, so this was mostly a harassing fire to give the enemy incentive, as Rocco put it.

Rocco fired another shell. Then another. Snow and clods of dirt flew into the air with each impact, mixed into shrapnel-filled blossoms of explosive light.

It didn't take long for the squad leader to decide the objective was too hot. They retreated, some individually, some helping others. But by standing, they provided aiming points for Griz, who made them pay the price for silhouetting themselves.

Learning their lesson, their retreat became a crawling movement, dragging wounded with them as best they could.

Neither squad was capable of offensive action anymore, unless they were suicidal.

"Sea Dog to all hands: Exfil to Rally Point Bravo. Last ones out will be myself, Mechanic, and Judge Dredd. Over?"

Those on the roof with him acknowledged directly. The rest by radio.

"Cannonball," Rocco said, "get on the north edge and give those guys something to think about."

Leon crawled over to the north edge of the roof while Jorge, then Carlos, climbed down the rope to the ground.

Rocco alternated firing shells at the north and south opfor to cover the retreat, while below Griz churned through his belt, six-to-eight rounds at

False Flag - Brown

a time, making life miserable for the enemy troops trying to fall back.

Rocco watched the ghostly figures of his unit moving out in a column on a westward azimuth, then turned to Leon. "Your turn, Cannonball."

Leon skootched over to where the rope was, slung the M21 over his back and climbed down. Rocco fired a shell at the northern squad, which was also pulling back, now.

When Rocco saw Leon disappear into the curtain of falling snow where the others had vanished, he radioed Griz. "Good work, Judge Dredd. Now your turn. I'll be right behind you. Over?"

"Wilco Sea Dog. Out."

The M60 chugged out one more burst, then fell silent. Rocco fired a shell after the southern opfor, watched Griz's huge form fade into the snow storm, then crouch-walked over to the rope, slinging his weapon. He slipped down to the ground and took off at a jog after the others.

Cavarra caught up to them at Rally Point B, and got a head count. Nobody missing; nobody wounded. But this was no time to push their luck, so they got moving again.

Less than a klick farther into the woods, and they came up against a fence.

"We can't be at the western boundary already," Frank said over the radio, checking his pace count for the second time. "There's no way, unless the map is wrong."

"You're right," Tony said. "We shouldn't come up on the fence for another three klicks."

"Maybe the map's not wrong about where the outer fence is," Griz said. "Maybe we're just not aware of everything inside it."

"What do you mean?" Rocco asked.

"Take a good look," Griz replied.

The fence was even taller than the one they had breached to get inside. It was topped with concertina wire, on leaning support brackets. Beyond the fence, camouflaged by the fresh snow, were several uniform structures: simple longhouses built to the same dimensions and lined up in perfect rows.

Rocco looked along the fence to the left and saw some sort of looming shape through the snowfall. He pointed along the fence and said, "Let's skirt this thing and keep moving. We can sight-see on the way."

They took a left turn and resumed their march. In short order they came to a corner of the fence. Just outside the corner was a 30-foot tall tower they could clearly make out through the snow storm as they passed below it.

"That's a guard tower," Griz said. "That concertina is angled inward. It's meant to keep people in, not keep them out. Those buildings are

Baracks."

"It's a doomed concentration camp," Jorge remarked. "It's just waiting for a staff and prisoners."

"One of those FEMA camps in all the scuttlebutt?" Butch asked, incredulous.

"FEMA, DHS, does it matter?" Carlos replied.

"That's why the commo building back there was pushed up so close to the gate," Griz said. "To make room for this facility back where nobody would know, until time comes to use it."

"Scum suckers," Frank grumbled.

"Don't be paranoid, guys," Griz quipped. "It's just an Amtrak switching yard. Move along. Nothing to see here."

They circumvented the fenced camp and made their way to the outer fence. This time they breached simply by cutting it, as Josh had taken care of all the electronic detection when he FUBARed the security system.

Once outside the fence, they changed course and drove on. Their tracks were filling in already behind them. After perhaps only another hour of snowfall like this, there would be no signs of their passing left in this winter wonderland.

They reached the small air strip well before sunrise. Phil Jenkins was waiting with a Cessna 441 Conquest II fueled up and ready to go.

Jenkins needed every inch of runway to get the passenger turboprop off the ground. It was built to haul up to 10 passengers, but with weapons and gear it was quite a heavy load.

They flew to another private airstrip, where Jorge's RV was now parked. Everyone transferred to the ground vehicle and drove for Josh's place where their personal vehicles waited.

False Flag - Brown

Lawrence Bertrand left his impromptu meeting with Harrison Travis, and eight other members from the Council, feeling like the whipping boy.

They had chewed him up and spit him out. A lot more than just his career was on the line, if Lightning Strike didn't achieve big results and earn him some redemption.

In addition to the abortive operation in Texas, the E.A.S. hijacking was a debacle of the first magnitude.

It was embarrassing.

Once it had been known that security was compromised, reaction teams were dispatched. Department resources were stretched thin, with everything going on. But still, the Quick Reaction Force should have been overkill for the job.

That the QRF was routed so handily, with nothing to show for it, confirmed that there were professionals among the DomTers.

And nobody figured out how to stop the broadcast for hours! Excuses flew like scattering geese about booby traps at the remote station, computer viruses in the Emergency Alert System, trouble finding a technician to sort it all out on short notice...

Finally power grids had to be shut down. But the virus had wormed its way through half the networks before it was stopped. Normal broadcasting resumed, but the damage had been done.

And speaking of viruses, somebody had hacked into the Data Center itself! It was diabolical--first cleaning the tracks of whoever the attackers were, then wreaking havoc on the intelligence gathered for the last few years. Unless there was still data somewhere, uncorrupted by the worm, on the most dangerous of the DomTers (such as the ones who hijacked the E.A.S.), Operation Lightning Strike wouldn't have nearly the effect needed.

Six of the nine Council members Bertrand met with had the burden of damage control resting on their shoulders, now. Their organizations not only had to withstand the onslaught of elements within the rogue media, they had to somehow make everyone forget about the nationwide pirate broadcast that looped for hours during prime time. Of course they weren't happy about this.

As far as making everyone forget, Harrison Travis told them, they'd be getting some help with that soon. But he made it clear that the DomTers had to be hit hard, and quickly.

False Flag - Brown

Bertrand assured them they would, and that Tommy Scarred Wolf and his accomplices would be among the first to go.

They asked how that was possible, since the Data Center had been hacked and the Threat Matrix destroyed. How could they be sure who the Indian sheriff's accomplices even were?

Bertrand was already on that, he assured them. Although outdated, they still had old, pre-Data Center intelligence to work with. And some Negro flunky in the C.I.A., DeAngelo Jeffries, had come forward voluntarily to share what leads he'd collected on the Scarred Wolf network.

As the limousine carried Bertrand to the airport and his private jet, he replayed, in his mind, his own speech about loose ends after he first hired Macmillan

Loose ends had been the bane of his efforts for half a century.

Previous operations always seemed to be plagued by overlooked details, or well-meaning people drawing attention to thin spots in the narrative. Special commissions had done some of the damage control, but the press had been instrumental in patching it all up.

With the rogue media challenging the official story every day, though, the loyal press organizations were losing their grip. Bertrand's colleagues in the Council had bought off who they could, planted others to discredit the rogues with straw man stories and lunatic fare, but they'd never be able to curtail the problem until they shut down the rogues completely—and that meant they needed a strictly regulated Internet. In fact, that was one of the objectives the Amarillo op was supposed to sell. They had put together a good backstory on how the DomTers had obtained their equipment, knowledge and hateful motivation all from the Internet.

Amarillo had backfired in the worst possible way.

But still, at least half the population—both liberal and conservative—accepted the narrative. And half was enough.

Everything would work out, in the end. All would forget McMillan's incompetence and the other embarrassments. The bad guys could slow things down, but not by much. They sure couldn't stop it. The momentum was unstoppable.

It was unfortunate that the phrase "New World Order" had been so profaned in recent years, because there didn't seem to be any better term so far. Whatever phrase was used, though, it was a done deal...by consent or conquest.

It looked like maybe a little of both, now.

Thoughts drifted to Bertrand's Collie; and all herding dogs.

Bertrand had watched many videos of modern livestock. There were

False Flag - Brown

often stragglers in any herd of cattle, which had to be dealt with according to their obstinacy. But with sheep, all it took was a loyal core that would respond to command, and the whole flock would follow.

Herding was easy. In North America he didn't need everyone to like him or even believe the narrative. He only needed them to follow the loyal core of the flock, until such time as what they wanted or believed was of absolutely no consequence.

As it should be.

False Flag - Brown

The sign hanging above the tent entrance read, "Helen's Hypnotheraputic Healing."

Inside, Terrance Handel reclined on a cot while Helen--an older blonde woman with Hindu-style clothing and a turban--sat facing him in a beanbag chair.

Helen had told him he had a very vibrant aura and that she might be able to unlock some of his lost long-term memories.

Now he was in a sleep trance and Helen was guiding him back to the early blank spots.

Terrance remembered standing in the corner during class, in elementary school. He'd been too aggressive on the playground again and the teacher put him in "time out."

He remembered staring into the texture of the paint on the wall, imagining each little bump and ripple was a hill or ridge to hide behind, from little microscopic soldiers. He imagined himself as a lone microscopic good guy soldier, waiting to spring up from hiding and shoot at the enemy army.

While the teacher read *Daddy's Roommate* to the class, Terrance visualized a whole microscopic war in the texture of the paint, with tanks, jet planes, artillery...and strange futuristic weapons as well.

A woman leaned in the doorway to the class and spoke to the teacher. The teacher called to Terrance. Terrance stepped away from the corner and his microscopic war, to face the teacher. The teacher told him to go with the woman.

As Terrance walked past the group of kids seated on the floor facing the teacher, embarrassed by everyone staring at him, Mandy Albright raised her hand. Mandy had naturally curly blonde hair, just like the girl in the *Peanuts* cartoons.

Yes, Mandy, the teacher said.

Mandy, sitting in the very front, listening with rapt attention when the teacher was reading *Daddy's Roommate*, asked why Terrance had to leave. Wasn't the time-out punishment enough?

The woman was going to help Terrance, the teacher said. Then he would learn to get along and be like all the other kids.

Terrance followed the woman down the hall, around a corner and into a private office. The woman was friendly, unlike his teachers, and attractive for a grown-up. She let him sit in an easy chair and make himself comfortable.

False Flag - Brown

She said her name was Jade, and she had come to his school to help kids just like him. She worked at a college, which Terrance knew was a school for grown-ups. So she was really important.

She asked him about the trouble he got into during recess, and he told her a little bit. She didn't condemn him for any of his behavior, but encouraged him to say more. So Terrance did.

"And then what happened?" Helen's voice asked, from the present.

Then Terrance went back to see the woman on another school day. She asked him more questions--this time about the games he liked to play at recess. She seemed fascinated with his answers, which inspired more questions--most of them about how he felt and why he felt that way, at a given time.

"Yes?" Helen prodded.

The woman, Jade, took acute interest in how cool Terrance thought soldiers were. And war. She questioned him about this a lot.

Then during one school day in her office, she had him lean back in the easy chair and watch Disney's *Fantasia* on the television.

It was a cartoon, which was cool. Terrance liked cartoons. But after a while, Terrance remembered drifting off to sleep. The cartoon played on in his mind, but changed. It was just shapes and colors flashing and blending, with noises and music...

Terrance sat bolt-upright from the cot, eyes wide open and forehead beaded with sweat.

Helen uncrossed her legs and leaned forward in her seat, alarmed. "Terrance?"

He looked at her. "What?"

"You came out of it? You weren't supposed to come out of it yet. What happened?"

Terrance blinked his eyes and wiped his brow. "I... It's like I hit a wall. A door. A locked door." He pointed to his temple. "And it hurt, up here."

He stood up. "I remembered more details about stuff I already knew. But you didn't help me remember any of the missing stuff."

Helen stood, too. "Well, this was just our first session. It might take a few. You were doing great--I could really see your aura engaged with what you were seeing." She handed him one of her cards.

Terrance took the card, but had stopped listening to her. Somebody was reading announcements over the loudspeakers outside.

"...Corporate meditation at 7:30. You don't want to miss it. It will open your mind for the rave tonight at nine. You can't really experience the beauty and power of the music if your mind isn't opened. Also, all

False Flag - Brown

Shinar Soldiers and *Montauk* Marines, you are invited to... let's see... Operation Lightning Strike? Yes, that's it. Anyway, that begins in five minutes over behind the Eternal Flame. Now don't forget that if you hear a song you just have to have tonight, to check the music table at the flea market for a compact disk or..."

Terrance exited the tent and shielded his eyes from the bright sun. He scanned over the area, and when he identified the Eternal Flame—basically a huge custom Bunson burner in a fancy altar-like structure with a gas-fueled fire—he marched toward it.

Behind the Eternal Flame some people were already gathered. Terrance joined them. Everyone behaved pretty much like him--standing and glancing around expectantly, briefly studying other faces looking for recognition or simply taking measure via eye contact.

Others approached and joined from all directions. They were all like him—relatively young; physically fit; male; with sober faces.

Finally a slightly older man arrived, holding a clipboard. He had the demeanor of somebody with rank, so all the healthy young men paid attention. Terrance had seen his type enough—the humorless military bureaucrat, as out of place in civilian clothes as a Muslim girl in a bikini contest. Such men had universal contempt for everyone except those of equal rank, yet obeyed, repeated, and enforced the most moronic, counterproductive orders without so much as a flash of critical thought.

"Alright, listen up," the man said, briefly rubbing his brow so that only one eye was visible. "Everyone here should be a member of the Baphomet Brigade. If anyone isn't, raise your hand."

Terrance had never heard of the Baphomet Brigade, so he raised his hand.

Everyone else did, too. Something weird was going on.

The man with the clipboard undid one of the buttons on his shirt and slipped his free hand into the gap, assuming a Napoleonic pose. "Alright, I'm gonna clear some things up for you. If you still aren't sure you belong here when I'm done, see me afterwards. Time is short, so be advised: The birdcage door is coming open. But the owl sees all and smiles. We have Christmas hams for 13 families. The average low this winter will be 33 degrees below, as above. There are gifts hidden for the widow's son. And the angel is in the whirlwind."

When the word "smiles" left the man's mouth, Terrance was gone. In his place was Adiur.

Adiur was a warrior from way back. He'd been waiting for Lightning Strike for most of Terrance Handel's life. He felt patterns of energy in the air and stretched out his arms to absorb them. He remembered.

All the blank spots in Terrance Handel's memory...Adiur knew what filled them. He remembered the early sessions with Jade, how she

325

established the triggers first, before guiding him to deeper levels.

He remembered the field trip, when most of Terrance's class went to a zoo and an observatory, but Jade took him to Disney World for an incredible day and night.

He remembered Ms. Greeley, who showed him unimaginable levels of sexual pleasure, all while reinforcing his training, and testing his capabilities.

He remembered the special advanced training he went through in Colorado Springs. He remembered the special duty assignment to transport the treasure in artifacts from the museum in Iraq; guarding an opium field in Afghanistan; guarding pallet loads of absentee ballots until the 2012 election was over; firefights with the Taliban; escorting V.I.P.'s around the Sandbox; training for counter-terror; training for wet work; training for black ops in the homeland...

And he knew why he was here, today.

Adiur recognized the other warriors around him. There was Adini, Zamana, Urukh and Nurval, to name just a few.

Zamana, the one with the clipboard, began calling them up by name. They formed a line in the order of the names he called. To each one he handed a sheet of paper and gave brief instructions. "Your first target is this sheriff in Phoenix," he told one. "Your target is the sheriff in this little podunk town in Montana," he told another. "Your target is this guy with the radio show in Texas. After that, there's a sheriff in the neighboring county..."

Nurval was just ahead of Adiur in line. When he reached the front, Zamana handed Nurval a manila envelope.

"You've got a big assignment in Washington, DC," Zamana said. "You'll be working with a ghost team that will link up with you there. All instructions are in the packet. Good luck."

Nurval saluted him. Zamana returned the salute. Nurval marched away toward his tent.

Adiur stepped up. Zamana pulled a sheet off the clipboard and handed it to Adiur.

"You live in Oklahoma," Zamana said. "This one's right in your front yard. There are other forces going after this same target. Regular ghost teams. You can work with them, advise them, or take over if need be. Just do whatever is necessary to terminate this sheriff."

"Yes sir," Adiur said, and saluted. Zamana dismissed him with a return salute and Adiur marched toward the tent Terrance had set up, looking over the text and images on the page.

Upon reaching the tent, Adiur set to taking it down and packing up.

He felt Kari approaching before he saw her. "You're leaving already?"

False Flag - Brown

she asked.

Adiur examined her physical form. He would like to enjoy that body. It was a shame Terrance hadn't been aggressive enough. Kari would have done it with him while her boyfriend danced at the rave, if he'd only pushed her buttons right. Well, there was no time, now.

"Something came up. But it was nice to meet you, Kari."

"An emergency?" she asked.

He shrugged and grinned at her as he stuffed the folded tent into the pack.

"You seem different, somehow," she said, breathily.

He looked her up-and-down, gave her another grin, and tossed his loaded backpack into the air with a flick of his wrist. He slipped into the straps as it hung suspended for a split second before gravity pulled it back toward Earth. Kari blinked her eyes as if she wasn't sure what she'd just seen. Adiur winked at her and marched off toward the parking area.

He studied the sheet of paper with more concentration as he went, this time. There was a color photo of a Native American man with intense, coal-black eyes, short black hair and a red-bronze face that betrayed no emotion. "Tommy Scarred Wolf," Adiur read aloud.

Nice that the target lived right on the reservation. Terrance was pretty familiar with the area.

Scarred Wolf was evidently one tricky character. Well, his tricks weren't going to help him now. He had no idea what he was up against this time.

False Flag - Brown

Linda was relieved when Tommy made it home unscathed, but she had to hit him immediately with bad news.

The reason Carl disappeared was he had been arrested. Carl called Linda from the jail the night after his arrest. Apparently Rachel White Bird had entrapped him on an alcohol-related charge. Carl told the whole story to his mother in Shawandasse, which none of the Tribal Police spoke or understood.

But when Linda arrived at the jail to bail her son out, she was told he wasn't there.

He was never there. It must have been some kind of prank, lady, like teenage boys are famous for pulling.

Tommy drove straight to the jail.

A sallow, haggard Jason Macmillan had arrived at the station just off the redeye flight to Oklahoma City the morning after the pirate broadcast. He was not in a polite mood, throwing his authority around and making threats when they weren't necessary. The Chief let him take over the interrogation of the Scarred Wolf Boy.

Macmillan took off the kid gloves almost immediately. The boy resisted being strapped to a chair and he had to be worked over a bit before they could secure him. Then the two experienced interrogators from the Department went to work on him.

The kid clammed up, and couldn't be tricked or scared into telling where his father was or who was with him. They worked on him non-stop for hours, and he wouldn't crack.

Macmillan had the Chief and all non-Departmental personnel leave the interrogation suite.

Young Carl's pupils dilated when the burning cigarette was ground against his flesh, but his expression remained blank and he refused to so much as squirm, as if the pain bothered him no more than the smell of burning flesh.

An interrogator told him there was a lot more where that came from if Carl didn't cooperate.

Carl spit in his face.

Macmillan was pondering what it was going to take to break this kid when he found out the man he was looking for was now at Tribal Police

False Flag - Brown

Headquarters, making a major stink.

The mountain had come to Mohammed.

As Macmillan and his two agents stalked down the hall toward the bullpen, they caught some of the heated exchange between the Chief and Mr. Scarred Wolf.

"Your brother doesn't work here and **you** don't work here anymore," the Chief said. "You got no business back here. Civilians come to the front counter."

The other officers at desks around the bullpen were frozen, staring agape at the scene. Most of them knew Tommy, and the officer at the desk let him in like she always had.

Today Tommy's holster was unflapped and his eyes were dead.

"Listen, shitbag," Tommy told the Chief. "You can charge him with something, or whatever you need to do. But my son is coming with me."

"Your son isn't here," the Chief said. "I don't know who told you that."

Some of the officers present knew that was a lie, but held their tongues, averting their gaze with ashen expressions.

The three arrogant visitors emerged from the hallway and nudged the Chief out of the way. They stood facing Tommy.

"Tommy Scarred Wolf?" asked the tall, bald, chunky one.

Tommy just looked at him.

"Yes, that's him," the Chief said.

The bald chunky one didn't exactly smile, but he appeared pleased on some level. "I'm Jason Macmillan, DHS. I'm afraid I need to ask you some questions."

"I'm afraid you've got bad timing," Tommy said. He chinned toward the Chief. "Your yes-man needs to give me my son. We can chat later."

Now Macmillan did smile. "This is a matter of Homeland Security. It's not a request."

Tommy cocked his head and fixed a sharp, scrutinizing stare on the bald chunky man. "Jason Macmillan. I've heard that name. On TV, maybe."

McMillan's face and neck flushed dark red. One of his agents had cracked and gave up Macmillan's name to the nation, via the subversive video played during the hijacked broadcast.

Tommy sneered. "Let's see some I.D., big boss man."

"Enough of the games, Tommy!" the Chief cried. "Don't play with these people!"

"You seem to be all mixed up, Scarred Wolf," Macmillan said, smugly. "You're not in a position to demand anything. I represent the

329

False Flag - Brown

Federal Government. **You** do what **I** tell you, **when** I tell you. Got that, boy?"

Tommy wobbled his head around to pop his neck, then flexed his back. "That depends on what country this is, I guess," Tommy said, in a flat, cold voice. "It looks like you and me are in a disagreement about that."

The Chief licked his lips and said, "Don't do anything stupid, Tommy. You're in a room full of police officers."

One of the agents with Macmillan eased his hand toward his sidearm. Tommy stared Macmillan in the eye. "If your goon so much as touches that gun..."

The man's hand moved away.

Officer Stark rose from his desk to Tommy's right. "That's it. This is too much," he declared, with a disgusted tone. "The Chief is lying. Carl is strapped to a chair in the interrogation room. They were torturing him."

"Stark!" the Chief roared.

Macmillan's jaw slackened and he turned his head to stare at Stark, confused.

Officer Lone Tree, Ralph's cousin, stood up behind his desk and pointed to a smoked plastic bubble protruding down from the ceiling. "Video cameras, dumbass. We have them in every room. I saw what you did to that boy, too."

"I never thought I'd live to see the day I was so ashamed," Stark said, then turned his head to the left. "I'm sorry, Tommy."

"Now listen here, everybody!" the chief shouted. "I don't know what you think this is, but I'm in charge here! I'm not going to tolerate..."

Tommy shifted his gaze to the other cops in the room, wondering who would break which way. One of the agents took that as an opportunity and went for his gun.

Tommy's M1911 blurred out of its holster and he fired while diving to the floor. The heavy slug hit the agent in the face, throwing him backwards, while a bullet snapped over Tommy's head.

Macmillan and the other agent pulled for their weapons.

Tommy hit the floor and fired again, hitting Macmillan in the groin. He raised his aim and fired, this time catching Macmillan in the neck. The other agent had his weapon out now and jerked the trigger. His bullet punched through Tommy's calf.

Tommy fired up through the underside of the man's jaw. The bullet pushed a big wad of brain and skull bone out the top of his head, to splatter on the ceiling.

Everyone's ears rang as the report of the last shot reverberated to silence. The smell of the powder hung in the air. Tommy rolled to a sitting position with his back against the wall, pistol still in hand while he scanned the room for any more threats. A couple of the officers had their hands up. Stark and Lone Tree had their guns out, but pointed at the floor for now.

"Oh, sweet lord..." the Chief muttered.

"You okay, Tommy?" Lone Tree asked.

"I'm good," Tommy said.

"I'll go get your boy," Lone Tree said.

The Chief stared dumbfounded as Lone Tree left the bullpen and disappeared down the hall. Tommy rose to his feet.

"I don't know what your deal is," Stark told the Chief. "But you pushed it too far. I kept my mouth shut for too long. You want a resignation? You want to take this in front of a jury? Let's go for it."

Tommy pointed at a female officer with her hands up. "Are you Rachel White Bird?"

The woman blanched.

"That's her," said Muroc, who Tommy recognized.

"You and me need to talk," he said. "After I get my son home. You can do it the easy way, or I can come find you, but you and me have business."

White Bird nodded that she understood.

While Stark covered for him, Tommy checked his leg. The bullet had missed his shin or he'd be in a lot more pain, probably. It had passed clean through—also welcome news. But he was bleeding pretty good.

A different female officer—Tommy couldn't recall her name—fished around in her huge purse, produced a couple feminine napkins and handed them to Tommy. He thanked her and pressed them onto the wound. Muroc handed him a roll of tape and Tommy secured the field expedient bandages to the wound.

Lone Tree returned with Carl. Son and father looked at each other.

Carl's gaze dropped to the floor. "Sorry, Dad."

"Get behind me, Son," Tommy said, softly. His lips trembled and he glanced around the room again. He raised his voice, and it throbbed with rage. "Anybody else got a bone to pick with me? Anybody want to be a hero for your Chief of Police?"

The room was silent, then Stark, his pistol still in hand, said, "Ain't nobody got shit to say, Tommy."

Tommy holstered the M1911 and stepped toward the Chief. "If you had a gun, I'd kill you. I don't know when you went dirty and I don't care at this point. You want to step outside with me, I'll hand my weapon over to Carl right now. You want to send somebody after me or mine, you better pack a lunch."

False Flag - Brown

The Chief said nothing, but tried to meet Tommy's glare with his own evil eye.

Nobody in the room saw the left hook. Suddenly the Chief was on the floor, his mouth bleeding and eyes glazed over.

"Let's go, Carl," Tommy said.

Before exiting, Tommy nodded at Stark and Lone Tree. "I know what this cost you. You are honorable men. Thank-you."

They nodded back. Father and son left the police station.

Carl sat in the passenger seat as Tommy drove them home.

"They hurt you, son?" Tommy asked.

Carl shrugged. "Knocked me around a bit. Cigarette burn. No big deal."

"You told Mom Rachel White Feather set you up for the DWI?"

Carl nodded. "Bitch." He looked out the window, then turned back, wiping a tear away. "I didn't talk, Dad."

Tommy reached across the cab to squeeze his son's shoulder. "What did you mean back there: you're sorry? You got nothing to apologize for."

Carl shrugged again. "I was stupid. Fell right into a trap. And I wasn't there to help when you needed me."

Tommy fought back the lump in his throat. "Shake it off, Carl. I couldn't be more proud of you."

Carl's face betrayed no reaction.

"It was me that was stupid," Tommy said, "going in there with no backup. Tribal police all around me and for all I knew they could have all been dirty."

"I could have fought back hard, Dad. Messed them up good. I thought about it. But they were cops..."

"Yeah, about that..." Tommy sighed. "Stuff is changing, fast, Son. The rules are gonna be different from now on."

Carl's eyes dropped to his father's leg. "You're bleeding. Did you get shot?"

Tommy nodded. "I'll let you handle the first aid when we get to the house. It'll be good practice for you."

"Shouldn't you go to a hospital?"

"I'd rather not," Tommy said. "If it's bad enough, me and your mom know doctors and nurses who can come by. I think we all need to be careful where we show ourselves from now on. Especially without backup."

After a few minutes, Carl said, "I heard somebody watching TV in the jail last night. Guys in jail are spreading some bizarre rumors. What's going on?"

False Flag - Brown

"War, Son," Tommy replied. "We're at war. First shots have already been fired."

False Flag - Brown

60
H PLUS 15
NORTHERN ARIZONA

Carlos, Leon and Rocco had carpooled to the Rennenkampf place, and they carpooled back. They were bone-tired after the operation and hours on end of stressed nerves, so they drove in shifts. Rocco was the lightest sleeper, and woke up when Carlos slowed down to take a freeway exit.

"What's up?" the older man asked, groggily.

"Just pulling over to get some gas," Carlos said.

Rocco stretched and yawned. "How far are we?"

"Just another hour or so, but I didn't want to risk it."

Leon stirred in the back. "It's cool. I gotta drain the weasel anyway."

Shotgun rose from the floor to put her paws on the armrest and look out the window.

"You **must** have to whiz," Rocco chided. "Your own bladder's about the only thing that can wake you up."

"Don't be hatin'."

Carlos pulled his gaze from the road ahead to glance in the direction of his friends. "Hey guys, straight up...you think we just saved the world?"

Neither answered him right away.

"I think we did everything we could do," Leon finally replied.

"If the world can even be saved at this point," Rocco added, "maybe what we did saved it for a little longer."

Carlos cussed in Spanish, as he turned off the ramp and the gas station sign became visible. "Look at those prices! They must have jumped 30 cents."

"Normally they jack 'em up for the weekend, then leave 'em be until Monday," Leon said. "Looks like they're still climbin'."

Rocco frowned thoughtfully.

Carlos pulled up to the pumps and got out to fill the tank. Leon went inside to use the restroom.

When Leon returned from the restroom, something in the newspaper rack caught his attention before he made it to the front door. He pulled the top paper from the stack to look at it.

The headline read: "INSANITY!" The subheader read: "DHS Says Depraved Right-Wing Extremists Want the World as a Captive Audience."

Leon read the accompanying article. According to the mainstream media, the broadcast Rennenkampf had pulled off was an elaborate hoax

False Flag - Brown

with actors pretending to be captured government agents and a manipulated informant. In other words: it was not the government, but **anti**-government extremists who perpetrated a false flag. They even called the confessions by Thatcher and the agents "shoddy acting."

It was all a tragic but incompetent attempt at deception on a grand scale, the story explained. Sensible people rejected it, of course, but still, there was a danger that some less sensible people might take it seriously, and act on it. Somebody needed to take steps to ensure nothing like this could happen again. And the perpetrators needed to be apprehended and prosecuted to the fullest extent of the law, according to the experts.

"Excuse me," called somebody with an Indian or Pakistani accent from the front counter. "If you want to read that you will have to purchase it. This is not a library."

Leon tossed the paper back in the rack. "Like hell am I gonna pay for that."

A white guy about Leon's height, with a pierced ear and a tattoo of a marijuana leaf on his neck, stared at Leon from where he stood by the coolers where the beer was kept. He laughed an ugly laugh. "That boy's never been in a library. You wanna hide somethin' from a spook, put it inside a book."

"That's a good one, Einstein," Leon replied, shaking his head. "I can tell you're a intellectual giant. You must read a lot yourself." He pushed the door open and trudged back toward the truck. He had a bad feeling, though, and turned back when he heard the door open again behind him.

The white dude who had been at the beer cooler rushed out, accompanied by another one, with long red hair spilling out from under a ball cap with a Confederate flag emblem.

"Man, this is too cliche," Leon said. "All you guys need is banjo music from somewhere."

The first guy sneered and said, "What's that? I know you ain't talkin' to me, boy."

"What you don't know would fill a library," Leon said. He wondered how tough these two were; if they knew how to fight as a team; or if they knew how to fight at all.

Leon knew he should have just swallowed the insults and turned tail, eating crow if necessary. That was the smart course of action. But he'd done that enough for one lifetime. He was tired of feeling like a coward because of being outnumbered and never knowing what other potential enemies might pop out of the woodwork.

"There's nothin' worse than a coon with a smart mouth," the first redneck said. It was obvious he was ready to throw a punch. His buddy looked ready for action, too.

False Flag - Brown

Shotgun began barking from inside the truck. Leon wished she was beside him now. It sucked being alone at times like this.

Rocco and Carlos arrived from the pumps to flank Leon.

"Is there a problem here?" Rocco asked, staring hard at the one with the tattoo and pierced ear.

"Oh, is that how it is? There's two of us so you have to go and get three?"

"There's one of him," Carlos retorted, nodding toward Leon, "so you had to go and get two?"

Leon was not alone. Why had he automatically assumed he was? His friends had his back.

The second redneck said to the first, "C'mon, man. Let's go."

The first redneck didn't like this, but apparently saw the wisdom in backing down. But he pointed his index finger toward Leon's face. "Boy, don't ever show your face around here again, unless you have a lot more than two Spics to hide behind."

Leon gave him the last word. By letting a belligerent ignoramus talk trash as he backed down, it allowed him to save face in his own mind, defusing the confrontation.

The two rednecks went back in the store.

Rocco clapped his hand on the back of Leon's neck. "I'm offended: I'm a Dago, not a Spic. He better get his euphemisms sorted out."

They returned to the truck. It was Leon's turn to drive, so he took the wheel and the other two climbed in.

"It's good you kept your cool, Cannonball," Carlos said. "We don't need police coming in and paying attention to us right now."

Leon said nothing for a while. Then, in a quiet, grieved voice, he stated, "Rocco is right: the world can't be saved at this point."

"C'mon, man," Carlos said. "They're just a couple of bigots."

"Yeah, exactly," Leon said. "They don't know me. Nothin' about me. Don't know what kind of life I lead; what I've done; what I believe; who I vote for. And they don't care. But they hate me anyway. If you can just look at somebody you don't know, and hate 'em...man, how can that be fixed? I put my life on the line for this country over and over again, so assholes like that are free to be assholes. But they just see a black man and think I'm the enemy."

Rocco bit his tongue. His friend was right; but it worked the other way around, just as often. And the animosity was sanctioned when going the opposite direction.

"You know what's worse?" Leon continued. "There's a whole lot of people out there who don't have a Confederate flag on their hat, but they ain't much different under the hat."

False Flag - Brown

Leon was right about that, too.

"And it's only gonna get worse," Rocco said.

COCCOCINO COUNTY, ARIZONA

They certainly didn't expect customers on Sunday, but after arriving at CBC Southwest Tactical, where they'd left two of their vehicles and all their cellphones, they hung out for a while after cleaning and re-oiling their weapons.

They sat around the lobby drinking coffee together as if it was just another day. But it wasn't just another day, and the atmosphere was heavy with that fact.

"You hear the news from the Middle East?" Carlos asked, checking the news feed on his phone. Leon shook his head, almost scoffing at the idea that a place so far away could pose any significance.

"Israel hit Iran's nuclear facilities," Carlos said.

Rocco took a sip of coffee. "So they finally did it." He spoke the words as if they were talking about a neighbor who finally repaired a hole in his roof.

"It's hitting the fan over there, too," Carlos added.

"Either of you notice the Dow Jones?" Rocco asked, eyes on his own phone.

Leon shook his head again. "All I'm hearin' about is that our video is all fake."

"Well, I'm not a stock market expert," Rocco said, "but keep your eyes on it. Looks like the petro-dollar is finally being replaced. When foreigners start dumping it, the whole house of cards comes down."

They heard a car pull into the lot. Carlos stood and strode to the window for a look. "Know anybody with a black Challenger?"

"That'll be Justin," Rocco said. "I told him to meet me here."

Justin knocked at the front door a moment later and Carlos let him in. They offered him coffee and a seat, but he hesitated.

"Does this TV work?" he asked, pointing to the flat screen in the lobby.

Rocco nodded. "Sure. What's up?"

"Just heard something on the radio as I was pulling in," Justin said. "Turn it on, please?"

Leon grabbed the remote and used it to turn on the TV. The image of a news anchor sitting at her studio desk appeared on the screen.

"...We have a camera on Capitol Hill and should be able to patch in the video feed momentarily," the news anchor said "As I mentioned there are reports from around the country of orchestrated attacks on local law enforcement. But by far the worst attack was on the nation's Capitol. Oh, alright, I hear that we're ready to go to our news team on site."

The scene changed to a woman holding a microphone with the Capitol Dome, fire engines, and police cars all in the background. Black smoke wafted by the scene.

"Now this can't be good," Carlos remarked.

H PLUS 18
LAS ANIMAS COUNTY, COLORADO

Joshua was so glad to have made it back home; and Jennifer was so glad to have him back, that the dogs staying inside the house while Josh was gone never came up in conversation. Jennifer wrote off going to church for the day. They spent some time doing what young healthy couples in love do pretty much whenever they get the chance, then ate together and talked for a while, before Josh's phone rang.

"That's different," Jennifer said. "It's **your** phone this time." She went to the kitchen to do the dishes.

Josh checked the caller I.D., saw it was Paul Tareen and took the call. "Hey neighbor," Josh said. "How's everything in your neck of the woods?"

"Josh," Paul said, speaking excitedly, "I know you don't watch TV, but you need to turn yours on now. There's a news broadcast on all the channels. Alternative media hasn't picked up the story yet."

Josh's eyebrows furrowed. "You mean the attempted false flag in Amarillo?"

"No. That's old news already. Things are happening fast. Just turn the news on. I need to make some more calls. I'll talk to you later."

The line went dead. Josh set down the phone, found the remote for the TV in the drawer of the end table, and switched it on.

He saw the reporter in front of the smoky Capitol Building, with fire engines and police cars in the background.

"It's still a state of pandemonium here," the reporter said, "but what has been confirmed is that a group of armed men shot their way into the Capitol Building, overwhelmed the security detail, and set off some kind of explosive inside. The terrorists used military weapons and tactics to spray bullets at everyone they saw. At least one representative from the House is dead, an untold number of Congressional aides and people who were visiting when the attack took place are dead or being evacuated to the nearest emergency rooms. Sources say the victims include members of an elementary school on a field trip were also caught in the gunfire. One of the terrorists was shot by security and left behind by the other terrorists. He has been identified as a member of a right-wing militia."

Josh leaned forward on the couch. "Jennifer! C'mere--you need to see this."

ABSENTEE-SHAWNEE TRUST LAND, OKLAHOMA

Tommy and his family were holding an impromptu meeting at his house when they got the call. Everyone who had accompanied Tommy to Texas was there, plus Linda, Carl, Uncle Jay, and every single member, active and inactive, of the Shawnee Militia. The meeting began as a mission debriefing, but evolved into a warning order for what might come next.

Michael Fastwater called Uncle Jay, who quieted everyone down and turned on the TV.

They watched and listened, dumbfounded by what they saw and heard. Gunther was the only one who spoke for quite a while.

"It was all for nothing," he muttered. "We stopped one thing, but they just went ahead with something else."

The Capitol Hill attack was the focus of most reporting, but one of the talking heads mentioned a simultaneous attack on hundreds of local sheriffs around the country. Everyone turned to Tommy when they heard it.

Tommy calmly addressed his oldest. "Gunther, take six of the guys and organize a detail to guard the property. Turn the dogs loose. Everybody packs a sidearm and his rifle. Everyone not on the detail, clean your weapons, reload your magazines, fix your gear and ditch your civvies. Put on your uniforms and whatever body armor you have. Who needs to go back home to get stuff, by show of hands?"

Most of them raised their hands.

"Nobody travels alone," Tommy said. "In fact, everybody goes to each house and pulls security for the guy who goes inside to grab gear. When you get back here, squared away, you relieve the men on Gunther's detail, and they go, as a group."

Linda, her eyes moist, began to say something.

"Hold that thought, baby." To the others he said, "We'll have more updates as time goes on, and I'll disseminate the relevant poop as you need it. In the mean time, be ready for anything."

"Roger that, War Chief," Uncle Jay replied, with solemn respect.

"Then move out," Tommy said.

Everybody stood. Gunther picked six men for guard duty. The others went outside to their vehicles.

False Flag - Brown

H PLUS 22
DALLAS, TEXAS

Clayton Vine was in an incremental process of epiphany ever since his forced retirement. He had become friends with both Doug Haugen and Gordy Puttcamp since meeting them. Vine had been disconnected from fellow Marine officers of commensurate rank (except for those he knew only online) or he might never have fraternized with the veteran pilots.

They talked about weighty stuff when they got together, and they disagreed on some matters. But he came to respect and trust them.

He was somewhat expecting Haugen's call that weekend after great steaming piles of dung hit the fan all over the United States.

Vine had a pocket copy of the US Constitution/Declaration of Independence creased open on the arm of his chair. He'd been reading it studiously of late, and after hearing a few points emphasized and reemphasized by people on the news networks, he thought he saw a pattern developing. He had penciled some checkmarks on the page with the Bill of Rights. The biggest check was next to the Second Amendment, because the phrase "military weapons" and "military assault weapons" were uttered too many times to count in association with the attack at the Capitol Building..

He had three checks by the First Amendment because the talking heads repeatedly stressed that the "right wing extremists" (also a phrase uttered too many times to count) behind all the domestic terror took advantage of the freedom of speech to network over the Internet, spread their hate speech to recruit some and intimidate others, and collect dangerous knowledge they used to deadly effect. Also, their hateful ideology was formed in evangelical Christian churches (freedom of religion), where some of their networking also took place. And they met together both publicly and privately to conspire (the right to assemble peacefully).

A checkmark was next to the Fourth Amendment because of the repeated claims that police and federal authorities "had their hands tied" even though those authorities suspected that the domestic terrorists had been "stockpiling weapons." But authorities were uncharacteristically adherent to the freedom from unwarranted searches in this one isolated case, despite their suspicions, and so the country was repeatedly reminded how those outdated Constitutional protections had prevented the Feds from apprehending the murderers **before** they could carry out this atrocity.

There were checkmarks by the Ninth and Tenth Amendments as well. Vine hadn't yet checkmarked the Fifth and Sixth Amendments, because those rights hadn't come up concretely in all the rhetoric yet. But from his research he knew that life, liberty and property could already be (and was, in many cases) deprived without due process—which included a speedy trial by jury.

"You watching this garbage on the news?" Haugen asked, after minimal small talk.

"Been watching for a while, now," Vine said. "The story so far, in a nutshell, is, right-wing extremists perpetrated a hoax in Amarillo to make everyone fear the government. When that didn't work, they decided to commit acts of terror. The other theory is that other right-wing extremists have been waiting to become active terrorists for years; so when they saw the Amarillo hoax, they were inspired to get started."

"How 'bout we grab a beer and talk?" Haugen suggested.

"Yes. I guess we should."

D PLUS ONE
AMARILLO, TEXAS

Jimmy and Bill were in evening service at church when they got texts from some of their heathen friends. They went outside to listen to the reports on the radio in Bill's truck. They stood there listening until after church let out.

The piano player found them and said the preacher would like to talk to them in his office. Bill and Jimmy exchanged a look, shrugged, and went to see him.

"Come on in," the preacher beckoned, from behind his desk. He was a short, rotund fellow with thinning hair and a sunburn.

Jimmy and Bill entered his office, shut the door behind them, and took seats.

"I noticed you two left a little early tonight," the preacher said, with a friendly tone and smile.

Jimmy explained about the news. The preacher turned grave, shaking his head over and over as he listened.

They exchanged some remarks about how horrible everything was. Then the preacher mentioned he heard rumors that the two of them had formed a militia unit. Jimmy and Bill didn't deny it, but didn't confirm it, either.

The preacher spent about 20 minutes telling them how wrong they were. He pulled a few verses out of his memory about submission to authority, and the sin of violence. Jimmy responded by bringing the context of those verses to the preacher's attention, and threw in a few biblical references of his own. After that the preacher tried to prattle on about doctrines he couldn't back up with text, but the two men had heard enough.

As they rose to leave his office, the preacher said, "Hey, I know things are bad. And we've got corrupt rulers breaking the law they swore to uphold. I get that. But taking up arms is not how you change things. That's not the way."

"I don't know what version of history you were taught, sir," Jimmy replied, "but there never would have been a United States of America if good men hadn't taken up arms."

The preacher began to sputter the usual platitudes about how that was acceptable for 1776, but not for the present day. Jimmy and Bill were halfway down the hall before he was able to fully develop this line of reasoning.

Once they had shaken off the preacher's spiel, Bill told Jimmy, "I'd say we're at DefCon One."

Jimmy sighed. "In a way," he said, "I'm glad. It's better that it happens now, while we're still pretty much ready. I'd hate to be looking at this from the age of 50."

They climbed in their pickup trucks and drove away to their respective homes with a simple nod to each other.

COCCOCINO COUNTY, ARIZONA

The narrative was pretty much revealed before the evening was over: Right-wing extremists were motivated by the racial tensions in Amarillo and other cities, to try taking over the government via acts of terror.

Cavarra turned the volume down on the TV and told his friends and son. "Well, I hate to be a party-pooper, but life as we know it is pretty much over."

Carlos nodded sadly. Leon was wrapped up in his own thoughts. Justin asked, "What happens next?"

Cavarra sighed. "Some time tomorrow probably, the alleged POTUS will give a speech. It might be worth listening to—he occasionally lets something slip that happens to be true. But the speech is to keep most people in their seats by the TV; and to tell his constituents what they want to hear. He has to show himself a 'strong leader' and all that. But the next event that really matters is, doors start getting kicked in. Camps like that one we saw out in the middle of nowhere? They're gonna be populated pretty soon. They've got to try taking out the potential trouble-makers as soon as possible. It might not be as convenient to find all of us now, with the Data Center out of action, but they'll find us if we let them."

"Trouble-makers," Leon said, with a scoffing laugh, staring at the

False Flag - Brown

floor.

"**Potential** trouble-makers," Cavarra repeated. "Folks who don't like the way government is going to work from now on, and **might** try to say or do something about it."

"Hope and change," Carlos mused, sardonically.

"What about us, Dad?" Justin asked. "What do we do?"

Cavarra began rolling his sleeves up. "I'd like you to come with me to get your sister. I need to get her out of the city, and I don't want her trying to travel alone. Sooner or later there's gonna be roadside checkpoints everywhere you go. There'll probably be more shooting going on, too. Like Amarillo, only worse. Once we get her...well, we'll have to figure it out from there. There's no place that's gonna be completely safe, but we'll need to reduce the risks as much as we can. Increase our chances to survive."

Leon raised his head to look at Carlos. "What about you, man? You gonna get with your family?"

Carlos shook his head. "My family's crazy. Mother and father been dead for a while. Brothers, sisters, cousins—they all signed on to this '*La Raza*' bullshit. They see all this as a chance for revenge against the Gringo. Gonna take back the southwestern states Mexico lost in the war. Actually, the leaders want to take over all of North America. It all sounded like ridiculous talk until now. It probably still is ridiculous. But I think they'll go for it. And my family is all on the bandwagon."

"What, then?" Leon asked.

"I'm going with Rocco," Carlos said. He turned to the older man. "Well, if you want me along, that is. I'd like to stick together."

"I could use you," Cavarra said, gratefully. "I'd love to have somebody with us I can trust."

"Trust is at a premium, now," Justin muttered.

Carlos chinned toward Leon. "How about you?"

Leon stared at the floor for quite a while. Cannonball was cool as ice when bullets were flying, but he looked deeply troubled right then. "There don't seem to be any place for me in the world, does there? I mean, some people will shoot me on sight. Other people will welcome me on sight...but I ain't buyin' what they're sellin'. If you could use another man, Rocco, I think I better stick with you."

Cavarra nodded. "Thought you'd never ask, Cannonball. I got your back. Okay?"

Carlos held out his fist to Leon. "Me too."

Leon bumped his fist.

Cavarra stood. "Let's pack our trash, then. We should take all the weapons, ammo and gear out of this place we can carry. Might as well toss our license plates, too. The less can be used to identify us, the better. And I won't be pulling over for anybody voluntarily."

They all got up and got busy. They had a mission to focus on: get Rocco's daughter and take her to safety somewhere. After that, they'd figure out the next mission.

***

There was a lag before the alternative media began reporting on the weekend's events, but when it did, the big picture was at least more reliable than the one the leftist press was painting. Joshua stayed up all night, piecing together what he could.

At zero-dark-hundred he called Tommy on their secure link and was surprised to get an answer right away.

"How's everything up there?" Tommy asked. "How's Jenny?"

"So far, so good," Josh said. "How about you?"

"Hoping for the best. Expecting the worst."

"Yeah, about that," Josh said. "I don't know how much you've paid attention to the attacks on local police..."

"It did pique my interest," Tommy said, dryly

Josh cleared his throat. "The state-approved narrative is that right-wing militias are attacking different sheriff's departments. But I recognized the names of a couple of those sheriffs, and did some checking. It just so happens that every one of the sheriffs being hit is somebody who's been resisting the federal takeover in their jurisdiction, or has gone on the record to say they won't participate in any civilian disarmament schemes."

"It just so happens," Tommy repeated, meaningfully. "Purely coincidence."

"You're catching on. Anyway, we may have slowed them down with what we did to the database, but they'll be coming after you sooner or later."

"Preaching to the choir, *nijenina*," Tommy said. "But if I'm hearing right, there's hundreds of sheriffs being hit at the same time. They've got that many death squads?"

"Obviously. We only cut off one head of the <u>hydra</u>. They had another one ready to do the job in Washington. If somehow we'd managed to stop both, who knows, they might have pulled another one. These guys are good at covering all bases. Just look at the elections in our lifetime."

Tommy thanked him for the heads-up. They went over commo contingencies for after the power grid went down, then signed off.

Josh kept a tab on his news sources and his head spun from all the chaos. On top of everything else, there were full-scale street wars underway in Detroit, Atlanta, Los Angeles and Cleveland. It wasn't just black against white against Hispanic against Asian, either. There were what sounded like Muslim hit squads attacking targets that weren't already engaged in a fight.

The big purge had begun in earnest. Feds and their local and state collaborators were kicking in doors. Patriots and other liberty-minded folks, along with veterans, and known and suspected gun owners, were disappearing in untold numbers in the dark of night. Hopefully most of them were bugging out on their own initiative. Others were undoubtedly being arrested.

But perhaps the most alarming news of all was of a financial nature.

Josh clicked the "Economy" button on a site he trusted and began to study this topic in depth.

Jennifer, in her nightie, stumbled out from the bedroom with tired eyes and sat in his lap. "Aren't you coming to bed, Sweetheart? I know you must be exhausted."

"You're right. I should."

"The world won't fall apart any faster if you take time out to hold me," she said, nuzzling against his neck. "I promise."

"I'm reading about the world falling apart right now," he said.

"I thought you'd be following the Capitol Hill thing."

"I am," he said. "But there's plenty more warm, fuzzy developments out there. Looks like the dollar may finally be collapsing. I'm really surprised it lasted this long."

"Is it because of the new Chinese currency thing?" she asked.

"The 'experts' are blaming all kinds of different stuff," Josh replied. "Blaming everything and everyone except what and who really caused it in the first place."

"Well..." she began, but didn't complete her thought.

"Oh boy," he groaned. "I suppose the Bible predicted this would happen."

"Not this exactly, in detail," she replied, yawning. "But it predicts a situation that requires something like this to happen, first."

"How much do you still have in your old bank account?" he asked.

"Less than a thousand," she said.

"We'll go to the bank tomorrow. Pull it all out, if they'll give it to you," he said.

"They better give it to me—it's my money, that I earned."

Josh shook his head sadly. As wise as she was about most things, she still didn't appreciate how differently bankers and politicians thought about private property, and who someone's honest earnings truly

False Flag - Brown

belonged to.

"There's gonna be a run on the banks, baby. They don't keep as much as what people put in, and everybody is gonna want their money when they realize what's about to happen. We only got a small window of time to get what cash we can and convert it to something with value. It's going to take a shopping cart full of Federal Reserve Notes to buy a loaf of bread, soon."

"You don't think the Fed can do something to stop the collapse this time?"

"The Fed is what **caused** it," Josh said. "It's what the Fed was designed to do in the first place, a century ago. Politicians have prolonged it for as many election cycles as they could, but everybody around the world understands how worthless our *fiat* currency is, now. There's no saving it, this time. Welcome to the Weimar Republic."

"The solution will be the regional currency," she said. "The 'Amero' or something like it. But that's just a transition to a global currency. And later a cashless economy."

So she **had** been paying attention, after all.

"You have to get your cash out, too, don't you?" she asked, rising to her feet.

He nodded. He had a bank account, but only kept enough in it to cover his bills. Thanks to his frugal lifestyle, those were minimal. The rest of his money went into food, supplies, and ammo, which he not only stored in the house but cached around his property. He'd sunk some of his earnings into silver, and in addition saved all his change when he bought items with cash, since there at least was some value in the metal of older coins.

Josh had invested in storage batteries, and generators to charge them. The smaller generators were powered by wind and water, respectively, and the big one turned thanks to the huge solar engine he'd built in the back yard. They already kept his light bill at minuscule levels, and when the grid went down, he would still have plenty electricity to handle the basic functions of his house.

Josh checked some of the mainstream news sites. They might actually have time to exchange their funny-money, because the lapdog media was keeping people in the dark for as long as possible. Meetings between the White House and the Federal Reserve were reported, and the implication was that the latest development would be smoothed over and life would continue as before once the right-wing insurrection was put down.

Yeah, right.

Some backhanded references were made about "irrational pessimism," but that was the only clue as to what was really happening.

False Flag - Brown

"We'll make a day of it tomorrow," Josh told her. "You clean out your account; I'll clean out mine. We'll do some shopping, then make like Hillary's emails."

"Fine, baby," she said. "Now will you come to bed with me?"

He turned off the desktop monitor and she stood. He rose, picked her up and carried her back to the bedroom.

There was no point completing his current I.T. consulting gigs, because he'd never get paid for them anyway. At least, he wouldn't be paid with anything he could use. The world may be spiraling to hell in a freight train, but he planned to sleep in the next day. At least his little corner of the world should be pleasant for a few hours.

False Flag - Brown

61
D PLUS ONE
TEXAS PANHANDLE

The order came down from the top.

The agents assigned to guard the F.A.P., until time came for the show trial, now had a different mission. They herded their prisoners into a concrete bunker-like structure with iron grating for windows. The men, women and children of the group who had bugged out of their homes and lives in Amarillo, because of Arden Thatcher's fake alert, were bound and blindfolded. Most of them wouldn't have believed what was in store, even if somebody had told them.

The agents locked them in the concrete compartment. Hundreds of spray nozzles in the walls and ceiling drenched them with a chemical very similar to lighter fluid.

When they smelled what they were being soaked with, panic gripped all of them and they began to scream.

After the contents of the bunker was set ablaze, most of the agents gathered to watch from a distance, upwind. The heat was very intense, especially when the fat in the people's bodies began to combust. But in time the smell was too much for all but the most hardcorps.

A couple agents were left behind to sweep up all the bones and ashes once the oven cooled down. The bones would be fed through the grinder. Nobody would ever know what happened to them, and the Free American Patriots could tell no tales.

Except, perhaps, as an example to other DomTer cells, who let their imaginations wander.

The other agents were freed up to join the teams converging on Oklahoma.

OKLAHOMA CITY, OKLAHOMA

As the various team members linked up around Oklahoma City, word spread that Macmillan was dead, at the hands of the primary target himself. Team leaders called the next step higher in their chain of command—Lawrence Bertrand. He gave them the location of a safe house and a time to meet there.

When they assembled at the safe house, they met an imposing young man who introduced himself only as Adiur—their new commander. He wasted no time laying out their new assignments.

Tommy Scarred Wolf was a war hero from the Special Forces. He had already bested the ghost teams twice, in two different confrontations.

False Flag - Brown

Adiur told them that was because they had fought on **his** terms. **His** kind of fight. They had played right into the Indian's strengths.

Tommy Scarred Wolf excelled at small-force-on-small-force engagements in the boonies. No doubt he'd already devised a defensive scheme for his home on the reservation; and he obviously had dedicated, capable followers. Most likely he was waiting for them.

Adiur's plan was to make Tommy come to them, against a fortified position in an urban environment. He outlined a plan to take over the county jail. Cynthia Greeley and some other key inmates would be freed and given assignments. Deputies and jailers who could be turned would be assimilated. Those who remained loyal to the sheriff would be slowly tortured to death, one at a time, until the crazy redskin had no choice but to attack the fortified jailhouse.

Some of the agents were surprised at this cavalier reference to death by torture. Macmillan and his predecessor had always been careful not to spell such things out.

Commander Adiur wasn't fooling around. They quickly came to admire his fearless, unadulterated belief in playing for keeps.

D PLUS TWO
BROOKLYN, NEW YORK

Huzayl reported to the mosque as ordered, and found about 15 of the other *mujahadin* had already gathered. He sought out Ridhwaan, who was from his own clan in the home country. Ridhwaan had just made his way into the U.S.A. three weeks ago through Mexico. They were still waiting on paperwork to be processed before he began collecting welfare, so Huzayl had to support him out of his own subsidy checks for now.

Something else had recently made it into the U.S. from Mexico—a very heavy metallic backpack. Everyone was curious, but it seemed nobody knew exactly what it was, nor who to ask besides Itqtidar. And Itqidar wouldn't tell them.

All the *mujahadin* were present, and had been waiting for almost an hour when Itqidar finally arrived that night. They knew he traveled around a lot, and assumed he must have just got back from an important trip.

When he addressed them, Iqtidar didn't give a rousing speech. The *mujahadin* didn't need to be convinced or reminded what they were doing was Allah's will. He just led them in a motivational chant, did the call-and-answer with some Islamic slogans, and went into task assignments.

Most of the warriors would be operating as units—three different units, in three different cities. Huzayl and Ridhwaan were selected for a special mission.

In a back room, Iqtidar showed them the big metallic backpack. He pointed to a switch and a lanyard on the object.

"The two of you must find a way to get this into the heart of Manhattan," he said. "Preferably Wall Street. When you do, flip that switch and pull this lanyard."

Iqtidar told them that pulling the lanyard would activate a timer and they would have two hours to evacuate the city.

This was a lie.

If there really were a timer, there was a chance the infidels could discover the device and disarm it. No, it had to be a martyr mission.

But Iqtidar wasn't just deceiving Huzayl and Ridhwaan. The infidel Lawrence Bertrand, who had been funding Iqtidar's network, believed the bomb was being detonated in Plano, Texas. Iqtidar had given Bertrand every reason to believe his orders would be followed to the letter. In fact, Iqtidar had never given Bertrand reason to doubt his loyalty in the last 21 years.

That was a long time to hide the fact that Iqtidar could think for himself.

An atomic blast in Texas would seriously cripple the Great Satan, to be sure. But an atomic blast destroying the heart of New York City would lay the Great Satan so low that it could never be raised from the ash— even in the fundamentally transformed state that infidels like Bertrand desired.

The eagle was going down for the count, and would not rise as a phoenix.

Infidels like Bertrand just couldn't conceive of a motivation stronger than their lust for power and control. To their own detriment, they underestimated the power of Islam.

Or, to paraphrase a famous old Communist: "When we have cleansed the Earth of all but the very last capitalist, he will lend us the money to buy the rope with which to hang him."

CHICAGO, ILLINOIS

Mac had a little difficulty finding the office building. It was tucked away in a warehouse district where nobody would expect an office to be. He drove around the back, checking numbers, until he saw the one he was looking for.

He parked, went up to the door, found it locked and pushed the button. After a moment the door opened and a stern-looking brother stood facing Mac. It was painfully obvious the guy was packing heat under his jacket. He asked for a name. Mac gave it to him. He stepped aside and Mac entered, ducking his head to clear the door frame.

The brother at the door gestured down a hallway behind him. Mac went down the hallway toward an open door with light and voices spilling out. He peeked inside.

Some 20 people occupied the room, mostly male; all black.

"Big Mac!" called a familiar voice. "You're right on time, man."

DeAngelo Jeffries appeared from behind a screen of other people. He met Mac halfway and rubbed skin before returning to the front of the room.

DeAngelo raised his voice and his hands, addressing the entire room. "Alright, we gonna get started. Settle down, now."

The mix of voices quieted.

"For those who haven't already met him," DeAngelo said, "let me introduce Mr. Lee Dickerson. He's been in the intelligence community for over 30 years—since back when you didn't see many black faces in clandestine service. He's helped many a young brotha and sista over the years, and I consider him a mentor. Go ahead, Mr. Dickerson."

An overweight bald brother in a sharp suit joined DeAngelo at the front of the room. They rubbed skin. DeAngelo stepped off to the side and Dickerson faced the people in the room.

Dickerson spent the first few minutes listing his credentials and accomplishments--which weren't all that impressive compared to the big words he used to describe them. He then transitioned to explaining that DeAngelo and a few others were instrumental in organizing this group; and they only recruited those who were exceptionally talented in their field and committed to the advancement of people of color.

After that bout of ego-pumping for DeAngelo and everyone else gathered, Dickerson said, "You may have noticed that the revolution has started."

A murmur of collected voices went through the room. A few people clapped—DeAngelo being one—but it never caught on to become outright applause.

"Before we get too excited, though," Dickerson went on, "keep in mind that we're outnumbered. And not just by the white man and his Jewish overlords.

"Now amnesty was a necessary tool, that in a sense took us in the right direction. But as we can see in Amarillo and other places, the Spanish got their own agenda, that don't always line up with what's good for black people. And let's be honest: they've been draining the resources that our people need. Their birth rate is much higher than ours. Not only that, but the rate that they've been coming across the border also exceeds our birth rate."

Mac was a little uncomfortable. This was a meeting of intelligence professionals, ostensibly to plan for contingencies to protect black lives in the developing crisis. It felt more like a campus rally of <u>Louis Farrakhan</u> supporters.

Mac sat in a chair with folded arms, listening to Dickerson use very diplomatic yet lofty language to outline a strategy to recruit the most violent gang-bangers from the 'hood for enforcers, and organize the inner cities into strongholds from which offensive action could be taken. They couldn't count on Hispanics or Asians as allies, Dickerson assured them. And yet their numbers and the impoverished condition of their brothers and sisters was such that they had to have help from somewhere. They had to put aside their prejudices, squeamishness, and differences, Dickerson claimed, and reach out to the Muslims.

So the similarity to a campus Farrakhan rally was not by accident. This whole surreal scene was something out of a B-movie scripted by some phobic white bigot.

And yet here I sit, Mac thought, seeing and hearing it live in the flesh.

When the official part of the meeting broke up, Mac pulled Jeffries to the side.

"Are you guys serious about this?" Mac asked. "The Muslims? DeAngelo, those people are crazy."

Jeffries shook his head and waved his hand as if to imply this was no big deal. "It's all good, Mac. He's not talkin' 'bout radical Islam."

Mac fixed a hard stare on him. "That is so weak, man. I don't know how long you were in the sandbox doing the spook thing, but 'radical' is normal for them. 'Moderates' are the ones who videotape the beheadings, or collect the rocks that are used to stone a teenage girl to death after she's been raped."

Jeffries closed his eyes for a moment and held out his hands, palms forward, in an assuaging gesture. "Alright, alright, Mac. But that's over **there**, man. That ain't gonna happen here."

Mac did find it hard to visualize Sharia Law executions taking place here on the block.

"And besides," Jeffries added, "the enemy of our enemy is our friend."

Somebody called Jeffries by name. He left Mac to attend to them.

Mac wasn't comfortable at all shaking hands with the devil. That's what an alliance with the Muslims seemed like to him.

False Flag - Brown

But a brother sure could use friends in times like these.

False Flag - Brown

Gary Fram invited all of his squad leaders over to his house for the speech. Several of the younger guys—just normal militia men, showed up as well. Most of them had been there for the standoff at the Bar G Ranch.

"This oughta' be good," was the common sentiment.

Gary and his wife set out drinks and snacks, and tried to be cheerful hosts despite the gravity of the situation.

They turned on the TV at the appointed time and all sat around the set. The boisterous ones were reminded, sharply, to be quiet so everyone could hear.

The individual who most of them referred to as the "Usurper in Chief" stood behind a podium emblazoned with the Presidential Seal, on a very elaborately built custom stage. Cameras flashed from the press box, but everyone hushed as he took in a breath just before beginning.

"I stand...before you...today..." he said, with painful, deliberate slowness.

"He likes to start speeches that way, don't he?" one of the men asked.

"Shh!" hissed several others.

"...With a...heavy...heart...and...profound sadness..."

Several of them rolled their eyes, but kept quiet.

SIERRA NEVADA MOUNTAINS, CALIFORNIA

Cavarra, Leon, Justin and Carlos rolled along the highway slowly, all within sight of each other and in radio contact. Their tanks were full; they carried extra gas cans full of fuel, and every vehicle was loaded with supplies, gear, weapons and ammo.

Cavarra had his stereo tuned to an FM station, as all the others probably did. Every regular commercial station was broadcasting the speech.

"...To...take this...nation...captive, with fear...and hate," the voice on the radio was saying. "These...hateful...deranged men...took advantage..."

Cavarra's satphone rang. This reminded him that he should probably throw the device into the next river they crossed, after finding Jasmine. But he answered anyway, curious about who, of everyone who had his satphone number, might be calling him at a time like this.

"Cavarra?" asked a familiar female voice in the earpiece.

"Speaking, he said. "Who's this?"

False Flag - Brown

"Bobbie Yousko," she replied.

He swerved slightly. "Holy crap. This line isn't secure, Bobbie."

"I know," sighed his old patron from the C.I.A. "There is no security. Never was, when you think about it. Anyway, that really doesn't matter anymore."

"You listening to the *Reichstag* Fire speech?" he asked.

"Don't need to," she replied. "I saw one of the early drafts a few weeks ago, by accident. You know: about 12 days **before** what happened in Amarillo. What **didn't** happen in Amarillo, I should say. Of course the speech writer couldn't have known that operation would backfire. I'd love to shake the hand of whoever spoiled that party. But anyway, even with the revisions, I know the gist of the speech: Thesis; antithesis; synthesis. Crisis; reaction; solution, yada yada yada."

"Are they coming for you, too?" Cavarra asked.

"I love my country," Bobbie replied. "What do you think?"

"Right," he said. "It is pretty cut-and-dried, isn't it?"

"And speaking of The List," Bobbie said, "That's another hand I'd like to shake someday, if somehow I live long enough. The suicidal genius who hacked into the Data Center and jacked it all up, I mean. But some of us are too high-profile for them to forget. Even before the Big List, there were thousands of little ones."

"I kinda' figured I'm still on somebody's," Cavarra said. "But I appreciate you thinking of me."

"You were farmed out to the NSA once—I figured you would know you're a target," Bobby said. "I'm actually calling so you can warn a couple of your buddies."

"Who is it?" Cavarra asked, his heart rate accelerating.

"Tommy Scarred Wolf. He's on the Sheriff List for one, of course. They're really concentrating some heavy firepower on him. If they haven't hit him hard yet, it's because they're winding up for a terrific haymaker. Think Desert Shield before Desert Storm."

"I'll let him know," Rocco promised.

"And a buddy of his from Special Forces is in the crosshairs too," she added. "Joshua Rennenkampf. You know him?"

"I know him. Good man. Somebody who deserves a handshake if you ever meet him."

She was silent for a moment.

"You have any idea when, where or how, on either of those?" Cavarra asked.

"I just know that they're priority, so it won't be long," Bobbie said. "Hey, I gotta go. I don't need to tell you to lose the phone, GPS, vehicle tracking gadgets and stuff like that as soon as possible, do I?"

False Flag - Brown

"Read you five by five, Bobbie. Thanks."

"And Cavarra?"

"Yeah?"

Her voice faltered as she said, "Thanks for your service." Then the line went dead.

Was that tough old broad crying just now? Cavarra stared at his phone thoughtfully as the voice from the radio droned on.

"...Some hard choices must be made...as we travel this unfortunate road...before we can reach a place of healing."

LAS ANIMAS COUNTY, COLORADO

The Rennenkampfs returned from town and spent some time hauling in groceries and other supplies.

All anyone could talk about all day, it seemed, was the scheduled speech at the White House. Joshua wrestled with whether or not to watch this episode of Snake Oil Theater, and finally decided he should hold his nose and do it—just for a hint at what the other side's next move would be.

Reality set in for Jennifer after the speech began, and she couldn't hide her horror. Josh held her while she stared in slack-jawed disbelief.

The polished, charismatic fraud on TV was saying, "...Grave threat...to members of Congress...cannot be ignored. For the protection of...these tireless, loyal men and women of the Legislative Branch...Congress is out of session...until further notice."

"Oh you big, brave hero," Josh remarked at the dirtbag on TV. "You're going to continue on with your noble leadership in the face of such a dire threat to all public servants, while Congress hides behind your skirt. If that means no checks and balances whatsoever, well, it's a sacrifice you're willing to make."

"Joshua," his wife complained, "I can't hear."

He bit his tongue and swallowed his anger.

"...A state...of national emergency," the slick grifter on TV was saying.

ABSENTEE SHAWNEE TRUST LAND, OKLAHOMA

Tommy took some time from his administrative and logistical duties to watch the speech with Linda.

"...Local law enforcement has done...the best job...it's been possible to do...with what leadership...and resources...were available," the popular man on TV said.

False Flag - Brown

"Oh boy," Linda muttered. "Here it comes, Tommy."

Her husband nodded.

"But tragically...they have been set up to fail. By leaving them...to their own devices...the policy makers with...misplaced paranoia...have deprived them of the tools...they need to counter this very real, and very dangerous threat. In addition...we've seen the same...culture of hate...that we're now at war against...infiltrate local and state level police...because there was no federal oversight...to safeguard against it. To our national shame...it was the ugly specter of racism...inside these unregulated police forces...that inspired the very first shots fired. We must seek...greater levels of cooperation...across all jurisdictions of law enforcement...local, state, and federal. And I know...some of you are worried. Change can be scary. Maybe you've heard...frightening speculation...about the dangers of a Federal Police Corps. But a comprehensive law enforcement structure...is needed. And let me be very clear: the safety of our people and our children demand it!"

The land line phone rang, and Rocco's caller I.D. showed on the screen.

Linda looked at her husband. "Let it go to voice mail, Tommy. Wait until after the speech and call back."

Tommy chewed his lip. "No, I better take this."

He picked up the phone.

AMARILLO, TEXAS

Bill and his girlfriend watched the speech together. There was really nothing worth gloating over, so Bill didn't throw any I-told-you-sos at Eva while she heard confirmation of his "fearmongering" and "conspiracy theory" right from the horse's mouth.

"...These new, proactive measures are no threat at all...to anyone's personal freedom. But they are essential...to the safety of every person. A new system of identification...must be implemented. I have experts...and professionals...joining forces from the scientific and law enforcement communities...to develop a means of universal identification...which can't be lost, stolen, or counterfeited. Because of the desperate need for...robust security enforcement...you may be occasionally stopped and checked. There are times when it will be necessary...to submit to a search of your vehicle, your house, or your person. Let me be very clear: these are not violations of your rights. These are simply common sense precautions...required by a responsible government...during the times in which we live...that might require a...sacrifice of personal convenience once in a while."

False Flag - Brown

Bill, pushing rifle rounds down into a box magazine with his thumb, glanced up to gauge Eva's reaction. She had scoffed at his predictions so many times in the past, he had simply given up on convincing her. If she could still deny the truth now, then there could never be any convincing her.

Eva's eyes were glued to the television screen, her face pale, her mouth clamped into a tight line.

"Some of you...are no doubt worried...about losing your guns. We are working very hard...to balance the need for safety...with the preservation of the privileges...you cling so dearly to. Those of you who act responsibly...and use guns for legitimate sporting purposes...will be permitted to continue just as before. But let me be very clear: the insanity...of allowing military weaponry on our streets...perpetuated by previous administrations...and by partisan political factions...sympathetic to a voter base of domestic terrorists...that insanity **MUST COME TO AN END**!"

Bill could hear the audience cheering through the television speakers.

"I know there's another situation...that's probably on your mind. During my time as President...I've worked hard and long...trying to repair the economic damage...of the previous administration. It's become obvious...that the damage is too severe. Two hours ago...I had no choice...but to declare a banking holiday. But even that isn't likely to stop...the failure...of the US Dollar. It's time we faced the facts: this grand experiment...this grand, tragic experiment...with a free market...has had disastrous consequences. It's too late...to avoid all the suffering...this reckless dereliction of duty has caused. The path is long...and recovery won't be easy. There are decisive actions...that must be taken. To begin with, we need a new, stable monetary base. Tomorrow...I'll be meeting with the national leadership...of our northern and southern neighbors...to discuss a new, regional currency. Together with Canada and Mexico, we share a common crisis...a common resolve...and a common destiny."

Finally, Eva puffed her cheeks and turned to her boyfriend. "I think I've heard enough, Honey. What do you need me to do?"

"I have a bugout bag packed for you," Bill said. "I'll bring it up from the basement in a minute. If you can get yourself dressed for a camping trip, I've got some calls to make."

The first call he made was to Jimmy. Neither of them mentioned the speech. "You know," Bill said, "I've always wanted to try bungee jumping. Think you might want to go?"

"I always thought bungee jumping was kinda' stupid," Jimmy replied. "But why not?"

They forced themselves to chat casually about banal matters for a couple minutes, then hung up. Message received and confirmed. They

False Flag - Brown

would link up at a predesignated rally point by midnight. They had a radically different life in front of them.

False Flag - Brown

After Rocco's warning, Joshua took Jennifer, the dogs, horses, and all the gear they could carry, and went up the mountain.

The simple alarm at the east gate transmitted a signal to Josh's old pager when the cable "gate" at the entrance to his driveway was disconnected, breaking the circuit. Like all his other precautions around his property, Josh had concealed the wiring well enough that it would never be noticed if somebody didn't already suspect it was there.

Josh dug the remote console out of his ruck and turned it on, slipping on his jacket, boots, and exiting the tent. When the screen flickered to life, he toggled through the camera feeds until he saw the SWAT vans and armored vehicle slipping and sliding their way up his private drive, slick with packed snow. The low level of light prevented much in the way of detail, but the dark shapes were easy to identify against the gray background of the snow-covered environment at night.

"What is it?" Jennifer asked, slipping outside after him, eyelids heavy with sleep.

"It's the storm troopers," Josh replied.

Jennifer raised the flaps on the pile cap he'd given her, and stared through the trees. Ragnarok and Valkyrie looked off in the same direction, heads tilted sideways. They could hear the truck engines. Josh's own hearing was sub-par, like so many men who'd been exposed to a lot of pyrotechnics up close without earplugs. He couldn't hear the approach this far away.

"It's all ground-based," he said. "I guess I don't rate heliborne assets. Too bad—I really wanted to see one of those black choppers I've heard so much about."

Jennifer was apparently not in a mood to appreciate his jocular remark. She stared through the trees down the mountain, toward the home she had hoped they would live happily-ever-after in, raising children and peacefully growing old together.

Josh tracked the vehicles' movement up the mountain, then toggled through the cameras to watch the Feds deploy. Their dark uniforms and armor made them easy to follow against the snowy background. His own mood turned dark, now. He activated all the buttons on the console.

He had planted and wired most of the mines years ago, and hoped they would still work. He had never told Jennifer about the ones at the front entrance to the house, so as not to cause her worry every time she came in or out.

False Flag - Brown

A team of blackshirts stacked on his front door. When they struck the first blow with the battering ram, he pushed two buttons.

Inside the front door of his dome home, six short lengths of thick steel pipe protruded from the inner wall—three on either side of the door. As far as Jennifer knew, they were just a crude hat/coat rack. Hats were hung on the top pipes, coats on the middle ones, and boots or shoes dangled by their laces to dry on the bottom ones. Jennifer sometimes complained about them because she bumped into the pipes while cleaning.

Indoors, the pipes were angled outward. But outside, on the front porch, the pipes were angled inwards. Each pipe was, in reality, a remotely activated smooth bore single shot weapon containing a 50 caliber armor piercing cartridge. These fired into the team at the front door; and the antipersonnel mines underneath them blew as well.

The breach team was shredded.

The effect of that countermeasure was similar to kicking an anthill. Federal blackshirts swarmed all over Josh's property. When one or more of those came within the effective range of another mine, Josh touched it off. The Claymores couldn't defeat their body armor, but the shrapnel sure wasn't kind to the unprotected parts of their bodies.

The assault force was roughly platoon strength on arrival, which was kind of flattering. Soon a good third of them were rendered ineffective.

Not bad.

Those who were still able opened fire, pouring hundreds of rounds into the Rennenkampf house. All the windows were shot out and the walls of the dome home became pockmarked with bullet strikes. They must have assumed Josh was holed up inside. But Alamo fantasies never really appealed to him.

The noise of the explosions and small arms fire were audible from his location. Valkyrie tilted her head at an angle and whined.

"Easy girl," Josh said. "Quiet."

"What are they doing down there?" Jennifer asked, now fully awake.

"Shooting up the place."

Her eyes were glossy. "They're destroying our home."

Josh could possibly have rendered all their vehicles inoperable, but he wanted to leave the option of retreat open to them. He triggered the antitank mines where the armored vehicle and the van with all the antennas were parked. The MRAP shuddered and the communications van hopped in place before it was engulfed in fire.

The assault degenerated into something barely more organized than a Chinese fire drill. The blackshirts did send another team at the front door. Those men successfully breached. Once they were inside, Josh waited for

False Flag - Brown

optimal timing and blew the small C4 charges stuck to the hard drives inside his computer towers. This caused a couple more serious casualties.

Then two of the federal blackshirts brought German Shepherds out of a van and led them into the house.

Josh turned to his wife. "Pack up the tent and everything else. Take both horses over to the creek and follow that uphill until you get to where I check the beaver trap. Wait for me there. Don't tether the horses near you. Hide them in the thickest trees you can find, then get about 50 meters away from them. Cover yourself with snow and lie very still. If you hear three short blasts on the whistle, escape and evade like we talked about."

"Cover myself with snow?" she repeated. "Joshua, it's too cold."

He reached inside the tent and grabbed his winter camouflage parka.

"So is death."

He pulled on his web gear, shrugged into the parka and let it drape loosely over him. He locked-and-loaded his tricked-out Mini-14 and checked the safety, then called to the dogs. "Ragnarok. Valkyrie On me—quiet!"

He trudged off down the slope, the two large hounds trotting alongside. Within seconds they had disappeared into the gloom of the winter night.

Jennifer got her anguish in check and began striking camp.

Josh went down their trail far enough to give Jennifer plenty of time, and took cover behind a snow covered boulder. He ordered the dogs to get behind the rock with him.

He waited.

Time went by; the clouds parted and the moon appeared, bathing the mountain with a pale blue glow.

In time Valkyrie began to whine again. He made a sharp cutting gesture with his hand and she flinched and fell silent.

When Ragnarok began to growl, deep in the back of his throat, Josh knew they were close. He silenced the hulking brute with another violent gesture. Ragnarok wagged his tail and smoothed his head, ears back, in an expression of contrition. But in seconds his instincts reasserted themselves. His ears hung forward, tail pointed straight down, and legs stiffened. But he kept quiet for the time being.

Josh pulled the hood of the winter camouflage parka over his head and scooted slowly over until he could see around the side of the boulder and sight down the slope.

The men and dogs appeared on the trail. Josh flicked off his safety.

Either the dogs heard the click or they caught the scent of their prey,

False Flag - Brown

because they barked and strained at their leads.

Josh's hounds began whining and growling again, on the verge of breaking discipline.

"Quiet!" he hissed. "Stand fast!"

The Mini-14 was a stainless steel model, originally, but Josh had it anodized flat black. He fitted it to a polymer pistol grip stock, and attached to the foregrip of the stock a folding bipod with telescoping legs, which were now extended. The trigger pull had been decent right out of the box, but he had modified it to be much lighter. In short, it was a nail-driver, and much more reliable in all weather and environments than the more popular AR15 variants.

For his opening round, Josh decided on a head shot. There was no armor there under the helmet, and he wanted at least one heavy body that other men would have to carry or drag back down the slope.

He got his breathing under control, willed himself not to shiver, and tickled the trigger.

The rifle thudded back into his shoulder. The first dog handler caught the 5.56 NATO round in the face and flopped backwards, sliding down the snowy slope.

Josh lined up his sights to below center mass on the other dog handler, in order to catch him under the ballistic vest. He fired as the handler was turning and caught him in the hip. The man winced from the impact, but didn't go down. Josh lowered his aim and shot him in the thigh. The man finally crumpled, rolling and sliding downhill, leaving dark streaks on the snow. Between the two dog handlers, four more blackshirts should be tied up pulling them back to the medics.

Both German Shepherds were loose, now, and bolted uphill barking furiously, making a bee line for the boulder. They were too low, and too fast, for Josh to draw a bead in time.

He raised his voice to his own dogs. "Attack!"

The two Pit Bulls launched down the hill in a blur. Ragnarok struck one of the Shepherds in a head-on collision, driving it hard back into the ground.

Valkyrie was more evenly matched in weight with her opponent, and the two tumbled over and over in the snow in a flurry of fangs and claws. When she wound up on her back underneath the Shepherd, Josh began to panic. But her powerful jaws had ahold of the other dog's snout and her paws ripped at its belly. The Shepherd yelped and instinctively tried to get away, but Valkyrie wouldn't let go. Meanwhile Ragnarok had the other dog by the neck and shimmied, terrier-fashion, whipping it back and forth like a stuffed animal. Pained choking gasps rattled out of the Shepherd's mouth as its throat was crushed in Ragnarok's monstrous jaws. Then with a mighty heave of his huge, muscular body, Ragnarok flung the dog a good four meters through the air.

Josh pumped two rounds into the Shepherd, finishing it, when it hit the ground.

Ragnarok pounced on it, realized it was no longer a threat after a few more bites and shimmies, then trotted over to help his sister finish off the other dog.

Josh called his bodyguards back to him and hid behind the rock once more. He checked them for wounds and found nothing serious. They wagged their tails and panted, looking at him for commendation for a job well done. He gave them each a pet and chest-scratch.

Josh waited some more.

It took a while, but he finally heard men moving up the hill toward him. Their noise discipline was lousy. He heard them exclaim as they found the dog handlers, and they openly discussed how to evacuate them, with much cussing and arguing.

They sent somebody forward to scout. When he appeared over the ridge, Josh held his fire. Josh wanted to let a few of them get well into the kill zone. If they were smart they would send a separate force up and around to flank or trap him from behind. The dogs would let Josh know if that happened.

After the lone scout advanced far enough to find the bodies of the dogs on the trampled, blood-smeared snow, he turned and retreated the way he'd come. Josh listened to him report his findings. There was more cussing, discussion, and squawking of radio headsets.

"Let's go," somebody with an authoritative voice said. "Leave the dogs. We're pulling out."

"But the perp is still up there somewhere," someone protested.

"We have critically wounded agents who need medivac, now. And there's still no damn choppers free. This is a bust. We gotta go."

They gaggled and scuffled back down the mountain to Josh's house. From this distance he could hear the truck engines start. He dug the remote console back out of his buttpack, turned it on and activated the buttons. He toggled through the camera feeds again. He caught an agent preparing what was probably an incendiary device to burn down his barn. Josh triggered the nearest Claymore. It wasn't perfectly placed for the circumstance, but it made the agent jump, drop everything and hold his arm. He backed away where another agent grabbed him, looked at his arm and steered him toward one of the vans.

The dogs found Jennifer's hiding place in the snow, greeting her with licks and wagging tails. Josh pulled her to her feet.

She shivered violently. He held her against him, wrapping his parka

False Flag - Brown

around her. He let her feed off his body heat for a while, telling her the blackshirts were gone for the time being and they would probably be okay for a while.

"What about the house?" she asked. "The barn?"

"Well-ventilated," Josh replied, sadly.

"Well, it can be repaired, right?" she asked. "I mean, we can..."

Josh shook his head. "We can't go back, baby. It's the wasp and hornet factor. A meter reader or utility man comes to do some work outside a house, opens the box he needs to work in and finds out wasps or hornets have built a nest there. They tear him up good and chase him back to his truck. But the guy is gonna come back there with bug killer, or whatever weapons he needs to make every last one of them pay for the hurting they gave him. It's the same deal with us, baby. We gotta let 'em have the nest, and escape. We'll sting 'em when they get too close, but we can't go back. Hopefully they'll decide we're not worth the trouble of chasing down."

"No white picket fences," Jennifer muttered with a faraway look, shivering hard.

In Joshua's mind he hoped they could return one day, if the war went better than anticipated. But he didn't want to get her hopes up. Or his own.

Sunup was only hours away. The most efficient solution for present circumstances was to get moving. It would put distance between them and the huge bullseye of his home. And physical exertion would warm Jennifer quickly.

He checked his trap, found a beaver in it, quickly gutted it and gave the innards as treats for the dogs. Then they led the horses deeper into the wilderness.

False Flag - Brown

Shortly after receiving Rocco's warning, Tommy Scarred Wolf got word that the county lock-up had been captured by Tier Zero teams. Word from the ninja Nazis was that those who were loyal to Tommy would be tortured to death until Tommy turned himself in.

Tommy knew a trap when he smelled one.

He deputized every member of the Shawnee Militia, and began to secure an operational area around the rez. Other volunteers sought him out, asking to join, including members of the Tribal Police.

There were a lot more responsibilities to consider besides just fighting bad guys. People had to eat, for one thing. Tommy found competent people and delegated logistical and some administrative duties.

When he first caught wind of the currency crash, Tommy had everyone scrape up all the money they had and raid the gas stations and grocery stores. They bought up every single package of seeds they could find for organic fruits and vegetables, because they would have to start growing their own. He visited every ranch in the area, seeing what the ranchers would accept in trade for horses. The ignorant ones accepted the funny money that was soon to be worthless. The less ignorant were willing to trade horses for vehicles. The fully awake ranchers asked for the protection of the Shawnee Militia from what was coming.

Once all that was in motion, Tommy began placing teams around the jail until every avenue in and out was locked down. Under cover of darkness, Takoda led a small team in to shut off the water and electricity to the building.

During a rare quiet moment of the siege, Tommy called all his sons together for a meeting behind the cover of a pumping station.

"It's a new world now," he said, in their native language. "You aren't just my sons anymore. You're my soldiers. My most trusted, to be sure, but you're still soldiers."

"Yes sir," Gunther said. Carl and Takoda nodded that they understood.

"Gunther outranks both of you right now," Tommy went on. "You may not like it, but that's just how it is. I'm not gonna be able to spend much time with any of you from now on. I'm gonna be busy pretty much 24/7." He pointed at Gunther, then Takoda. "I can't keep you two separate all the time. I'm not gonna be around to play referee. The two of you are gonna have to work together. There's no compromising, here: you **will** work together. Whatever petty grudges you're holding are done as of now. I need you. I have to be able to trust you."

The four of them stared at each other for a moment, then Gunther looked at Takoda. "Brother, everybody who knows you would want to have you on their side in a fight. Especially me."

Takoda's gaze dropped to the ground and his face twitched a few times. Then he looked up and said, "I'm sorry for what I did, before. It was wrong. I'm ready to do whatever you or Dad need me to. I won't give you any trouble."

"Well, not too much, anyway," Carl quipped. Despite his joke, he knew how important Takoda's words were, and how hard it was for him to say them.

Tommy nodded at his sons. "Okay. Let's get to work, then."

Every time somebody tried to make their way out of the jail complex, they were interdicted by two or three-man teams of the Shawnee militia and either retreated or were captured or killed.

A Tier Zero squad outside the complex, however, surprised one of the interdiction teams, killing Charlie Drake and wounding Jason Lone Tree. Tommy stepped up the patrols in the area. The next time the opfor struck outside the jail complex, their intended victims were ready for them. While the two forces shot it out, one of Tommy's sniper teams moved in. Carl Scarred Wolf—a superb shot—took out the leader and two others with the old Russian sniper rifle his father had taken as a trophy in another conflict long ago and far away.

At night, the Shawnee Militia donned anti-night vision camouflage and opened sections of the fence surrounding the county lock-up. One of those nights one of Tommy's deputies, Sanford, escaped from the jail and linked up with his boss.

He had pretended to switch allegiance and assimilate into the group led by the man known only as Adiur. They forced him to take a blood oath before they would trust him.

"I kept my fingers crossed," Sanford explained.

He painted a frightening picture of what was going on inside. Inmates were loose, beating and raping everyone who had balked at assimilating. Adiur had tortured one person to death every day since they took over.

The siege and the loss of power and water was having an effect on morale. Cynthia Greely, who'd been put in charge of Adiur's *de facto* harem, had candles burning all over the place and conducted weird religious rituals. Adiur participated in these to one degree or another.

Tommy grilled Sanford on what weapons were inside, how much ammunition, and where Adiur's shooters were deployed.

False Flag - Brown

One afternoon while Tommy was visiting his interdiction teams, a brightly colored van rolled up into his area of operations. It was rare to see any sort of vehicle on the streets anymore. This one was emblazoned on both sides with the name of a local surround-sound equipment dealer.

A long-haired white man in perhaps his late 30s got out of the truck with his hands up, facing the militia men.

"What's your business here?" demanded John Saxton, flank covered by his brother.

He approached slowly, scared but determined. "I've been hearing that this is free territory over here."

"Yeah, so?"

"So I'd like to come over to this side," the man said. "Between the gangs and the Muslims and these federal...soldier/police, it was only a matter of time before somebody got me. I loaded up everything I could fit from my store and got out of there."

When he drew close enough, Mike Saxton pulled him behind cover and searched him. Tommy watched the whole process unfold warily. More and more people were escaping Oklahoma City and other areas and joining the community roughly covering Tommy's jurisdiction, for the same reason this man gave. All had been sincere so far. Some of them even came armed, equipped, and ready to help defend "free territory." Tommy was grateful for the added strength. But it was only a matter of time before the Feds started sending over moles to infiltrate.

"He's clean," Mike said.

Tommy nodded to Mike, who went back to pulling security. Tommy beckoned the man over, and sat, encouraging the visitor to do the same.

"You escaped with a van load of stereo equipment," Tommy asked, searching his face, "not food, clothes, toilet paper and drinking water?"

"I live in Norman," the man said. "My store is in OK City. I've been holed up there for days. I'm starving. But I should have some of that stuff at my house, if nobody broke in and stole it all."

"That's a big 'if' in this new world," Tommy said.

"Yeah, I know," the man said, and chewed on his lip for a moment. "Look, I hear that Sheriff Scarred Wolf is still in charge, here. That he's keeping the Feds and gangs out."

"The gangs, yeah," Tommy said, then wobbled his head back and forth. "The Feds...well, that's a taller order."

"That's better than back there," the man said, thumbing over his shoulder toward OK City. "I should be allowed to stay, right? I mean, I'm a resident of this area, anyway."

Studying his eyes, Tommy was pretty sure the guy was on the level. He said, "Well, maybe. We try to respect everyone's free will and property over here. But the situation requires us to be more strict than we'd normally like to be. If you're working for the other side...well, this is wartime, and espionage is a capital offense."

The man gulped, but shook his head, showing his palms. "No, no. Oh hell, no."

"And there's no such thing as the welfare state anymore," Tommy added. "We can't afford to support freeloaders and deadbeats. If you want to eat, you're gonna have to contribute in some way." Tommy glanced back toward the van. "Are you pretty good with wiring? Simple electrical stuff?"

The man brightened. "SImple? I was a licensed electrician before I got layed off. That's why I went into business for myself. But boy, if I'd have known about all the bullshit regulations, and the taxes..."

"Okay, okay," Tommy interrupted. "Maybe we can use you, then."

"To be honest, What I really need right now is something to eat and drink. Is there some message you can broadcast, so nobody shoots me while I drive to my house?"

"Let me think for a minute," Tommy said.

"I wasn't able to pull my money out of the bank in time," the man said, "so that's all gone. I guess nobody's accepting paper money anymore, anyway. I got nothing to trade for food, except a bunch of high-end electronics. Something tells me there's not going to be much demand for that, now."

Tommy looked toward the van again, glanced at the jail complex, and almost smiled.

Leon Campbell had once told Tommy about Operation Blue Spoon (better known as "Just Cause"). Specifically right now, Tommy remembered how a psyops detachment had blasted heavy metal and American pop at the Vatican Embassy in Panama City where Noriega was holed up, waiting for him to crack and give himself up.

Tommy oversaw the setup of the sound equipment at points around the jail complex. His newest recruit worked with some militia volunteers to wire it for power. Tommy had the word spread throughout the area that they needed CDs or MP3s of a very specific music genre, and the citizens who had what he needed gladly made an offering of it.

So loud that it echoed all across the landscape for untold miles, the Shawnee Militia assaulted the besieged enemy with the most obnoxious old-time Gospel music that could be found in the county. They played it non-stop, day and night.

***

False Flag - Brown

The situation in the cities grew worse. Neither Federal Reserve Notes, nor food stamps, were accepted as payment by anyone within a few days. Nor were the cards that digitally represented those resources accepted as payment. Life savings and other investments were rendered worthless before most citizens who had them could pull it out and exchange it for anything useful. Millions of people around the country couldn't get refills of their prescriptions. Whether the drugs were truly necessary or not, folks were dependent on them just the same. Without them, the worst of human nature began to show itself.

Gradually, cell towers went down; phones quit working; internet connections failed; and power went out.

Starvation was a strong motivator, but almost nobody had the skills to accomplish the most basic task of survival without calling in a specialist. Life turned cheaper by the minute. Out in the country it wasn't quite as bad, but bad enough. Suddenly people with highly specialized jobs that paid big salaries in white collar fields had absolutely no skills that could benefit themselves, their families or communities. After what material goods they could trade for food and firewood were gone, they had nothing left to bargain with.

And a bad winter was coming.

Small armies of urban looters went to war with each other over who would ransack grocery stores for what food was still on the shelves. They tended to divide along racial and ethnic lines. Fewer and fewer local and state police reported for work, as their salaries were suspended. The departments didn't have the new regional currency to pay out.

The unchecked anarchy spreading through the country made the Amarillo riots look tame by comparison.

Active and reserve military units, supplied with fuel and food paid for with the new regional currency, were deployed to replace police. The forces participating in Jade Helm had their exercises interrupted by new orders. Like good soldiers, the C.O.s of the relevant units transitioned from training to peacekeeping duty without missing a beat. Nobody in the establishment used the phrase "martial law." Military troops were not just ordered to crack down on the gang warfare, but to clear the cities house-by-house, confiscating weapons, ammo and any hoarded supplies missed by the federal units executing Operation Lightning Strike. People were relocated out of the cities by the thousands, and interned. Initially, most city-dwellers volunteered for the camps, if it meant they'd be fed and kept warm.

First they came for the gun owners. Then they came for the veterans. Then they came for everyone considered to be right-wingers. Then they came for "fundamentalist hate groups": anybody with an evangelical

False Flag - Brown

Christian worldview.

As the most potentially troublesome individuals were removed, new categories of domestic terrorists were created, and people who fit the new classifications were snatched and relocated. It seemed nobody was safe. Anybody with any belief which didn't line up with state-approved dogma might be suspected of hateful thought at any time and turned in by a neighbor hoping to be rewarded with food, drinkable water, drugs or brownie points.

The threat (real or imagined) of some personnel or units causing mutiny among the ranks of the armed forces, against Washington, prompted the new "streamlined" government to bring in multinational peacekeeping troops as a precaution. Some foreign military forces were already in-country, and set about their duty right away.

Almost as if that was their intended purpose all along.

When Manhattan was consumed in an atomic fireball, even Washington was stunned into paralysis. The currency change and peacekeeping troops seemed inadequate to salvage what was left of civilization in the United States of America.

False Flag - Brown

Rocco Cavarra and his small crew had to run a roadblock checkpoint on the way up to reach Jasmine. On a rural backroad they stopped at an old country gas station and traded some 12 gauge and 22 LR ammo for a gas fill-up. They also shot it out with a small gang there who thought they could steal one of the vehicles. The major interstate highway had too many checkpoints, so they bypassed it. They had to take a long, roundabout course to reach Sacramento, filled with detours and delays. The precautions they took made their journey even slower.

They rolled up into the parking lot of the apartment complex and positioned their vehicles for a quick exfil. The place had been a clean, modern facility not long ago, but now it looked like a tornado had passed through, smashing windows, tearing off doors and scattering garbage everywhere. In fact, all they could see of Sacramento looked like a battleground—pretty much like every other city, now.

The four men and one dog dismounted. Justin wrinkled his nose. "What's that smell?"

"Death," Carlos replied. "We're downwind of dead bodies. Quite a few, I would guess."

Rape, murder
It's just a shot away
It's just a shot away...

Cavarra couldn't get the song out of his mind.

All of them were armed and armored. They pulled on their web gear as they stretched their legs. If there was a firefight, they wanted to have loaded magazines handy.

Faces appeared in windows. A few men around the complex wandered tentatively outside to see what was amiss.

Leon and Carlos remained with the vehicles while Cavarra and Justin advanced warily toward the staircase.

"Yo, boss, you affiliated?" somebody called to them from a balcony.

"What you lookin' for?" asked somebody else.

Rocco and Justin ignored these and other questions and demands as they climbed the stairs to the second floor. They strode down the balcony until they reached her apartment. Like many others, the door hung wide open. The window was smashed in and the drapes hung out through the opening.

False Flag - Brown

Anger, fear, and dispair tore through Jasmine's father and brother. They entered the apartment with weapons ready. After searching every room, it was painfully obvious that Jasmine and her roommates were long gone. The place had obviously been looted. Every closet and drawer was thrown open and ransacked, with unwanted items left strewn all over the floor.

Justin sat heavily on the couch in the living room, face in his hands.

Rocco paced for a moment, then went back to Jasmine's room. He came out with the dress he had bought her a couple Christmases ago. He spoke over the radio.

"Cannonball, we're coming out. Gonna need to borrow Shotgun. Over?"

On their way back to the vehicles there were more questions, challenges and demands from a growing number of people emerging from apartments. It was doubtful many of them were paying residents, here. More likely they were squatters who had left even worse conditions in the inner city.

This time Carlos and Justin guarded the vehicles while Rocco and Leon followed Shotgun, after letting her sniff the dress.

Shotgun led them back up to the apartment and Rocco's heart sank all over again.

"No. No, you stupid bitch. You're not supposed to find her apartment. You're supposed to find **her**."

Leon held up his index finger to Rocco, but spoke to Shotgun. "No. This ain't it, girl. Where else?"

Shotgun growled, then barked, baring her fangs, staring toward the front door.

It was a chilly day, but the belligerent-looking young black man in the doorway stood bare-chested. One hand held a snubnose pistol hanging at his side.

Leon hushed Shotgun.

"Yo, I know you heard me talkin' to you out there," the stranger said, just dripping with truculence. "You deaf or somethin'?"

"You got our attention now," Leon said. "Speak your piece."

"I wanna know what you doin' here, yo," he said. "You come rollin' up on my turf wif guns an' shit, I'm askin what your business is here."

"Why?" Rocco replied. "Are you offering to be helpful?"

"I ain't offerin' shit. But you needa answer my questions, fool." His angry gaze shifted from Rocco to Leon. "I don't care if you got guns, dog. You better show some respect."

"Mind your own business, scrotum head," Rocco spat.

"What? What you call me, fool? I'm 'bout to take all yo' shit, then use you for bitches!"

He raised the snubnose, but he held it sideways like the thugs in the movies did, evidently believing it was the cool thing to do. Rocco brought the barrel of his *Galil* down hard on the back of his hand and the snubnose dropped from his grip.

Leon strode forward, driving his rifle butt into the man's face.

The man staggered backwards through the door and against the balcony rail, blood spurting from his busted nose and ruined mouth.

Rocco followed him, and landed a kick to his solar plexus with such force that the balcony rail gave way and the man fell one story to the ground below.

All the yelling in the complex came to a stop.

"Anybody else wanna show us how bad they are?" Rocco rasped, voice echoing off the building walls.

Leon pocketed the snubnose and held the dress down for Shotgun to sniff again. "Where else, girl? Where else?"

The Shepherd spun in place a few times, looking up at Leon after each revolution.

Leon shook his head. "No, Shotgun. Where else?"

She put her nose to the ground and went through the doorway. She paused, then trotted down the balcony walkway. Leon followed.

Shotgun paused, looking back until Leon caught up, then surged on with her nose to the ground. Rocco brought up the rear, turning periodically to evaluate potential threats.

Shotgun led them down a staircase at the opposite end of the building, then stopped facing a metal door. Leon tried the door, but it was locked. It was one of those locks that took a key card with a magnetic strip. With the electricity out, now, it wouldn't even work if they had a card.

"I got some primacord back in the truck," Leon offered.

"Save it," Rocco said, pulling a strip of what looked like gray taffy, sandwiched between celophane, from his jacket pocket. He pulled a simple detonator out of his buttpack.

Tempering the normal "P" factor (plenty) with situational frugality, Rocco crammed the charge into the gap between door and jamb where the lock was, and "wired it for sound." He ducked around the corner where Leon and Shotgun already waited. Cavarra covered his ears. Leon had inserted earplugs, and now clamped his hands over Shotgun's ears.

"Fire in the hole!" Rocco yelled, out of habit.

The charge blew with a loud *blang* and they stepped around the corner. Leon pushed the door open and Shotgun led them down an inner staircase to a below-ground level.

The stairs fed out into a long room with a concrete floor and washing

False Flag - Brown

machines lining one wall, driers lining the other.

"Oh that's just great, Cannonball," Rocco said. "I wasted some ordnance so she could lead us to where Jasmine forgot some laundry."

"Daddy?" a tired, weak voice echoed off the concrete walls.

Shotgun barked and ran to a dark corridor which separated two different laundry rooms. She barked some more.

Both men rushed into the corridor, eyes still adjusting to the darkness. A trembling, wraith-like figure rose up from a fetal position on the floor. Leon used a red-lensed flashlight to illuminate the young woman, then told Shotgun to be quiet.

Father and daughter recognized each other and fell into an embrace.

They returned to the vehicles. Sister desperately hugged brother like she feared never seeing him again. Hiding out in the basement for days with no food or water and only other people's laundry to keep her warm, that had been one of her recurring fears.

The family reunion wasn't a happy event for everyone, however. Growing bolder by the minute, a crowd of squatters had emerged from the surrounding apartments, swaggered toward the small convoy and now moved to surround it.

One of the squatters, a big one, leered at Jasmine and licked his lips meaningfully. "Oh...see, now, I didn't even know that sweet little thang was nearby." He rubbed skin and exchanged muttered comments with those on his left and right.

Some of the squatters had pistols. Others had knives, pipes and improvised weapons.

Leon opened his truck and placed the M21 in the rifle rack. He came back out, faced the mob, unflapped his holster, then pulled the captured snubnose out of his pocket and snapped open the cylinder to check the load. It still had four live rounds.

"Y'all ain't affiliated," a squatter said. "Y'all look like some a' them militia fools or somethin'."

Rocco turned to Justin, speaking calm and low. "Get her in your car and get ready to go."

Justin helped his weakened sister into the Challenger, slid behind the wheel and shut the door.

The squatters watched this happen and visibly grew antsy—like watching a bear escape a bear trap. One of them nodded to the others and began advancing closer. The others followed suit and the cordon closed in. Shotgun growled and bared fangs.

"Yo, man, they ain't getting outa' here with all these goodies, y'all," the leader told his followers. "You know why they ain't popped any caps, yo? 'Cause they ain't got bullets. They tryin' to scare us, like we're punks."

"I bet that dog would taste real good, sliced up and cooked on the barbeque grill," another one remarked, coaxing ugly laughter out of his buddies.

"Carlos; Cannonball," Rocco said. "Leader at one o'clock. Pistols at eleven, six and three. You see anything else?"

"That's what I got," Carlos said.

"I got another zip gun at nine o'clock," Leon said.

Rocco turned to confirm. "Roger that. I'll take one and three."

"I've got nine and eleven," Carlos said.

"Six is mine, then," Leon said, sidling around to his truck's passenger door.

"That's far enough, 'original gangster'," Cavarra told the head squatter. "You come any closer, it's on."

The leader cussed, laughed, slapped skin with those on his left and right...and kept coming.

Cavarra shouldered his rifle and shot the leader between the eyes. Pivoting at the waist he pumped two rounds center-mass into the squatter with the pistol at three o'clock.

At the first shot Carlos opened up, catching the gunmen at nine and eleven o'clock, and most of the individuals in between.

Leon didn't stop at just one, either. He took out the one with the revolver at six o'clock with his Ruger, gunned down those who tried to retrieve the fallen revolver, then emptied the captured snubnose into the crowd.

With their leadership destroyed in a matter of seconds, the remaining squatters ran, with a few more well-placed shots as encouragement.

Knowing they could use the guns for trading down the line, Carlos and Leon policed up the dropped weapons. Then they climbed in their vehicles and laid tracks out of there.

They found another gas station abandoned along a rural road outside the city, with dead bodies strewn around it. The pumps no longer worked. Cavarra had Justin use a foot pump and plastic hose to siphon fuel. They topped off their tanks and filled their gas cans.

They headed south and east toward Yosimite, with no specific destination in mind—just getting as far away from major population centers as quickly as possible

It had been a hell of a ride.

The small party pulled into a lonely rest stop, dismounted, took turns making head calls/latrine breaks, then congregated around a picnic table

False Flag - Brown

to look over a AAA map of the region, trying to figure out their best course of action. They were all exhausted from lack of sleep. Their fuel supply might not get them back to their place in Arizona on a circuitous route. There was certainly no guarantee they could find more fuel along the way, and they might run into a situation they couldn't shoot their way out of this time.

The consensus was they had probably pushed their luck far enough. But they had to figure out where they **were** going to go.

The younger veterans looked to Rocco for an idea. He had proven himself an excellent planner in the past. He was crafty as a fox, could think on his feet and make the right calls under pressure. Surely he could work some magic again.

But it was Justin who piped up. "Where are we?" he asked, pointing to a spot on the map with his index finger. "Here, right?"

Carlos nodded, blinking bloodshot eyes.

Justin traced his finger along the thin blue web-like representation of a river until he found what he was looking for. "There's a construction site within sight of the bend in this river here. About 40 miles from here as the crow flies. Probably 90 miles on the roads. Construction was halted about seven years ago. I passed it on a canoe trip one summer. Got curious after I was back home; looked it up. The permits were revoked—some big environmental concern about mining on federal land. There was going to be a mine there, and some buildings were going up nearby. Warehouses or something. Just frames when they had to quit. I seriously doubt the permits were ever reinstated. It's probably still abandoned. Only a handful of people even know about it, and I doubt any of them live nearby."

"What good does that do us if they never finished the buildings?" Jasmine asked, feeling much better now with some food in her.

"They didn't finish the permanent structures," Justin said. "But the first thing they did was build a construction office on the site. They parked a trailer there, probably for a security guard to watch the equipment at night. I paddled by there on the river at least a year after it had been abandoned, and there was still a big propane tank sitting on the site. If it's full, that could give us heat for the coldest months. Even if not, we can still get out of the elements. There's a source of fresh water nearby, full of fish. I'm sure there's game in the woods around there. It might not be perfect, but we'd have a good chance to survive there."

Rocco clapped his son on the back, a smile wrinkling his haggard countenance. "No Son, I disagree. I think it **is** perfect." He turned to the others. "Anybody got an objection, or a better idea?"

"Call me Daniel Boone," Leon said. "Or Grizzly Adams. It sounds good to me. We should have gas left over afterwards, too."

False Flag - Brown

"If we can find the access road," Justin said, and chewed his lip. "I don't know how to get there on land."

"We can find it," Carlos assured him, studying the map and pointing. "You said it's right here by the bend of this river?"

Justin nodded.

Carlos moved his finger in a circle around the indicated point. "There's only so many places it could be. What makes the most sense to me..."

Rocco leaned back and put his arm around Jasmine's shoulders as the younger men figured out the best place to search for the access road.

There was hope.

They could survive—indefinitely, if nobody discovered them. But at least they could find shelter for a few months--the next few months that would prove to be the most important of their lives.

After all, there was a bad winter on the way.

False Flag - Brown

Gary Fram and his unit, part of a larger organization which went by the name "Defenders of the Republic," had a perimeter established on a wooded hilltop.

Only one of the men was wounded, and him not critically. It was a small price to pay for the successful ambush of a U.N. supply convoy. They had scored medical supplies, rations, water purification tablets and cold weather gear. All of it was stuff they could use. The gravy was, it was a treasure that would be deprived the enemy.

In a hasty command post dug into the cold ground, reinforced with dirt and collected logs, and winter camouflaged by a white sheet, Gary read his map and made notes on a pad he normally kept in a zippered plastic bag. His wife slept, wrapped tight in a mummy bag sandwiched by space blankets. The other women, and children, were in the big dome tent camouflaged in the center of the platoon's position.

A runner from Second Squad arrived. Gary glanced up. "Everything okay?"

"LP/O.P. says we got visitors," the runner said.

They needed to get some better commo, so these kind of reports could come straight to Gary; not the nearest squad to the Listening Post/Observation Post.

Gary's forehead wrinkled. His next panicked thought was that somebody had tracked them from the ambush. "SALUTE?"

"Um, two guys. They look to be searching for something—probably us. They're approaching from the west. Uniform is kinda' mixed up, like most of ours," the runner reported. A live example of that which he spoke of, he had civilian mossy oak cammie pants on, black Bunny Boots, a tiger stripe fatigue blouse, and an old West German field jacket over that. On his head was an old U.S. Army surplus soft cap, with the inner flap pulled down to protect his ears from the cold. "Cowboy boots. One has a cowboy hat. Not carrying much but their rifles. One is a CAR15. The other is some old lever-action job. Maybe a '94 Model Winchester."

"Sounds like our link-up from the boys in the Chapanee Valley," Gary said, relieved. "Give them the old pre-war challenge. But don't light 'em up if they don't remember the password. Disarm them if you have to and let me take a look at them."

The runner nodded and left.

The cowboys remembered the old password and were escorted back to the CP to meet Gary.

False Flag - Brown

He climbed out of his hole to greet them. He shook the hand of the older one with the lever-action rifle. "Rusty."

Rusty gave him a nod. "Gary."

Gary turned to the younger one, shaking his hand as well. "Mike. It's good to see you guys. Where are your horses?"

"We left 'em a ways back," Mike said. "Thought we might have to sneak away if we ran into somebody besides you. Can't sneak too good on a horse."

"Got any hot coffee?" Rusty asked, blowing into his hands.

Gary frowned. "Sorry. We're already low. And we don't want to waste heat tabs right now."

"I reckon that's understandable," Mike said.

"Sorry I don't have much in the way of furniture, either," Gary said, wiping snow off the seat of his pants.

"Y'all come all this way on foot?" Rusty asked. "That's a lot of walkin'."

Gary shrugged. "We're light infantry. A lot harder for the Traitors to find than if we had trucks and such. We can go more places, too."

"You should get some horses, at least," Rusty said.

"Hey, if you can hook us up, that'd be great. How're you guys doing?"

"Well, they done left us alone, so far," Mike replied.

"They ain't worried 'bout us," Rusty said, then chinned toward Gary. "They must not even be worried 'bout you, yet. Got bigger fish to fry, and they'll come for us afterwards."

Gary nodded. "Are you ready for it?"

Rusty shook his head. "I don't see how we could be. Horses and rifles against tanks and helicopters and artillery? They ain't scared of us. We'd have to take off to the hills like you, to be any threat. Then what happens to our herds; our grass; our families?"

"Exactly right," Mike said.

Gary kicked at a tree root bulging the snow. "Well, any news?"

"There's a big war in the Middle East," Mike said. "I don't know who all's involved. Israel against everybody else, I guess."

"Because they attacked Iran's nuclear program."

"That's what everybody thinks," Rusty said. "Who knows?"

"You hear about New York City?" Mike asked.

"Something about a nuke there, right?" Gary replied.

Mike nodded. "Ever'body thinks it was us. Get this: we joined forces with the Moslems, accordin' to the experts. Ain't that a hoot?"

They all shook their heads, sadly.

"Anyway, there is some good news," Mike went on. "Some American military folks are comin' over to our side. Texas National Guard, for

False Flag - Brown

starters. I heard the same thing about Montana and Idaho."

"Maybe Arizona," Rusty added. "Kentucky, Tennessee, the Carolinas. Don't know how much of that is true, though. Could be just wishful thinkin'."

"Heard about any active duty units coming over?" Gary asked.

"Not yet," Mike said. "'Course, some of them are still overseas. But we do have our own general, now."

This got Gary's attention. "Our own general?"

"Yeah. Some retired marine, name of Vine or Vaughn or something. Says he's organizin' a guerrilla resistance. Some of the militias are joinin' up with him."

"We could use something like that," Gary said. "If it's legitimate."

"My boy's got one of them HAM radios," Mike said. "Fancy rig. It can jump or skip or something."

"Frequency hop?" Gary asked, getting excited.

"That's it. Anyway, the other side can't listen in. So my boy hears about this hoppin' plan for his radio. So he programs it, and hears this general talkin' one night."

Rusty adjusted his hat. "A bunch of us been goin' over there to hear his show ever night. It's like a 'fireside chat' I guess."

"He teaches about tactics and strategy and such," Mike went on. "He must have his own generator, like us."

"He better be careful," Rusty said. "They'll find out where he's broadcastin' from and come after him."

"He's probably ready for 'em," Mike said. "Like I said, militia groups like Gary's here are hookin' up with him. He calls them the 'Patriot Resistance.' Somethin' called the 'Special Forces Underground' is trainin' 'em. And soldiers from the Army and Marine Corps are desertin', joinin' up with him one by one. Don't know how they're findin' him, but I guess they are. Some of those boys who were trainin' with Jade Helm? They're defectin', too."

Gary locked eyes with Mike. "I'd like to talk with this guy. Think that could be arranged?"

Mike thought about it, then said, "Yeah. I'd have to take you back with me. Would it be just you or the whole outfit?"

"I'd prefer to keep everybody together."

Mike turned his head to the side and spat, staining the snow brown with tobacco juice. "Well, I can put up some of ya. I know Roy Jr. will be glad to help. We can do it. Might be good to get your folks out of the weather for a while, anyway. There's a bad winter on the way."

"I'll get everybody ready to move," Gary said. "We'll leave right away."

False Flag - Brown

Joshua and Jennifer rode down into a thickly wooded valley. Both animals and humans were tired from the rigorous journey of the last few weeks.

Josh was able to get enough meat for them by hunting and trapping, and Jennifer already knew a lot about what local fauna was edible. Plus, Josh had hidden caches all around his mountain stuffed with ammunition, dehydrated food and other necessities. He and Jennifer, and even the dogs, would be fine on the mountain. But the horses weren't doing well on just grain and pulped tree bark. They needed grass. Grass was pretty sparse that high up the mountain, at least where they could get to it without sliding down to their deaths on the snow-slick slopes. The snow also made the sparse grass all the more difficult to find.

They needed to get down to where the grass was thicker and where it wasn't as cold, so the snow wouldn't stick as tenaciously.

And so their migration began.

From high up on a ridge they had spotted a patch of green in a valley below, where the sun had melted off enough snow to expose grass. The plan was to ride down there and let the horses graze and rest while they figured out what to do next.

Jennifer's hearing was still superb, and Josh was learning to interpret subtle changes in behavior from the animals. There was something going on in the woods ahead, in between them and the grass.

Josh called a halt. He dismounted and handed his reins to Jennifer. He told the dogs, "Stay with Mom," then picked his way through the trees.

As he drew close, he began to recognize the sounds of an encampment. There wasn't enough noise discipline for it to be military, but he proceeded with caution anyway. When he drew close enough to have a visual, he saw it was civilians—maybe 40 of them, with less than half as many tents set up in a clearing. A lot of the civilians had horses.

Just as he was wondering why there were no dogs, a group of canines came at him from the side, yapping and growling, alerting everyone in camp. Josh stepped out in the open with his hands up, rifle slung over one shoulder. Gun muzzles swung his way from everywhere.

It was amazing he didn't get shot, or eaten alive by ravenous dogs. A young man ran forward with rifle leveled, and stopped a couple meters from Josh.

"Who're you?" the kid demanded. "What're you doin' here?"

"Relax," Josh said. "I'm not from the government, but I was afraid

False Flag - Brown

you all might be, until I got a look up close. I've been up in the mountains for three weeks and just came down today. I was trying to get over east of here a bit. I'm just passing through."

As he spoke, more men showed up, of various ages, all with weapons trained on him.

"And you just happened to stumble across our camp?" another man asked, obviously skeptical.

"Well, yeah," Josh said. "It happens a lot, actually. Haven't you ever come across somebody you didn't expect?"

They all studied him like Bedouins about to stone a heretic.

"How do we know you're not with the Traitors?" someone else demanded.

Josh drew half of the fish symbol in the snow with his foot. They watched this, but none of them drew the other half. They looked at him like he was not only a probable enemy, but crazy, too.

No Christians. Great. Or maybe they just don't know their own history.

His thoughts drifted back over the last few weeks he spent with Jennifer. Sometimes in camp during daylight hours, she read aloud from her Bible. At that moment one of the stories she read him came to mind.

Joshua liked he story of Jephthah for two reasons: because the Hebrew judge reminded him a little of himself, and because it was interesting from a communication angle. The story was the source of a now-archaic household term for "password."

Jepthah went to war against the tribe of Ephraim, and routed them. When the Ephraimites tried to escape back to their own land across the Jordan, they pretended to be from a different tribe. But when Jephthah's men commanded them to say "shibboleth," they couldn't pronounce the "sh" sound and were exposed for what they were.

"Okay, let's try this," Josh said, meeting the gaze of several people in the growing crowd. "We hold these truths to be self-evident: that all men are created equal; that they are endowed by their Creator with certain unalienable rights; that among these are life, liberty and the pursuit of happiness. That to secure these rights, governments are instituted among men, deriving their just powers from the consent of the governed. And whenever any form of government becomes destructive of these ends, it is the right of the people to alter or to abolish it."

This raised many an eyebrow among the people who confronted him.

This was a variation on the old "who won the World Series" shibboleth from generations past, when G.I.s used their horse sense to test for German spies.

One of the men lowered his rifle. "I doubt a Traitor would have bothered to memorize that."

"You never know," another one said. "Besides, that wasn't the whole thing."

"You want me to recite the whole Declaration?" Josh asked, incredulous. He had surprised himself by being able to recite the words, after they had collected dust in his memory for so long.

"That wasn't even the whole preamble."

"When in the course of human events..." Josh began.

"How 'bout Article II in the Bill of Rights?" another man interrupted.

Josh sighed. "A well regulated militia, being necessary to the security of a free state, the right of the people to keep and bear arms shall not be infringed."

Two more men lowered their weapons.

"Lot's of people know that one," the suspicious one said, "because we quote it everywhere, all the time."

"Yeah, but the Traitors edit out the part about 'the people'," another one said. "Or they don't even know it's there."

"And you didn't say 'Second Amendment'," somebody pointed out. "You have to actually read the Bill of Rights to identify it as 'Article II'."

Another man lowered his weapon, but said, "Tell us about the separation of church and state."

"No such phrase in the Constitution," Josh replied. "That was taken from Jefferson's letter to the Danbury Baptists...ironically explaining that the First Amendment forbids the government to mess with churches. Article I says, 'Congress shall make no law respecting an establishment of religion, or prohibiting the free exercise thereof; or abridging the freedom of speech, or of the press, or the right of the people peaceably to assemble, and to petition the Government for a redress of grievances'."

All but the suspicious one lowered their weapons after that.

"C'mon, Pete," one of the suspicious dude's compatriots said. "Ain't one person in a hundred could answer that one so good. Some people right here couldn't, I bet."

"They might have coached him," Pete said.

"Well he at least earned you takin' that rifle out of his face."

Pete reluctantly lowered his weapon.

Josh lowered his hands and let out a relieved breath when Dan and Reuben Tareen arrived from the other side of the camp and recognized him. Paul Tareen was called. He emerged from a tent, followed by his wife, and hurried over. Terry appeared from a tent with some other girls of various ages. They all vouched for Josh. The whole community relaxed after that.

Josh went back to his family and brought them to the camp.

False Flag - Brown

Everybody was hungry for news. Josh had picked up broadcasts now and then on his small shortwave receiver, and knew some of the big stories--like the nuking of Wall Street and the Marine Corps general organizing a resistance movement. Then it was time to exchange personal stories. They did that for a while, and Josh certainly was glad to find friendly faces out here, but he worried about his horses.

Josh left Jennifer in the camp and took the horses to find that thawed grass he'd seen from the mountain.

When Josh returned to camp, after dark, Paul and a group of men gathered around him.

Paul made introductions, then said, "Josh, we've been puttin' our heads together. I told the rest that you were a Green Beret. It was your job to train native forces to fight, the way an army fights." He made a sweeping gesture that included the whole camp. "You can see what we have here is one big cluster fu..." He stopped abruptly before finishing the word, gaze shifting to some eavesdropping children.

"A gaggle," Josh said. "What you have here is a colossal gaggle. This is a pond full of sitting ducks."

"Exactly," Paul said. "Anyway, we'd like you to pitch in with us. We're here. We're willin'. We're armed. Would you be on board with trainin' us? Get us ready to fight?"

"Think of us as the *Montagnards*," another man said.

Josh scanned over the men gathered around. He took a look around the camp. He studied some of the women and children. He glanced over to where Jennifer had set up their own tent.

Well I guess I know what **she** wants to do, he thought.

This wasn't a very promising start for the Patriot Resistance. If this remained the state of it, they'd never be able to strike back at the Traitors. And if they couldn't take the fight to the enemy at some point, resistance would collapse. The great military thinkers said every successful resistance movement needed popular opinion on their side, and the support of a foreign power. They didn't have either, and as Josh saw it, they weren't likely to pick up either of those along the way. That was two strikes against them already.

His mind went back to what he'd studied about the American Revolution—yet another cluster of memories that had lay dormant for many years after he soured on the American Dream.

At first General Washington wasn't able to challenge the British effectively. It was everything he could do just to hold the Continental Army together. During the bitter winter at Valley Forge, he did all he could to scrape up food and basic supplies for his starving troops.

False Flag - Brown

Meanwhile, he assigned Baron von Steuben to drill them in the tactics of the day. The Continental Army may have been lacking in some basic necessities like shoes for all the soldiers, but it began to develop discipline, and *espirit de corps*.

The priority was to keep the Patriot Resistance alive for the immediate future. At the same time, they would have to be disciplined and educated very quickly. If they could survive until the spring thaw, maybe they could begin to sting the enemy, here and there.

This would have to be their Valley Forge. Guys like Joshua Rennenkampf would have to be the von Steubens this time.

"I'd be willing to talk about it," Josh said.

Being around other people would probably be better for Jennifer, anyway. And there was a long, rough winter coming.

False Flag - Brown

There was too much going on for Tommy Scarred Wolf to concentrate all his attention on the siege of the county lock-up, but his men managed to keep anybody from getting in or out of the complex.

There was no electricity in the jail. One of Adiur's men took a battery powered radio up to the roof, but Carl managed to pick him off with the sniper rifle.

Somebody else must have tried again, but stayed low enough to keep out of sight. That's how Tommy figured they must have called the chopper in.

When the old UH1 "Huey" was heard flying toward the jail, Tommy was notified. He radioed his commanders and had all but a skeleton force at assigned posts break off and assemble near the jail.

But before everyone arrived, Adiur's force, spearheaded by inmates, attempted the breakout.

Power was down most everywhere now, but the music still blared at the jail thanks to a diesel generator. The annoying music was partially drowned out as the approaching helicopter drew closer.

Carl and his spotter were already in place, and went to work right away, dropping the inmates as they flooded out the doors and toward the gate. Gunther arrived before the mob reached the gate. The team he brought had the homemade rocket launcher captured in Amarillo, and the M1928A1 Thompson submachinegun from Tommy's personal war trophy inventory.

They wasted no time. The crude antipersonnel rounds from the rocket launcher didn't land with pinpoint accuracy, but they hit amidst the surging mob and exploded with impressive shrapnel spread. After the second such explosion, the mob's charge stalled.

Another team arrived. Gunther directed them to a good overwatch position and told them to fire at will.

Between the shock of the explosions and the increasing small arms fire, the inmates lost their enthusiasm and broke, most of them attempting to get back in the building. This created an ideal turkey shoot for a few moments, until a couple Tier Zero teams forced their way through the trampling chaos and got the herd moving toward the gate again with threats and a few Soviet-style hasty executions.

By that time both Takoda and Ralph White Feather had arrived with their teams of recent recruits. They got into position behind cover and opened fire.

False Flag - Brown

"Carl!" Gunther yelled. "Concentrate on the guys in military uniform!"

"Okay," Carl replied, still sending rounds downrange.

The chopper came in to buzz over the jail compound just inside the fence. Gunther had always thought those old Hueys were good-looking birds. But this one had rocket pods and machineguns on both doors. One of those machineguns now swung toward the Shawnee Militia and opened fire.

"Get the door gunner!" Gunther told his comrades.

Gunther's men were behind good cover, and none were hit by the chopper's machinegun. The door gunner was laying suppressive fire, and as such, it was effective. Those not hiding from the gunner were occupied trying to pick him off. Adiur's mob used the distraction to rush toward the gate.

The Huey finished its gun run and banked for another pass. This was when the chopper was at its most vulnerable. The men came out of hiding and poured it on, until Gunther noticed the mob at the gate.

Gunther ordered Carl to prioritize the door gunners, but everyone else to concentrate on the mob. They were close enough now that Gunther nodded to the man with the Thompson. He opened up with the old museum piece, ripping a bloody swathe through the ranks of inmates.

Gunther called Takoda over the radio. "Bowtie, this is Blue Oval. Over?"

"This is Bowtie. Over?"

"Time to rock & roll."

Takoda's men opened up with Ingram M10 submachineguns that his father had hung onto after the rescue op in Sumatra. They fired heavy, jacketed .45 ACP slugs like the Tommygun. Adiur's cannon fodder was cut to ribbons.

But the surviving Tier Zero teams dropped to the prone and returned fire. Meanwhile the chopper completed its turn and came back, this time firing rockets.

"Incoming!" a dozen men screamed.

The rockets streaked in, one blowing a pothole in the ground and the other destroying an abandoned Volkswagen. Fortunately nobody had been using the Volkswagen for cover, but Gunther still heard somebody cry out, "I'm hit!"

And now the chopper was coming in for his second gun run, the opposite door gunner now lighting them up.

Gunther himself had to make like a cockroach as a burst of 7.62 NATO snapped by too close for comfort. Then another sound swelled in the noisy ambiance.

False Flag - Brown

An old Dodge pickup truck with a camper shell came barreling around a corner and bore down on the parking lot below Carl's rooftop perch. Tommy's voice came over the the radio. "Blue Oval, this is Hammer One. Be advised: friendlies are entering your A.O. in a mobile anti-aircraft platform. Make a hole. We'll take care of the chopper; you concentrate on the ground-pounders, over?"

Gunther pointed at the truck and yelled, "Friendlies in the truck! Make a hole; pass it down!"

The men to his left and right repeated his statement, which was in turn passed all along the line. At Gunther's direction, they tried to ignore the impending ground-to-air action and continue to engage personnel.

With the chopper's machinegun stitching the ground seemingly all around it, the truck careened into the parking lot and cut a hard turn, rocking to a stop with the tailgate facing the general direction of the enemy.

Both doors swung open. Tommy and Sanford stepped out. Tommy limped back to the bed on one side of the truck; Sanford hurried back to the other.

"You're not ready?" Tommy hollered, then laced his next remark with creative profanity. The gist of it was: "They're lighting us up while you're taking your sweet time in there!"

There was a muffled retort, then Tommy and Sanford each grabbed a side of the camper shell and lifted it off the bed. This revealed Uncle Jay, in the act of positioning himself behind a large machinegun on a makeshift monopod. "If you crazy bastards didn't drive like total maniacs," Uncle Jay bellowed, "I'd have had it unclamped already!"

Nobody was used to seeing Uncle Jay in a foul mood. Unless you knew him well, it was rare to even find him in a serious mood. But he was a crotchety bastard right then, pissed off and smarting from the pain of being tumbled around in the truck bed like a pinball. But the old fart knew what he was doing with a belt fed weapon.

The gun was called "the Dover Devil"—Tommy's most impressive souvenir from the Sudan mission. A gunner could feed belts of SLAP (Saboted Light Armor Penetrator) ammo from either side, and it had other features that were just too high-speed for words.

In the midst of the firefight, men took notice of the heavy pounding noise of the Devil—a new instrument in this symphony of destruction. The Snare Drum From Hell.

The Huey visibly lurched when the SLAP rounds tore through the nose. The old Air Cav trooper worked over the entire fuselage of the chopper, and the hapless gunners in the open doors. Glass and sparks and chunks of metal flew off the old bird as the .50 caliber saboted rounds punched through one side and out the other, sucking debris out with

False Flag - Brown

them. Then Uncle Jay bullseyed the tail rotor and down she went.

While this was going on, Adiur's forces made it through the gate. They were mowed down in droves, but several Tier Zero operators made it out of the death funnel.

Tommy called to Sanford, who by that time was acting as assistant gunner to Uncle Jay, up in the bed of the pickup. "Tell me if you see their C.O!"

Jay ceased fire. Sanford, still holding the belt up out of the big ammo can, scanned the opfor's faces as they charged through the gate. "Don't see 'im!"

The Huey crashed, blocks away.

"Wolverines!" Uncle Jay bellowed, striking a heroic pose.

"Okay, Colonel Kilgore," Tommy said. "Get your big fourth point down, before it gets shot off."

"Charlie don't surf," Uncle Jay replied, easing himself down to a sitting position.

Most of the inmates were littered over the space between the jailhouse and the mouth of the gate. Adiur's Tier Zero teams didn't continue the charge toward the Shawnee Militia, but took hard left or right turns once outside the gate and scrambled away as fast as their feet would take them. Two of them inadvertently drifted back into Takoda's sector of fire and were torn nearly in half. Several more were dropped or winged by Gunther's sharpshooters, but plenty made their escape good.

Gunther signalled for a cease-fire, then assigned a couple teams for pursuit.

"Blue Oval, this is Bowtie," Takoda called. "Over?"

"Go ahead, Bowtie."

"Permission to recon the crash site. We can use those door guns, if they're still good."

Gunther gave permission, and added that they should secure the site until somebody could come by to salvage the rocket pods or whatever else might be of use.

Tommy had the music stopped and the generator killed to save fuel. He found Gunther while he was busy getting a head count and ammo check.

"Sitrep?" Tommy asked.

"Pretty sure we got some wounded," Gunther replied. "But I haven't heard back from everybody. Some of the opfor made it out of the gate and got away."

"I know," Tommy said.

"I sent a couple teams after them to hunt them down, but no luck yet."

"Call them back," Tommy said. "They might be anywhere out there, and your boys could walk into an ambush. Worse—they might get ambushed and cut off."

"Okay," Gunther said, dejectedly.

Tommy gave his son a light slap on the back. "Hey, we got 'em out of the jailhouse, didn't we?"

"Yeah, but I sure would have liked to get them all."

"I know. Me too. But that's war, Gunther." Tommy swept his gaze over to the jail compound. "Keep eyes on that place for a couple hours before you send anybody in. Then make sure whoever does go in has all the backup you can spare. You've got to see if any bad guys are in there, or if any friendlies are, or both."

"Okay," Gunther said, still glum.

"Keep all the approaches interdicted until it's clear," Tommy said. "Then let me know. We're gonna need to redeploy your teams, now that we have Tier Zero units in our A.O. Also get me a casualty report ASAP. If any of it's bad, they can ride with us to the rear. We have an aid station established where the clinic was."

"Will do," Gunther said.

Tommy left him and climbed up to check on the sniper team. Both were healthy.

Tommy made sure to spend more face time with the spotter than with his son, to make sure the other man knew he was no less important than even Tommy's own family.

But Carl had a long face, too.

"How much ammo did you use?" Tommy asked, looking over the brass spread across the area to the right of Carl's hide.

"I think about 70 rounds," Carl said. "Maybe more."

Tommy whistled. "Wow. Did you get 70 kills?"

"Over 50, easy," the spotter said.

"I just couldn't hit the door gunner," Carl grumbled, as if ashamed and prepared for a reprimand. "I don't get it. It's like he had a force field or something. Sorry, Dad."

"You got to lead it according to the aircraft's speed," Tommy said. "And the rotor wash is like a powerful wind. Could be you have to aim high. When you're relieved from your post and get some chow, see about hooking up with Uncle Jay. He can probably give you some tips about engaging choppers with small arms."

"Okay, Dad."

Takoda was still out with his team scavenging weapons, ammo and gear off the chopper, and two other teams were returning from their aborted pursuit. Tommy checked on everyone else personally before returning to the truck.

There were three wounded men, and one dead—one of the new recruits. Tommy had the wounded put on the gun truck and he drove them back to the aid station. There would be a brief funeral service for the dead man once everything was stabilized a bit. Enemy dead...there would have to be a burial detail composed of men who would rather be assigned some other task, and were needed elsewhere...but it had to be done or the stench, vermin, and possibly disease would contribute to more problems.

Gunther had handled things pretty well. Any death on their side was tragic and unwanted, but it would have been much worse had he not taken charge and made some good calls. All his riflemen gave good account, too. Their fire was disciplined and effective. He believed they had all honestly tried to make every shot count. And most of their shots **did** count, judging by the bodies massed around the gate and farther back. They didn't panic when faced with superior numbers and air support. After taking automatic weapons and rocket fire, they came back swinging. That meant not only had he disciplined his original shooters well, but they were doing an outstanding job training and leading the recruits.

Recruits were sorely needed, because there was a lot of terrain and resources to protect. And he was getting a lot of volunteers, mostly from OK City. A few of them even had their own weapons. A couple were veterans, thank God, and got up to speed quickly.

But nothing was happening quick enough for Tommy. And he didn't have enough men for the ground he had to protect, while at the same time, he had too many to feed.

Tommy had reduced rations to one meal a day and still didn't think that would get them through the winter. He had made deals with farmers in the area and was seeking deals with more, but their crops wouldn't be coming in any time soon and it would be stupid to eat all their livestock, not leaving them enough to breed more. He and his sons all knew how to hunt, and there was an overpopulation problem with deer and other game in the area. They would just have to be careful not to go too far. It was better to stay a little hungry than get greedy and wipe out all their food supply for the future.

There were also the problems of fuel, electricity, and medicine. Or the lack of it, more accurately. Meanwhile the mysterious Adiur and his elite killers were on the loose.

OKLAHOMA CITY, OKLAHOMA

False Flag - Brown

Adiur called a halt when Cynthia Greeley and the other surviving members of his harem could no longer continue the march. They had complained incessantly and lagged farther behind until they just gave up outright.

Already in a foul mood, Adiur considered killing at least one of them as an example to the others that complaining wouldn't be tolerated. But his anger should rightly be focused elsewhere.

He let four teams into a hotel building.

They rounded up the owners and security force guarding the place against looters and squatters. Once all were stripped and zip-cuffed, they were put in Cynthia's custody and locked in a closet. They would be used in subsequent ceremonies. Their energy was needed.

Adiur set up his headquarters in the Presidential Suite and established radio contact with the ghost teams that had escaped in a different direction from the jail complex. One at a time the surviving teams converged on the hotel.

The opportunity to release some of his rage presented itself when one of Adiur's subordinates did the unthinkable.

With witnesses all around, during a briefing, the agent said, "You're not exactly the genius you're cracked up to be, whatever-the-hell your funky-ass name is. I thought Scarred Wolf was supposed to blunder right into your brilliant trap. But we all saw you turn tail and run with everybody else after he kicked your ass."

Adiur lifted the agent over his head, gear and all, and hurled him across the suite to hit the bar with such force he knocked it over. Hardly had he bounced off the bar and hit the floor before Adiur was on him. He tore the agent's helmet off and began to beat him with it.

The agent was unconscious after one blow. He suffered fatal head trauma not long after that. But Adiur kept beating him with the helmet, blood splattering all over the area. By the time he stopped, now with a satisfied gloating grimace, the agent's skull was caved in.

Adiur stood, hardly even breathing heavy, and raked everyone in the room with a chilling glare.

"That's the last time anybody is going to disrespect me in any way." He pointed with index and middle finger at the closest ghost team leader. "Your incompetence is why my plan didn't succeed. All of you! You're spoiled! You always have the advantage of surprise, and strike against targets that don't fight back. If they do fight back, it's only token resistance. And if you run into the slightest difficulty you call in support from any number of sources and it arrives withing minutes to bail you out."

With a gutteral cry, Adiur stooped to lift the toppled structure of the bar, then slammed it down on top of the dead agent. His subbordinates squirmed. Some of the harem girls and inmates averted their gaze or closed their eyes to avoid seeing the atrocity. Some in the room were filled with an awe not unlike sexual attraction. The dressing-down they suffered made Adiur seem all the more admirable.

"You were humiliated by **militia men**!" He roared. "And I guess one helicopter in support just wasn't enough to tip that match-up in your favor!"

Adiur paced, clasping his hands behind his back. "It was a perfectly simple, reasonable plan. Unfortuanately, this Indian Chief and his 'braves' are a determined opponent. They didn't take the bait. They're clever. You stupid shits underestimated them!"

He stopped pacing and faced them, in a stance similar to parade rest. "But they've got weaknesses. We're going to regroup. I'm going to train you candy-assed door-kickers how to fight somebody who fights back. Then we're going to exploit those weaknesses. We're going to drain the blood out of Tommy Scarred Wolf's lifeless body if we have to slaughter every single person on the reservation to do it. In fact, we might just do that anyway."

ABSENTEE SHAWNEE TRUST LAND, OKLAHOMA

As Tommy passed the little church where his niece had been married a lifetime ago in a different world, he saw people standing in line to get in. Snow was falling now and they shivered in the cold.

Well, at least one place is still open for business, Tommy thought.

He suddenly noticed his own feet were freezing, and his wounded calf was throbbing with pain made worse by the cold.

Instead of driving to his own house, or his temporary headquarters, he went to Michael Fastwater's property, pulled up in the yard and killed the motor.

"Good idea," Uncle Jay said. "Michael's probably not handling the cold real well."

"We're gonna have to put him with somebody else now that Louise is helping out at the aid station during the day," Tommy said. "Somebody who can look after him. Make sure he's warm, clean, and well-fed."

Louise was Michael's great-great granddaughter, who used to take care of him year-round.

Neither man made a move to step outside, yet. Tommy gazed out over the prairie, now being covered with snow.

"Ironic, huh?" Uncle Jay asked.

"What's that?"

"Tecumseh was in a similar position once," Jay explained. "Didn't work out so well for him, did it? Not for us."

"That's why we wound up in Oklahoma, ultimately," Tommy replied.

"I hope you're planning to do things differently," Uncle Jay said, rubbing his shoulder with a pained expression.

"A lot differently," Tommy said. "Because a lot is different. Back then it was all about our tribe. For the whites it was all about **their** tribe. Freedom isn't about tribes. America's not. Some people want to make it about that. But it's not. It can't be. America is an idea."

"You sound like your friend, Rennenkampf," Uncle Jay said.

Tommy shook his head. "Not anymore. Joshua hasn't talked like that for a long time."

"Well, he picked a hell of a time to give up on the idea."

"Not just him," Tommy said.

Uncle Jay sighed, stretching his neck. He attempted a straightforward smile and cheerful tone. "I see you got plenty of white folks coming over to our side."

For just a moment, Tommy's lips curved upwards. "They think we're on the right side of this. Or at least we're the best option they see. Folks from all over are hearing about us, and they're stepping up to do what they can. Red people. White people. All colors, I guess. I wish it didn't have to come to this, for that to finally happen."

"Now that it has, you think it'll be enough?"

Tommy continued staring out into the prairie. "I don't know, Uncle. Not my call, and not much I can do about it. All we can control is our little piece of the puzzle here. Do the best we can and,,,we'll see."

Uncle Jay lit up a cigarette, cracked the window and did some staring into space of his own. "If anybody can pull this off, Nephew, it's you."

"Wow. Was that a compliment? With a straight face, no less."

"Hey, I'm too cold and sore to figure out how to hide it inside an insult." Jay opened his door. "Let's go get the old crippled Jarhead. If I'm cold, he must be freezing."

They both stepped out and walked to the trailer. It felt like the temperature had dropped another 20 degrees. The wind kicked up and Tommy felt like his body was being stabbed with icicles.

The bad winter was finally upon them.

THE END

False Flag - Brown

It is easier to deceive a man than to convince him that he has been deceived.

In the beginning of a change the patriot is a scarce man, and brave, and hated and scorned. When his cause succeeds, the timid join him, for then it costs nothing to be a patriot. - Mark Twain

At what point shall we expect the approach of danger? By what means shall we fortify against it? Shall we expect some transatlantic military giant, to step the Ocean, and crush us at a blow? Never! All the armies of Europe, Asia and Africa combined, with all the treasure of the earth (our own excepted) in their military chest; with a Bonaparte for a commander, could not by force, take a drink from the Ohio, or make a track on the Blue Ridge, in a trial of a thousand years. At what point, then, is the approach of danger to be expected? I answer, if it ever reach us it must spring up amongst us. It cannot come from abroad. If destruction be our lot, we must ourselves be its author and finisher. As a nation of freemen, we must live through all time, or die by suicide. - Abraham Lincoln

Still, if you will not fight for the right when you can easily win without bloodshed; if you will not fight when your victory will be sure and not too costly; you may come to the moment when you will have to fight with all the odds against you and only a precarious chance of survival. There may even be a worse case. You may have to fight when there is no hope of victory, because it is better to perish than live as slaves. - Winston Churchill

We just cannot rely on our military to achieve our national security objective. We need a civilian force that is just as well trained and just as well funded as our military. - Barack Hussein Obama

In the next century, nations as we know it will be

False Flag - Brown

obsolete; all states will recognize a single, global authority. National sovereignty wasn't such a great idea after all. - Strobe Talbott (1992)

Today, America would be outraged if U.N. troops entered Los Angeles to restore order. Tomorrow they will be grateful! - Henry Kissinger (1991)

We shall have World Government, whether or not we like it. The only question is whether World Government will be achieved by consent or conquest." - James Paul Warburg

The only thing necessary for the triumph of evil is for good men to do nothing. - Edmund Burke

False Flag - Brown

AFTERWORD

Hello from the author! Since you evidently read all the way through my third novel of Rocco's Retreads, I guess I didn't offend you too much.

This series wasn't originally meant to be a series. *Hell & Gone* was written with the intention of getting it traditionally published, because that was the only game in town at the time. Plus, I killed off all but five characters. But over time I was convinced I should write a sequel, and *Tier Zero* was a lot of fun—partly because I knew from the start it was not going to be traditionally published, so I need not kowtow to the thought police of the industry.

That realization has sunk in a little deeper now, so I wrote this novel in a way that guaranteed it could never be published if every book was still filtered through the gatekeepers of the New York Publishing Cartel. Or any gatekeepers anywhere, for that matter. As the recent controversy over science fiction's Hugo awards have shown, sooner or later every governing body in the arts comes under the iron-fisted control of left-wing tyrants who not only suppress the work of any who disagree with them, but throw quite a tantrum when their monopoly is threatened.

So as you can tell. I'm moving these characters through a genre transition, now. Whereas *False Flag* is speculative fiction with a dystopian flavor, I anticipate a sequel that is full-blown TEOTWAWKI. But I don't plan on writing a survival manual disguised as a novel—that's been done, and personally I'd rather read one or the other, not a fusion of the two.

A technical note: back in the day, during a cross-M.O.S. bull session, a helicopter crew chief informed me with authoritative confidence that a chopper can be brought down with a rock. (And during my first years at Fort Bragg there was an epidemic of fatal Blackhawk crashes. This was during peacetime conditions—no hostile fire contributed to the disasters. We grunts came to call the UH60 "the CrashHawk.")

While it is true that the tail rotor is the Achilles' heel of a helicopter, bringing one down is not as easy as the crew chief made it sound. So while it may be improbable that two choppers could be brought down as depicted in this novel (one by rifle fire), it's far from impossible.

[Begin mini-rant.]

And isn't reading about exceptional individuals accomplishing improbable feats a keystone of enjoyable adventure fiction? Wasn't our

False Flag - Brown

victory in the American Revolution rather improbable? Wasn't it improbable that the mighty and hitherto undefeated Japanese Navy, in the span of a couple minutes at Midway, would be struck a blow it could never recover from? Both fiction and real life would be unbearably depressing if what is probable didn't get pushed around once in a while.

[End of mini-rant.]

If you liked this book, please consider leaving a review. It doesn't even have to be a "review," really. Just a sentence or two of your honest thoughts is fine.

Until next time,

Henry Brown

False Flag - Brown

ACKNOWLEDGEMENTS

Heartfelt appreciation to John Scott for the beta read. His feedback made this a better book.

False Flag - Brown

CHARACTER REFERENCE

The cast of primary characters is large. Some readers may find this list useful.

THE RETREADS:

TOMMY SCARRED WOLF – A Special Forces veteran who has since worked in various branches of law enforcement. Previously participated in covert operations in Sudan and Sumatra (Indonesia) as part of a small paramilitary unit.

DWIGHT CAVARRA ("ROCCO") – A former SEAL Team commander who retired from the Navy and opened a tactical shooting school and supply business. After recruitment by the CIA, led the covert mission in Sudan. Also participated in the unsanctioned operations in the Malacca Strait and on Sumatra.

JOSHUA RENNENKAMPF – SF veteran who, as a civilian, has gone Galt. Harbors strong anti-government sentiments. Was instrumental in the success of the Indonesian mission.

JACOB McCALLUM ("MAC") – Delta Force veteran, and survivor of the above-mentioned paramilitary operations. Increasingly tribal, distrustful of whites, and hostile toward Americans with patriotic inclinations.

CARLOS BOJADO – A retired Force Recon Marine and participant in the Sudan mission. Participated in the major War on Terror deployments almost from start to finish.

LEON CAMPBELL ("CANNONBALL") – A sniper who served in the Airborne, and veteran of the paramilitary operations in Sudan, Sumatra and the Malacca Strait.

False Flag - Brown

THE INSIDERS:

LAWRENCE BERTRAND – A behind-the-scenes administrator. He's been on the classified payroll of various secretive agencies, but his mission has remained the same: provide stimulus for the public to accept policies and change that they wouldn't ordinarily tolerate.

JASON MACMILLAN – An ambitious, apolitical professional who has climbed the ladder from state-level law enforcement to working directly for Lawrence Bertrand. Now a planner and supervisor of covert "black" operations.

JADE SIMMONS – Also works directly for Bertrand. Made the transition from academia to (clandestine) government programs after a career building on the post-war work of German scientists.

DEANGELO JEFFRIES – A field operative for the C.I.A. He does some unofficial networking and recruiting on the side in preparation for a race war he believes inevitable. The system is useful for taking down his people's enemies, and providing him a paycheck, but a day is coming when his use for it will end.

JUSTIN – A tech-savvy NSA employee hard at work on a data mining project. What he does and sees might be disturbing for some, but he has no interest in politics. What interests him is keeping a career with job security in a train wreck of an economy.

THE TEXANS:

JOE TASPER – A guy who minds his own business and tries to make an honest living, but frequently suffers encounters with agents of the police state.

KEN FOWLER – somebody who is tired of walking on eggshells and playing along with institutionalized bigotry against those who are allegedly privileged.

False Flag - Brown

ARDEN THATCHER –White and proud of it. He's always wanted to make a difference for the Aryan race, and his opportunity is at hand.

CLAYTON P. VINE – A an apolitical brigadier general forced to retire for political reasons. The ignominious end to his career has inspired a self-education about the change sweeping the country, making collateral damage of lives like his.

BILL – A USMC veteran who returned home to a country he is starting not to recognize. From his perspective the future looks grim, but he is determined to prepare for it as best he can.

JIMMY – Bill's best friend who also spent the cream of his youth on deployment. Now he wonders just what the sacrifice was for. Together, he and Bill devise contingencies, warily observing a system that evidently considers them potential enemies.

THE ABSENTEE-SHAWNEE:

JENNIFER SCARRED WOLF – A human trafficking survivor with a law degree, recently convinced that the criminal justice system has little to do with justice, but sure is criminal. Her father was first framed for murder, then was himself murdered. She has abandoned the notion that either a positive attitude or burying her head in the sand will ensure a bright future.

RACHEL WHITE BIRD – An officer of the Tribal Police on a special assignment from the Chief. She will accomplish said mission one way or the other, even if she has to get creative.

GUNTHER SCARRED WOLF – Tommy's firstborn and a participant in the mission to Indonesia. He is living his life and chasing his dreams as best he can, with the constant awareness that life as he knows it could end at any time.

TAKODA SCARRED WOLF – Tommy's second son, an alpha dog with a chip on his shoulder nonetheless. The world may end tomorrow or it may not, but he is going to crush it either way.

False Flag - Brown

CARL SCARRED WOLF – Tommy's youngest, who lives under three giant shadows. With anyone else for a father and brothers, he likely wouldn't recognize a universe larger than one big enough to contain friends, girls, video games and his dirt bike.

UNCLE JAY – An Air Cavalry veteran from the Vietnam era who is normally content to let his nephew Tommy handle the dangerous stuff. But deep down, he's still a soldier.

THE CITIZENS:

GARY FRAM – A veteran, leader, and patriot. If he had a million men who shared his convictions, he would take the government from the elitists and give it back to the people, to whom it rightly belongs.

TERRANCE HANDEL – A USMC veteran with huge lapses in his long-term memory and occasional, disturbingly random compulsions. What memories are intact seem to be getting triggered a lot lately, though.

ROY GARBER, JR. – A rancher whose father simply wanted to put a duck pond/water hole on his own property, at his own expense. Now his father has been pushed to the breaking point and Roy Jr. finds himself in an intense confrontation with the federal government.

WILLIE MAE HARRIS – A victim who has been deprived of her fair share for much too long. But long-needed change is bringing retribution within reach.

CPSIA information can be obtained
at www.ICGtesting.com
Printed in the USA
LVHW081354020720
659542LV00026B/2991